For Evil to Exist

Christine Schmidt

Reginald Russell Press
Blue Bell, Pennsylvania USA

For Evil to Exist

Published by
Reginald Russell Press
Blue Bell, Pennsylvania
USA

For information, contact: reggieschmidt@verizon.net
ISBN: 978-0-692-33140-8
First Edition: March, 2015
Book Cover Painting: Deb Hartmann-Healy
Interior Book Design by www.integrativeink.com

DEDICATION

To all Children . . . they carry the weight of the words
and actions of their parents and all other *teachers*

The Year 2010

Chapter 1

BETH LOOKED OUT the kitchen window of her apartment and watched the windswept leaves dance around the only car in the parking lot—hers. She shifted her eyes to the knife she held under the spigot and used her thumb and forefinger to wipe off the excess peanut butter. She felt the comfort of routine, as she dropped the knife into the plastic utensil container of her dish rack and then pumped some soap onto her hand to wash off the oily residue. She tore off a paper towel; dried her hands and then swiped the moist cloth over her mouth. She opened the junk drawer in the kitchen and took out her chapstick and ran it back and forth over her mouth. She couldn't stand having dry lips. When she started to speak or smile, it felt like her lips were stuck to her gums. Ironically, she had no one to speak to other than her dog and she rarely had a reason to smile on these slow, quiet winter days. She shivered and pulled her sweater tighter as she returned to her chair in front of her only hope for a productive day (apart from household chores) and that was her computer screen. Beth had been out of work now for a year and a half. Her unemployment compensation from the state of Massachusetts had dried up. The Christmas holidays were fast approaching, so she had to take money out of savings to buy presents for her nieces and nephews, who lived with the rest of her family in Pennsylvania.

Fortunately, Beth's husband, Henry, had a good job and he never expected her to take money out of her savings to pay the bills and buy the groceries. For this, and other good reasons, she stayed in her marriage.

She loved Henry; his job provided health insurance, which in 2010 was already mandatory for all residents of the state of Massachusetts. Henry wasn't all bad. In fact, when she told him she was laid off from her job, he had encouraged her to "write that book you've always talked about." The tradeoff was that Henry was the king of his castle (which was currently a pleasant-enough one bedroom apartment) and Beth was the haus frau. She did all of the cooking, cleaning, laundry; shopping for groceries, household items, and weekly table wine—white for him and red for her. She was responsible for paying the bills with Henry's money, and she did precise bookkeeping to ensure the household checkbook balanced. The fair amount of money that was left over after these expenses went into Henry's pocket. Henry was not a saver, and he spent money like it might burn a hole in his pocket. But he wasn't hanging out at bars or gambling. He spent his money on eBay purchases of used boats; boat engine parts; machining equipment to make and modify guns; and all the various parts and powders required to fire them up.

The bad part about Beth staying in her marriage was putting up with Henry's violent temper and the physical and emotional abuse suffered at his hands.

During his rages, Henry yelled out a slightly different version of the same litany: "Everyone at work—everyone who knows me for that matter—says I'm easy to get along with. It's *you* who can't get along with anyone. You can't get along with your own parents or your sister. You can't get a job because you don't have any marketable skills. Sure, you were in sales, but who can't sell Merck's drugs? What a joke that job was. You even told me you were basically like a UPS man delivering samples to doctors' offices. You have no interests or hobbies and that's why you're always worried about what I'm doing."

Inevitably, Beth would rationalize Henry's bad behavior as being a direct result of her own bad behavior. She would remind herself she wasn't easy to live with because she was very insecure and possibly insanely jealous. It was the kind of jealousy that made her worry about who Henry might meet at work or anywhere else for that matter. She felt anxious not just by the presence of an attractive woman but sometimes even at the mention of a female coworker. And it wasn't just women who worried her. She even feared that Henry might secretly be gay and it was possible he might run off with a guy from the shooting range; so she was even jealous of his male acquaintances. It filled her with the opposing emotions of anger that rattled her and depression that made her lethargic. Her anger was not directed at other women, it was always directed at Henry because, the way she saw it, he might somehow give the wrong signals—as if he was still looking for something better. They would argue, with Henry yelling she was not only wrong but crazy. Then Beth slid into depression because she was certain she would lose him in the end; so she resigned herself to defeat, as Henry yelled she was creating a self-fulfilling prophecy.

Beth had convinced herself that events in her childhood were to blame for her insecurity. If anger and worry weren't tangled in her DNA at birth, they were at least imprinted on her brain during childhood and adolescence. Those unhealthy emotions gave rise to aggressive behavior that made her feel powerful in the moment—like when she yelled back at Henry, who would yell even louder. Their emotions escalated until she slammed a door or he drove away; or she threw something or he hit her. Men are given one dimensional labels of lover or fighter. If women were given the same labels, Beth's would be a fighter. She admired and envied women who were assertive. She knew that true confidence and self-respect would allow her to calmly state her needs and impose boundaries on herself and others. If Beth had self-respect and confidence, she would have walked away from this abusive and violent man. Instead she would curl up on the bed and cry until she couldn't cry anymore and then panic set in. She had to win him back. If he didn't leave the apartment, she would sheepishly approach him as he sat at his desk in the living room—deeply immersed in the world of the internet. She nervously twisted her shirt around her fingers, like a child, and said, "Henry . . . I'm sorry . . . I was out of line and . . ."

"Not now!" Henry would snap; never taking his eyes off the computer screen.

If he had driven away, she would call his cell phone again and again but he wouldn't answer. Whether he was at home or finally answered his cell phone from the garage he rented, (to tinker away at his projects) she knew he would forgive her if she listened attentively to his fatherly lectures about what she had said or done wrong.

It was then that Henry was the most manipulative. He would motion for her to come sit on his lap or lay in bed next to her and calmly remind her of all those bad things about her, while stroking her hair and ending with, "Sweetie, I try my best to make you happy. I'm supporting you financially and you can stay at home and write your book. I'm the one who really loves you. Your family doesn't care about you. I know you believe you have a close family but, in all the time we've lived here, have your parents ever visited you? You're the one who's always chasing after them; taking the train or driving down with me, when I go to Maryland; then driving to Pennsylvania to go to another birthday celebration or to watch your nieces and nephews play some ball game." Beth would point out, "My brother has visited a few times when he's been in Boston for work and the rest of the time he's busy with his own family. I don't expect my sister to visit because she's always traveling to Europe or somewhere for her job, and we're not close anyway." But Henry persisted in a gentle tone, "You make excuses for everyone who disappoints you but me." It was true that in the four years Beth was living in Massachusetts, her parents had not visited her once and yet when her brother played football, they drove to various states, including Massachusetts, for nothing more than an overnight stay to watch his game. Henry would then look into her eyes and quietly say, "But you have to learn to forgive your parents and your sister for whatever they've done to hurt you. I think that's why you have a hard time forgiving me, because you've carried anger and resentment toward them for many years."

Beth would ask for forgiveness because she knew she was lucky to have him, and she had to admit . . . everything he was saying about her was right.

The day had finally arrived when Beth finished editing and revising her first novel. She had not registered for any night classes that spring or summer because she would need to devote herself to the task of finding an agent to represent her. This is what she had learned about the book publishing process—just like an actor—a writer needs an agent to shop the book around to all of the big publishing houses in New York City. Sure the going rate was 15% for the agent, but it was 15% of big bucks. With dreams of a guest spot on Oprah to discuss her novel, she bought the 3 inch thick book, "Writer's Market" and determined which agencies would surely have an interest in representing her. Over a period of months, Beth excitedly carried 25 to 30 manila envelopes at a time to the post office. They were being shipped to potential agents with the required 50 pages; or first three chapters of her manuscript. She grinned coyly when customers at the post office puzzled over the pile of envelopes resting on her forearms as she stood in line for proper postage. She would remember those inquisitive looks some day when she smugly recounted them to an interviewer.

But the rejection letters slowly crept in. Even *those* created excitement initially when she spotted the self-addressed envelope in the mail, because writing was her niche; writing was her hope. She sliced through the envelope and grasped the letter inside. Too excited to read every word, she skimmed for the part that asked for "more pages"... or ... "to set up an appointment to discuss a contract" ... or ... "I would like to represent you." Instead, she read "... not what we're looking for at this time" ... or "good luck finding an agent who would be better suited to your material." It only took half a dozen of those letters to realize they were form letters; but even that brought a glimmer of hope. Beth told Henry, "they probably didn't even read the pages I sent," and she reassured herself that once an agent took the time to read her chapters, she would get a call; sign a contract; and decide what to wear on Oprah.

Beth began to attend weekend writers' conferences in Boston and New York City that cost hundreds of dollars (withdrawn from her savings), but it was worth it for the networking the brochures and emails promised. The guest speakers were successful authors; and there were agents, editors and publicists in attendance. For several dollars more, you could have a *sit-down* with a real-live agent who would read your first few pages and assess your book's potential. There were lunches and receptions that promised vital networking opportunities. It didn't take long for cynicism to set in, as Beth went from writers' conference to writers' conference and recognized a familiar feeling of not wanting to be a member of this club—a club of writers with aspirations of greatness who hadn't yet recognized their transparent desperation. It took her back to the 70s when she was a novice runner, milling around the crowd before a 10K race. She was disgusted by the incessant spitting, grunting, leg limbering and crotch picking of the mostly male crowd. She wanted to accomplish something by finishing the race and yet she would be happy to return to the lonely runner's life once it was over.

The only people who were approachable at the lunches and breaks of writers' conferences were the writers who had finished writing their great American novel years before and were still trying to get the book published. Only the writers who had just recently written their final chapters were naïve enough to appear nonplussed by all of the agents in their midst. And the agents were snobby and aloof. They treated the writers like fleas. Beth would manage to get a sentence or two out of an agent, after she bravely edged her way into their cliques at a reception—only to have their eye contact stray, as they pretended to have the urgent need to speak to someone across the room. Their presentations consisted of mocking the style and content of the writers of the millions of manuscripts they could no longer bear to read.

Once, as she commiserated with another aspiring writer, who had endured years of rejection; he suddenly took a deep breath and straightened his posture in a manner that Beth recognized as a pause to gather the courage to ask her out. She was prepared to disappoint him and wondered why a wedding ring is never a deterrent; but then he blurted out, "You know you'll never be published by anyone in New York City with a German last name like Hardt."

"What do you mean?" Beth asked, but she feared she knew the answer . . . and she did.

He said, "The publishers are all Jews, Beth. You might as well forget it."

Her heart sunk when she recalled the one student in her Fiction Writing course at Harvard's evening school, who had nonchalantly shared with the class that her book would be published. Her name was Iris Goldenberg. Now a new misery overcame Beth.

Her first novel was supposed to lift her to new heights; finally the opportunity to be where a little part of her dared to know she belonged— among the winners of the world. She didn't need to be Oprah-rich; just rich enough to buy a house with a big dining room. She would fill it with an eclectic mix of intelligent, creative and devoted friends. She could shed her current life of rejection, joblessness and spousal abuse. People would like her. She just wasn't motivated at the moment to cultivate friendships. Besides, the stereotype of cold and cliquish New Englanders rang true. They were only *renters* in their condominium development of mostly *owners* but apparently qualified for the occasional invitation to neighborly pot-luck dinners or a Sunday brunch. As one neighbor introduced her, "This is Beth. She and her husband *rent* here." As if that wasn't bad enough, they would also find out that Beth and Henry were both *Catholic!* Occasionally Beth agreed to a cup of coffee or a glass of wine and a couple hours of chatting with people she had met in her evening writing classes. But she always found an excuse not to go a second time—she had to walk her dog or get dinner started; or go to a doctor's appointment. Beth told herself she was just going through a phase of being a home-body. She wanted to have friends on the few occasions when it was convenient for her. But friendship required maintenance and that maintenance required time and money and constant reciprocation of whose turn it was to have dinner; buy lunch; or treat for a coffee; and she couldn't possibly be unavailable when Henry had free time. She always made herself available for him; and yet Henry would come and go as he pleased. They used to do day trips on his old boat and cruise along the Mystic or Charles River; or go on a hike and have a picnic with their dog, Jake; but in the past year or so, it seemed that Henry only had time for Beth when he was in the mood for sex or needed assistance at the garage; or when he was in one of his manic moods when he wanted Beth to listen to his idea for a new project or a new job; or a new place to live. Finally, she had his attention. But it was Henry who needed attention at that moment, and it always played out the same way. If she interrupted with a comment, he cut her off. If she tried to speak again, he talked louder. If she was persistent, he screamed, "*Listen to me!* I know what you're going to say and you're wrong!"

Exasperated, Beth would say, "But what I meant was . . ."

Again he would cut her off. Only now, he was furious. He paced around the room and shouted, *"NO! No. No. No. No!"* He would suddenly stop and glare at her with a frightening intensity as he continued. Then she sat quietly, not even daring to let her eyes stray from him. If she lost eye contact with him for only a moment, he would lean toward her and demand, *"Listen to me. Try to focus and learn something god-dammit!!"* When he finished, an hour later; sometimes 45 minutes; sometimes an hour and a half had gone by; he would soften . . . and sit by her. Now Beth could relax. Her eye contact could stray; her muscles could relax; and she always felt sleepy after one of his dissertations. He was calm now and even affectionate. Then the advice portion would start with, ". . . so that's why you have to listen better before you jump to conclusions sweetie. I'm just trying to help you. Your father always told you how you think you have the answers before you know all the facts . . . right sweetie?"

Beth grinned. "He's right. They're both right," she thought to herself. "I'm too impatient." She didn't have to say anything. Henry knew she got the point. He could see it in her eyes. "I love you sweetie," Henry said in a soft voice.

"I love you too" Beth said softly. She was in a stupor of calm.

Henry kissed her lips and said, "Should we go to bed now?"

"Yeah." If he wanted to go to bed now, it was because he wanted to have sex. Sometimes she wanted it too. Other times she was just happy because it meant he had chosen her over his computer screen.

Henry was a night owl and Beth was a morning person. The first thing she did each morning, after turning off the alarm clock, (which was strategically positioned so it required her to get out of bed) was to take Jake for a walk. When she returned home, she fed Jake; made coffee; and then chopped up apples and sliced oranges, and made muesli with cereal grains, nuts, pineapples and yogurt for Henry to take to work. Henry hated to get up in the morning, so when Beth went in to awaken him again, he would motion for her to join him in bed. "Ah, come on Henry. I'm already up and dressed and I want to exercise now." It wasn't that Henry wanted to have sex in the morning; he just wanted to stay in bed.

By 9:00, and sometimes later, Henry would be off to work. Beth often marveled at how flexible the workplace seemed to be for brilliant software designers like Henry.

Beth's job searches yielded nothing but recruiting site applications or responses from financial institutions or insurance companies. Beth thought to herself, "Everybody knows the only reason they have job openings is due to an attrition rate that requires a revolving door at the front entrance." The newspapers advertised sales jobs that are "entry level" (code for—only young people need apply) or promised earnings of 150K the first year. Beth knew that, in reality, these commission-based jobs yielded little income, with expectations of growth designed for failure so that new employees would bring in money for the first three months by hitting up their families and friends for sales. Once that dried up, the company had made some money and when the new employees eventually failed to bring in business; they would be fired; and the cycle continued.

Somehow Beth had managed to turn an uncertain future into a rigid pattern of day-to-day living; yet Friday felt different from the other days in the week. She was excited by the idea that the weekend was coming and she never knew what to expect from Henry. Hot sex if Henry was in the mood or maybe an excursion to another state or city to pick up his latest eBay purchase; or total neglect if, for some unknown reason, Henry was angry again.

"Sweetie?" Henry called out.

Beth had just finished closing the plastic container with Henry's muesli. "I'll be right there." She put the container and a spoon into the little black, nylon bag that Henry carried into work each morning. She set it on the little table in the entryway so he could grab it, along with his keys, on his way out the door.

As Beth walked into the bedroom, Henry was lying in bed picking at the skin around his fingernails. He continued to do this, as he said, "Sweetie, I've been looking at apartments in New Hampshire because it's really nice, and I think it would be a good idea to move up there."

"Why?" Beth was immediately filled with dread—another move—and this time even further away from her family; and when had Henry been driving around New Hampshire looking at apartments?

Henry heard the panic in her voice. He jumped out of bed. "Goddamit! There you go again! Restricting my freedom and never growing! Never growing because of you! You and your goddam family!"

"But I . . ."

Henry waved his hands in the air and shouted, "I don't want to hear your voice!" He slipped out of his underwear and again he said, "You just want to restrict my freedom."

Beth panicked. She followed him into the bathroom. Henry yanked at the shower curtain and drew it back with such force that he almost brought down the rod. Fortunately, there were so many coats of paint over the screws in the wall that it only managed to crackle a few chips onto the floor. Henry switched on the water.

"Why do we have to move to New Hampshire now? All we do is move from one place to the next and . . ."

Henry shouted, "*Leave me alone!*"

Beth paced back and forth in the hallway outside the bathroom. Then she walked into the bathroom and stood on the little rug between the sink and the shower. She pleaded, "Would you please tell me why you want to move to New Hampshire?"

Henry said nothing as Beth stared at the shower curtain and listened to the falling water. She left the room and walked down the hall to the kitchen, talking out loud to herself, "Why the hell does he want to move again?" Then a lightbulb went on. She rushed back into the bathroom and yelled loudly, "I know why! It's probably got something to do with the gun laws. Doesn't it?"

Silence . . . no response . . . just the sound of water.

"Henry? Can you answer me please?"

About ten minutes later, the water was turned off and Henry slowly pulled back the shower curtain. He wiped water from his face and spit a little, as he pulled at his towel on the rack. Beth was still standing there . . . waiting. If she remained silent, he would relent and speak. And finally, he did; but in an all-too-familiar crescendo that was a low voice initially, until it grew louder into his fierce anger. "I do *not*—I repeat—do *not* owe you any explanations of why I want to move to New Hampshire, or why I want to buy a boat engine, or why I . . ."

Beth interrupted in a whining, pleading tone, "But I *do* have the right to ask . . ."

Henry screamed, "NO! No!"

"But I . . ."

"No. No! I don't want to hear your voice. Stop!" He had partially toweled off and wrapped the towel around his waist as he made his way to his chest of drawers in the bedroom.

Beth yelled at him, "I want to know why you want to move to New Hampshire. What about your job?"

"I can still get to work from New Hampshire. I've timed it and it's about a 45 minute drive."

"You *timed it?* So, does that mean you've already picked out a place?"

"Yes I have. And you can just move back to Pennsylvania with your goddam family because that's all you care about anyway."

Beth started to cry. "That's not true. I love you but I'm tired of all this moving and . . ."

Henry had stepped into his briefs and was now tucking his undershirt into the waistband of his briefs. Suddenly, he came at Beth and started screaming so fiercely, that spit flew onto her face. "You are not the decision maker in this family. Remember, he who makes the money, makes the decisions. And I am sick of you restricting what we can and cannot do. It always the same thing—no, no, no! That's you and your pathetic little world. You don't know anything. You don't want to know anything. You don't want to try anything. You don't want to grow and live and enjoy life, you just want to be miserable like your goddam mother!"

Beth screamed, "No I don't! That's not true."

"Yes it is! And I'm sick of it! I'm sick of you and your excuses."

"Excuses! Excuses for what?"

Henry pushed her forcefully toward the bedroom doorway. She flinched. "What are you doing?"

"Just get out of here. I don't want to look at you. Look how you're dressed. You look like a hag!"

"What?" Beth cried out.

"You're a loser! What am I doing with you anyway?"

Beth was horrified. She stood with her mouth open. Suddenly, Henry shoved her with such force that her back slammed against the wall and, as she struggled for her footing, her leg turned into a little wooden magazine box by the bed and then her butt slammed onto the floor. Her shin had caught the edge of the wooden box and started to bleed. All the while, Henry continued to yell; but it seemed they both noticed the bleeding shin at the same moment. Suddenly, Henry reached for the phone and shoved it at her. "Here. Call the police! I don't care. I can't live with you anymore."

"I'm not going to call the police!" Beth said; hoping Henry would see this as a sign of her abiding love. But he hit her shin hard with the phone and she screamed. Then he slammed the phone onto the floor; knelt down and pounded his head against the floor saying, "I can't do this anymore. I can't do this anymore."

Beth sometimes thought he was crazy but she told herself it was the cruel underside of his brilliant mind. He would calm down soon. She was sure of it.

Now he sat there, slouching and holding his head in his hands. In that momentary silence, she thought, "I shouldn't get him so angry.

Why do I have to be so rigid? What's wrong with New Hampshire anyway?"

She watched him; the same way she watched her father after he hit her mother. She was waiting for him to be strong again. Instead, he stood up with the attitude of a teenage boy—resentful of life's responsibilities—as he sluggishly finished dressing.

She followed him into the entryway and stood there with hands clasped around her sweatshirt—afraid that he might leave and never come back.

With a sullen expression, Henry pulled on his jacket and mumbled, "I have to go to work." And with that, he shut the door behind him, but he had grown so listless that he didn't even use enough energy to click the knob into place to lock it.

Beth walked over to the door and gently pushed it shut, until the knob clicked. Then she ran to the window in the kitchen to watch him walk to his car. His head was hanging until he lowered himself into the car and pulled out of the parking space. She worried, "Should I call his cell phone?" She struggled to think of what to say. "Something light," she thought, "something to make him happy again." If he was happy again, then he would be happy about *her* again. He wouldn't strike up a conversation with some young, attractive woman at work. Beth picked up the phone in the kitchen. Her heart sunk. She couldn't think of something to say—something that would make him say 'I love you' before he hung up. She needed reassurance; but she thought better of it. "Maybe I better wait. Maybe I'll wait until this afternoon."

She could hardly wait to finish her peanut butter and jelly sandwich. By then it would be 1:00 and she would call him. Her heart was pounding as she picked up the phone. She imagined him calling her sweetie. That would make her calm. Then she could concentrate and get something accomplished today. She pressed the numbers into the phone and listened to the first ring. "I hope he answers." She hated getting his voicemail. She wouldn't be able to find out what his mood was like and right now she didn't know what to say if she had to leave a message. Then she heard, "Hi sweetie." It was as if nothing bad had happened that morning. A weight lifted and Beth said, "Hi Henry." He sounded so pleasant and normal that she had to think of something quick—something trivial—no heavy topics—no mention of the morning's fight . . . "I took Jake for a walk before lunch, and we saw a skunk in the distance and he started yanking on the leash."

Henry laughed a little and asked lightheartedly, "Don't tell me he got sprayed?"

"No. No. Thank God." Beth was doing her best to sound pleasant too. After a couple of minutes, Henry said, "I have to get ready for a meeting at 2:00 sweetie."

Beth felt the gentle stroke of his voice. "OK. I'll let you go."

Henry lowered his voice and said, "I love you."

Beth grew serious and said, "I love you too."

Henry's voice returned to a light intonation, "I'll see you tonight my love."

"OK. Have a good day."

"You too. Bye."

"Bye." Now all was right with the world. She had the reassurance she needed. Henry loved her. She walked into the living room, where Jake was asleep on the couch. She went over to her desk and thought, "It *is* a good book. If I can't find an agent, I'll just start mailing chapters directly to publishers." She sat down and got to work.

Chapter 2

HENRY ARRIVED HOME around 6 p.m. each evening. It was a dramatic change in work culture at Thorpe Medical Care, a dialysis care company; versus the fast pace biotech world where both Henry and Beth had previously worked. The hours at Thorpe Medical Care were regular and the deadlines and demands for Henry's software projects were reasonable. Each night, Beth cooked "good food; simply prepared" as Henry described it. He never talked during dinner which still managed to make Beth uncomfortable. But a glass of red wine eased her nerves and by the time he was clearing his plate, Henry's expression softened as he focused on their dog Jake. Encouraged by this change in mood, Beth would tell an anecdote about something cute Jake had done during the day. With no children, Jake was her only hope to interest Henry in home and hearth. He never asked how her day went and if, on occasion, she talked about mundane things like her trip to the grocery store and someone or something that caught her attention, she would see his face slide into boredom. This nonverbal response was intended to let her know to shut up. She would quickly find a stopping point that felt contrived, but at least Henry could now rise from the table and give her a kiss on the mouth and say, "Delicious." If he was in a particularly good mood, he would move his chair back from the table and tap on his thigh to let Beth know she could come over and sit on his lap. They would look at each other for a moment and hug as she lay her head on his shoulder. After a quick kiss, he tapped her butt to let her know to get up. Then he too stood; happy to retreat to his own plans for the evening.

Every night, as Henry left the kitchen, Beth wondered what he had in mind for the rest of the night. She hid her anxiety by continuing with her routine. She took the dishpan out from under the sink and hit it with a long squirt of liquid soap. While the hot water filled the pan, she walked over to the radio and turned on NPR to listen to an evening interview program. On Friday nights, it was a recap and discussion of the week's politics and other news. Knowledge soothed Beth's nerves; whether it was from reading or studying or, in this case, listening to the information relayed via the moderator's soothing voice.

She heard Jake's paws on the floor in the hallway and turned to glance in his direction. Henry had changed into the clothes he wore to the garage. Lately he was machining a hand gun, which was probably illegal, given they were living in the anti-gun state of Massachusetts. But Beth was starting to learn to choose her battles with Henry because it seemed he was always raising the bar in terms of the location and cost of his hobbies and projects.

Henry started to say something so Beth had to turn off the water to hear him over the din of the radio.

"What?"

Henry shook his head with irritation and, after a dramatic pause, repeated himself. "I said, I have to go to Maryland for three weeks." Beth was immediately panic-stricken and, in a flash; indignant. What was Henry up to now?

"Three *weeks!*"

They shouted at each other in the kitchen until Henry stormed out of the room. Beth slipped off her Playtex gloves and slapped them onto the side of the sink. They travelled to Maryland at least once a month and stayed at Henry's dilapidated cabin for a week at a time. He had lied to his boss and told him that Beth's mother was being treated for late stage colon cancer and they needed to help with her care. His boss allowed him to work remotely as often as he needed to. This afforded Henry the opportunity to nurture one of his current obsessions—his guns. He would shoot them on the back end of his property by the river's edge; but only after cleaning and polishing the bullet shells; then filling them with a precise amount of gun powder, which Henry adjusted according to the velocity of the bullet in flight.

In truth, Beth's mother had long since recovered from Stage 1 colon cancer; but their time in Maryland allowed her to drive up to Pennsylvania to see her nieces and nephews quite often. However tonight, it sounded as if Henry planned to go without her. She followed him into the living room where he was sifting through a pile of paperwork on his desk. Without turning around, Henry said loudly, "I'm leaving early tomorrow morning. I have to go over to the garage tonight to pack some things."

Beth knew there was no chance of changing his mind, but she persisted. "Why do you suddenly have to go?" She knew it had something to do with their horrible fight that morning.

To her surprise, Henry seemed to calm down a bit as he guided her to a chair. "Here, sit down for a minute." He sat on the couch across from her.

"Aren't you going to take me with you?"

"No."

"Why?"

"It's none of your goddamned business!"

If Henry had used that phrase with Beth once, he had used it a thousand times. Beth attributed it to the fact that he was born and raised in Germany and, from what she had witnessed when they visited his family in Germany, men were the decision-makers in the family. Or maybe it was something in the blood of eastern European men; after all, her father was 100% Russian and he too was domineering with a bad temper. During Beth's childhood, her Irish mother thought she ruled the roost because her father was always home, where she wanted him, when he wasn't working one of his two jobs. He didn't golf, or go out drinking with the boys. But his day job was selling beer to Philadelphia bars; and, as a former professional athlete in the good-ole-boy era, it was highly possible that he had quite a bit of down time during the day which likely provided the freedom he otherwise didn't have. In turn, he happily participated in all the required socializing with her mother's family; as the grandparents, aunts and uncles of choice. His family, consisting of a twice widowed, working mother and a sister eighteen years his junior, took the required backseat to family priorities.

All of the little victories won by Beth's mother paled in comparison to her father's success in the marriage battlefield because, in Beth's family (as in Henry's family), women were second class citizens.

In any event, it was Henry's way or the highway, and his German accent only embellished the stereotype of a demanding tyrant when he screamed at her, as he often did. The combination of Beth's anxious demeanor, coupled with Henry's volatile temper and frequently erratic behavior was a dangerous mix. Now Beth was consumed by anger and panic. She had to do something to stop him.

Henry and other gun advocates were stocking up on supplies in anticipation of dramatic changes in gun laws now that a Democratic President was in office. Several times a week, UPS was delivering cartons and cartons of cartridges and bullet shells, which Henry hauled down to Maryland for cleaning and filling. "That's it!" Beth thought. She glared at Henry and said, "If you leave for three weeks, I'm going to call the police and tell them about all the bullets and ammunition you've been getting from eBay."

Suddenly, Henry jumped out of his seat and brought his fists down heavily on her head. Fortunately, she flinched as he came at her so he only managed to hit her forehead as his fists then landed on her eyes.

Beth screamed and jumped out of the chair. She couldn't see out of her right eye. "Is it still in my head?" she wondered, as she staggered with a sensation of dizziness. She had to get to the mirror in the bathroom; but even in her state of panic, she was relieved that Henry seemed concerned. He was no longer pursuing her but seemed to be following and backing away at the same time. As she crossed over the entryway and headed toward the bathroom, Henry flung open the front door and she thought she saw Jake run out. But she had to continue to make her way to the bathroom which now seemed so far away. She swayed into a closet door, and she could only see out of her left eye. "Oh God, is it there?" She flipped on the light switch and looked into the mirror. Both eyes were still in her head, but her right eye was closing under a puffy lid. She was already crying and now she screamed, "You bastard!" She turned toward him, but Henry was gone and so was Jake. She wasn't dizzy anymore as she headed for the living room. She sat down and then jumped up again. "I should call the police!" She had done that several years before when they lived in Delaware. They had been arguing in the bedroom until each of them seemed to calm down a bit. Beth had been sitting on the edge of the bed and, as she stood up, Henry repeated a comment that had started the fight, and they were back to square one. She turned to look at Henry in disbelief, when he suddenly yanked at a clump of her hair and shoved her to the bed. He slapped her face left to right. Then he started pounding on her arms and chest with his fists. Beth caught a glimpse of his face—red and contorted with anger, as she tried to block him from her own face. He was shouting as he punched at her. Beth was frightened by the strength of his blows and screamed, "Stop it! Stop!" Henry finally backed off and slumped onto the bed, which allowed Beth to escape down the stairs. She grabbed the phone from the wall in the kitchen as Henry started down the stairs. They looked at each other for a moment as Beth hesitated. Henry knew what she was doing. He shouted, "Go ahead! Call the police. I'd rather be in jail than live with you!"

"Alright I will!" Beth cried out.

The police had handcuffed Henry and slipped him into the backseat of the police car. But Beth didn't feel relief; instead she felt regret. How could she do such a thing . . . and humiliate Henry like this! "He'll never speak to me again." She cried but didn't dare call anyone to tell them what had happened. She would do that tomorrow. By then, maybe it would all be over and Henry would forgive her. Beth didn't know that the State of Delaware issued an automatic PFA (Protection From Abuse) Order against the alleged perpetrator in a domestic violence call. Apparently advocates of the law were savvy enough to know that victims of abuse typically did not report their abusers and when they did, they quickly regretted their decision to do so.

Henry was released from jail the next day but he had to get a lawyer for his arraignment on charges of domestic violence. He pled guilty and had to get counseling and take anger management classes. Henry and Beth were not allowed to communicate for six months as required by the PFA; until Henry secretly called her using someone else's phone. Beth was relieved to hear from him and know that he still loved her. Henry had cried to her that his career might be over because of the charges against him. He asked her to call his lawyer and explain what *really* happened. Fortunately, Beth had stiffened when he said this. She refused to lie about what he had done. Then his quiet demeanor changed and he yelled, "You made me do it! You know you provoke people. Your father and mother tell you that. Your sister tells you that, but you always blame everyone else for your problems. Nothing's ever your fault. When are you going to learn? When are you going to see it?" Henry knew the silence meant that Beth was realizing he was right. Then she said, "Henry, I know I'm partly to blame for what happened because I got you upset; but I went to my neighbor's house the next day and she started to cry when she saw how black and blue my arms were turning. Even my neck and face and chest . . ." Soon Beth became aware of the silence on the phone. "Henry? Are you there? Henry?" Her heart sunk. He had ended the call. Beth panicked. She hit the redial button on the phone. He didn't answer. She called again. He didn't answer; but this time she wrote down the number so she could reach him again. Henry knew he had her back. He had given her just enough hope in him, and doubt in herself, to stir her emotions. He had pushed just the right hot buttons that made her confused and insecure. She needed him to love her and he needed someone who would always come running back. She fed his ego and he fed her desperate need for what she thought was love. Eventually they reunited when Beth rationalized that she had surely caused his violent outburst.

It wasn't long before the front door opened, and Henry walked back in with Jake. "I'm sorry sweetie." It was the first time he had ever apologized for hitting her. She was comforted by his gentle voice and she felt a sense of relief. But this time was different. It wasn't relief that he still loved her; it was relief that she was finally ready to leave him. She had been mired in quick sand for so long. She needed to be loved by him, but the screaming fights happened again and again. Almost anything could set him off. It was no longer just about getting his way. It could be a discussion about a current news event that began with a difference of opinion but would always blossom into a tirade about what was wrong with Beth. In moments of clarity, Beth knew there was a disconnect between what she had said and how Henry reacted. Finally, at this moment, she saw things clearly, and it was long past time for a change.

Henry said quietly, "Why don't we sit in the kitchen and talk."

"Alright."

"You can't call the police because they'll throw me in jail and I'll lose my job."

"I know. I know."

With Henry providing their income, Beth would not do anything to endanger that.

They both knew what was coming next and now they both wanted it. Beth said plainly, "We have to separate. But I need you to help me with finances and health insurance until I get a job."

"Don't worry about that sweetie. You know I will."

Beth was happy to have the leverage of his violence to use against him. He didn't love her anymore and she knew it. Maybe he never did. So many times he had shouted, "You think you're morally superior!" Yet she knew she wasn't any better. Her conscience told her it was a sick relationship but it was easier to stay than to start her life over again. But in this moment, Beth felt ready for change. She knew Henry was afraid of losing what he valued most—his freedom; and *her* greatest fear was financial ruin. If he could give her a monthly stipend until she found a job, she could finally get back up on her own two feet. She had worked hard over the years and had made a good salary in pharmaceutical sales, before the cutbacks—before she was laid off. Then it was time to take Henry up on his offer of moving up to Massachusetts. He had only been there for about six months working for a biotech start-up company.

Beth had sacrificed a lot to build up her savings. Of all the bad things she had internalized from her mother's behavior, she had also adopted some of her admirable traits—like *not* trying to keep up with the Joneses. Beth thought, "I have to get my own place right away. I'm *not* going to move in with my parents in the meantime. Maybe now is the time to use my savings to buy a condo or a townhouse."

She looked at Henry. She knew she must look ridiculous sitting there with her face and eye all puffy and bruised. She said, "I guess I'll move back to Pennsylvania. At least I'll be near my family and I'll just look for a job there."

Henry nodded in agreement and said, "I have to stay here for my job."

A familiar, quiet, calm had washed over Henry, which always followed his violent episodes. Beth figured it was OK to ask at this point. She had to satisfy her curiosity. "Why did you say this morning that you wanted to move to New Hampshire?"

Henry sighed. "I've looked at a couple of places and it's much cheaper to live there."

"Oh." Beth was certain it really had something to do with gun laws and she had hoped he would admit it; but she decided to just let it go. Instead she said, "The lease is up at the end of May and it sounds like you've found a place. If I start looking now, we could be out of here by then."

"Let's go into the living room," Henry said.

As soon as Beth sat down, Jake jumped onto her lap. Henry pulled a blanket around their shoulders as they huddled on the couch. Beth looked at Henry's long, thin legs that wore faded, navy blue mechanic's pants. She was filled with a sense of melancholy as they sat in the silence of imminent change.

Chapter 3

CHARLES BRACED HIMSELF against the cold as he made his way to the bus stop. His hands were curled inside the front pocket of his hoodie that he tugged downward, so it would hold tight against his wet hair. He refused to run, even as the bus was already loading kids from the curbside. He subtly quickened his step when he saw the last girl in line move forward. He knew his mother would give him a rash of shit if he missed the bus again. He was still a short distance away when a gust of wind rushed against his face causing his eyes to water, as he noticed the bus was now just sitting still; waiting for him. "Oh shit!" he panicked. In one swift motion, he rounded past the bus door and ascended the first step, when he quickly halted. That weird nerd, Shelly, had bent down to pick up the books she dropped, when she tripped onto the bus steps. This gave Charles enough time to catch his breath and even look like a hard ass, as he shook his head with impatience and waited for Shelly to pick up the mess. He didn't dare to assist her. He sniffled and wiped the snot from his ice cold nose.

He spotted an empty seat just past the middle of the bus. Charles, like all the other students, avoided eye contact when choosing a seat on the school bus; yet each of them could have found their comfort zone in the dark. There was an unwritten rule that delineated who sat where; and it hadn't changed for decades. The front seats were for the nerds and bookworms; followed by the jocks and cheerleaders; followed by the in-betweens who didn't quite have a category; and finally the back-seats for the burnouts and bullies. He settled into the warmth of the overheated bus and immediately wondered if Leah was looking at him. She sat at the start of the burnout section; vaguely tethered to Charles's world of the in-betweens. Suddenly, he was filled with dread when he heard, "Hey there's Chuck! How the fuck is Chuck?"

He turned and gave a half grin to the guy who said this every day without fail. And without fail he thought, "Why the hell did my parents have to name me Charles. Nobody is named Charles anymore." His mother told him it was the name of her favorite brother, who also happened to be Charles's godfather.

If the rest of his friends were preoccupied, David Reilly would let him go. But if just one other person—and that was usually John Rablinski—paid attention to David and started to laugh, he'd keep it up. And on days like today, when Charles could smell the aroma of pot coming from the back of the bus, it turned into a no-holds-barred attack. David would eventually move up a few rows to sit in back of Charles and say, in a stage whisper, "Hey Chuck, wanna fuck?"

John Rablinski laughed as he said, "No way man. You don't do that shit."

David leaned into the back of Charles's head and said loudly, "I like girls but you could change my mind Chuck. Let's meet in the gym and I'll ride you like a fuckin goat!"

John Rablinski roared with laughter. Charles moved his head forward to get away from David. Today, he felt brave, so he turned around and said, "Come on man. Back off."

David made a mock-startled look at his audience. "Back off! I want to back on!"

Finally, Leah, who always carefully assessed Charles's reaction to this routine and wondered how he could stand it day after day, said, "Why don't you leave him alone David?"

David pretended to be hurt and said, "Why? Do you want me to save him for you, Leah?" At which point David returned to his seat. As he passed by Leah, he murmured, "Yeah, I guess now that I'm done fuckin you, it's all downhill from here."

John laughed and Leah shouted, "Shut up David! You asshole."

Charles felt his heart skip a beat. "David Reilly?" He worried to himself. "Leah slept with him? Ah Jesus . . . how could I be so stupid? Maybe it's not true. Maybe he just said it to make people think she did it." Now the bus felt too hot. Charles slipped his fingers between his collar and his throat and tried to let some air in. The bus driver made another stop and more students made their way down the aisle. Charles started to feel nauseated as he caught a whiff of diesel fuel, mixed with marijuana. He heard the hydraulic door hiss shut and the bus lurched forward, when he felt a chunk of his breakfast cereal reflux into his mouth. His stomach contracted in a reflex of panic and he slowly exhaled through his nostrils while discretely chewing on the toasted oats. He looked out the window with mock interest and swallowed his breakfast for a second time. Oddly, it was a comforting reminder of home—not that he had much happiness there either, but at least it was better than this.

When the bell rang at 3:00, Charles reluctantly made his way to his math teacher's classroom. His mother had insisted that he get tutored in Algebra after she found his last report card. "You wanna be a loser like your father? Just keep it up! Don't study. Don't do your homework. Get some girl pregnant by the time you're 17 and end up a miserable bastard like him." Then she had softened for a minute and said, "Oh, I'm sorry." She took a long drag from her cigarette. "Just do me a favor and find out if they have some kinda tutoring at your school. Hell, I'll pay somebody if I have to. But don't ya see? You won't be able to make anything of yourself if you don't get into college." Then she poured herself another glass of that sweet white wine he always smelled on her breath—like juice mixed with morning breath; mixed with cigarette ashes.

"Hi Charles."

He turned his head slightly to the left and saw Leah approaching him. "Hi Leah." He felt awkward when he heard the unguarded enthusiasm in his voice.

"Are you staying after school?"

"Ah yeah. Are you?"

"Yeah. I have cheerleading practice." Leah was one of those girls who fit in everywhere. She was cool enough to be liked by the burnouts; athletic enough to be liked by the jocks; and smart enough to be admired by the nerds. Her long blond hair, angelic face and shapely figure made her the object of desire for most of the boys of the 6th grade class.

"What are you staying for?" Leah asked.

Charles didn't want her to think he was the object of bullying *and* stupid, so he had to think of something fast. "Um. I'm just going to head to the library for a little while because I have a history report due soon."

"Alright, well I guess I'll see you later," Leah said. She gave him a flirtatious look and, for a minute, Charles was the happiest man on earth . . . until he saw Matt Howard meet up with Leah at the end of the hall and she gave him a kiss on the lips. With that, his life returned to misery, as he watched Leah and Matt stroll arm in arm around the corner.

By the time he arrived at the doorway of the math teacher, his head was hanging.

"Charles. Good to see you. Come in. Have a seat."

Charles made his way to a seat just to the right of Mr. DeLeon's desk. He felt no inclination to hide his mood. He dropped his backpack onto the floor as he flopped into the chair.

"Bad day?" Mr. DeLeon asked.

"Sorta." Charles was leaning over to pick up his backpack when Mr. DeLeon said, "Don't bother with that now. Just sit and relax a minute."

With that, Mr. DeLeon stretched his arms into the air, pushed his chair back, and stood. He pulled his V-neck sweater back into place; walked to the front of his desk and then sat on the edge of it and crossed his arms. "What seems to be the problem Charles?"

He squirmed a bit in his chair and diverted his eyes from Mr. DeLeon. He etched his thumb on the top of the small desk that jutted out in front of him. After a moment he sat upright and looked at Mr.

DeLeon for a second. Then he lowered his eyes again and said, "My mother basically said I'm gonna ruin my life if I don't get this Algebra thing."

Mr. DeLeon made a nasal snorting sound and Charles looked up at him. Mr. DeLeon seemed to be amused and said, "Well I wouldn't go that far. After all, there are lots of successful people in the world who basically sucked at Algebra."

Charles laughed a little. It was the second time he felt happy that day. After all, Mr. DeLeon was a cool guy—everybody thought that. He had a swagger. He was good looking, tall, athletically built and seemed to have a perpetual tan. He was the coach of the boys' tennis team and one of those popular teachers, who made even nerdy kids feel cool by association.

Mr. DeLeon said, "That's not what I was referring to when I asked what the problem was. I was referring to the way your head was hanging when you entered my classroom."

Charles felt a little embarrassed. "Oh that. It was nothing."

Mr. DeLeon took a deep breath and stood up straight. As Charles raised his head, their eyes met. "Charles. You can trust me. Lots of guys tell me what's going on in their lives. Sometimes it can feel like you're all alone . . . but you're not."

Charles wanted Mr. DeLeon to like him and now it seemed like he might. "It's just a girl thing that's all." Now Charles was nervously picking at some lint on his shirt.

Mr. DeLeon said, "I know how that goes. But don't give it another thought. I can help you with that too." Then he returned to his seat at the front desk and said, "But first, why don't you take out your math book and we'll try to make a couple of things more clear."

Charles took out his book and a pencil and asked, "What chapter?"

"Why don't we start at the beginning? But don't worry, we'll skim through a lot of stuff."

Charles smiled and they proceeded with his first tutoring session.

At 4:00, it seemed like he had only been there for 15 minutes instead of an hour. A buzzer sounded and Mr. DeLeon said, "Looks like you're a free man Charles. Just do me a favor and try the first five problems at the end of the chapter."

"OK."

"And don't stress over whether you can work all of them out. Just do what you can and that will help me to evaluate what we need to spend more time on when you're here again on Thursday."

"Alright. Thanks Mr. DeLeon."

"No problem Charles. Have a good couple of days." Mr. DeLeon stood up and reached out his hand. Charles shook hands with him. "And we'll talk a little more about that girl too."

"Sounds good." Charles made a shy grin and then quickened his pace through the halls. He didn't want to miss the activity bus.

By the time he walked out of the front lobby, a bus with number 25 was sitting outside. He climbed onto the bus and was relieved to see just three other students on board.

"Great." He thought. "I'll be home soon. I hope mom cooks tonight. I'm hungry." He rubbed his nose, which was running a little. He lifted his hand again because he noticed the smell of cologne. He liked it. "But where . . . oh, it must be Mr. DeLeon's cologne." He remembered shaking his hand. He thought, "How cool would it be if he could help me with Algebra *and* with figuring out a way to get Leah to go out with me someday." He caught his reflection in the window when they passed a row of trees on the right, as the sun's rays now lowered behind the trees on the left. He admired his reflection. He was a handsome young man whose weight had not yet caught up with his increasing height. Now his slender fingers wrapped around the cold, metal pole at the front of the bus. The next stop was his. The bus door hissed open and the early darkness of another cold winter night made Charles shiver. He jogged toward his house and then kicked a stone against the wall of his front porch. As he opened the front door, his heart sunk when he heard his parents shouting at each other. He thought, "Another night with the battling tops." It was just a nickname he had given to his parents.

His father's voice grew louder, "Yeah well I'm outta here you fuckin bitch!" On his way toward the front door, his Dad's mood changed when he saw him. "Hey, how's it going Charlie?" His tone was genuinely friendly.

"Alright I guess."

"I'll catch ya later." And with that, his father was gone . . . again.

He turned toward the kitchen. "Hey Mom. I'm home."

His mother had been crying, but she wiped her face and said, "Don't get too comfortable. Let's get in car. We're going to Burger King. I'm not cooking tonight." She finished off the wine in her glass and grabbed her cigarettes.

"What happened?" Charles asked meekly.

"Don't worry about it. Just hurry up so we can get you back home to do your homework. I told you I don't want you turning into an asshole like your father."

Charles wasn't sure how doing his homework would prevent him from becoming an asshole but he tended to side with his mother's opinions since his father was hardly ever there.

Chapter 4

O**N SATURDAY MORNING**, Beth took Jake for a walk and returned home to find Henry standing in the kitchen drinking a tall glass of water mixed with just a small portion of orange juice, while he nibbled on chocolate chip cookies. For an exceptionally intelligent man, his logic on most things was a puzzle to Beth. He didn't want to drink too much orange juice because "it's full of sugar," Henry would say; and yet he constantly nibbled on cookies and candy. Beth found it annoying that his metabolism had never changed as he matured because he was able to eat vast amounts of sweets and still maintain his thin frame. Most people would reason that his 6 foot 5 inch height allowed him to consume a high intake of simple carbohydrates but Beth knew differently as a 5 foot 11 inch woman, who now had to exercise and watch her calories if she wanted to stay in shape.

"Hey there he is!" Henry said, referring to Jake.

Beth was relieved to hear his pleasant tone so she figured it was safe to ask, "Aren't you going to Maryland this morning?"

Henry walked over to her and said, "Sweetie, I can't leave you now. I'm going to wait until Monday and I'll just stay there for a few days."

"That's good news."

"I love you," Henry said as he hugged Beth close to him.

"I love you too." Beth hoped this might mean the whole idea of their separation would be forgotten, but then Henry said, "And don't worry. You know I'll take care of you and Jake. Right now money isn't an issue."

Beth still wasn't sure where he was going with this, so she said, "You mean, you'll help out until I find a job in Pennsylvania?"

Henry stood back from her and started to say something until he looked at her face more closely. "Wait a minute." He turned on the overhead light and said, "Oh sweetie, your right eye looks pretty bad."

"I know. I saw it in the bathroom this morning." Her eyelid was still puffy, but now looked as if she had done a sloppy job with purple eye shadow because the color purple spread across her eyelid, until it circled under the eye and around to the bridge of her nose.

"Does it hurt?"

"A little. At least I can see out of it. That's what I was really worried about last night when you . . ." She caught herself.

Henry said, "I'm so sorry sweetie. I don't want to hurt you. But you were threatening my freedom." His voice got progressively louder.

"Your freedom? How was I threatening your freedom?"

Henry yelled, "You said you were going to call the police about my shells (referring to the bullet shells) if I went to Maryland."

"Yeah, but I still don't understand why you decided to go to Maryland for three weeks."

"I told you—it's none of your business!" Henry walked out of the kitchen and was pacing around the living room. He turned to look at Beth. He shouted, "And what right do you have to tell me what I can and cannot do!"

Beth just sort of crumbled into a chair and started to cry, while Henry continued his rant. Finally, he said "Come on Jake. Let's go back to bed. At least we'll have peace there." Jake followed him into the bedroom and Henry slammed the door shut.

Beth sat and cried for a while, but then she had an idea. "I'm going to take a picture of my face." She knew Henry well enough to know that he would eventually deny what he had done or, at the very least, convince her that she deserved it.

There was a walking trail behind their apartment that stretched for miles. It was one of many "Rails to Trails" paths in Massachusetts. These were old, unused rail lines that had been converted into bike paths. They were less crowded during the week, but on weekends, they were cluttered with people jogging, walking, biking or roller skating along the trails. Beth figured she could slip out and, if Henry noticed, she would simply tell him that she had gone for a walk. She didn't have to mention that she had asked someone to take her photograph while she was gone. She found her digital camera and realized she hadn't used it in quite some time. As she was fumbling around with it, she decided to try taking some photos of herself while holding the camera at arm's length.

She took one photo but became nervous when the camera made audible beeping sounds as the photo was taken. She held her breath and crept to the hallway to listen for any sounds of Henry stirring. It was quiet. With that, she slipped out the sliding glass door and made her way to the walking trail. After no more than five minutes, she came upon a threesome of middle-aged women who were strolling along the path and chatting. "Excuse me," Beth said tentatively. She felt awkward as the women turned in unison and looked at her. They seemed to have an attitude of "Why are you bothering us?" so she knew she better get right to the point.

"I had a fight with my husband last night and . . ." She could see their expressions soften and hoped their judgment would be on her side. "My husband hit me and I wondered if you could take a picture of it so I can show the police if I have to."

One of the women was indignant, "You should call the police right now! They should see what he did to you. Nobody deserves that." The other women shook their heads in disgust.

Beth was afraid the women would force the issue so she tried to dissuade their intensity. "It's the first time he's done something like this," she lied, as she handed the woman her camera. "Where do I push the button . . . Oh here it is." Then she instructed Beth, "Turn to the left a little so I can get a good view of the right side of your . . . OK, that's good." She snapped a couple of pictures and, as Beth looked off into the distance, she wondered what the passersby were thinking.

"Here." The woman handed Beth her camera unceremoniously.

"Thank you."

"You really should get rid of him," the woman said scornfully.Beth's eyes filled with tears and she uttered, "I know." One of the women touched her arm and said sympathetically, "It's not the first time either, is it?" Beth looked at her and confessed, "No. It's not." The woman grimaced and, after a brief silence, they turned away from her and continued on their walk.

The next day was Sunday. Beth went to the 7:30 mass by herself. She sat way in the back, which made her feel odd because she usually sat in one of the first three pews; but that morning her eye was worse. The purple color had deepened and spread into the upper part of her cheek. Fortunately it was cold enough to warrant a hat; so with her glasses on, and a hat pulled down far enough to meet her eyebrows, Beth convinced herself that the priest wouldn't be able to see anything. It wasn't until she had to walk up the aisle to receive communion that she felt worried. But as luck would have it, there were enough people in attendance to warrant a Eucharistic Minister—a member of the church who assists with distribution of communion. Beth turned toward this man and said, "Amen," as he lifted the communion wafer in front of her eyes. She blessed herself and returned to the back of the church, where she quietly slipped out just after the final blessing was given.

Beth had prayed for the strength to get away from Henry—not just physically by moving back to Pennsylvania, but emotionally. She had gazed at the statue of Mary, the Blessed Mother of God, and silently promised her to do the right thing. But as soon as Beth crossed the threshold of her front door, the promises in her prayers were forgotten. Beth was addicted to Henry; or maybe the addiction was her craving for the love of a man who would protect her. She didn't see how illogical this was. She didn't know that what she needed protection from, was him.

Beth made her usual Sunday breakfast of eggs, bacon, toast; tea for Henry, coffee for herself. She lit a candle on the table in the kitchen, which was always covered with a white linen tablecloth. The apartment didn't have a dining room, so she did her best to make the kitchen table an acceptable substitute.

Henry was quiet, as usual, while they ate breakfast. She was grateful that he seemed to be in a better mood than the day before; but for the rest of the day, he sat at his desk in the living room and ignored her. Although it was normal behavior for him to be intensely focused on his computer for hours, Beth knew his neglect was a way to punish her for upsetting him. She did her best to distract herself by reading and then going for a long walk in the afternoon. At dinner, Henry was morose and only grumbled when Beth tried to make conversation. She grew more and more depressed and tired so she went to bed early, with the television left on to provide the company of people in the background.

At 4:00 a.m. on Monday, the alarm went off. Henry was quick to leap out of bed and prepare to leave for Maryland. Beth stayed in bed, while Jake followed Henry around. She could hear him stacking the cartons of bullet shells by the front door. She felt a mixture of sadness and anger as she wondered, "How can someone who is so well educated, and from an upper middle class family in Germany, behave like a gun crazed hillbilly?"

To say Henry's cabin in Maryland was rustic would have been a compliment. It was one of his many unfinished projects that Beth had helped him with over the years. Henry insisted that they do the work themselves. But once they moved up to Massachusetts, he decided to enlist the help of his friend, who was a building contractor. However, he neglected to consider whether or not he had the money available to pay him for the work. When he had asked Beth to pay the $35,000 bill out of her savings, she refused. Henry became violently angry and eventually chased her up the cabin stairs with a long-handled flashlight that he smashed against her back. Fortunately, just as he pulled back to strike her, she had tripped onto the floor mattress that served as their bed and so the blow hit her muscles instead of her spine. But the worst was yet to come when Henry told her if she didn't lend him the money, they were finished. So Beth loaned him the money which he would pay back a few years later. But even after all of this, the cabin languished with no insulation and nothing but drywall sheltering the great room that Beth had paid for.

Henry was always getting distracted by a new hobby or a new project. They had had a big fight the weekend he taught Beth how to fill the bullet shells with a precisely measured amount of gun powder. The original plan for the weekend was to work together to do some inside construction work on the cabin, but, instead he decided to drive to Virginia to pick up a machine he bought on eBay, that would spin the shells and cartridges to shining, clean perfection, at which point they were ready for filling. In the meantime, Beth was assigned to sit at an old wooden desk, under a lamp and fill the shells, while stopping periodically to load more wood into the wood-burning stove for heat.

Beth got out of bed, after hearing Henry make a few trips in and out of the apartment. She wanted to say goodbye.

Henry pet Jake and then looked at Beth and said, "I'm going to miss you guys."

Now Beth was tearful as she said, "We're going to miss you too."

Henry hugged her and said, "I'll call you tonight when I get there."

Beth started to say something but stopped. Henry asked, "What is it?"

"I was just wondering how long you'll be gone." She was suddenly afraid and desperate at the thought of him leaving.

Henry hugged her again and said, "I love you sweetie. Don't worry. I'll just be gone a couple days."

By Wednesday, Beth found herself going to church again because it was Ash Wednesday (the beginning of Lent for Catholics). Again, she felt self-conscious in church because the colors on her face continued their metamorphosis. Deep purple now encircled her eye and there was an inflated pouch that had formed in her upper cheek that must have been from pooled blood. It was green, purple and yellowish at the edges. These same colors were now evident on the left side of her nose and above her eyebrow into the temple area. That afternoon, she took several more photographs of her face, and then took the tiny camera disk to her local pharmacy to be developed.

The next day, as she sat in her car, reviewing the photographs, she was surprised. Somehow, looking at her bruised face in the photos made her more aware of Henry's brutality. It was like looking at someone else instead of her own image. "That bastard stayed for the weekend because he wanted to be sure I didn't go anywhere or tell anyone what happened. As usual he was nice initially but already blaming me for what happened by Saturday." She knew it would happen again and again. She knew she was repeating what she had lived with in her parents' marriage.

Beth's mother was quite beautiful; yet she was an extremely insecure and jealous woman. Her father was 6 feet 7 inches tall with a muscular physique and a handsome face; but it was his charm and charisma that made him a successful salesman and the life of the party. Yet he was a good father and faithful husband; but like Henry, his downfall was his temper. His children received the typical warnings from mom when a test was failed or, once when a pumpkin was stolen. . . "Wait until your father gets home . . ." This amounted to being yelled at and, depending on the severity of the offense, a slap, a shove, and when they were little, the belt came off now and then for a few lashings on the behind. But as children of their era, this was considered good parental discipline and certainly not abuse. However, fights between her parents inevitably escalated from yelling at each other to violence. In the beginning, it always happened when the children were asleep—maybe because her father worked two jobs for at least a dozen years. But Beth always woke up when the shouting started. Her little brother slept in the tiny third floor bedroom of their modest split level twin home, where he apparently couldn't hear their parents. Her sister shared a room and a bed with her, but always told Beth to "go back to sleep" whenever Beth nervously shook her sister's leg to wake her up. Beth would then lean out of bed where she could see the small staircase and the green, leather recliner in the corner of the living room. It was really "Daddy's chair" but her mother took refuge in it, while she waited for her father to get home from work. On most nights, Beth was relieved to see her mother relaxing in the chair; sometimes half asleep with the television on; sometimes reading a book. Then she too could relax and go to sleep. But when the fighting started, the chair was empty. Beth would creep out of bed and stand at the top of the stairs with a slight tremble and a nervous stomach, as her hands grasped the sides of her pajama pants. But she was always brave enough to intervene. As soon as she heard slapping or her mother yelping in pain, she would descend the stairs without hesitation and yell at her father to stop. It seemed as if they never noticed the waiflike figure in between them; except maybe the time that her father punched her mother in the nose and she started to bleed. Beth yelled louder that time. Her father backed away a little and brought his fist to his face that winced as if *he* was in pain. In that split second, he seemed to be making a decision. Suddenly his mouth twisted into an ugly grimace. He growled, "*Jesus Christ!*". . . as he started forward again. "Stop Daddy! Stop!" Beth shouted. Then he turned and kicked the kitchen chair away from the table and then slumped into it; shaking his head in despair. Her mother had retreated to the couch and sat crying. Beth was frightened by the blood splatters on her mother's blouse. She asked meekly, "Are you alright?" She ignored Beth, but the attention seemed to give her mother fresh courage. She yelled at her father, as she made her way into the kitchen to get a paper towel. Her father jumped out of the chair and started toward her mother again. Beth's heart was beating wildly as she ran to get between them. Somehow it worked, and her father changed direction; this time he flung open the refrigerator and before the door shut on its own, she heard the crack of the aluminum tab being pulled from the beer can. It was a sound that meant trouble—a sound that came to signal either the start of a fight or the continuation of a fight.

It was that same night, when Beth's father acknowledged her presence. For the first time, this tiny referee got the attention of this giant. He even pulled her close to him and sat her on his lap. She could smell his beer breath as he spoke softly. And then her mother yelled, "You leave her alone!" Up until that moment, her mother had also completely ignored her. And yet Beth was certain her mother wanted her there. The rest of the scene that night grew dim and almost faded from memory . . . almost.

Beth was well into her 40s when her sister Laura came to visit. It was an episodic closeness they shared; because most of the time Beth saw Laura as an enigma—a person who would never truly open up about herself or her feelings. On this visit, Laura was there to comfort Beth who was experiencing a particularly rough patch during the divorce process (from her first husband Bernard, an alcoholic). Laura was going to stay overnight and they were upstairs getting ready for bed when their conversation erupted into an argument. Beth began to cry and, as always whenever she argued with her sister, or her parents, memories of childhood came gushing at her and stirred an old anger that lingered with a quiet burden on the edge of her mind. Maybe she would have been freed of it, if she ever truly forgave her parents. . . or her sister. She could never forget all those Sunday afternoons when she heard the sound of his car keys as her father announced, "I'm just going for a ride." Then he would turn to Laura and say, "Come on" and the two of them would be gone for a couple of hours. Where did they go? What did they do? It seemed as though they always went on those rides after her mother and father had a horrible fight. She was always afraid to ask her; when suddenly, out of nowhere, Beth heard herself screaming, "What happened when you went on those car rides with Dad?"

Laura responded indignantly, "Nothing!"

Beth forced herself to lower her voice. Maybe this time Laura would finally tell her what really happened if she could just bear the weight of Laura's stoicism at moments like this when Beth tried to pry at whatever was going on inside Laura's mind. Laura sat rigidly on the edge of the bed with her big brown eyes fixed on Beth. It felt as if she wanted to say something more. Beth said softly, "Well, what did you talk about?"

"I don't know," Laura whined and then looked away.

Beth moved closer, "Did he ever . . . touch you?"

"No!" Laura screamed. She stood up and immediately began gathering her things. She was leaving. The moment for intimacy was gone and now Beth had nothing to lose, so she shouted in frustration, "Well how come he always went on rides with you when him and mom were fighting?"

"I don't know!" After a moment of silence, Laura stopped for a minute and offered, "I guess he just needed someone to talk to because mom was so crazy . . . he said when they had sex all she would do is just lay there!"

"He *said* that?" Beth shouted.

"Yeah." But Laura now stood still, looking strangely calm, as if she expected Beth to see how normal it all was.

But Beth said defiantly, "What father says that to his daughter?"

"Oh Beth . . ." Laura's tone insinuated that Beth was entirely too provincial.

Beth sat down and said, "You know, one time when mom and dad were having a really bad fight, I remember Dad telling me to sit on his lap. And mom said 'You leave her alone' and I don't know exactly what happened but there was something in the tone of her voice I never forgot." She was almost afraid to continue but she felt she had to; if not now, then when would they ever talk about it. "I remember these little round circles with a design in the center all over his white boxer shorts. Sometimes I don't know if it really happened or if it's one of those false memories, but I think he told me to touch it."

Laura, who had returned to sit on the bed, suddenly stood up and said, "How can you say that about Dad!"

Beth was suddenly defensive and she shouted at Laura, who was now turning to leave the room, "Then why do I remember that I pulled my little hand away from this hard thing and he guided it back . . . "

Laura was now running down the stairs shouting, "You're crazy Beth!"

Beth stood at the top of the stairs and screamed, "Why am *I* crazy? What about what *he* did?"

But Laura had slammed the front door and was gone.

Beth stood crying and then ran to the bedroom window and pushed the curtain aside to look at the empty parking space left by Laura. She didn't feel regret about what she had insinuated. Instead she felt the same frustration about the unsolved mystery. She thought, "If nothing ever happened on their long drives, then why was Laura so bizarre as a teenager and even as a young woman, when it came to boys." She could still see Laura, on one of those many nights, incapacitated—almost catatonic—as she sat on the floor leaning against her bed; ashen and tormented with nausea and occasionally vomiting into her trashcan; while Beth selfishly tried to coax her into going out to a dance club to meet up with the guys they had met on the boardwalk the night before. But it wasn't always selfishly motivated. For some strange reason, Beth felt compelled to help Laura when she worked herself into such a state before a date. She would notice that Laura had not come out of her room and it was getting close to the time that her date was supposed to arrive. Beth would find Laura in her bedroom, so crippled with nausea and fear about the date that she would say she wanted to call the guy and cancel. Then Beth would get aggressive, "Oh no you're not. Come on. Snap out of it. It's too late to cancel. You have to go!" Finally, Laura would stand up and, white as a sheet, she would slowly finish getting ready. But the next day, she would tell Beth that she had excused herself to go to the bathroom during the dinner date and she threw up in the restroom. Even when Laura worked at her father's office one summer and he drove her to work with him; Laura would have to take a grocery bag and set it on her lap for the ride to work, so she could vomit into the bag along the way. Laura told Beth it was because she was nervous because she liked a young guy at work.

Beth wiped tears from her cheek and, as she pushed her hair from her face, she could see herself gently moving her mother's hair from her face. But now, instead of being the child reassuring her mother, she wondered out loud, "Maybe it wasn't *always* his fault." It seemed that, other than family events (and sometimes even those), every social outing resulted in a fight between her parents.

Beth remembered so many scenes as if they happened yesterday. This time it was a big picnic at a swim club many years before. It was hot and sunny and the kids were all laughing and shouting as they jumped into the pool. All day they were swimming and eating hot dogs and drinking soda. By nightfall, the parents were having fun dancing to the live band. As it began to get dark, her mother started to round everybody up to leave. Beth got into the car with her brother and sister and they were all still buzzing with energy. She remembers her mother smiling and saying goodbye to a few of her uncles who were there. Her father shut the car door and started to drive away when her mother started on him. "Did you have fun dancing with that slut?" It escalated from there and the yelling got louder and louder. They were stopped at a traffic light when her father turned toward her mother. Beth could see in his profile the ugly face he made with gritted teeth and fury in his eyes; it always meant that in a matter of seconds, his hand was going to hit someone hard. And sure enough, he slapped her mother across the face. She cried before she started yelling at him. "You danced with that woman in front of your children!" He shouted sarcastically, "Yeah and I wanted to go make out with her in the bathroom but you were watching us like a hawk!" Her mother gasped and the light turned green; and as he steered into a turn with his left hand, his right hand suddenly pulled her hair that had looked so pretty pulled back with her red and white scarf. He drove forward as he yanked her head back and forth. Beth felt embarrassed for her mother, whose hair was now messy and her scarf was now crumpled around her shoulders. Then there was that moment of silence that hung in the air . . . they might stop . . . or . . . then her mom taunted, "She was so ugly, at least you could have picked someone good looking."

"Jesus Christ!" Suddenly, her father flung a backhanded slap against her mother's face.

"Oww!" And then crying . . . . more crying . . . and finally quiet.

Beth could only remember her own anxiety as she watched them. She never knew how to stop them when her father was driving. She couldn't even say whether her brother had fallen asleep; maybe he was scared too. She didn't wonder about Laura because Laura was able to ignore them, or so it seemed. Beth only concentrated on keeping watch. The old car had no air conditioning and the cool summer night air rushed through all the open windows and brought the ambient noise of peace. It was when the car came to a stop that the summer crickets warned of more fighting when they got inside the house. For now, Beth's hands clenched around the hem of her shorts and rested against her skinny, little legs.

Beth was learning that violence and jealousy were normal parts of a marriage. She was learning that it was normal to keep those secrets locked inside the walls of a family home. When her mother talked with the other women at a neighborhood block party, someone gossiped about a woman in the news who had been beaten by her husband. Beth noticed her mother was as shocked and disgusted as the other women; and she began to wonder if her mother was the only one hiding a secret. "Maybe half the women here get hit," she dared to wonder. And this taught her that living with domestic abuse, and hiding it, was just the way women lived.

It was the memory of one fight a couple years later that still brought with it a palpable feeling of dread. This time Beth was too afraid to do something and she only watched, as her father hit her mother who was sprawled across the staircase. He was wearing a suit and tie, and her mother had on that green and purple dress with a fold at the hip line that simulated a belt. Her black hair was teased up in the back with bangs that highlighted a face of fine features and Irish freckles that she hid as best she could with makeup. They must have been at a dinner with her Dad's sales team. "Stop it! . . . Stop it! . . ." her mother cried. She tossed her head from side to side, as her father slapped her face from right to left. He had that same ugly grimace as he slapped her again and again and then punched at her. Beth stood there, speechless and shaking because lately, her parents had begun to notice her. They had both been angered by her presence during their fights. Not only did they notice her, but they would each yell at her to go back to bed—even her mother, which she really couldn't understand. Suddenly her father looked up and yelled at her, "Go to bed!" She remembered sitting on the floor in the kitchen the next day, pressed against the cabinet, as she watched her mother pace around the kitchen with the long, white phone cord extended to follow her as she cried into the phone to her *own* mother, "He raped me! He tore my dress and he raped me!" Beth didn't know what the word rape meant, but judging by her mother's hysteria, she knew it was something really bad. After a while, her mom calmed down and hung up the phone, but she started crying again as soon as she sat on the couch. Beth followed and sat quietly on the floor next to her mom's white, freckled legs. Her mother ignored her presence, but Beth was certain they shared a secret, silent bond.

Whereas Beth saw herself as mom's brave defender, her mother *and* her father only saw Beth as an embarrassing reminder of their bad behavior. And Beth's father didn't hide his resentment for her mother's protector. Like most kids, Beth felt the excitement of Friday nights—no school for two whole days. Friday was a break from cooking for her mother. They usually got pizza and were allowed to stay up late enough to watch "Sing Along with Mitch!" One Friday night, Beth was going to be the one who got to hold the pizza in the front seat of the car. She was dancing and twirling around in the shop while they waited for the pizza to come out of the oven. The man behind the counter said, "Somebody looks happy tonight." Beth smiled and the man talked to her daddy about her and they were all laughing and happy. When they left the pizza shop, her father's mood changed in an instant. He became monstrous, and he threw the change onto the parking lot. As the coins scattered around, he yelled to Beth, "Now pick that up!" Apparently, she had gotten on his nerves again; and it would happen a lot. It was usually when she was happy and talkative. He either sneered at her and shook his head in disgust or hollered, "Jesus Christ . . . what's wrong with you?" It was the most embarrassing when it happened at the dinner table. Her smile would slip away and she would quiet down. She would feel the weight of her face—suddenly so heavy that she couldn't stop it from drooping into a pout. She would swallow hard but it felt like stones in the top of her throat and now it was beyond her control—suddenly she was crying—again. Then her father would say, "Oh Christ, now she's crying! There's something wrong with that kid."

Beth became more emotional and sensitive. "I think she's emotionally disturbed!" her father yelled to her mother in the kitchen one night. Ironically, her mother never took her side. It seemed that as long as her father was *in* the house and paying attention to her, her mother didn't care if Beth was hurt. "What's wrong with you now?" she would say in a nasty tone. Then Beth would start crying again and run upstairs to her room. Still, whenever her mother was sick, Beth would sit by her bed. There was a time when her mother was suffering severe back pain and, as Beth held vigil sitting on the floor in front of the bed, her mother yelled, "Why are you sitting there? Just get out of here and go play!" Beth felt embarrassed and hurt, as she slowly stood up. "Now don't start your crying!" her mother snapped.

One time her father slapped her across the face in front of her first boyfriend, Mark. They were standing in the kitchen on a Saturday afternoon and Beth's mother had already said no when she asked if she could go over to Mark's house for dinner the next day. Beth turned to her father and playfully pleaded, "Please Dad . . ." Suddenly he was angry and shouted, "Your mother already said no!" and then he slapped Beth. She stood frozen, holding her hand to her face and looking at the floor. Her father just walked out of the room and her mother said nothing. Fortunately, Mark did not interpret that as license to do the same to her.

Yet even into her teenage years when her parents raged at each other, Beth was quick to defend her mother. One night, Beth woke up when she heard the front door slam shut. The worst of it must have happened in the car this time because her mother looked disheveled. The good thing was, there seemed to be less violence by then; the bad part was that something had changed about her mother. She actually began to talk to Beth. "I don't think your father wants to be married anymore," she cried, as she sat on the edge of Beth's bed at 2:30 in the morning. Her mother said fearful, angry things to Beth that a young daughter should not have been burdened with.

The morning after was always the same. Her mother never seemed to notice that she dragged Beth into the twisted emotions of domestic violence. She never spoke to Beth about what she had said the night before; it was expected that Beth just pretend it never happened. Her parents fighting and being happy again became the normal routine. What confused Beth the most was that Laura had become her parents' obviously favorite child. They even seemed to compete for her. Maybe her mother wondered about those car rides too. Maybe she thought they talked about her and if she was nice enough to Laura, she would help to convince her husband to stay with her. One time after a fight, her mother took Laura to the mall for a shopping spree. That night Beth and her brother watched as Laura modeled her new clothes in the living room. The highlight was the new gray maxi coat, with faux pockets and sleeve cuffs—the fashion rage of the day!

"Wow! I love it!" Beth stood up to touch the material. She was happy because she knew she could wear it once her sister outgrew it.

As Beth watched the favoritism toward her sister over the years, it did eventually fill her with envy. And her sister's long drives with her father were viewed with gnawing suspicion. The seeds of anger and self-doubt had been planted.

Chapter 5

"Hello Charles," Mrs. Kerbowski called to him from her front porch, as he walked home from the bus stop.

"Hi Mrs. K." His voice trailed off at the end of his greeting and he started to look away, until the sound of laughter came from Mrs. K's porch. She lived by herself and didn't typically have visitors in the middle of the week. He saw two other women standing on the porch. Mrs. K. must have seen his inquisitive look. She called to him, "Charles, would you like to meet your new neighbor?"

"Sure," he said, with only slight interest.

The women strolled down the short driveway to meet him. Mrs. K. said, "This is Joyce Batrone. She's a real estate agent."

"Hi Charles. Nice to meet you."

"Nice to meet you too," and then he grinned politely.

Then Mrs. K. motioned toward the tall woman with shoulder length blonde hair and said, "And this is your new neighbor, Beth Hardt. She's going to buy my house."

Beth reached out to shake his hand. "Hi Charles. Nice to meet you."

"Hi. Nice to meet you too." He looked puzzled. "Where are you going Mrs. K.?"

"Oh it's time for me to move into a smaller place. But I won't be too far from here. I'm moving into Haverford Arms—just about a mile or two from here."

Charles hadn't paid much attention to the "For Sale" sign that had been posted on Mrs. K.'s front lawn for several months. For a while now his focus was on Leah, who lately seemed to be making a point of being by his locker at least once a week after the lunch break. He was sure she was doing it on purpose so he would eventually ask her out. He just couldn't work up the nerve because he still saw Leah walking the halls with Matt Howard. They always had their arms around each other, but Charles imagined that Leah secretly needed him to rescue her from Matt. He figured she was such a nice girl that she just couldn't manage to break up with Matt; even though she was really in love with Charles. He hoped Mr. DeLeon could offer some advice about what to do. He just had to find the right moment to bring up the subject.

It seemed that Leah's attention had a very positive effect on Charles. His grades were getting better; partly because Mr. DeLeon's tutoring was helping him to make sense of Algebra; but mostly because he was happy, and that gave him more energy—energy to study and even put his clothes in the hamper; both of which meant his mother wasn't constantly nagging him. Since his grades were improving, it even improved *her* disposition, and when his father showed up a couple weeks ago, he had actually *stayed* since then. With both of his parents at home and not fighting in the middle of the night like they used to; Charles was able to sleep through the night without being awakened by the "battling tops." Life was good.

If he had been a bit younger, he would have asked Mrs. K. if Beth had any children. He would have wanted to know if there were going to be any new kids to play with in the neighborhood. But by 6th grade, it wasn't cool to appear so eager. Instead, he had another thought. He squinted with a bit of uncertainty and looked at Beth, "If you need someone to cut your grass I could probably do it." His mother always complained in the summer about the grass getting too high because his father didn't cut it often enough. She kept telling him, "I can't wait till you're old enough to fix things up around here." When he had turned 12 back in April, she told him to ask his father to show him how to use the lawn mower. He was thrilled. He figured when Beth paid him, he could meet Leah at the mall and maybe buy her something.

Beth said, "Oh that would be great." She looked toward the house. "As long as everything goes okay with the property settlement, I'll be moving in by the summer." Then she looked at Charles and said, "Wait a minute, I just realized I don't even have a lawn mower!"

"That's OK. I have one," Charles said eagerly.

Beth smiled. She was charmed by his youthful energy and excitement. "Alright then. Sounds like a deal."

Charles smiled. "OK. I'll see ya later." He started to walk away but then he turned around and said, "Bye Mrs. K." He wasn't sure if he would see her again with all that talk about her moving. But the thought didn't linger more than a moment and he was on his way home again.

The realtor, Joyce, looked at her watch and said, "I have to be going. I've got another showing soon." Then she asked Beth, "Aren't you happy you don't have to look anymore?"

Beth smiled and said, "Oh definitely."

Joyce said, "Well I'll get moving on the paperwork tonight and don't forget to fax your bank statement to me as soon as possible. I need that as proof that you can make a lump sum payment for the house." Beth had decided to use the bigger portion of her life savings to pay cash for the small house because she had no guarantee of finding a good job that would provide enough money for monthly mortgage payments. It was a bold move for someone who was such a careful, frugal saver.

Mrs. K. said to Joyce, "Make sure you keep things moving because I'd really like to settle by the end of May if possible."

"It shouldn't be a problem."

"It was so nice to meet you Mrs. Kerbowski," Beth said.

"Well it was my pleasure. I'll miss this place but I'm happy to see such a nice young woman moving in. You're going to like it here a lot. The neighbors are good, simple people." She hesitated for a moment and then added, "And hey . . . you already have someone to cut the grass for you." All three of them laughed and, with that, Mrs. Kerbowski waved goodbye and went inside.

Joyce asked with mock concern, "Are you sure Henry won't give you any trouble about moving out?"

Beth was a little embarrassed to admit it, but she said, "Yeah, I'm sure." She knew Joyce was more concerned about getting the deal done.

"Was Henry able to find a place or is he going to stay there—at the same apartment?"

Beth was a little uncomfortable with Joyce's prodding but she answered, "No, he's moving to an apartment in New Hampshire. It's an area he once talked about moving to with me and now he's going by himself."

In a weak moment shortly after she had met Joyce, Beth had shared with her some of the truth about Henry. But now she regretted it because she knew Joyce saw her as a weak and needy woman. Now more than ever, it seemed that her old confidence was gone. Beth had not stayed connected to any old friends, and she didn't put any effort into making new friends. The only people she had stayed connected to, outside of her marriage, was her family. She didn't have anyone else to turn to. Her brother had his own family now and neither Beth nor Laura made any effort toward repairing their relationship. She had allowed herself to become isolated and again made the mistake of latching onto a man, who was only bad for her; and she built her world around him.

She didn't even know if her family was really happy that she was moving back to the area. She had felt so independent when she had decided to move to Massachusetts with Henry. Her family had said that it would take some time to get used to the idea that Beth had gotten back together with Henry because of the violence that had ended their relationship in the past. There were countless times when Beth breathed a sigh of relief that she hadn't confided in anyone that the violence and neglect had started all over again. Once it was over, there was always a brief honeymoon period—until the next time. Beth felt she had to tell someone because somehow, confessing to someone who could validate that she was doing the right thing by leaving him, would help her to finally do it. Telling a stranger made it too easy not to do the right thing because if she was never going to see that person again (like the women on the bike path who took a picture of her bruised face); she didn't feel accountable to them. Whereas if she told her mother, her mother would never let her forget how awful Henry was.

Beth had stayed at her parents' home for long weekends, while she was in Pennsylvania house-hunting. One night, she found herself in a rare private moment with her mother. It seemed her parents were always in the same room, even if they weren't paying attention to each other. She owed this to her mother's anxiety that she had the need to be wherever her father was and he had given up years ago on any chance of the slightest independence. Maybe he felt it was his penance for what he had done to her mother. But on this night, her father had been dozing off in his chair for over an hour when Beth began to talk to her mother.

She told her about a couple of the incidents when Henry had lost his temper—not the worst ones—but enough to provoke her mother into saying the words she needed to hear. Beth's mother did just that. "You should have known he would never change. He's an idiot. You have to think enough of yourself to leave him."

The irony in those words coming from her mother just filled Beth with resentment.

Her father began to fumble his way out of his chair, as he shifted his aching joints. He didn't want to be a part of the impending discussion and now was his chance to escape. Beth's mother looked up at her father when he said, "I'm gonna head in hun." Her mother fidgeted and said, "I'll be right there."

"Goodnight Dad," Beth said.

"Goodnight," he said and raised his head slightly as he made an expression of a goodnight kiss. After he had gone down the hallway, Beth knew her mother would soon follow, so she only had a minute or two to ask. She was nervous and felt as if the words were stuck in her throat . . . but this might be her only chance to *really* talk to her mother. Her mother started to get up from the couch, so she blurted out, "Well . . . you know what it's like."

Her mother sat down again and asked, "What?"

Beth swallowed. "You know . . . the temper thing."

"What do you mean?"

Beth fumbled for the right words. Was her mother pretending not to know what she was talking about or was she serious? After all, she and her sister had noticed that their mother was getting more and more forgetful. Now Beth was twisting her hands in her lap. Her mother was looking at her, with clear eyes and no sign of deception, so she gave her the benefit of the doubt and said bravely, "Dad's temper. I mean, you know what it's like to live with a husband who has a temper." She really wanted to say that her mother knew what it was like to live with a husband who slaps and punches and pulls her hair, but she didn't dare. She was hoping her mother would read between the lines. Apparently she did.

"Oh . . . that was only that one time Beth." Her tone was almost pleading.

Beth's heart sank. What was the point of arguing about it at this point? Her mother was 75 and her father was 77. It seemed her mother wanted to continue to pretend he had only hit her once and therefore it was forgivable. She wanted Beth to continue pretending too. Yet Beth was certain that if her mother had ever acknowledged what had happened during her childhood, she would be able to forgive her mother and free herself of the weight of it. She had more anger toward her mother than her father. Her mother was only a victim of her father's violence. Beth was a victim of witnessing his violence and feeling her mother's neglect. By ignoring the protection of a little girl; by not caring about how confused she must have been by violence at night and then pretending it didn't happen by morning; by favoring the daughter who did nothing to protect her; by never admitting that she lived with an abusive husband and then telling Beth should never make the same mistake; and by never thanking her for her bravery. Instead, her mother wanted her to think that an abusive husband was Beth's problem. It had never been hers. The distance between Beth and her parents had become like a raging river and the only way to close the gap would be to cross it on foot, which was impossible.

Joyce Batrone called first thing in the morning. "You're flying back to Boston tomorrow?"

"Yeah. I'll be back in Lexington by about 4:00 in the afternoon."

Joyce said, "Listen, I know you won't forget to get me that bank statement, but I forgot to ask how the job search is going?" After an awkward silence, she quickly added, "I just don't want to see you get the house and then lose it because you can't pay your bills."

Beth was embarrassed to reveal her *deal with the devil,* but she had to because she had not yet found a job, and she would have to provide proof of income. Finally, she said, "Henry and I have a written agreement—in fact we had it notarized in Massachusetts—that he will support me with $500 per month for rent or living expenses, until I find a job." As she spoke, Beth relaxed a little because she realized she didn't have to tell Joyce *why* Henry had agreed to do so. She didn't have to tell her that Henry had agreed to pay $500 a month because Beth agreed not to report him to the police.

Fortunately Joyce didn't pry. She just said curtly, "OK good. I'll look for your fax tomorrow night then."

"Alright. Thanks again Joyce."

Chapter 6

IT WAS THURSDAY afternoon and Charles was sitting at a desk in front of Mr. DeLeon for another tutoring session.

"How did you make out with the problems I gave you last time?"

Charles said, "Not bad. I had a couple questions but um . . ." He looked at his notebook and played with the frayed edges . . . "I wanted to ask you . . . well . . . remember the time you said you could help with um . . . some advice about girls?" He finally made eye contact with Mr. DeLeon.

Mr. DeLeon smiled. "No problem. What's up?"

"Well, there's this girl Leah and I think she likes me because she's always giving me these looks and talking to me on the bus. And she even stops by my locker sometimes."

"It sounds like she's into you," Mr. DeLeon said cooly, as he played with the tip of his pencil.

"The problem is that she has a boyfriend."

Mr. DeLeon smirked, "That's not a problem. You just have to move right in."

Charles felt hopeful. He laughed a little and said, "Yeah, but what if this guy kicks my ass?"

"He won't. See, you have to strategize. The best way to play it in these situations is to let the girl do the hard part—no pun intended." Mr. DeLeon gave him a slick sideways glance.

Charles made a cautious laugh. He thought he knew what Mr. DeLeon meant but he wasn't a hundred percent sure.

Mr. DeLeon continued, "Look . . . a guy can tell when a girl's into him. So you already know she's into you. Just start giving her more compliments when you talk to her—like how shiny her hair is or how perfect her teeth are—how green her eyes are—you know what I mean. Then after about two weeks of that, ask her if she wants to go to a movie with you. Now you have to be prepared for her to say no the first time. So you just play dumb and ask her why she can't go. Then she tells you she's dating . . . whoever this guy is. But the important thing is that you have to be Mr. Nice Guy and just say, 'that's cool.' Just keep up the charm. Wait another two weeks and ask again . . . eventually you'll wear her down and she'll say yes. Then, if things are going well when you get together, ask her if she's still dating that guy. But don't ask in a desperate way; just say it the same way you would ask if she . . . oh, I don't know . . . if she likes Algebra." They both laughed. Mr. DeLeon continued, "If she says she's still dating him, then you tell her you just don't feel right about sneaking around—that she should do the right thing and tell her boyfriend that she wants to see other people. She probably won't agree immediately, so just tell her to think about it—no pressure. That night she'll go home and think about what an honest person you are—in addition to everything else she likes about you. The next time you see her, she'll agree to tell her boyfriend that they should see other people, and that will probably lead to a breakup because no guy wants to share his girlfriend. And boom. Your problem is solved."

Charles smiled and said, "Sounds good."

Mr. DeLeon smiled and gave him a lingering look. Then he said, "Do me a favor and help me with something back here." He rose out of his chair and headed toward the back of the classroom.

"Sure thing." Charles got up and followed.

Mr. DeLeon opened the door to a large closet and flicked on the light. There were bookshelves on two sides of the room, filled with binders, books and paperwork. One of the walls was partially covered with framed awards for the tennis teams that Mr. DeLeon had coached over the years. The more recent ones were hanging in a display case in the front lobby of the school. A couple of filing cabinets stood under the frames and about half a dozen cardboard boxes were stacked just to the left of the doorway.

"Do me a favor and give me a hand with these." Mr. DeLeon picked up two of the boxes.

"Sure," Charles said, as he bent over to lift another two but quickly realized they were too heavy for him.

Mr. DeLeon had placed his two boxes on top of one of the filing cabinets and turned to see Charles struggling. He rushed over, "Here, just get one and I'll get the others."

"Which cabinet should I put them on?" Charles asked.

Mr. DeLeon guided him to the cabinet on the right. "Here this is good." He put two more boxes on top of the one Charles had placed there. Charles turned to be sure they had gotten all of the boxes when Mr. DeLeon put his hand on Charles's shoulder and said, "That's all. Thanks." But Charles felt his hand linger on his shoulder and then Mr. DeLeon put his other hand on his left shoulder and began massaging his shoulders. Charles instinctively moved away but immediately felt embarrassed for being so skittish.

Mr. DeLeon laughed a little and said, "Hey relax man. I'm not a pervert. I give massages to my tennis team all the time. It's good physical therapy after a match, but it's also a good idea to release tension and anxiety."

Charles lips protruded as he nodded in agreement. "That's cool." It wasn't until the phrase came out of his mouth that Charles felt awkward. For a moment, he felt like he was trying to be someone he wasn't. He was relieved when Mr. DeLeon led him out of the closet again, and he quickly followed.

As he neared the front of the room Mr. DeLeon said, "Alright let's get to those questions you had about your Algebra homework."

Later that afternoon, Charles was lost in thought as he walked through the halls and headed toward the front entrance to catch the activity bus. He jumped up the bus steps and flopped into one of the first rows. The seating hierarchy was a moot point on the activity bus because there were usually less than a dozen kids spread throughout the bus. Charles turned to pull his backpack off of his shoulders when he noticed that same familiar aroma. He recognized it immediately as Mr. DeLeon's cologne and he thought about the awkward massage. After a moment, he realized he was making too much of it. After all, now he felt like he was becoming part of Mr. DeLeon's crowd—the jocks—not that the tennis team consisted of the same type of jocks who played football or basketball—but the girls still seemed to go for them. Sure, Charles couldn't afford to wear the preppy polo shirts and khaki pants they wore to school, and he wasn't even actually on the tennis team, but he was beginning to feel like he fit into that clique, and Mr. DeLeon seemed to think so too.

After a couple of weeks of mutual flirtation and stolen glances Charles said to Leah one day, "Would you like to go to the movies with me some time?" Leah gave him a surprised look. Charles began to feel an immediate sensation of warmth, followed by a chill going down his back.

Leah turned a little to the left and a little to the right as if she was checking to see who was around. But then her face lit up with a smile. "Sure." Then suddenly her expression changed and now she seemed nervous, which made Charles nervous.

"What's wrong?" Charles blurted out in desperation.

"Nothing. Nothing." Leah was no longer making eye contact and her fingers were fidgeting with his locker door. She was looking at the floor.

But Charles persisted, "Is this about that guy . . . Matt—Matt Howard?" There! He said it. He didn't care. It's not what Mr. DeLeon had told him to do, but it was too late. Besides, he wanted Leah to know he had seen them together. Charles was surprised to suddenly feel angry.

Leah looked incredulous. "Well, I . . . I . . . I guess so."

Charles grabbed at her arm. "Leah, I know you like me. So . . . so just dump this guy! Get rid of him!"

Now it was Leah who got angry. "How dare you tell me what to do!" She started backing away from him.

Charles was dumbfounded. He swallowed hard and stood with his mouth open.

Then Leah looked away from him and toward the crowd of students now rushing through the halls. She looked at Charles again, only now she had tears in her eyes, and she yelled at him, "Just forget it!" And she stormed away.

Charles felt a cold chill and realized he had been sweating. His stomach cramped and then he felt a gurgling sensation. He turned and jogged toward the nearest bathroom. He flung open the door and didn't even bother to look at the guys who were hanging around smoking. Instead, he looked at the floor as he said, "Excuse me" and quickly made his way to the stall at the end of the room. He was careful not to slam the door of the stall because he didn't want anyone to notice his panic. As he locked the door of the stall he felt as if he might not get his pants down fast enough . . . and just as he hovered over the seat . . . he had a horrifying thought . . . all the guys hanging around in the bathroom would hear him taking an explosive shit! A second later, a bell sounded and one of the guys said loudly, "Let's get outta here man." And with that, Charles let it go. Fortunately, he was alone in the room when he finished and then made his way to the sink. He was hunched over, mindlessly watching as the soap suds caressed his hands and he felt a small comfort, until he decided to look up into the mirror in front of him. He could see beads of sweat over his lip and his hair looked greasy as it swept over his pale face. "Oh my God . . . now I ruined everything with Leah. She hates me. I'm such a dick!" He immediately straightened up when he heard someone enter the room. He dried his hands and smacked the wet paper towels into the metal trash can as he left the bathroom.

As he neared his locker, he saw that he had left the door hanging open. He wanted to go home, until even that thought made his stomach feel tied up in knots because lately he never knew whether his parents would be fighting or getting along. He grabbed at his books on the top shelf; slammed his locker shut and made his way to his next class.

At the end of the day, he was relieved that it wasn't one of his days for a tutoring session. "Mr. DeLeon is going to think I'm such a loser when he hears about this."

He caught the regular afternoon school bus and hoped that Leah would have cheerleading practice so she wouldn't be on the same bus. But it just wasn't his day. It seemed that David Reilly was fueled by a sugar rush or a caffeine rush or maybe he had smoked too much pot; but whatever the case, he was relentless with Charles. He had barely sat down, when David yelled, "Chuck! Hey it's Chuck you guys!" He rushed up and sat in the seat next to Charles and got right in his face as he swung his arm around him and puckered his lips, "Fuck me Chuck. Fuck me Chuck please. Pretty please. I promise you'll like it too."

Charles tried to shrug him off as he turned away from him to look out the window. But David pulled the collar of his jacket and slammed Charles back against the seat. "Come on Chuck. Give me a fuck."

Suddenly a voice called out, "Leave him alone you asshole!"

Charles couldn't believe it! It was Leah.

Only this time, David ignored Leah and continued taunting Charles, until finally, he leaned close enough to whisper into Charles ear, "I'm not kidding man. I've got a hard on for you. I want it man." Then he kissed Charles on the ear.

Charles sprung up and shouted, "Get away from me you homo! Get the fuck away from me!" He shoved David aside as he got out of the seat and went to the front of the bus where he stood holding the cold metal pole. He saw the bus driver look at him through the rearview mirror. Charles looked away and consciously slowed down his breathing because he was afraid he might get that gurgling feeling again. He felt a glimmer of hope when he thought of the possibility that Leah might be impressed that he had finally stood up for himself. David Reilly had sauntered to the back of the bus to smoke some more pot. Charles stared out of the bus windows, and began to feel a sense of relief—an unfamiliar feeling of calm. He felt . . . like a man. A moment later, he became aware of his surroundings again and saw that his stop was next. He got off the bus and turned toward Mrs. K's house and this time he noticed a "SOLD" sign on her front yard. And then another strange thing happened. When he opened the door to his house, he smelled food cooking. He recognized the scent of boiling potatoes and when he turned the corner to the kitchen, his mother looked happy when she said, "Hey, guess what Charles? We're having a family dinner tonight. Your father will be home any minute." Charles stood perfectly still and breathed in the scent of a good meal, and then he smiled.

Chapter 7

BETH TOOK A taxi from Boston Logan Airport to her apartment in Lexington. Henry's car was gone because he was still at work. It was a rainy, gray day and she felt a heavy sadness as she put her key in the door and heard Jake barking. He jumped at her as she entered. "Hey Jake. Oh I missed you so much." He whimpered and barked with excitement. "Should we go for a walk?" Beth left her suitcase in the entryway and, after using the bathroom, she grabbed Jake's leash from the hook on the kitchen wall and they walked along the bike path. She began to feel melancholy and when they headed back home, she looked toward her apartment through the wooded path. She felt sorry for herself, "Here I am again. Lost really. No home. No kids. Soon no husband; back to square one again and again . . . I just wish I didn't still love him."

By the time Henry got home from work that night, Beth was happy to see him. He looked so handsome in his leather bomber jacket. Henry was blessed with the facial structure of a model—with a strong jaw line and those manly curved frown lines around his mouth. He had blue eyes and sandy blonde hair and the lithe, muscular body of a tall man. He smiled at Beth as she walked toward him. They held each other by the door, without saying a word. Now Beth felt a surge of desire. She looked at Henry and suddenly they were kissing passionately. They made their way into the living room and started unbuttoning each other's clothes. "Wait," Beth said, as she made her way to sliding glass door to close the curtains. Henry went to the windows and turned down the blinds. Then he turned on the light by the couch and Beth grinned because they both liked to look at each other's naked bodies when they had sex. They were each removing their clothes unceremoniously until Henry saw that Beth had started to reach back to undo her bra. He grabbed at her breasts with just enough pressure to make her groan with pleasure. She reached back and pulled his buttocks close to her as they kissed deeply. Suddenly, Henry dropped to his knees and began pulling at her panties with his teeth. He pressed his face against her and she bent at the knees so she could spread her legs a bit more and he began to move his tongue over her panties and then licked the skin around them. She groaned and laid back on the couch, as Henry stretched his body over her and kissed her neck. She squirmed because it tickled and then Henry thrust himself into her. He moved his hands underneath her and squeezed her buttocks, as he moved back and forth, faster and faster. She held back as she felt an orgasm starting. "Tease me. Oh tease me." Henry stopped for a second. Then he groaned and started thrusting back and forth and she felt herself about to come. Both of them were crying out, "Oh yes! Oh yeah. Oh God. Oh God." They collapsed onto the couch and, after a couple minutes, Henry pulled the blanket over them as he said, "Oh Beth. That was great." Beth smiled and they held each other, until she could feel Henry's breathing slowing, as he fell asleep.

Jake heard a noise outside and started to bark, which stirred them Henry awake. They sat up and pulled the blanket tightly around them for a moment, until Beth shivered. "Are you cold?" Henry asked.

"Yeah. I think I'll get dressed." As she got up, she asked, "Hey, how about pizza for dinner tonight?"

"That sounds good to me."

"Alright. I'll call. How about a steak bomb pizza?"

"Oh yeah. How's that sound Jake? A steak bomb pizza?"

Beth got dressed again while Henry used the bathroom. She felt happy and comfortable until the phone rang. "I'll get it." As she picked up the phone in the kitchen, she wasn't surprised to see her mother's number on the caller I.D. There were moments when her mom seemed genuinely concerned about her but, oddly, it happened whenever Beth was leaving her mother's house or already in another place. She was rarely close or affectionate when Beth was right there in front of her. Beth felt a pang of guilt as she picked up the phone. She made sure her voice sounded neutral—not sad and certainly not happy. "Hi Mom. Sorry I forgot to call you when I got in."

"That's okay. I just wanted to make sure you were alright."

"Yeah. The flight was on time and I just got home a little while ago." She started nervously rambling because she knew what her mother would say next.

"Did *he* get home from work yet?"

Beth swallowed. She thought, "Oh God. If only she knew I just had sex with him." She pushed the words out, "Yeah. He got home a few minutes ago." Beth glanced at Henry, who was now walking toward her. He had been grinning until she mouthed to him, "My mother." His expression immediately changed to a grimace and he turned to go into the living room. Now she was caught in the middle. She worried, "Henry's mood will have undoubtedly changed by the time I get off the phone. But if I'm too short with my mother, she'll think I've changed my mind." Then she heard her mother saying, "I guess you can't talk now." Beth was relieved. Fortunately her mother had perceived the pause in the conversation as being a sign that Beth couldn't say much because Henry was eavesdropping.

"Right." Beth used an inflection in her voice to insinuate an obvious attempt at discretion.

"Well don't let that jerk bother you tonight. Just keep your distance and don't let him egg you on. He'll probably try to start a fight. But just don't let him get to you."

Now Beth felt riddled with guilt. "I won't Mom. I'm tired anyway so . . ."

"Alright. Well just give me a call tomorrow whenever he's not around."

"Alright Mom. Thanks. And thanks for letting me stay with you guys."

"Oh, you're welcome honey. Goodnight."

"Bye Mom."

As she walked into the living room, Henry had his back to her as he sat at his desk on the other side of the room. Beth had a sick feeling in her stomach. She felt torn. She was no longer happy; instead she felt guilty—guilty that she so desperately needed Henry's love and attention and yet guilty that she lied to her mother. Struggling for the right thing to say to Henry, she suddenly realized she had forgotten to order the pizza. She was relieved by the tedium of routine and thought it might lighten things up a bit as she broke the silence, "Oh! The pizza!" But Henry didn't turn around. She proceeded to the kitchen and found the phone number in a drawer with the other take-out menus. She ordered the pizza for delivery and now Henry had actually spoken from the living room.

"What did you say?" Beth tried to sound light.

Henry's tone was dismal. "I said, was your mother calling to make sure you hadn't changed your mind?"

"No." Beth lied, because she knew her mother was subtly doing just that. "She just wanted to make sure I got home okay. I told her I would call her when I arrived, but I forgot."

Beth walked over to Henry and tried to be nonchalant, but she recognized the familiar, awkward feeling of desperation as she began to speak. "Henry, what we do is our business." She paused and then added, "I love you and I know you love me." She knew she was really asking him more than telling him. But she knew she had the advantage of a sex hangover. And she was right. Henry turned away from his computer and the grin was back on his face again. "Come here." He hugged her and then nestled his face into her stomach. She felt warm and safe for a moment and even tried to convince herself the feeling would last.

On Saturday morning, Beth was pouring her second cup of coffee when she heard Henry coming down the hall. He yawned and stretched and said, "Good morning sweetie." He gave her a quick kiss and asked, "Did you guys already go for a walk?"

"Yeah."

"Good."

"Do you want me to make some breakfast for us?"

"Why don't you wait a couple minutes until I'm awake."

"Alright."

Beth sat in the living room with her coffee and a book. After more than an hour had passed, Henry was still nestled at his desk. She felt hungry, but she knew it was better not to bother Henry at that point, so she quietly made her way into the kitchen. Just before she sat down, she called out, "Breakfast is ready." Henry made no reply and gave no indication that he had heard her, so she sat down and began to eat. When she finished, she went into the living room and said, "How about if I join you at the garage today?" Henry didn't say anything and he didn't turn around. "Henry, did you hear me?"

Suddenly, Henry lashed out at her. "Now there you go again! Demanding attention!"

"Demanding attention? Are you kidding me?" Even though there was truth in it, Beth was suddenly indignant. "You've ignored me from the moment you sat down at that dam computer!"

Henry yelled, "Oh now it's that dam computer! Little miss doesn't get her way so it's the computer's fault!"

"What? What are you talking about?"

Henry pushed back from his chair so hard that it slammed into the wall. He started screaming as he neared her. "You know exactly what I'm talking about. You just want me to stay home and sit with you and give in to your demands!"

"My demands! What demands? I said I would join you at the garage."

"You don't want to go to the garage. You just want to make sure that's really where I'm going. Besides, after a half hour, you'll be huffing and puffing and saying you're tired. You're always tired!"

"Always tired! How am I always tired? I just made you breakfast and . . ."

Henry interrupted, "Made me breakfast? What did you make? I don't smell any food cooking?" And with that he stomped into the kitchen and yelled, "What breakfast?"

"Look in the refrigerator."

Henry flung open the refrigerator and said mockingly, "Museli? Are you kidding me? You poured cereal into a bowl and mixed it with yogurt and that's 'making me breakfast'!"

"I cut up apples and oranges and added nuts and . . ." Beth felt silly as she attempted to describe some sort of labor intensive project.

Henry shouted, "Do me a favor and don't make anything for me anymore. It's not worth it! Whether you mix some cereal together or cook a steak. I don't need it! I can take care of myself. I don't need a mother. I don't want you to cook anything for me ever again!"

"Henry, please. I thought . . ." She stopped herself.

"You thought what?" Henry shouted. "You thought everything was OK again, even though you're running down to Pennsylvania to look for a place to live after you leave?"

Beth moved toward him, but Henry waved her away. "Leave me alone goddamit."

"But Henry . . ."

Now they were only inches away from each other, when he raised his fists above her head. She cowered and Henry yelled, "Oh my God. You're crazy! Just leave me alone!" He went into the bedroom and slammed the door.

Beth sat in the kitchen in stunned silence, until she heard him come out of the bedroom. She looked up and saw him dressed in jeans and a flannel shirt. He took his coat from the closet and then stood in the kitchen doorway and said calmly, "Just enjoy your day Beth. I'll be back tonight." Then he shut the front door.

She said out loud, "When am I going to learn? He's never going to change. He's happy if we have sex and maybe for an hour afterwards, or an entire night if we fall asleep, but then it starts all over again the next day." She went into the living room and sat down at her computer and looked up the Amtrak schedule for the following week. The phone rang and it was her realtor. Joyce said, "I didn't get your fax."

Beth felt guilty and irresponsible. "I'm sorry Joyce. I forgot by the time I got in yesterday, but I'll do it right now." She didn't forget. She had actually been reconsidering. She added, "In fact, I was just about to look at the train schedule for next week."

"You're coming down again so soon?"

Beth hesitated, but she said, "Things aren't going so well here, and I've got to start looking for a job down there. I think I'll just go to some businesses and hand them my resume. Who knows, maybe I can actually apply in person the old fashioned way."

Joyce said, "I hear ya."

Beth said, "I'll send the fax to you now. Can you call the title company and Mrs. Kerbowski so we can figure out a settlement date?"

Joyce said, "Sure."

"Great. Thanks Joyce."

After she sent the fax, Beth perused the Amtrak schedule. She mumbled out loud, "OK. Here we go. It looks like I could leave Tuesday morning from Boston."

She made the reservation and suddenly felt energized. She threw a load of laundry into the washer and then opened her closet and started thinking about the job of packing for the move. She pulled out a bunch of flattened cardboard moving boxes that she had stored under the bed. Big clumps of dust scattered around the floor and she started to sneeze. Jake sniffed around the boxes as she dragged them to the center of the room. "Well, Henry's going to know I'm serious this time." She looked at the chest of drawers and the armoire and thought, "He's not going to have any furniture after I move out." She looked over at the bed. "I'll just leave it here. I don't want this stuff anyway."

It was a very productive day. She went to the store and bought packing tape and a black magic marker to identify the contents of each box. She stopped at a liquor store and loaded up her car with used boxes and after unloading them into the apartment, she started packing them. As it grew dark, she was hungry and decided to make spaghetti, sausage and meatballs for dinner. She thought, "If Henry doesn't want me to cook for him, I'll cook for myself." She breathed in the garlic and onions and sipped a glass of wine while she listened to music and fantasized about a flourishing new life. All of this put her in such a good mood that when Henry arrived home, she was genuinely smiling. "Hi Henry."

His expression softened. "Smells good." He walked up to Beth and kissed her softly on the mouth. "I'm sorry sweetie."

"It's alright." But this time was different. It wasn't alright because she forgave him again; it was alright because she felt ambivalent.

Henry said, "I'll go wash up before dinner." She thought it was ironic that just that morning, the topic of food had ignited a war and now, Henry was even interested in sitting down to a meal with her.

Beth stood by the stove to put the food onto their plates, when Henry walked up behind her and slipped his arms around her waist and said softly, "Sweetie, I'm sad to see the moving boxes in the bedroom."

Beth hesitated before she turned to face Henry. She reminded herself in that moment, that by morning, Henry would be a changed man and would surely be angry or miserable with her about something. "I know Henry. I'm sad too." She knew his mood could change very quickly if she pursued the topic, so she said, "Let's just take it a day at a time and see what happens." But this time her mind was made up.

Henry made a charming pout and said, "Alright."

On Monday morning, Beth was chopping apples on a cutting board and placing the slices onto a plate for Henry to nibble on as he got ready for work. Henry was in his briefs and buttoning his shirt, as he entered the kitchen and took an apple slice. He then put his hands on Beth's shoulders and gently moved her away from the cutting board. He picked up the knife and slowly, methodically sliced tiny, even pieces of apple and even diced them without making a sound. He said, "What do you hear?"

A familiar feeling of dread swept over Beth. She didn't want to answer him, but she had to; otherwise things would escalate. And yet for some reason, she remained stubbornly silent. Henry was patronizing when he said, "Sweetie. I'm asking you. What do you hear?" Before she could answer, he made a few more slices and dices and then grinned at her. "Come on. What do you hear sweetie?"

Beth felt like a child being reprimanded, but she knew she had to answer before Henry started shouting. She mumbled, "Nothing."

Henry was getting angry and said loudly, "I can't hear you."

Beth shouted, "Nothing. I hear nothing OK? You made your point. I'm cutting the apples too loudly."

Henry shouted, "See how you get! Nobody can tell you anything. You just can't stand to be told how to do something better. You always know everything. Why do you think you can't get along with your sister or your father? It's because you always know better. And then you have a little hissy fit if somebody tries to help you to learn the *right* way to do things." He was like a broken record. Henry continued with his harangue until he left for work. Beth's nerves were shattered and she wondered how any sane person could keep coming back for more.

Chapter 8

CHARLES PULLED OUT a chair to sit at the kitchen table for dinner when his mother stopped him. "Go wash your hands. That's what decent people do before dinner."

Charles shrugged. "OK Mom."

When he returned to the kitchen, his father was already seated at the head of the table. "Hey Charlie, good to see ya buddy."

"You too Dad."

His mother was shooing away the steam from the colander that held the potatoes. "Here, gimme your plate."

"Easy, easy hun. You're getting water on my plate from that thing," his father was saying lightly.

"Well I'm not going to dirty a bowl just to plunk the potatoes in it for five minutes. It's easier just to dump them on your plate from this thing."

As she moved the colander over to Charles's plate to serve him, he was already saying, "Pass me the butter Dad."

His father cut wedges of beef from the roast. "Here Charlie. A couple a slices of this stuff will put some meat on your bones."

Charles held out his plate. "Thanks Dad."

His mother took the last of the potatoes and then followed the same procedure to dispense the peas from the colander. In the meantime, Charles was shaking salt and pepper onto the potatoes and he laughed when his father reached over and mashed them into chunks that oozed through the spokes of his fork.

His mother caught them in the act as she sat down at the table. "Cut that out you two fools." But she wasn't angry and Charles ate heartily as he sensed a spirit of happiness around the table.

"Hey Charlie, how'd ya like to go to a Phillies game with me?"

"Whoah! Are you kidding? Yeah!" Charles shrieked with excitement.

"Alright then. It's a little ways off—in June; the Phils versus the Pittsburgh Pirates. Oh and it's pink cap day so we can bring home a baseball cap for your Mom."

"Pink cap? What's that for?" Charles asked.

"I guess it's to raise money for women's cancer so they give out pink hats."

His mother said, "Hey wait a minute. You two go to a baseball game and all I get is a pink baseball cap!"

"Ah Cassie, c'mon." His father reached for her hand and gave it a quick kiss.

"So in June Dad? When's that?"

"It comes right after May you idiot!" His mother laughed a little and added, "He's so excited, he can't think straight."

"Oh, it's ah June 8; I think it was. Wait a minute." His father stood up from his chair a bit so he could reach into his back pocket for his wallet. He sat down again with a sigh and said, "I've got the schedule in here somewhere."

Charles watched with anticipation as his father fingered through money and miscellaneous papers.

His mother said sarcastically, "Make sure you hide all those scraps with your girlfriends' phone numbers on them."

Charles felt a knot in his stomach. He thought his mom was probably just being weird again but he wasn't sure. He felt relieved when his father responded, "Cassie, you're my only girl . . . you know that."

"Sure I do. Sure I do."

"Oh here it is." His father unfolded a tiny piece of cardboard paper that revealed the Phillies iconic red and white colors and lots of tiny printed type all over it. "Yep. Saturday, June 8, it is my man."

"Awesome. I can't wait." Charles said.

A little while later, his mother started to gather their plates. Charles looked out the window and said, "Shoot! It's almost dark."

"What? What do you mean?" His father asked.

"I was gonna ask you if you wanted to have a catch?"

"Ah . . . it's a little too cold for that tonight Charlie."

His mother said, "Don't be worrying about having a catch. You have homework to do."

"I don't have much tonight Mom."

"Yeah, well get your butt upstairs and do what you have to do."

"Alright." Charles hesitated before leaving the room. He wasn't sure if his father would leave after dinner. As if he read his mind, his father said, "I'll stop by your room to say goodnight before bed Charlie."

"OK Dad." He darted up the stairs to his room and threw open his closet. He rummaged through some sneakers, dirty socks and a really smelly pair of slippers on the closet floor. His baseball and glove were lodged in the corner and he grabbed them and immediately started tossing the hard ball against the leather glove. Now that it was dark out, he could see his reflection in the window as he wound up to pitch the ball. He imagined he could hear the cheering crowd around him and his jeans and t-shirt were magically transformed into white, cropped pants with red Phillies stripes and his shirt had a bright red letter P across his heart. He went back into his closet and took his red Phillies baseball cap off the shelf. Once again, he wound up and pitched the ball toward the window but stopped short of actually throwing it. The crowd went wild as the umpire yelled out, "SttttEEeeeRIKE one!" He stood up straight with a confident grin and looked toward the first baseman as he rubbed the tip of his nose with a horizontal forefinger (the signal for a curve ball pitch). He wiped the moisture from his hand on his hip; took a deep breath; and wound up to throw another 90 mph pitch. "SttttEEeeeRIKE two!" screamed the umpire and now the crowd was on their feet, waving and cheering, as the organ played "Dunnt dunnt dunnt dunnt . . . dunnt dunnt dunnt dunnt . . . badah badah . . . BADAHhhhhhhhhhh" He spit a clump of tobacco onto the dirt and this time he looked at the first baseman as he brushed his right ear. It was going to be knuckle ball this time. But could he do it . . . he hadn't thrown a knuckle ball yet this season. He looked straight down the line that led to the batter, who was nervously straightening his batting helmet, before he moved in closer to the mound, and his hands choked up around the bat. Charles looked away for a few seconds and then watched his feet dig into the sand a bit. It was time. Charles slid his thumb around the ball and felt his fingers grip the stitches on the opposite side. He wound up and let his infamous knuckle ball fly. "StttEEeeeRIKE three!" cried the umpire. The organ blared and the crowd roared, "Yay Charlie!" Somehow he could distinguish Leah's voice from the throngs of cheers. He looked toward her in the third row, just midway down the first baseline. Her blond hair was flowing in the spring breeze and she stood up smiling and waving at him. He gave her a quick wave and he felt so happy as he turned toward the dugout, that his eyes welled with tears. He looked down at his cleats as they skimmed across the green turf. A circle of clean appeared on the tip of his dirty cleat from a fallen teardrop. He instinctively looked upward to make sure no more tears could fall and hoped that no one noticed the one that did. A couple of the guys were slapping him on the back as the pathway to the batter's box narrowed. They called him, "Knuckle Chuck," and one player said, "Way to hold 'em Charlie," just before he spit out a hunk of chew. Charlie was just about to take a seat on the bench when he heard a knock and looked up to see his father standing in his bedroom doorway.

"Hey Charlie, how's the studying going?" His father smiled when he saw Charles's expression. "You look dazed man. Did ya get a little distracted buddy?" Charles saw his father looking at his baseball glove. He felt a little embarrassed. "Oh I was just thinking about the game that's all."

"Yeah. It's gonna be a blast."

"You leaving now?" Charlie sounded worried.

"No. No. I just thought I'd check in on you before your mother and I hit the hay."

"Hit the hay? It's only 7:00." Charlie said naively.

"Yeah, well, she's still doing the dishes so I thought I'd crash in bed and watch a little TV before she comes up."

It didn't make sense to him but he liked the idea of his parents being back together again, so he said cooly, "Alright. Like I said, I just have a little homework to do so . . ." Charlie walked over to his desk and turned on the lamp.

"Yeah, well, your mom's right about that. You gotta keep studying so you don't turn out to be an idiot like me."

Charles felt the need to defend his father. "You're not an . . . you know . . . you know a lot Dad . . . so don't worry about what mom says. She's just weird sometimes that's all."

They looked at each other across the room and smiled. Then his dad quietly shut the door and Charles was alone again. Only this time, he picked up his backpack, sat in his desk chair, and took out his history book.

Chapter 9

IT WAS LATE in the day on Tuesday, when Beth stood up to put her backpack over her shoulders and then used both hands to steer her dufflebag in front of her, as she wedged herself down the aisle of the train to wait for the next stop. The incessant swaying motion of the train had made her queasy hours before, but by now she had gained her sea legs. It was probably the first trip to the restroom that tested the strength of her quadriceps as she hovered over the swaying seat, adding to the sprinkles of sticky urine around the toilet. Now she positioned her hip near a seat that cushioned the blow when the train suddenly banged against the switching rails. She was sweaty, tired and thirsty. She was always one water bottle short of feeling properly hydrated and her breath was stale with a slight aroma of P&J sandwich mixed with bad, overpriced coffee from the café car.

She took a taxi to her parents' house because she knew she would quickly wear out her welcome if she required pickups and drop-offs from the train every time she traveled back and forth from Boston, while she was house hunting. Her mother always answered the front door. Beth kissed her on the cheek and then followed her into the room that adjoins the kitchen; where her father sat in his chair watching TV. A side table was positioned between his chair and the loveseat, where her mother sat by herself. If it was early evening, before their dinner, her father would have a martini sitting on the side table. If it was after dinner, they each had a cup of tea on the side table. Beth kissed her father on the cheek and he said hello and reached for his tea cup. Beth always had the feeling that her parents were gritting their teeth as they said hello and secretly hoped it was just another short stay.

She was disappointed, but not surprised, that her parents had already eaten dinner and she was told to help herself to some lunchmeat and potato chips. Her parents sat silently and watched the evening news that blared from the television. It was as if Beth had just come back from an errand and they had just seen her earlier that day because they didn't even make conversation with her. Beth sat by herself at the kitchen table and choked down dry mouthfuls of sandwich. She spotted an open bottle of red wine on the counter. She got up and surreptitiously filled a wine glass with a healthy portion, and her mood lightened with each deep swallow of wine. She joined her parents and quickly realized they weren't in the mood to socialize, so she excused herself and went up to bed. Too tired to shower, she peeled off her jeans and a heavy sweater and just slept in her socks, underwear and cotton turtle neck.

The next day she borrowed her mother's car and drove over to Joyce's office for their scheduled meeting at 2:00 to go over some paperwork. They stayed only a short time before they left to take another look at Mrs. Kerbowski's house. Joyce parked the car by the front curb and said, "It's going to be yours soon."

Beth smiled. It would be a quiet, peaceful life and she felt excited about a new beginning.

A school bus slowly lumbered up the road and the young boy who followed behind it gave her a polite grin as he passed them. Beth remembered they had agreed he would cut the grass for her. "What was his name again?" she asked Joyce.

"Oh, um, I forget."

Beth watched him for a minute and then said, "Charles! That's it. Charles." Beth looked at her watch. "Oh Joyce, I have to get back to my parents' house because we're going to meet my sister and have an early dinner. Tomorrow I'll start pounding the pavement for a job."

Joyce said, "I'll keep my eyes and ears open too. Unfortunately the job market is pretty tight right now."

Beth said, "I know. I just hope I have better luck here than I did in Massachusetts."

An hour later, Beth sat in the backseat of her father's car and her parents were bickering, as usual, about one thing or another. Suddenly, her father interrupted her mother and said, "Hey did you see that?"

Beth said, "Yeah, I did."

Her mother asked, "What? What are you talking about?"

Her father checked the rearview mirror and then pulled over to the side of the road. He asked, "Do you have something to write with?"

Beth was searching through her pocketbook. "Yeah I found a pen." She took out an envelope and scribbled on it to see if the pen was working.

Her mother strained to turn her neck to see what they were both talking about. "I still don't see . . ."

"It's a sign about a job opening." Her father said with a tone of annoyance at her mother.

"OK. Got it." Beth said, as she finished writing the phone number for Ajit Medical Center.

"Do you have your cell phone with you?" her father asked.

Beth knew what he was thinking. She said, "Well, I guess I could call them now."

In unison, her mother and father instructed, "Call them. Call them now."

After half a dozen rings, a voice instructed the caller to "please listen to the selections, as our menu has changed. . ." Beth pressed "3" to "make an appointment;" that way she knew someone would answer the phone.

"Ajit Medical Center, can you hold please?" a pleasant voice asked.

"Sure." Beth had barely uttered the one syllable word when she heard a click and assumed she was not disconnected but, rather, put on hold. Her father pulled into the parking lot of the restaurant and her mother said something barely audible. Beth wasn't sure whether her mother was talking to her or her father. "What did you say mom?"

Her mother repeated, "What did they say?"

"Nothing yet. They put me on hold." Her mother and father were already opening their doors to get out of the car. Beth started to get out and her father said loudly, "Just stay there. We'll wait for you." Beth sat down again and heard, "Thanks for waiting. Did you need an appointment?"

"No. I'm calling about the job opening for a front desk receptionist." There was a moment of silence and Beth thought, "Maybe she doesn't know about the sign," so she said, "I just drove past your office and you have a sign on the lawn that says . . ."

The woman interrupted her, "Oh sure! Sure. What's your name?"

"Beth Hardt."

"Do you have experience working in a medical office?"

"No, but I've worked in the pharmaceutical industry so I'm very familiar with medical terminology and . . ."

The woman interrupted again, "Alright, well you'll need to talk to our Office Manager, Kathy Hallahan."

"OK. Great."

"She's on the other line, so I'll have her call you back. Can I have your phone number?"

"Sure. It's . . ."

"Well that was lucky." Beth's father said as she got out of the car smiling.

"I know. What are the chances that we pass a sign about a job opening!"

Lunch was pleasant enough until her sister, Laura, and her mother left the table to use the bathroom. While they were gone, Beth's father swallowed a mouthful of his martini and then said wryly, "So you think you're *in* again?"

"What?" Beth furrowed her brow and pretended not to know what he was talking about. She knew her father was referring to her status within the family. It never ceased to amaze her when her father behaved as if he was the patriarch of some uber rich family. Even her mother, at times, had some delusional idea that just because she was a pretty, Irish, Catholic woman of a certain age; she was a descendent of the Kennedy clan. In reality, her mother only resembled the Kennedy's in her ability to hide the dirty truth of what her husband was really like. Her father was indeed a patriarch, however not of an uber rich family; but a typical 60s era success story for a guy who never went to college but had enough natural personality and business savvy to get promotion after promotion that brought his family from the city to the suburbs. He had a beautiful wife; a son who seemed to adore his father and two daughters—Laura, who was Daddy's little girl and had never married because no man could compete with Daddy; and finally Beth, who had long ago stopped adoring either parent. Her brother had grown up to be smart, athletic, handsome, respectable and funny. Beth was certain it was his sense of humor that had kept her sane when she was growing up. He was now happily married with four children and lived and worked within a ten mile radius of the house they grew up in. It was his four children who kept the family tied together because they were the only grandchildren; and the only children Beth and Laura would vicariously "parent" because neither of them had children of their own.

Her father seemed to be keeping a watch for the return of her mother and Laura, when he said, "You know what I mean. You move away with Henry and don't tell us until you're settled into Massachusetts. Then when things don't work out, you expect to come back and be part of the gang again."

Beth knew there was truth in her father's comments, but it only made her feel more lost and insecure. She felt a lump in her throat and tears filled her eyes as she looked down at the tablecloth. She quickly looked up so the tears wouldn't fall; and she tried to be tough, as she said sarcastically, "Oh that's nice." She took a gulp from her wine glass with the hope that she would soon be buzzed and relaxed. It was just like being around Henry; the more wine she drank at dinner, the happier her life appeared to be.

Her mother must have sensed something as she sat down at the table again because she asked, "What's wrong?"

Her father said, "What do you mean, what's wrong? Nothing's wrong," and he shook his head with annoyance. Laura steered the conversation to her favorite subject—her brilliant career. Beth ordered another glass of wine as she listened to Laura bragging to big Daddy about the latest amazing thing she had accomplished at work.

The next day Beth received a call from Kathy Hallahan, the Office Manager for Ajit Medical Center. Kathy conducted a phone interview and it went well; so she scheduled Beth for an interview with Dr. Ajit the next day.

Beth arrived at the office ten minutes early. She walked up to the reception desk, which jutted out into the waiting area in a semi-circle. There was no fingerprint laden, sliding glass window in front of the reception desk like most offices. Beth liked the openness; it was much more patient-friendly. However Lydia was not exactly warm and friendly when she greeted Beth. "How can I help you?" Lydia snapped, as she continued to look at the paperwork on her desk, rather than make eye contact with Beth.

"I'm here for my interview with Dr. Ajit."

Lydia flashed a smile and said, "Oh great." Then she lowered her voice to a conspiratorial tone (which Beth would later recognize as the precursor to some disparaging remark about Mrs. Ajit or "the father" Ajit).

Lydia said, "It's pronounced Ah-JEET—like a long e sound."

Beth was embarrassed that she had pronounced it something like "Ah-shit." She emulated Lydia's tone and said quietly, "Oh thanks."

Lydia continued, "It's OK. Most of our patients are Indian so they know how to pronounce it."

Beth grinned. She would be sure not to mispronounce the name ever again.

"Are you meeting with 'the father' or 'the son'?" Lydia asked.

"Ah . . . I . . ."

Fortunately, Kathy Hallahan had overheard them, as she neared the desk. "She's meeting with Arvind." She explained to Beth, "Dr. Deepak Ajit is 'the father.' He's been in practice here in Lansdale for 33 years. His son, Dr. Arvind Ajit, joined us about a year ago. To avoid confusion, we use their first names and refer to them as Dr. Arvind and Dr. D. Lydia just calls him D." Then Kathy lowered her already quiet and demure voice, which required Beth to lean over the counter to hear. Kathy said, "Dr. Arvind will be taking over the practice when Dr. D retires. So he's really the one running the show these days."

Beth said, "Alright. Thanks for explaining that Kathy."

"Sure." Kathy then formally introduced Beth to Lydia, who worked at the front desk in the mornings and, if Beth was hired, Beth would work at the front desk in the afternoons, evenings and Saturday mornings. "Why don't you have a seat for a few minutes because Dr. Arvind is with a patient right now."

"OK. Thanks Kathy." Beth sat in a chair within a row of seats that faced the front desk. It reminded her of her days in pharmaceutical sales as she sat there waiting, with a full view of the office activity. She felt a little embarrassed that she now had to interview for jobs that she had, at one time, thought to be *below* her. But even with a Masters Degree, and successful experience in sales, she was now 52 years old and no pharmaceutical company would hire women her age as a sales rep to call on physicians because the medical profession was still predominantly male. Doctors were more likely to endure the interruption of a sales rep if she was *young* and beautiful. Beth knew she had several factors working against her hopes of finding a good paying job. The economy was bad and unemployment was on the rise, as pharmaceutical companies like all major corporations, were laying off—not hiring. The pool of unemployed, college educated professionals had swelled so the few jobs that opened up for that level of education brought hundreds of competitors. Beth's age worked against her because employers perceived a new-hire-at-50 as a performance risk (surely she was motivated by desperation rather than aspiration); a health insurance burden (surely her health was declining) and, as-yet-unseen, a woman her age was probably overweight and unattractive. The only one of these factors that was applicable to Beth was desperation. In fact, Beth *was* desperate insofar as her willingness to take a job well below her education and experience just so she could make some money and have a paycheck coming in sooner versus later, in order to end her dependence on Henry.

An attractive, professionally dressed Asian woman was chatting with Lydia at the front desk. An oversized Dooney & Burke pocketbook dangled from her forearm and Beth could only catch bits and pieces of what she said. Beth couldn't hear a word coming from Lydia's mouth because she was a soft-spoken woman, whose voice belied her obesity. Lydia was fairly tall at 5'8"; and Beth stood at an unusual height of 5'11". But whereas Beth exercised and passed on desserts in order to maintain her attractive figure; Lydia never turned down the lunches, desserts and yummy treats brought to the office by the pharmaceutical sales reps; and it showed. She weighed a sturdy, big-boned 230 pounds.

Beth heard the Asian woman say something about pharmacy school but Beth was immediately distracted from her eavesdropping when she saw a young doctor walk a patient to the threshold of the waiting area. On either side of the front desk semi-circle there was a doorway, but they were unencumbered by doors. This was also unusual and quite welcoming. She straightened her posture as she anticipated being called back to meet with the doctor at any moment. But the doctor disappeared and the patient moved toward the front desk, which caused the lovely Asian woman to make a hasty goodbye. As she turned, Beth noted that the woman was probably in her mid-40s so the comment about pharmacy school must have been a reference to her past. The patient who now stood in front of Lydia would prove to be more typical of the patient population. He was a frail Indian man who appeared to be in his mid-60s but was actually only 47 years old. He had requested to be seen by "the father" Dr. Deepak Ajit, but he was diverted to "the son" at the last minute. Beth would initially feel embarrassed for Dr. Arvind Ajit because none of the patients were requesting to be seen by him. In fact, it was quite the opposite. They wanted to be seen by Dr. Deepak "the father" or, even more often, they requested Dr. Vishnu, whom Beth would meet later. In order to build up the number of patients seen by "the son," they would do a "bait and switch" on patients. Lydia would say, "You'll have to wait a while to be seen by Dr. D or Dr. Vishnu but Dr. Arvind can see you now." Many of the patients depended on a ride to the office with a friend or family member, because they didn't drive or didn't own a car. They would agree to be seen by Dr. Arvind so their ride didn't have to wait too long.

For several minutes, Beth had been staring at the enormous painting of two tigers making their way through a vast jungle. She had only ever seen a painting of this size in a museum. It stretched from the ceiling to the floor and was probably eight feet wide. She figured they must have brought it into the office before the very large, front windows were installed because it would never fit through a doorway. It was a fairly new building that was a split level design. The first floor was nothing more than the landing from the parking lot; where you could go up a flight of stairs to the second floor, which housed the physician practice; or you could go down a flight of stairs to the basement level, which housed Mrs. Ajit's business, "Lansdale Labs" at the very back end of the basement; and the rest of the basement level was a very large office space rented by New Day Physical Therapy. The path from the parking lot branched out toward a handicap ramp or, alternatively, to a longer walkway with a small flight of steps. Both paths led into the front entrance of the physicians' office.

Dr. Arvind "the son" was embarrassed by his father's tiger painting. It was so ethnic; and yet he made every effort to be seen as a typical American-born, up and coming professional. He and his wife had a lot in common; in fact, so much so that it would seem they had a traditionally arranged marriage—not so; they say. They were both Indian, both Internal Medicine physicians; both the offspring of wealthy physicians (although her father was an even wealthier specialty physician) and both flaunted their success, wealth and good looks. They lived in a condo at 17th & Chestnut Streets in Philadelphia and they enjoyed the restaurants and nightlife of the city's very wealthy, Rittenhouse Square area. Dr. Arvind's wife drove a white Mercedes and he drove a new Audi sports car. His watch, briefcase and the clothes beneath his lab coat revealed expensive tastes. Dr. Arvind's demeanor was aloof, intolerant and impatient with office staff, patients, pharma sales reps and even with other physicians in telephone conversations held on the fly in the hallway between exam rooms. He slowly and grudgingly learned that the pretense of friendliness and tolerance with those well below his education and income level, could bear fruit in terms of patient requests to be seen by him; dinner invitations from sales reps and cooperation and optimal performance on the part of his lowly office staff.

"Beth?" It was a summons; not a question.

Beth shot up from her seat and smiled as she neared Dr. Arvind with an outstretched hand. "Nice to meet you," Beth said, while at the very same moment he said, "Why don't we go into my office." He led her down the hallway to an office with a bookcase, two desks, a window and a small playpen area for Dr. Arvind's miniature Yorkshire Terrier, whom he brought to the office every day. Apparently "the father" and "the son" shared this office with "the dog." The playpen area had a soiled doggie pee pad in it and Beth would discover that, unless she picked it up and threw it out, the same soiled pad would stay there for days while it collected even more doggie urine.

"Hi there cutie." Beth fussed over the little dog for a couple of minutes before Dr. Arvind ushered him back into the area behind the little white, plastic fence where he settled in with a tiny chew toy. He latched the gate and said, "My wife got him when she was doing her residency and now that she's started to work part-time, she can't take him to work with her; so I bring him here every day."

Later, after Beth met his stunningly beautiful wife and became accustomed to her being the same temperament of Dr. Arvind, she would think that a lap dog with a Burberry sweater was yet another accoutrement well suited to their personalities and lifestyle.

Beth was a little bit nervous as she talked about her work history during the interview. She had expected Dr. Arvind Ajit to be impressed;

yet he appeared to be nonplussed. Now and then she was encouraged by a half smile, but she didn't know where she stood by the time he ended with, "Well we have several well qualified candidates, as you can imagine, so we'll take a look at everyone and then make a decision."

Beth had honestly expected to walk out of the interview with a job offer. She worried, "Maybe he's wondering why a former pharma sales rep wants to work for just $13 an hour. Don't people realize there just aren't any jobs out there?" She did her best to wear a pleasant expression despite the fact that she was disappointed. Dr. Arvind stood and continued, "But I want to wrap this up by the end of next week; so you can expect to hear from us one way or the other by then."

"Thanks for your time Dr. Ajit." Beth smiled with confidence; knowing she had properly pronounced his name (Ah-JEET).

Lydia was busy with patients at the front desk so Beth wasn't surprised that she didn't have a moment to say goodbye. But Kathy turned around as she heard Dr. Arvind speaking. She walked over to Beth and smiled. "Thanks for coming. We'll get back to you soon."

"Thanks Kathy." As Beth turned toward the waiting area, she noted that it was a bit busier now, with at least half a dozen Indian men and women chatting rather loudly in their native language and one elderly White man reading a magazine in the corner.

The next morning Beth had a message on her cell phone, which she had left inside her parents' home while she was outside doing her rigorous exercise walk. It was Kathy's voice saying, "Dr. Arvind wanted me to give you a call to offer you the position of front desk receptionist. As we discussed, it's a permanent part-time position at a rate of $13 per hour. Give us a call as soon as you can."

Beth felt such relief now that the weight of finding a job had been lifted. The pay rate was terrible when compared to her previous salaries, but at least she would be working again. She could continue to look for a better job, but now she had the advantage of being employed. It seemed employers were only interested in considering you for an interview if you already had a job. Beth figured that 28 hours of work per week at $13 an hour would help to pay some bills and buy groceries;

but she knew it would never cover her oil heating bills, or her cable and cell phone bill. When she called the cable company about setting up service at her new address, she had whittled her bill down to the basic level, which provided not much more than being able to turn on her television. She had access to channels 3, 6 and 10, as well as the least desirable, nonsense cable channels. Although she had been able to buy her house with her savings, she had the scary high real estate and school taxes to pay each year; homeowner's insurance; car insurance, along with all her other household expenses. She still had some money in savings but what would happen when that was gone? She decided she would tell Henry she expected to continue to need his financial help, until she found a better-paying job. She worried, "What if he refuses and says the agreement was just 'until I find a job'?" Then she panicked, "I'll just tell him about the photos I have from when he punched me in the head. He better not refuse." She immediately called Kathy to accept the job offer.

Kathy reminded her, "Now because it's a part-time position, it will not include health insurance benefits, but I think you had said you're covered under your husband's plan?"

Beth said, "Yes I am." During her phone interview with Kathy, she had sensed that Kathy was a warm and caring person and, she secretly hoped that Kathy would take pity on her when she shared, "I don't think he's ever cheated on me but . . . he has a bad temper," at which point she paused; hoping Kathy would understand what she was insinuating. Apparently she did, because Kathy had said, "Well nobody should have to put up with that." Beth had responded, "Well he's not all bad because he has agreed to help me out a little bit financially and, of course, I'm covered under his health insurance."

"When do you want me to start?" Beth was apprehensive because she had lied and told Kathy she was already in the process of moving her things from Massachusetts back to Pennsylvania. Kathy said, "Ideally, next week; but I know you're in the process of moving."

Beth worried she might lose this opportunity if she prolonged her start date too much. She said, "Can I start the week after next?" She had no idea how she could possibly manage this.

Kathy responded, "Sure. I've told Dr. Arvind a little bit about your situation and I'm sure he'll be fine with waiting another week."

For a moment, Beth felt uncomfortable hearing that Dr. Arvind knew about *her situation*, but she said, "Thanks Kathy. I'm really looking forward to working with you."

"Great. Give me a call next Thursday and we'll just confirm the time for your start the following Monday."

"I'll do that." Beth thought, "I guess they really liked me because Dr. Arvind said they had other candidates." She felt happy for a moment, until she was suddenly struck with a surge of melancholy. She welled up with tears and thought, "Why did he have to be such a jerk?" Beth was only kidding herself when she thought she was now a shrewd, manipulative woman who was getting financial payback from Henry for all of his abuse. She was, in reality, not simply tethered to Henry for financial reasons, she was still deeply, emotionally dependent on Henry because of her twisted perception of what love is and what is acceptable behavior in a marriage. The only thing she was right about was that it wasn't going to be easy to leave Henry.

Chapter 10

CHARLES SWALLOWED HARD when he saw Leah approaching him. He took a book off the top shelf, scratched his face a little and tried to occupy himself in this moment of anticipation.

"Hi Charlie. Haven't talked to you in a while. You haven't been on the bus."

He tried to play it cool and said, "Yeah. My dad's been around lately and he wants to drive me to school in the morning. Kinda like making up for lost time I guess." He had told Leah that his mother and father were sometimes separated and sometimes back together. He was more than happy when his father offered to drop him off at school on his way to his construction job because he could avoid being tortured by David Reilly every morning on the school bus. He would never tell his Dad about it. He was sure he'd think he was a wimp.

Leah said, "Oh that's nice." They had just started walking together when the bell rang for the start of the next class period. Students were shuffling into their classrooms but Charles didn't care. Then Leah blurted out, "If you still want to go to a movie or something . . . that would be great."

He felt dazed for a minute and thought to himself, "Did she just say what I think she . . ." and then he heard himself saying out loud, "Yeah sure. I . . ."

Leah thought he was probably wondering about her and Matt so she said, "I broke up with Matt."

A smile spread over his face. "Great. That's great. I mean . . . sorry . . . I . . ."

"It's OK. I know what you mean." Now Leah looked directly into his eyes and Charles felt his heart leap. By now the hallway was quiet and they seemed to be the only two people in the world for a moment. It was Leah who brought them back to reality. "Well I better get to class."

"Yeah me too . . . ah, do you want to go this Friday night?"

"That sounds good."

"Alright. I'll ask my mom or dad to give me a ride to the mall. We can meet there."

Just then a teacher was closing the door to her classroom when she called out, "Don't you two have a class to get to?"

Leah said, "Yes. We're going."

The teacher gave her a knowing grin. Then Leah handed Charles a piece of paper. "That's my phone number. Call me."

"OK. I will." As Leah walked away, Charles stood motionless. Now he knew what it felt like to be in love and he liked it. Just then, Mr. DeLeon rounded the corner.

"Hey Charles. What's up? What are you doing hanging out in the hallway?"

Charles smiled. He was about to tell Mr. DeLeon what had just happened but, in an instant, he changed his mind. He lied. "I forgot my history book so I had to get it out of my locker."

"Alright. Well, I'll see you this afternoon." Mr. DeLeon remembered it was a tutoring day.

"Sure. Great. I'll see you later." Charles walked off to his next class slightly delirious. It seemed that absolutely everything was going his way. He was going on a date with Leah. His father was back at home and he felt like he had a normal family. He was even going to a Phillies game with his dad that spring. And Mr. DeLeon seemed to think of him as a member of his clique.

When he arrived for his tutoring session, Mr. DeLeon seemed to be as happy as he was. "Hey Charles. Good to see you. Have a seat."

As he settled into his chair and pulled out his Algebra text and notebook, Charles was grinning. He thought to himself, "Mr. DeLeon is going to ask me about what's going on with Leah . . . he'll never guess that it happened so fast."

For his part, Mr. DeLeon was thinking, "He's such a handsome kid. He seems really comfortable around me now. He's not intimidated the way he was when we first met." Mr. DeLeon had just started working out with the boys' tennis team; doing inside drills in preparation for the upcoming season. It was still too cold and windy to play on the courts outside; so he had the boys doing agility drills and strength training. Yesterday, they set up a temporary net on the basketball court and practiced their serves. He grinned when he thought about his meeting with Blake after practice the day before. Blake was a tall, svelte, olive skinned 7th grader who had confided in Mr. DeLeon; telling him he was homosexual and a virgin. Blake seemed to be embarrassed by his virginity but surprisingly comfortable with his homosexuality. Now he wouldn't have to be embarrassed about being a virgin. Mr. DeLeon could feel himself getting hard just thinking about how Blake had caressed his penis with his warm lips and sucked him into his soft, pulsating throat . . . back and forth . . . back and forth . . . now he could feel himself getting wet . . .

". . . so we're going to meet each other at the mall Friday night; and maybe go to a movie if my mom lends me the money," Charles was saying.

Mr. DeLeon cleared his throat and surreptitiously moved his erect penis to the right a little bit as he pulled his chair further under his desk at the front of the room. He pretended he had been listening to what Charles had been saying. "That's sounds good Charles. And what's her name again?"

"Leah. Leah Godwin."

"Yeah. She's a very pretty girl. So it looks like my advice worked."

Charles was a little confused. He had just explained to Mr. DeLeon that, initially, everything went wrong. He didn't want to embarrass Mr. DeLeon or hurt his feelings; so he just grinned.

"Hey Charlie, before we get started today, could you help me in the back again?" Mr. DeLeon was again referring to that closet in the back of the classroom with the stuffed bookshelves and all those trophies.

Charles felt uncomfortable. He thought, "*Charlie?* Why did he just call me *Charlie?* My dad's the only one who calls me Charlie." Then he remembered the last time; when Mr. DeLeon started giving him a massage . . . and then he visualized himself later that same day . . . on the activity bus when he wiped his nose and smelled that cologne . . . Mr. DeLeon's cologne.

"Charlie? Hey c'mon man." Now Mr. DeLeon was standing up and it no longer felt like a request but a requirement—not a command—a requirement; that he just ignore his gut feeling.

"Sure." Charles heard himself say, as he followed Mr. DeLeon to the closet.

Mr. DeLeon opened the closet and, just after Charles stepped in; it seemed that Mr. DeLeon suddenly realized that the tennis teams' shirts were hanging on a short pole that jutted out from the back of the door. He shut the door and started to lift one of the hangers that contained a team shirt; still wrapped in plastic from the dry cleaners. Mr. DeLeon said, "Hey, why don't you try one of these on?" He quickly added, "If it fits; you can keep it."

"Really?" Charles couldn't believe it. The shirt was a cool, nylon replica of the 'Abercrombie & Fitch' shirt that all the jocks wore to school. The only difference was that, instead of the brand name 'Abercrombie & Fitch' plastered across the front of the shirt, it said "Forest Hills M.S. Tennis" (the M.S. for middle school).

Charles tried to pull the shirt over the long sleeve shirt he was already wearing, when he realized it was too snug.

Mr. DeLeon laughed a little and said, "Hey man, I think you have to take off your shirt."

"Ah yeah; I guess so." Charles pulled his shirt up from the waist and raised it over his head.

"Here ya go." Mr. DeLeon handed him the tennis shirt.

Charles put it on and looked down at his chest and saw the blazing white letters sewn onto the green nylon. It felt comfortable. He said, "I think it fits."

"Great. It's yours."

"Wow. Thanks Mr. DeLeon."

"No problem man."

Charles started to ask, "But . . . how?"

Mr. DeLeon said, "Don't worry about it. We always get extra shirts and besides, you can keep stats for the team at our home matches and that way you'll earn the shirt."

"Cool. I'd love to do that!" Charles hadn't been on a school team at all this year because they had started to charge parents for the privilege of participating in the sports programs. Charles's mother had said, "Jesus Christ, I can barely afford to pay the bills and now the goddamned school is going to charge me so my kid can play sports? No. No way. Sorry Charles. You can find some kids to play with in the neighborhood instead."

Charles felt a pang of anguish and asked sheepishly, "How much will it cost for me to do the stats for the team?"

"Don't worry about it. I'll take care of it." Mr. DeLeon could see Charles was still worried. "It's only a nominal fee for the auxiliary team members. I'll pay for it myself."

"Ah you don't have to do that Mr. DeLeon."

"I know. I know Charlie. But I like you, so don't give it another thought. Oh and here you go." Mr. DeLeon reached into his back pocket for his wallet and he took out a ten dollar bill. He said, "This will help with the cost of the movie." He handed Charles the money.

Charles hesitated for a moment and then said, "Are you kidding?"

Mr. DeLeon laughed and said, "Hey, it's no big deal. Just take it."

"Thanks Mr. DeLeon." Charles took the money; never thinking there were strings attached.

Mr. DeLeon looked at the top shelf of the bookcase in front of him and said, "Hey, Charles, do me a favor a grab that binder up there."

Charles didn't know how he was going to reach it, when Mr. DeLeon said, "Here. I'll hike you up." He stood in back of Charles and, within seconds, placed his hands around his waist and hoisted him into the air just as easily as if he was picking up a cup of coffee.

Charles looked at the binders and asked, "Which one—the blue one?"

"Yep. That's it." As Mr. DeLeon lowered him to the ground, he tugged at the bottom of Charles's shirt and said, "Tuck this in."

But before Charles could react, Mr. DeLeon was tucking his shirt into his pants the way a mother would dress a child, with slow, deliberate movements.

Charles's heart skipped a beat when he thought he felt Mr. DeLeon's hand linger for a minute as he tucked his shirt into the front of his pants. He was startled by how warm Mr. DeLeon's hand felt as it brushed against the front of his underwear. But instead of taking his hand away, Mr. DeLeon suddenly pushed downward and now Charles was sure he touched his penis. Mr. DeLeon said loudly, with a slight laugh, "You'll need to wear a protective cup for that when you come to our tennis matches." Then he quickly took his hand out of Charles's pants and said, "C'mon, let's get back to that Algebra." He flung open the closet door; walked to the front of the room and said very matter-of-factly, "Turn to chapter 6."

Charles obeyed, but he was confused and distracted. So much had happened in the last few minutes that he didn't quite understand; and he didn't quite know what to think about it. But he forced himself to concentrate on the Algebra instructions. After all, he didn't want Mr. DeLeon to think he was making a big deal out of nothing.

They had been working on a particularly difficult problem when Mr. DeLeon said, "Hey it's already 4:00 Charlie. You better get moving so you don't miss the activity bus."

Charles glanced at the clock. "Oh yeah." He quickly stuffed his books into his backpack. He wondered if Leah would be on the activity bus today. As he was pulling his backpack over his left shoulder, he glanced at his shirt and said, "Oh shit! I mean . . . sorry Mr. DeLeon, but I . . ."

Mr. DeLeon realized Charles was talking about the fact that he was still wearing the tennis team shirt. "Just put your jacket over it and put your other shirt in your backpack."

Charles stuffed it into his backpack and said, "Thanks again Mr. DeLeon."

"Sure thing."

They exited the classroom together and Mr. DeLeon said, "Hey have a nice time at the movies tomorrow night."

Charles smiled and said, "We will. Thanks."

They began to walk in opposite directions when Mr. DeLeon called out, "Hey, don't forget to come to our tennis practice on Monday."

Charles seemed to have already forgotten. He said, "Oh yeah. I'll see you then." Then he stopped short and said loudly, "What about the Algebra stuff?"

Mr. DeLeon seemed to have that figured out. He said, "Our practice is only an hour so we'll get to your Algebra after that."

"Yeah. OK."

Charles was nearing the front lobby doors and glanced down at his shirt as he opened the door. He thought, "I can't believe he gave me this shirt! And $10 for the movie!" He was struck by an uneasy feeling in his gut. He thought about Mr. DeLeon tucking in his shirt and the way his hand brushed against him. He wondered for a moment if Mr. DeLeon was one of those weird dudes. Then he thought, "Nah. He's a cool guy. It was nothing." Then he started to jog toward the activity buses that were lined up out front.

Sure enough, Leah was sitting on the activity bus and smiling at him as he got onto the bus. He sat next to her and asked, "How was your cheerleading practice?"

"Good. What did you stay after for?"

At this point, Charles knew that Leah liked him, so he wasn't ashamed to admit, "I've been getting tutoring in Algebra from Mr.

DeLeon." Then he looked at Leah and continued, "I guess I was a little embarrassed about it before, but, I . . ."

Leah didn't want him to be uncomfortable, so she interrupted, "It's OK. Math has never been my best subject either. But my older sister is really smart, so she's been helping me."

Leah said, "A lot of the girls have a crush on Mr. DeLeon."

"Yeah Mr. DeLeon's a pretty cool guy." Then he knew he would impress her with, "He asked me to do the stats for the tennis team when they play at home." Not only would Leah think he's cute, but now she would know he was smart enough to do the stats for the team. As he looked at her, he couldn't believe how beautiful she looked when the sun streamed in from the opposite window, across the aisle. Her greenish-blue eyes sparkled and widened for a moment, until she blinked slowly, and Charles felt himself floating.

Suddenly, as if he had regained consciousness, he just started rambling, as he shifted his gaze to the back of the seat in front of them.

It wasn't long before he saw the bus turning into his neighborhood. He wished he could have stayed on that bus with Leah forever. Then he thought about Friday night. "So do you think your mom can give you a ride to the mall tomorrow night?"

"Oh yeah. She does it all the time . . . I mean, you know, when I meet my friends there." Leah didn't want Charles to think she was referring to her dates with Matt Howard.

"So what time do you want to meet there?" Charles asked.

"7:00 is usually a good time to go because we're finished with dinner and my mom doesn't have to rush around too much so she's in a good mood."

Charles imagined Leah sitting at a formal dining room table with her parents and sister and passing mashed potatoes and vegetables around to one another in those fancy bowls that you always see on TV. Then each of them would put a big piece of steak onto their plate. Then he flashed on the usual scene at his house—with him and his mom taking their burgers and French fries out of their fast food bags. They were always done dinner by 6:00 or even earlier because his mom was always hungry after standing on her feet all day at work.

As he stood up for his bus stop, Charles said, "OK. I'll see you at the main entrance to the mall, by the fountain, at 7:00."

Leah smiled and said, "OK. See you then."

As planned, Leah was waiting for him by the fountain at the mall's main entrance. Her long, blonde hair fell loosely around her shoulders. She was wearing a light blue sweater and jeans. She smiled and gently took Charles's hand as he neared her. "Let's just walk around for a little while before we go to the movies."

"OK." Charles said. Then he slipped his fingers through hers without any hesitation or awkwardness. They strolled around the mall, sometimes talking; sometimes saying nothing.

They never made it to the movies. The time had passed so quickly that, if it hadn't been for the clock on the wall in the frozen yogurt shop, Charles would have been late to meet his mother at the end of the evening. Leah had just returned from the restroom and, before she sat down again, she turned to say hello to a friend who had called out her name. That's when Charles saw the clock. "Oh shit! 9:55." He pictured his mother sitting in her car parked against the curb and tapping her fingers impatiently against the steering wheel, as she took a long drag from her cigarette.

He stood up before Leah sat down again. "Leah, I have to go."

"What time is it?"

"It's almost 10:00 and my mother is going to be waiting for me. She'll be mad if I make her wait."

"Yeah. I know what you mean. My mom's the same way. Come on. I'll walk out with you."

Charles was surprised when he didn't see his mother's car waiting by the mall entrance. "That's weird. She's never late," he said.

"There's my mom's car," Leah said.

"Where?"

"The black BMW over there."

"Oh, sweet."

"Hey, my mom could probably give you a ride home."

"Really?" Charles liked the idea of prolonging his time with Leah. He was a little embarrassed to say it, but he had to. "Ah, I don't have a cell phone so . . ."

"Oh, here, use mine." Leah handed him her cell phone. Charles called his mother. After three rings, his mother answered. She sounded sleepy as she said, "Who is it?"

"Charles, Mom. It's Charles." He figured she had been drinking wine like she does most nights and probably passed out on the couch.

"Oh Charles. Sorry, I . . . was I supposed to . . ."

Charles interrupted, "Don't' worry Mom. It's OK. Leah's mom is going to give me a ride home."

"Alright then. Are you on your way now?" His mother asked.

"Yeah. I should be home in about 15 minutes."

"OK. I'll see you soon." Charles wondered why his father hadn't answered the phone if his mom had been sleeping on the couch. He thought, "I hope they're not fighting again."

In the meantime, they had reached the BMW and a very attractive, older woman was sitting in the driver's seat.

"Hi Mom. This is Charles. Can you give him a ride home?" Leah asked.

"Sure honey."

When Leah opened the door to the backseat of the car, the inside light shone on her mother and he could see how beautiful Leah would look in twenty years.

"Hi Charles. I've heard a lot about you."

"Hi Mrs. Godwin. It's nice to meet you." Charles said shyly.

"Where do you live honey?"

"On Warren Avenue. It's just off of Eagle Road. Near Lawrence Avenue."

"Oh sure. Sure. I know where it is."

Thankfully, Leah's mother turned on the radio so they could talk quietly to each other in the backseat. Again, Leah reached for his hand and their eyes met. Charles leaned over and kissed Leah's lips. He felt like he was dreaming when he felt how warm and soft her lips were. He was spellbound, until he heard her mother say, "What's the address again honey?"

"134 Warren Avenue. There it is—the one with the Toyota Corolla out front."

The car slowed to a stop and Charles boldly kissed Leah on the mouth again. "Goodnight. I'll call you."

Leah smiled and said, "Goodnight Charlie."

Charles saw the light on in the kitchen as he shut the front door. He walked toward the kitchen and found his mother standing at the sink, smoking a cigarette. She smoothed her hair back when she saw him.

"Hi Mom."

"Hey. How was the date?"

"Good."

She stood silently and he could see that she was upset. He asked, "What's wrong?"

"Oh, it's just your father again—as usual."

"What do you mean?"

"Well, he doesn't seem to think that he has to stop dating, even though he's married."

Charles felt his stomach knot. But, in an instant, his attitude changed and he blurted out, "Maybe it's you! Maybe he's just sick of your drinking and smoking and complaining!" Then he stormed out of the kitchen and ran upstairs to his room and slammed the door.

Within minutes, his mother flung open his door and waved her finger at him, saying, "How dare you blame me! After all I do for you, and you're going to take his side!" She stalked around the room and then stopped short and said, "If I ever told you half of what I put up with, with him, you wouldn't be so quick to take his side. Do you know he . . ." She stopped herself because she thought better of it.

But Charles shouted with tears in his eyes, "What? What did he do? Tell me!"

His mother slumped her posture. She looked defeated. "Never mind. What's the use. You men all stick together anyway." She stopped in his doorway and said quietly, "Goodnight."

He didn't answer her. He just got up and shut his door and locked it this time. He laid on his bed and thought, "She better not mess things up again. I don't care how mad she gets. She's not stopping me from going to the Phillies game with him . . . bitch!"

After a few minutes, he calmed down and started to think about Leah. He laid back on his bed and looked at the ceiling, as he re-lived every moment of the evening and soon, he fell fast asleep.

On Monday morning, Charles left for school in a good mood. As he neared the bus stop, he felt a bit apprehensive. Since his father wasn't home all weekend, he had no choice but to take the school bus. Then his mood lightened. He thought, "I can sit with Leah and talk on the way to school." The bus screeched to a stop and he climbed the three steps and turned to look for Leah. Suddenly, David Reilly yelled out, "Hey Chuck! Wanna fuck?" He couldn't believe it. For some reason, Matt Howard was on the bus. And what was worse, he was sitting next to Leah. But she looked upset. Charles brazenly walked up to them and said to Matt, "What are you doing here?"

Matt said cooly, "I stayed at my cousin's house last night so I decided to take his bus to school. Is that alright with you Charlie?"

David Reilly was listening to the exchange and he shouted, "Hey man, he's my cousin. Don't mess with him. Besides, you're *my* boyfriend—not his."

Charles ignored David. He was undaunted. He asked Matt, "What are you doing sitting next to Leah?"

Matt said defensively, "What's it to you?"

Leah looked upset. She started to stand up but Matt put his arm out in front of her and said, "Where do you think you're going?"

Leah pushed past his arm and said, "Get away from me Matt!"

"What the fuck?" Matt looked exasperated.

"Come on Charlie." Leah took his hand and they moved to a seat near the front of the bus and then sat together.

David Reilly shouted, "Oh. Them there's fightin words girl!"

Charles got up and started toward the back of the bus when Matt shouted, "Fuck it David. Fuck her too. She's a fucking bitch anyway."

Now Charles wanted to defend Leah. He walked right up to Matt and demanded, "Stand up!"

Matt looked at him in disbelief and said, "What? What the fuck? Are you fucking kidding me?"

"No. No, I'm not." Charles said bravely.

"Look man. Just get the fuck out of my face," Matt said.

David Reilly suddenly jumped up and shoved Charles to the floor. He tried to get up, but David was now on top of him and started to punch him.

"Get off me you asshole!" Charles shouted. He threw a punch at David.

The bus driver had apparently been watching this scene in his rear-view mirror. He shouted, "All of you guys better sit down in the next two minutes, or I'll see to it that all of you are suspended."

Fortunately, that was enough to dissuade David Reilly and he backed away from Charles, as he mumbled curses at the bus driver.

Charles got up and brushed himself off. He heard Leah's voice, "Charlie?" He turned in her direction and went up front to sit next to her.

Leah asked, "Are you alright?"

"Yeah. I'm fine."

"Don't let them get to you Charlie. They're jerks. Spineless jerks."

"Yeah. You're right about that for sure."

When they arrived at school, Charles remembered he was supposed to meet up with the tennis team after school. He asked Leah, "Are you staying after school for cheerleading practice?"

"No. We don't have practice today."

"Oh."

Leah could see that Charles was still upset. She wanted to reassure him. She said, "Charlie, I really like you a lot so don't let whatever Matt said, or that jerk David Reilly, bother you."

Charlie smiled and said, "Alright. Oh and . . . I like you a lot too."

"I know." Leah smiled.

They walked into the school building and only moments later, the bell rang for classes to begin and Leah said, "Call me tonight."

"Alright. I will. Bye Leah."

Chapter 11

BETH WAS SURPRISED to see Henry outside with Jake, as she got out of the taxi she had taken from the train station. It was 4:30 on a Sunday afternoon and Henry was typically still at his garage until somewhere around 6:00 in the evening.

"Hey sweetie?" Henry called to her and walked up to the taxi with Jake. "Let me help you with your bags."

"Oh thanks."

Henry leaned in for a kiss. Beth wasn't surprised by his affectionate greeting. He was always nicer to her when he thought she might be fed up with him. Even the fact that he was home this early on a Sunday afternoon meant that he was trying to get on her good side and charm her into changing her mind.

"We missed you. Jake and I were just about to go for a walk. Do you want to join us?"

"Yeah. Sure. Let me just put this stuff inside and go to the bathroom." Beth was dreading the conversation she had to have with Henry about the job and the move. Then she thought, "Actually it would be the perfect time to bring it up—when we're outside because he's less likely to freak out."

The daylight was starting to fade and they had been walking through the woods off of the bike path. "Maybe we should start heading back," Beth said.

"Yeah. Hey, how about Chinese takeout for dinner?"

"That sounds great."

The three of them fell in line with the others on the bike path. They kept to the right and were mindful to "share the path" as the intermittent signs reminded everyone to do. Joggers passed them on the left, followed by some really fast moving bicyclists. Jake started to bark when he saw the roller skaters approaching in the distance. Henry tightened his grip on the leash and pulled Jake further to the right as they whizzed by.

Finally, Beth summoned the courage to say, "I have to finish packing up my things in the apartment."

"Well, there's no rush is there?" Henry said, but then he stopped suddenly and had a worried look on his face. He asked, "When are you thinking of moving?"

Beth felt nervous as she said, "Well . . . probably by the end of this week."

"Oh." Henry started walking briskly and Beth had to quicken her pace to keep up with him; but it seemed that Henry purposely walked even faster.

"Hey wait up." Beth started to jog, just to keep up with him. Breathlessly, she pleaded, "Henry, could you slow down so we can walk together?"

Suddenly Henry stopped and shouted at her, "It's you! You're purposely slowing down. I'm just trying to get home before it gets dark."

"Henry, come on. You started walking fast just to get away from me once I told you about the move."

Now Henry yelled, "You just like to piss people off! You just like to start a fight. We were having a perfectly nice walk and then you had to start walking like you're in a funeral procession. Everyone is trying to pass you. Can't you see that?"

"What?" Beth was incredulous. She knew this wasn't about the pace of her walking. But now Henry was growing progressively more angry. He stopped and Beth saw that he was getting those crazy eyes; when his eyes actually lost focus and he glared *toward* her but his eyes couldn't seem to look *at* her. Now there was spit flying out of his mouth as he got up in her face and screamed, "You're impossible to get along with!

Nobody likes you! Your own parents don't even like you! You can't get a job. You just expect me to pay your way. Now I guess you expect me to help you move all of your stuff back to Pennsylvania. Well count me out! You're on your own. You selfish bitch!" A few people on the bike path slowed down and looked on timidly; as if they were afraid to get involved with such a madman. Then Henry's face contorted and he shoved her before he ran off toward their apartment.

Beth lost her footing and fell hard on her right side. She sat there for a moment absolutely stunned. Then she noticed her jeans were ripped around her right kneecap and her knee was bloody. A jogger had stopped short and asked if she was alright. Beth started to cry. The woman helped her get to her feet and Beth said, "My glasses . . . my glasses . . . where . . ." She looked at the grassy area next to the path where she had fallen. She pushed her hair from her face and heard the jogger say, "There! Are those your glasses?" Beth looked at the brown frames. "Yeah. Oh, thank you." The jogger asked, "What happened? Did that guy push you?" Beth started to cry and said, "Yeah. Yeah. He did."

"You should call the police!"

Beth shook her head. "No. No. It's alright. He's my husband."

The stranger said, "Well I hope you can get away from him."

Beth looked at the woman and said resolutely, "I am. I am finally getting away."

"Good."

"Thanks for your help."

"Are you sure you're OK?"

"Yeah. Thanks."

When she got inside, Henry was pacing around the living room. Beth knew she was safer if she got out of the same room, so she headed for the bathroom. She purposely left the door open because she knew he would get angrier if he thought she was shutting him out and ignoring him. She turned on the spigot in the tub and started to take off her jeans.

"What are you doing?"

She didn't answer. She just stepped out of her pants and got into the tub. That's when Henry saw the blood. "Oh God! Oh my God! Now I'm done. Now you're going to call the police!"

Beth ignored him and tested the temperature of the water. When it was lukewarm, she splashed water on her knee and picked up the soap and gently washed it. Then with a completely different tone in his voice, she heard Henry say, "I'm sorry sweetie." She looked up and saw that Henry was in tears. Beth said, "It's OK."

"Can I help you?" he asked.

"Could you get me the bottle of peroxide under the sink?"

Henry quickly found the bottle and handed it to her. "Do you want a bandage?"

She said, "Do we have any gauze? It's pretty bloody."

Henry opened the drawers until he found a first aide kit. He took out some gauze and a spool of adhesive tape. Beth had shut off the water and was now sitting on the side of the tub. Henry bandaged the wound and apologized again and again. Beth knew he was sincerely worried—maybe not so much about her wound but about the fact that he had shoved her in front of people and she might have found a witness after he ran off. But she was happy for the peace and calm. She said, "I'm just going to lie down now." She got into bed and under the covers and eventually fell asleep.

By the following Saturday morning, Beth had rented a small Uhaul truck and she started to make the first of many trips back and forth from the apartment to the ramp that led up to the inside of the truck. Box after box of clothes, sheets, towels, shoes, and all sorts of miscellaneous items, quickly started to fill up the space inside the ten foot deep truck. She carried paintings wrapped in layer upon layer of bubble wrap and even took a small table, two chairs and a desk that folded in just such a convenient way, as only Ikea furniture tends to do.

Henry had long since calmed down and convinced Beth that he would not have reacted that way, if he hadn't been so upset about her leaving him. There was the crying and pleading and Beth reconsidered her decision at least a hundred times during the course of the week. When he knew she was really going, Henry had offered to help her with the move. He would drive the Uhaul truck and Beth would drive her car down to Pennsylvania. They planned to leave in the early morning hours on Sunday.

As she looked around the apartment one last time on Sunday morning, Henry put his arm around her and said, "I'm going to miss you sweetie. I'll be so lonely."

Beth started to cry and they hugged each other for several minutes. She calmed down and said, "Well, who knows what the future will bring. Maybe we just need some time apart."

Henry was happy to hear this. He said, "I love you. You're my wife. Let's not be apart too long, OK?"

They looked into each other's tear-filled eyes. "Alright. Let's just take some time and figure out how to get along better."

After a few minutes she said, "I guess we better get on the road."

Henry said, "Are you sure you want to leave all this furniture?"

"Yeah. It's just easier right now."

Henry asked, "When do you make settlement on the house?"

"Joyce managed to get it moved up to a week from Wednesday." Beth was going to stay at her parents' house until then.

Henry asked, "Are you going to unload the stuff at your parents' house?"

"No. Thank God I don't have to because my brother knows the manager of the local Uhaul franchise down there. He agreed to let me store the stuff in the truck for just over a week, so I don't have to unload the truck twice. God, I'd go crazy if I had to do that."

Henry asked, "Don't you have to work on Wednesday?" (Beth had finally told him about her new job and Henry had agreed to send his monthly stipend when he heard her hourly pay rate).

"No. Thank God the doctors' office is closed on Wednesdays, so it works out perfectly as far as that goes."

Beth took a deep breath and said, "Well, let's hit the road."

"Are you taking Jake or am I?" Henry asked.

"I'll take him. But don't worry. You can walk him when we get to our first rest stop."

Henry smiled and said, "Alright. I'll drive in the right lane and just try to stay behind me."

"OK. I will. But don't worry if we get separated because I know the way."

Henry said, "Alright, but just try to stay behind me anyway."

After hours of driving, and a few rest stops for coffee, sandwiches, restroom breaks and brief dog walks, they finally arrived at Beth's parents' house. Her parents had agreed to let Henry stay there overnight since he had helped Beth by driving the truck for her. Beth would drop him off at the Septa train station on her way to work the next day. Henry would get off at 30th Street Station in Philadelphia and then connect with an Amtrak regional train for the trip back to Massachusetts.

Henry parked the truck in her parents' driveway and when he got out, he stretched and yawned and then walked up to Beth as she got out of her car. He said, "Hey, after we say hello to your parents, do you want to drive past the house? After all, I haven't even seen it."

Beth said, "Oh yeah sure. That's a good idea." But she had a bad feeling that it really wasn't a good idea.

Sure enough, on the drive back to her parents' home, after showing Henry the house from the road, he got very quiet. Beth knew this wasn't a good sign. She nervously tried to think of something to say. "It's a shame I don't have the key yet because I could show you what it's like inside—not that it's so great or anything—it's just an older house." Henry remained silent. Beth continued, "I mean, it needs a lot of updates, but I can't afford any of that right now." That must have hit a hot button because Henry said loudly, "Sure. You don't want to fix it up now. Wait until we're back together again so you can get me to pay for it!"

"What? What are you talking about?"

"Oh come on Beth. You know you're really just moving on. Maybe you'll meet somebody at the doctor's office. Maybe one of the doctors is single and then you can divorce me and marry him and then 'little miss' will have everything she wants."

"Henry, this is crazy. Stop it. First you say I just want you to pay for everything and then you say I want to meet a doctor to pay for everything. You're not making any sense."

"*I'm* not making sense? You're the one who doesn't make sense. No wonder you were unemployed for so long. You'll probably mess this job up too. You're such a loser. What am I doing with you anyway!"

"Henry stop it, please."

"Yeah. I'll stop it. Let me out!"

"What?"

"I said, let me out of this car right now!"

"But Henry your stuff is at my parents' house and what's going to happen when I walk into the house without you?"

"Oh that's all you care about—appearances. Let's not let mommy and daddy think that I don't have Henry wrapped around my finger."

"Henry, please stop it."

He started to open the passenger side door, while the car was still moving.

Beth shouted, "Stop it! Stop it right now!" She looked in her rear-view mirror and fortunately there were no cars behind her, because she had already started to pull over. Just as she stopped the car, Henry pulled the door shut again. She turned to look at him, and he slapped her across the face.

"Oh my God!" Beth cried out.

"You deserved it you bitch. You goddamned princess!" Henry got out of the car and started walking down the street.

Beth sat and cried for a minute, before she looked at her face in the rearview mirror. There was a red mark on her cheek but she was relieved not to see any blood. She straightened her hair and wiped her face. She pulled the car back onto the road and very soon, came upon Henry, now walking slowly on the side of the road. She pulled to a stop and put the passenger side window down. "Henry?"

He leaned down to look into the car. His face was full of anguish. He had been crying too. He said, "I'm sorry Beth. Are you OK?"

"Yeah. Yeah. I'm OK Henry. Get in." Beth was relieved that he had calmed down.

"I'm sorry sweetie," Henry cried.

"I know. I know you are." She hugged him. She knew he was just sad and afraid of what was going to happen to them. She almost said it, but he was in such an erratic mood that she worried it might set him off again, so she was silent.

Fortunately, her parents were already upstairs in their bedroom when they got back to the house. Beth was grateful that they had been cordial to Henry, but she knew they didn't want to spend any more time with him than was necessary. Given what had just happened, Beth was relieved to have privacy. They quietly went into the kitchen and Beth foraged through the refrigerator to look for something to eat. They nibbled on some cheese and crackers and each of them had a glass of wine, before calling it a day.

Chapter 12

BETH HAD WALKED Jake; showered and dressed; all while Henry was still sleeping; then she sat on the bed to put on her socks and reached over to shake Henry's leg. "Wake up Henry."

He groaned and then raised his head from the pillow to look in her direction, "You're dressed already? What time is it?"

"It's 6:45. We have to leave by 7:30. I would have gotten you up sooner, but you said you could get up at the last minute."

"Yeah. Yeah. It's OK."

"I'm going downstairs to get something to eat," Beth said.

"OK. Let me take a quick shower and I'll be right down."

Beth was a little bit nervous about her new job, but she was also looking forward to it. As they approached the Lansdale train station, she felt pangs of anxiety. Henry did too. When she stopped the car, Henry said softly, "I love you sweetie. Please don't give up on us."

They hugged each other and for a moment. Henry said, "Hey, I'll come down to visit you once you're settled in your new house."

Beth felt a little uneasy. She knew it wasn't the right thing to do, but she said, "OK," and then suddenly she became aware of the time. "Oh God. It's 7:40. I better get going. I have to be there at 8:00."

"OK. Don't be sad. Call me tonight and let me know how your first day went."

"OK, I will. Bye Henry."

As Beth pulled away, she felt butterflies in her stomach. She was literally separating from Henry and starting a new job and maybe even a new life.

This time Lydia gave Beth a welcoming smile when she saw her come through the front door. "Hi Beth; boy am I glad to see you. I've been working both shifts and I'll be happy when we're done with your training so I can get back to just working the mornings."

Beth smiled. "I'm happy to be here." For the purpose of training, Beth and Lydia would work the morning, afternoon and evening shifts together all week. By the following week, Beth could start to work on her own in the afternoons and evenings. Kathy's hours were from 11:00 a.m. until 5:00 p.m., which would provide an overlap, from the time Lydia left, in case Beth had a question or a problem.

Kathy came walking up the hallway on the right with Dr. Deepak Ajit "the father."

Kathy said, "Beth, I don't know if you've met Dr. Deepak Ajit."

"Hello Beth. It's nice to meet you." Dr. Deepak had maintained a heavy Indian accent even though he had lived in this country for close to 40 years. He had a slight build, black, wavy hair, glasses, and a mustache that rested over an easy smile. He gave Beth a hearty handshake and welcomed her to the practice. While they talking, another Indian doctor walked passed them and gave Beth a courteous nod. Lydia said, "Oh and this is Dr. Vishnu."

Beth shook his hand. "Dr. Vishnu?"

"Yes. That's it. You pronounced it perfectly," he said with a little giggle.

Beth said, "Oh good. I wasn't sure if I should pronounce the "i" like an "e.""

"No. No. No. It's fine. It's fine. The way you pronounced it with a soft "i" is fine." Dr. Vishnu was a bit taller than Dr. Deepak Ajit and he had a stocky build; a bald head and glasses. He was younger than Dr. Deepak by at least a dozen years.

Beth smiled and Dr. Vishnu walked toward the other end of the office—by the back door. Beth assumed Dr. Vishnu had his own separate practice and just rented the office and exam rooms at that end of the very large floor space. She made this assumption because his name was not on their sign; their business cards; prescription pads; or anything else for that matter. When she was a pharma sales rep, there were a couple of practices with Indian doctors who seemed to have a similar arrangement. She assumed these foreign doctors shared office space for their separate practices because it saved them a lot of money as they tried to settle into their new country.

Lydia moved a second chair with castor wheels into the space behind the front desk. "It's going to be a little tight with the two of us sitting here, but it's the only way I can train you while we're seeing patients."

Lydia and Beth squeezed together in front of a large desk with the computer screen in the center facing them. The phone was to the left of the computer, along with a half dozen metal bins stacked on top of each other, which contained frequently used forms. To the right of the computer screen were the usual containers of paper clips, rubber bands, pens, sticky notepads, as well as coffee cups. The desk extended on both sides of Beth and Lydia; so there were really essentially three desks. The one to Beth's left contained a centrifuge for spinning tubes of blood, a rack for holding tubes of blood, a black box that could have held index cards but it contained prescriptions, in alphabetical order, to be picked up by patients. The desk to the right of Beth contained more racks for tubes of blood and a series of containers with empty blood collection tubes—some large and some small and different colored rubber caps; apparently for distinguishing one type of blood sample from another. There were containers full of empty urine cups and lids; and the pipettes used to extract urine from the sample container, which was then squirted into the same cylindrical tube that is used for blood samples. There was a little machine used to print the labels with the patient's name on the blood and urine tubes. Beth assumed all of this lab stuff had nothing to do with her job, but she would soon find out differently.

These three desks had "walls" that surrounded Beth and Lydia on all three sides, like a fortress. It would have looked like a typical office cubicle if it weren't for the 12 inch-wide counter that jutted out and ran along the top of the entire semicircle. The doctors used the right side of the counter to pick up or deposit patient charts. There was a little machine that printed out prescriptions that had been typed by the doctors on their computers. Many prescriptions were just sent electronically to the patient's pharmacy but, the ones that were printed out were soon to become mysterious to Beth, like many things in the practice. The counter directly in front of Beth and Lydia stretched out an additional 12 inches. This is where patients interacted with the front desk receptionist to sign in for appointments; to schedule appointments; pay copays; complain or just chat; before they either sat down in the waiting area in front of Beth; or exited by the front door; or used the patient restroom in the foyer. The counter to the left of Beth is where a giant plastic bag of labwork (blood tubes and urine samples) sat until the courier picked it up.

The hallway to Beth's right had a series of rooms; one of them was a kitchen that was used as a multi-purpose room where pharma sales reps were directed to deposit their drug samples into the bins labeled for their products. The sales reps were to linger there until the doctors stopped in to chat with them, in between seeing patients. The kitchen had a full size refrigerator that often contained more labwork than food. This was the labwork for Mrs. Ajit's lab business. She had a nasty habit of storing Friday's labwork there because she wouldn't get to it until Monday. She didn't work on the weekends so the blood and urine samples to be processed by her lab business were stashed there until she got to it. Beth wondered how this waiting period of a few days might affect the integrity of the samples. The kitchen also had a large folding table, which was pushed up against the wall and pulled out for lunch, which was provided almost everyday by pharma sales reps. Two chairs were always shoved against the wall and additional chairs would be moved in and out to accommodate the people around the lunch table. This room always had literature about various prescription drugs scattered on the counters; but some of the materials were kept in an orderly fashion in old-fashioned metal filing bins that at one time were used to collate materials. The tiny sink contained cups for tea or coffee that were rinsed out and used each day by the doctors. There were large cabinets that contained lots of paper plates, cups, napkins and bags of stale pretzels and potato chips. When lunches were over, Lydia and "the father" would schlep the leftovers back to the unused exam room at the opposite end of the office, where a sheet of paper was drawn across the exam table to keep some of the sauces, condiments, and crumbs off of the table. Dr. Vishnu often took some of the leftovers, but he never stayed for lunches with sales reps. He lived very close to the office (a five minute drive door to door) so he always went home for lunch.

Just beyond the kitchen were three separate patient exam rooms—one for each doctor. Beth would quickly learn that Dr. Vishnu was in fact part of the practice; thus one of the exam rooms was his. They never switched rooms; each of them always used their own particular exam room to see patients. The far end of the hallway had a very large floor to ceiling window, in front of which were two scales for weighing patients—one of them electronic and broken, and the other a traditional metal doctor's office scale, which was never calibrated for accuracy. The office shared by father, son and dog was also in this hallway, as well as another patient bathroom, which was mostly used by patients to pee into urine cups which they then deposited onto the counter to the right of Beth.

The hallway to the left of Beth contained the copier, the water cooler and the staff restroom. Beyond that were two additional exam rooms; the one at the far end of the hallway is where lunch leftovers went, and sat for the rest of the day, as staff stopped in to scoop up a snack or fill containers for dinner that night. This room was used as a catch-all for a variety of things. Lab supplies (for Lansdale Labs and also for the doctors' use) were stored in large, half opened cardboard boxes on top of, or under, every piece of furniture in the room; including a second exam table, which was shoved up against the opposite wall. Dozens of tissue boxes, paper towels, toilet paper, and more lab supplies were stuffed onto the table. There were Christmas decorations and straw flowers and dirty vases in the corners. There was a counter with a tiny sink and above it, and below it, were cabinets filled with more lab supplies. There was a filthy microwave oven that looked like it hadn't been cleaned in years, despite the burn marks from overcooking food and overheating tea. There was always a patch of spilled sugar near the large container of sugar that was apparently the property of "the father" and "the mother." This room was directly across the hall from Dr. Vishnu's office; and in between these two rooms was the back door at the end of that hallway.

In between the catch-all room and the water cooler was a mysterious; apparently unused exam room. It was fully stocked with the same equipment as the other exam rooms, but patients were never directed there; and yet Beth would later discover evidence that the room had been used; just never during regular office hours.

Dr. Arvind Ajit walked up to the front desk with a patient he had just seen. Lydia busied herself with setting up a follow-up appointment for the patient, while Dr. Arvind "the son" welcomed Beth to the practice. He lingered for just a moment and then returned to his exam room.

Kathy asked, "How did your move go?"

"Oh good. Thanks for asking."

Lydia asked, "Are you moved into your new house?" (Apparently Kathy had filled her in on Beth's *situation*).

"No. I'm staying with my parents until next Wednesday. That's the day of my settlement."

Kathy said, "So it works out perfectly that your settlement is on the day we don't have office hours."

Lydia said, "You can put your pocketbook here." She pointed to an empty space on the shelves under the desk on her left. As Beth squeezed her bag into the space, she noticed a couple of Tupperware containers.

Lydia said, "Oh yeah, bring a Tupperware container with you so you can fill it with food from our sales rep lunches."

"Oh, OK." Beth cringed at the idea. At one time, *she* had been the pharmaceutical sales rep bringing lunches to doctors' offices and she was always amazed at how the office staff stacked their plates with food. They had no qualms about taking two sandwiches or three desserts. Beth had always thought it was rude; so she knew she would never bring a Tupperware container to the office. Besides which, her shift was afternoons, evenings, and Saturday mornings. Beth always ate at home before her shift and by the time she arrived at work, the rest of the staff had already eaten or hoarded away most of the food from the lunches brought in by the sales reps. It was only the food they didn't like, or couldn't stuff any more of into their containers, that sat for hours on the exam table in the catch-all room.

At the end of her first day, Beth followed Lydia into the kitchen, where Lydia opened a cabinet and pulled out a large trash bag. They proceeded to go in and out of each exam room, as Lydia emptied the trash baskets into the larger trash bag. Beth watched with apprehension as she saw Lydia's ungloved hands empty trash that contained bloodied bits of gauge, plastic wrappers; partially filled blood tubes and urine cups; used bandages, sticky notes, crumpled 8 1/2" x 11" papers, and an occasional tear-off sheet from the exam table. The doctors rarely changed the paper sheets on the exam tables—only if there were obvious splatters of bodily fluids.

Beth asked sheepishly, "Do *I* have to empty the trash at the end of the day?"

Lydia said, "Yes." But then she laughed a little and said, "If it sticks, it stays," referring to gum or whatever else might stick to the plastic, white trash bags in each exam room waste basket.

Beth had an idea. "Can't I just replace the bags in each waste basket at the end of the day?"

Lydia smirked and said, "Are you kidding? They would never want to pay for that. Just empty it and only replace it if there's a puddle of something in it. Otherwise, we have a housekeeper who comes in once a week and she's supposed to replace the bags that are in bad shape."

Beth would notice that this didn't happen too often because she would see the same coffee stains in the same spot for weeks at a time. When they got to the room with the lunch leftovers, Lydia asked, "Did you want any of this?" She was referring to the large aluminum pans that contained small portions of mushy salad, stale-looking pasta, a half dozen rounds of white bread (the kind of slightly crusted white bread that's served in cheap Italian restaurants) and plastic containers of salad dressings and tomato sauce.

Beth said, "No. No. I'm fine." She didn't dare tell Lydia that she had been a pharmaceutical sales rep because she didn't want Lydia to think she was bragging or, worse, wondering what had happened that caused her career to plummet to the level of front desk receptionist in a doctor's office.

Lydia put one tray into the other; tossed all of the condiments into them and then shoved all of it into the trash bag. She said, "Follow me."

Beth followed her through the back door and down the steps to the exit door. If they had continued down another flight of stairs, that was where New Day Physical Therapy, and Lansdale Labs were.

There was no dumpster outside; just 4 oversized, plastic trash cans and Lydia took the lid off of one of them and threw the bag in there. She said, "Just bring the trash out here each night. After office hours on Saturday, you have to drag the cans over to the corner over there, where it will be picked up on Monday." Not only were there no hazardous waste receptacles at Ajit Medical Center, but the office trash, mingled with bodily fluids, was left to stew on the curb for a couple of days.

As they entered the building again, Lydia said, "By the way, this is where you should enter the building each day, instead of through the front entrance—that's just for patients. All of us enter through this door. Kathy is going to have a key made for you because you will have to lock up at night."

That night Beth stopped at the local Walgreen's on her way home to pick up a few toiletries. Next door was a small bookstore and, as an avid reader, Beth had to stop in to check it out. She came across a display with an odd assortment of laminated crib sheets, one of which contained a few anatomical illustrations and lots of medical terminology in both English and Spanish languages. Beth bought it; thinking that Ajit Medical Center would surely have a few Hispanic patients, since the news is constantly reporting on this ever-expanding demographic.

But by her second day at work, she would learn from Lydia that 97% of their patient population was Indian and the other 3% were White; with just a few who were Black or Chinese. Beth was shocked by the number of Indian patients—not just long time patients—but always more and more new patients who were also Indian. She had no idea this demographic existed in Lansdale and surrounding towns. She would begin to notice a similarity in the zip codes and addresses of patients. Whereas the more educated, middle class Indian patients lived in mixed race neighborhoods; the low income Indian patients (and they comprised the majority of the patients in the practice) clustered in homogeneous communities. The towns of Hatfield and Lansdale, in Montgomery County (a suburb of Philadelphia) had large swaths of Indians living there. The local White people called Hatfield "Little India." Certain streets, with a radius of several blocks in Lansdale, had an exclusively Indian population. It was Dr. Vishnu who told the staff that two or three Indian families crowd into small townhouses and even apartments that don't have enough bedrooms to accommodate the number of people living there; so people sleep on floor mats and blankets. They bring relatives from India who stay for months at a time and crowd into these tiny quarters; along with children, teenagers, parents and elderly relatives. Dr. Vishnu spoke of an apartment complex in Hatfield that had to evict family after family for violating occupancy rules. But there were no rules or restrictions on individually owned townhomes, or twin or single homes; usually purchased by a family member with a good job, who brought in family from India who stayed and multiplied.

By the afternoon of her second day, Beth met Mrs. Ajit, who was very cordial. Lydia giggled when Beth stood up to shake her hand. Lydia said, "Look how tiny she is next to you!" Mrs. Ajit was all of 5' tall and seemed shorter because she always leaned over on her right hip and walked with a limp because she had problems with her left hip. She wore blouses with paisley floral prints or vivid stripes and black or navy blue pants. If she was going to a special occasion after work, she wore a traditional silk sari. Every day she wore the same diamond earrings, shaped like flower petals and a subtle gold necklace. She dyed her long, black hair, which was braided down her back, but she always had a line of white hair showing her roots in a middle part.

Beth hovered over Mrs. Ajit and asked, "Do you work up here in the afternoon?" She knew Mrs. Ajit ran Lansdale Labs the rest of the day downstairs.

Mrs. Ajit laughed a little and said, "No."

Lydia asked, "How do you like having another large White woman working here?" Beth thought it was a crass way of putting it, but Mrs. Ajit said, "Oh it's good." She looked directly at Beth and said, "You can't trust Indian people. They lie."

Lydia laughed but Beth felt uneasy. She wasn't sure how to react to this since Mrs. Ajit was Indian. So she just smiled and Mrs. Ajit left to go into the kitchen.

When they sat down in their crowded space next to each other, Lydia whispered, "She's going in there to take all the food home. She doesn't do it everyday; just when she's having company at her house."

Just then, Dr. Vishnu walked by and Lydia said to him, "I was just telling Beth about Mrs. Ajit taking the food."

Dr. Vishnu giggled and then looked to make sure Mrs. Ajit wasn't coming out of the kitchen. He said, "Oh, she's unbelievable. I've already been invited to their house with a large group of people, and she serves leftovers from the rep lunches. Some of the food has mold on it because she's kept it for several days."

Beth grimaced. Dr. Vishnu said, "Oh yes. And I know it's leftover food so my wife and I won't even eat it."

Mrs. Ajit came walking out of the kitchen with a large, brown paper bag with handles. It was full of containers of food that she would store downstairs in the lab, before taking it home at the end of the day.

As Dr. Vishnu walked away, Beth said, "I noticed his name isn't on the business cards or on the sign out front; or anything else for that matter."

Lydia didn't explain anything. She just sort of waved away any notion of impropriety and said, "Yeah, Yeah. He's been with Dr. Ajit for about 18 years. In fact, Dr. Vishnu leads most of the patients here because he's very active in the Indian community and the word spreads. Indian patients want to be seen by Indian doctors. That's why they borrow cars or get rides from friends to get to this office."

Then Lydia changed the subject. She said, "The last appointment of the day on Tuesday and Thursday is 6:00 p.m. On Monday and Friday, the last appointment of the day is 4:30. On Saturday, the doctors have hours in the morning only, so you have to be here by 7:30 a.m. and they start seeing patients at 8:00 and the last appointment is at 11:00 a.m. After the last patient is seen, it takes about an hour or so for you to get caught up on paperwork, labwork and phone messages. You will also have to begin preparation for the morning's appointments by verifying insurance for each person scheduled. And since you are the last person to leave everyday, you have to empty the trash and do your light housekeeping duties." Lydia stood up and pointed to the waiting area, saying, "You know, like putting the magazines back in the racks, aligning the chairs and picking up any trash that patients or their children may have left behind . . . oh and refilling the soap dispensers in the bathrooms or refilling the toilet paper and paper towels. And the docs insist that we lock the front door as soon as the last patient leaves. They want to avoid the possibility of a patient walking in at the end of the day, and bothering them with a question or last minute paperwork they need. Basically, the docs want a patient-free hour to update their charts and return phone calls before they leave for the day. Since I work the morning shift during the week, I have to lock the front door after the last patient is seen; then the docs have a two hour break before they start seeing patients again at 2:00. You have to transfer the phones to the answering service before you leave and use the keypad by the back door to turn on the security system." Beth looked toward the back door.

Lydia said, "I'll show you how to do it before we leave tonight and I'll give you the code. Once you input the security code, you have ten seconds to leave and shut and lock the door behind you. Then on your way out, you lock the door to the building; unless of course it's a night when New Day Physical Therapy has hours, in which case they lock the building door when they're finished."

Beth asked, "What time will I finish up then?"

Lydia sighed and then said, "Well of course it varies a little, depending on how busy it is on any given day, and whether or not D is seeing patients because he's always so slow getting his charts finished. But generally, you should finish up by 8:00 p.m. on Tuesday and Thursday and by 6:00 on Monday and Friday. Saturdays you'll finish by 12:00—12:30 if D works, but don't worry, he never works on Saturdays unless he's covering for Dr. Arvind."

During her first week, Lydia stayed late enough to lock up the office and then walk out with Beth. It was 8:15 p.m. on Tuesday, when Beth and Lydia were walking toward their cars and Dr. Deepak Ajit called to them.

"Oh shit!" Lydia mumbled. "He's going to keep us here for another half hour."

But when he caught up with them, Lydia smiled and said, "Hey D. What are you doing here so late?"

Dr. Deepak said, "I went downstairs to the lab to get Mita (Mrs. Ajit) and then I saw Vijay Rahman (referring to a patient) and we talked." He looked at Beth and asked, "How was your second day?"

Beth said, "Great. It's a lot to learn but Lydia is a good teacher."

"Good. Good. You know she's been with us now for 2 years and she knows everything about this practice. She knows how to use the electronic medical records and, you know, we used to do all of that by hand." He laughed a little and said, "Remember that?"

Lydia said, "Oh yes I do. Beth doesn't know how lucky she is!"

Beth asked, "What do you mean?"

Lydia said, "When Dr. Arvind started, he quickly switched us over to using electronic medical records instead of paper charts. But before that, all of the visit summaries and medication notes that the doctors write up had to be done by hand."

Beth was confused because one of her duties, in preparing for the next day, was to pull charts from the massive floor-to-ceiling, rolling filing cabinets (there were three of them and then 3 more in Dr. Vishnu's office for patients no longer with the practice; however their files had to be retained for 7 years).

Beth asked, "But what about all of the charts that we still use?"

Lydia said, "Well right now most of our patients have both—paper charts *and* electronic medical records. But if they're new patients, they *only* have an electronic medical record. So we pull the paper charts for all of the patients because the docs want to review their history before they see the patient. There's a little icon on the electronic chart that lets you know if they also have a paper chart. I'll show you tomorrow. It's cute. It looks like a little manila folder."

Dr. Deepak changed the subject. He said, "I've seen some of the same patients for 33years. Now I see their children and grandchildren." He pointed toward two older houses across the street, now lit up by streetlights, and said, "My office used to be in that house over there. I had a little office on the first floor. We just built this office three years ago because we knew Arvind would join the practice when he finished medical school. We still own the houses over there and we converted them into apartments that we rent out."

As he talked about some of the history of his practice, Lydia, who was now standing next to Dr. Deepak, looked at Beth and rolled her eyes impatiently. Beth pretended not to notice and continued to listen, but she could understand that Lydia probably heard all of this more than a few times before. It was getting chilly as they stood under the bright lights of the parking lot. Dr. Deepak saw Mrs. Ajit coming out of the building. He called out, "Mita. Let's go."

They were all smiles as they parted. Dr. Ajit and Mita (pronounced "ME Tah") got into his Mercedes and pulled away.

Lydia said, "You can never get away from him once he gets started. I'll be making dinner at 9:00 tonight!"

Beth laughed a little.

Lydia continued, "You know, they're never here this late. I wonder what's up. I guess Mita was busy in her lab downstairs. But they're usually out of here by 4:00 or 4:30."

Beth asked, "Do they always drive together?"

"No because D's been cutting back his hours and sometimes he'll come in for a little while in the morning and then leave to play golf. Mita drives separately most of the time. Oh, and you'll notice that D sometimes stops into the office later in the day because he likes to check up on us. He was supposed to retire soon after Arvind started but so far he doesn't seem to want to let go."

Beth said, "I guess it's tough to let go after all these years."

Lydia said, "Yeah. It's an ego thing too. He likes to waltz into the office and socialize. But he really gets on Dr. Vishnu's nerves because he'll cherry pick the patients he sees and then he'll spend an hour talking with them in the exam room. You'll get an earful from Dr. Vishnu, I'm sure. He's always complaining that D sees one patient to his 8 patients. Oh well, let's get out of here." They each walked to their cars and then Lydia shouted, "Don't forget to stay home tomorrow because we don't have office hours on Wednesday."

Beth smiled and shouted back, "I can't believe I have a day off already—not bad after two days. Goodnight Lydia. I'll see you on Thursday."

During her second week, Dr. Arvind Ajit stayed late enough that he was still in the office when Beth left so he was able to lock up at night. It wasn't until her third week that Beth was given a key to the office. She figured it was because they wanted to have the feeling that they could trust her with the responsibility of locking up the office.

Chapter 13

WHILE CHARLES WAS eating his sandwich in the cafeteria, he remembered he should have told his mother he would be home later than usual. It was his first day doing stats for the tennis team and afterwards Mr. DeLeon would do his Algebra tutoring. He finished his lunch and proceeded to the administrative office. He felt a little embarrassed because most kids his age had a cell phone. He walked up to a woman's desk and asked, "Can I please use your phone? I have to call my mom."

"Oh sure. Here." She handed Charles the receiver and then turned her phone toward him. "Just dial nine first."

"OK. Thanks." Charles breathed a sigh of relief when his mother answered her cell phone.

"Mom, it's me. I forgot to tell you that I'm going to be a little later than usual today." He didn't dare tell his mother about the tennis team at this point because she would start yelling about how she's not going to pay for that. He figured he could explain everything to her when he got home and he didn't want to be further embarrassed by her screaming into the phone while this nice lady pretended not to hear her.

His mother said, "Yeah I know. You have your Algebra tutoring today."

"Yeah but my teacher can't start at the usual time because he coaches the . . ." He stopped himself and then nervously coughed a little to create a diversion from the topic. "He's . . . he's gotta start a little late today so he told me I should take the late activity bus. I'll be home a little after 5."

"Well what does that mean . . . 5:30 or what?" his mother asked. She sounded annoyed and he could hear loud machines from the factory in the background.

"Yeah. I'll be home by 5:30." In that instant, Charles realized he sounded like his father. He wasn't asking anymore . . . he was *telling* his mother what he was doing.

"OK. I'll see you then."

"Alright. Bye mom." Charles noticed a change in her tone. It worked. His mother had realized that Charles was becoming a man. She was losing her power over him and he liked it.

When Charles got home that evening, his mother was heating up a frozen dinner in the microwave oven. He asked, "Is Dad here?"

"No. But he said he might stop by later."

"Oh good."

His mother must have read his mind because she lit a cigarette, took a long drag and started to speak while smoke puffed from her nose and mouth. "I hope he doesn't disappoint you with this Phillies game. I hope he actually takes you when the time comes."

Charles's heart skipped a beat. But instead of giving a moment's credence to what he perceived as her usual, miserable attitude, he said, "You don't have to worry about that."

"Yeah. We'll see."

Now Charles felt angry. It seemed his mother wanted his father to screw up. His anger emboldened him and he blurted out, "I'm going to be doing stats for the tennis team."

"You're doing *what*?" his mother asked, with her hand on her hip.

"I said, I'm doing stats—you know keeping track of who scored and whether the tennis ball went over the net." Now his tone was sarcastic.

His mother's face twisted into an angry snarl. She pointed a finger at him and said, "Now don't you get flip with me. And what did I tell you about playing sports at school? I'm not paying for it. Sorry Charlie. We can't afford it."

"You don't have to pay for anything. Mr. DeLeon said because I'm keeping stats, it doesn't cost as much as it would if I was playing, so he's going to cover it. Besides, it's just for their home games. I won't go to the tennis matches at other schools."

She straightened her posture. "You better be careful. Why is he paying for it?" She didn't give him a chance to answer. She said, "You know a lot of these teachers nowadays like young boys. Look at what's happening at Penn State. Do you ever watch the news? He might be looking for something in return."

Charles was mad at her and yet a little self-conscious because he had a faint worry about Mr. DeLeon too. But he said, "Mr. DeLeon's a cool guy. He's just trying to give me a chance to sorta be on the team. I told him you don't want to pay for it, so that's why he offered to pay. Besides, he said doing stats is like math and he's my Algebra tutor."

"Yeah. Well you better make sure he doesn't try to tutor you about anything else!"

Charles shook his head in disbelief for a moment. He was hurt, and he didn't want his mother to be right. He shouted, "You just don't want anybody in my life but you. You don't like Dad. You don't like Mr. DeLeon. Pretty soon you'll find a reason you don't like Leah. Face it mom. I'm growing up and you better get used to me not being around!" With that he raced up the stairs and slammed his bedroom door shut. He was breathing heavily and started to cry. After a few minutes, he calmed down. He was surprised and relieved that his mother hadn't run after him. He had expected to hear her pounding on his locked door.

Mr. DeLeon was being firm but pleasant, as he patiently taught Charles how to keep proper statistics for the boys' tennis team. He said, "You're a fast learner Charlie. Don't worry about asking questions. It's better to ask a question when you're not sure about something, than to be silent and make mistakes because you were afraid to ask."

Leah was already sitting on the activity bus; as he sat down next to her. He felt like a real jock sitting there in his Forest Hills Middle School tennis team shirt, while resting the green stat notebook on his lap that had the same white lettering for FHMS Tennis.

Charles noticed that Leah had been silent for a few minutes. He sensed that something was wrong because her expression had become very serious and, as he looked closely, he saw tiny beads of sweat over her lip. "Leah? What's wrong?"

She swallowed hard and finally said, "I just felt sick to my stomach for a minute. But then it went away." She sighed. "I think I might be getting the flu or something because I felt the same way yesterday and even this morning. I almost didn't stay for practice but I started to feel better and . . ."

"What?" Charles asked.

"I wanted to see you."

Charles reached over for her hand and whispered, "I love you Leah." He couldn't believe he said it! But then Leah said, "I love you too."

The next day Leah wasn't on the activity bus, so Charles called her as soon as he got home.

"Hello?" Charles recognized the voice of Leah's mother.

"Oh. Hi Mrs. Godwin. Can I talk to Leah?"

"Is this Charles?"

"Yes. Yes it is."

"Oh honey. I'm sorry but Leah isn't feeling good right now. Oh . . . wait a minute . . . here she comes. She wants to talk to you."

"Good."

"Here she is. It was nice to talk to you again Charles."

"You too, Mrs. Godwin."

"Charles?" Leah's voice sounded weak.

"Yeah. Hi. It's me." Charles sounded anxious. "Are you OK Leah?"

"Yeah. I'm fine. I just felt sick again this morning and . . ."

"What?"

"Well, I threw up." She felt embarrassed. She quickly added, "I felt better right away, but my Mom heard me get sick so she made me stay home from school."

"Do you feel better now?"

Leah said, "Yeah. I'm sure I'll be at school tomorrow."

"Are you going to stay for practice?"

"Yeah. I'll stay for cheerleading practice, so I'll see you on the activity bus."

"Oh wait! Tomorrow's Thursday, so I have to stay later, after tennis for my Algebra tutoring and . . ."

"Oh. OK. Then I'll just call you tomorrow night," Leah said.

For a moment, Charles thought he might just be brave enough to take the bus to school in the morning. That way he could sit with Leah. But then he thought about how humiliating it was to have David Reilly harassing him in front of Leah. He'd never admit it, but he was afraid of David Reilly ever since he shoved him to the floor on the bus. He was sure he would have gotten beaten up pretty badly if the bus driver hadn't finally yelled at them and threatened to have them suspended. But what if the bus driver didn't get involved the next time? It was better to stick with having his mother drive him to school. He had lied to Leah when he told her his father insisted on driving him to school in the morning, although it was partially true. His father had only driven him to school twice; and that was when he had stayed at their house a couple times. After that, Charles had managed to convince his mother to drive him. She only agreed after he confided in her about David Reilly. But he hadn't told her about the bullying. He just said that this kid, David Reilly, was always smoking pot on the bus with some other kids and the smell made him sick to his stomach. First his mother called the school to complain. The administration made an announcement over the loud speaker that smoking any substance on the bus would not be tolerated; nor would bullying or harassment of any kind. All of that sounded good but, in reality, all kinds of things happened on the school bus and the good kids had to put up with whatever the bad kids decided to do. Charles's mother had agreed to drive him to school if, and only if, he was ready to leave 20 minutes earlier than usual because she could not be late for work. He agreed.

Finally Charles said, "I'll talk to you tomorrow night then. And I hope you feel better Leah."

On Thursday, after the tennis team finished up their practice, Mr. DeLeon said, "Hey Charlie. Why don't we just sit in the office over there today to work on your Algebra?" He pointed toward the physical education office at the other end of the gymnasium.

"Sure."

"Alright. Just wait for me in there. I'll be over in a couple minutes."

It was a tiny office and Charles settled into one of two chairs in front of the desk. He perused the room and looked at the wall lined with team photographs—football, basketball, baseball, wrestling and tennis. There must have been two dozen trophies lined up along the bookcase on the opposite end of the room. The rest of the bookcase, as well as the desk in front of him, was a mess of paperwork and Charles began to notice an odor of something familiar—like sweaty socks. Sure enough, when he looked at the wall in back of him, there were half a dozen pairs of dirty sneakers and muddy cleats tossed along the baseboard.

"So what chapter are we up to Charlie?" Mr. DeLeon asked, as if he had been in the room for some time and was just continuing the conversation.

Charles realized he hadn't even opened his Algebra book yet. He quickly did just that and flipped through several pages, past the middle of the book. "Oh, um, Chapter 17."

"You know what they say about Chapter 17, don't you?" Mr. DeLeon asked.

"No."

Mr. DeLeon smiled. "Somebody once said, 'Life is like a Dickens's novel. All the important people show up again in Chapter 17."

Charles gave him a patronizing smile. He didn't know what that meant but, judging from the pleasant smile on Mr. DeLeon's face, he assumed it was something he should pretend to be happy about.

Forty five minutes had gone by, when Mr. DeLeon asked, "Hey, how are things going with Leah?"

"Great." Charles smiled. But then he remembered she was sick this week, so he added, "Well, except that she was sick a couple days this week."

Mr. DeLeon feigned concern. "Really? I hope it's nothing serious."

"No. No. She just threw up once; that's all." Charles looked down at his paper. He felt a little awkward after telling Mr. DeLeon about his girlfriend throwing up.

Mr. DeLeon started looking threw a couple of drawers in the desk. He mumbled, "Now where do we keep those?" Then he got up and said, "Hey Charlie, follow me."

Charles followed him into the locker room; where Mr. DeLeon opened one of the larger storage lockers. "Here we go."

Charles couldn't quite see what was in there. Then Mr. DeLeon turned around and said, "Here. This one should fit. Try it on."

Charles reached out and took the athletic protection cup from Mr. DeLeon.

Mr. DeLeon said, "Remember I told you it was a good idea for you to wear one of these because you really could get slammed by a tennis ball. I mean, these guys can smack the balls pretty hard." They both laughed at the obvious pun.

Charles looked around as if he didn't know where to go.

Mr. DeLeon said, "Hey man. We're in the locker room. Just try it on over there." He was pointing to the bench in between a row of lockers.

"Alright." As Charles unzipped his pants to try on the jock strap, he remembered what his mother had said, insinuating that Mr. DeLeon might be one of those weird guys. He felt a little bit nervous because no one else was in the locker room. But he immediately pushed the thought out of his mind. He didn't want Mr. DeLeon to think he was a momma's boy. After all, he had seen the guys on the team walking around the locker room naked. He took his pants off and next his white briefs and laid them on the bench in front of him. He began to extend the elastic bands of the jock strap when Mr. DeLeon moved closer and stood on the opposite side of the bench in front of Charles. He said, with his usual slight laugh, "Here. Let me help you with that." Mr. DeLeon took the jock strap from him and stretched out the bands and said, "Now just lift your right leg."

As Charles lifted his right leg, he could see that Mr. DeLeon was holding the outstretched elastic in such a way as to direct him where to insert his leg. Then he did the same with the left leg. But once the straps were around his legs, instead of letting Charles pull up the band, Mr. DeLeon held on to the waist band as he moved in closer to Charles. Then he leaned into him as he hoisted the jock strap up so tightly that his balls and anal area hurt at the same moment. "Ouch!" Charles called out.

Mr. DeLeon immediately let go of the band and said in an oddly quiet tone, "Oh sorry man." He gently put his hand on Charles's butt. Charles instinctively moved away.

Mr. DeLeon laughed a little and said, "Hey, relax Charlie. Are you alright man?"

"Yeah. Yeah. I'm fine." He didn't make eye contact with Mr. DeLeon but immediately started getting dressed, when Mr. DeLeon asked, "Does it fit?"

Charles had already put his briefs on, over the jock strap. He was beginning to feel comfortable again, but when he looked at Mr. DeLeon to answer, he noticed that Mr. DeLeon seemed to be glaring at his underwear. Then Mr. DeLeon put his hand on his own crotch and made an adjustment of some kind. When he looked at Charles, he had a strangely serious expression and then started to speak, "Charlie . . . I . . ."

Charles didn't like the look on Mr. DeLeon's face. He grabbed his pants off the bench and started to put them on. Mr. DeLeon started to move toward him, "Charlie, I'm sorry." He was about to put his hand on Charles's shoulder when Charles nonchalantly turned to lift his backpack off the hook in the locker behind him. He hadn't even finished buckling his belt when he swung the backpack over his shoulder and said, "It's OK Mr. DeLeon. It's OK. Really." Charles looked for the exit and then realized he could just go through the door to the office and then into the gym. In seconds, he was in the office. Mr. DeLeon was right behind him. "Charlie. Hey man. I'm sorry if I you got the wrong impression . . ." Now Charles thought Mr. DeLeon had started to sound like himself again, but he had continued walking and was by now in the gymnasium. He stopped and turned to look at Mr.DeLeon and said, "No. It's OK." Mr. DeLeon looked relieved and said, "Hey you should wear that thing to practice from now on." Charles said, "Oh yeah. OK." He grinned a little and then turned to make his way toward the exit from the gym. Mr. DeLeon called out from the distance, "I'll see you on Monday. There's no practice on Friday." Charles detected the almost desperate tone in his voice. Then he mumbled, "I know. See you Monday," but he didn't turn around as he walked out of the gym. Now it seemed possible that Mr. DeLeon was *one of those guys that liked kids.*

Charles breathed easier as he approached the front doors of the school and saw the relative safety of the activity buses waiting outside. There was no Leah on the bus today, but no bullies and no weird teachers either. He sat down and discovered he was panting. He thought, "God, I can't tell my mother about this . . . or my Dad . . . and definitely not Leah." In his mind, he could hear David Reilly calling out, "Hey Chuck, wanna fuck?" He thought, "Maybe it's me. Maybe there's something wrong with me that brings it out in people. No. David Reilly's just an asshole and Mr. DeLeon . . . he's . . . I don't know . . . maybe . . . maybe he wasn't going to do anything . . . but why did he pull the strap up so hard?" He remembered how much it hurt. Then he thought, "Maybe it was an accident . . . but why did he have to stand so close to me . . . and then he put his hand on my butt . . . that was weird . . . then again maybe I'm too skittish . . . he was probably just trying to help me." As the moments passed, he began to calm down.

Leah stood naked in front of the full length mirror in her bedroom. She caressed the tiny bump that had been forming in her belly. Then she got dressed and turned again to look at her silhouette. "That's better. You can't see a thing," she mumbled. Leah knew her nausea and vomiting was due to morning sickness. But she wasn't expecting the feeling to creep up on her in the middle of the afternoon, as it sometimes had. She sat down on the edge of her bed and brushed her long hair. For the hundredth time, she replayed the scene of that night with Matt Howard.

They were lying naked on the couch in his basement, and Matt was playing with her hair. He always liked to do that after they made love. This was going to be the night she finally told him. She lifted her head from his chest and spoke softly, "Matt, I have a surprise for you." She pursed her lips coyly, and Matt put his arm behind his head so he could look into her eyes as she spoke.

"I'm going to have your baby."

Matt sprung up and Leah almost fell off the couch. Matt stood bent over, as if someone had just punched him in the stomach. "Jesus Leah! Are you serious?" He brushed the hair from his face and looked at her in horror.

Leah sat upright. "Of course I'm serious. I thought you'd be happy." She started to cry.

Matt sat down next to her and smoothed her hair. "I . . . I . . . it's just that . . . well, you know . . . we're . . .

"We're what?" Leah shouted.

"Shhh. Shhh. It's OK. It's OK. I just meant . . . we're so young for this to happen that I . . . I . . ."

Now Leah jumped up. Her face contorted as she cried out, "You don't want our baby!"

Matt lunged at her and covered her mouth. "Shut up goddamit! Do you want my parents to hear you? Jesus Christ! That's all I need!"

Leah was pinching his fingers around her mouth and trying to free herself from his grip.

"Oww!" Matt took his hand away after she pinched it hard.

But it seemed Leah now realized it wasn't a good idea for his parents to hear them. So she blurted out in a stage whisper, "You want me to have an abortion, don't you!"

"Leah, honey . . . I . . ." He moved toward her.

"Stay away from me. Just answer me . . . answer me!" She demanded.

"Well yeah. I think you should."

She hoped he meant she should have the baby, but her gut told her otherwise. Still, she said in a hopeful, desperate voice, "You think I should have our baby . . . right?"

Matt shook his head. Now he said in an angry tone, "Stop saying *our* baby."

"What?"

Matt said, "Well it's not like it was my choice! You're the one who decided to get pregnant!"

"Oh. I decided to get pregnant! Well I think the fact that you fucked me had something to do with that!"

"Shhh. Shhh. Alright. I'm sorry. Come on Leah." They sat down and Matt put his arm around her. After a few minutes, Matt held her face in his hands and said, "Look Leah. I love you, but we just can't have a baby right now."

Leah started to cry again.

"I mean. We're not even in high school yet for Christ sake!"

That must have struck a nerve, because Leah stopped crying. She stood up and started to get dressed.

Matt watched her with apprehension. He hoped she realized they had no choice. But then Leah said, "Well, I'm not having an abortion."

Now Matt panicked. "Why not? Well what . . . What are you going to do?"

She tucked her shirt into her pants and then stood up straight. "I'm having this baby. That's what I'm doing."

Matt was relieved that at least she was no longer saying "*our*" baby.

As she started up the stairs from the basement, she stopped and turned to Matt and said, "I hate you. I'll never forgive you for this—not the baby—but your reaction to it and what you wanted me to do."

Matt swallowed hard. He just hoped his parents hadn't heard anything. Leah slammed the basement door. He stared blankly at the wall for a moment and held his head in his hands. Then he jumped up with a start. "She better not tell anybody it's mine!" He spotted his cell phone on the table next to the couch. He punched in Leah's number.

"Leah?" He tried to sound sweet and caring.

Leah was still angry but she felt a twinge of hope. "What Matt?"

"I . . . well . . . I'm sure you're not going to tell anybody that it's mine, are you?"

"What! You bastard. God! I hate you Matt Howard! I hate you!"

Leah finished brushing her hair and walked over to her bureau and picked up her cell phone. But before she called Charles, she thought, "He's probably still a virgin. I better not wait too long before I get him to have sex with me. He *has* to think the baby is his."

Chapter 14

"**H**ELLO BETH. How did your property settlement go?" Kathy asked.

"Great. The settlement was in the morning and by mid-afternoon I had all my boxes and stuff out of the Uhaul truck. I didn't take any furniture other than a few small things. In fact I ordered a single bed that will be delivered Saturday afternoon." She paused for an uncomfortable moment because she felt self-conscious about having a tiny, single bed now; then she felt more awkward when she realized they were probably visualizing her sleeping on the floor. She quickly added, "Then I returned the truck and my parents gave me a ride back to the house because they wanted to see it."

"Did they like it?"

"Yeah. They said it was nice and cozy for an old house; and my mother said it had more space than she thought it would because it looks so small from the outside."

Kathy grinned. Lydia was on the phone but she motioned for Beth to come sit by her. As Beth sat down, she could hear someone yelling at Lydia on the phone. Lydia rolled her eyes and held the receiver out in front of her. They both giggled as they listened to the woman who continued to yell into the phone in a heavy Indian accent. Beth whispered, "Do you ever have trouble understanding patients?"

Lydia said, "Eh, it depends. There are some patients that I've talked to so many times that, even though the accent is thick, I can kinda make out what they're trying to say. And guess what?"

Beth smiled, "What?"

Lydia said, "Today's your lucky day. I'm going to let you answer the phones so you can get used to how we triage calls from patients, physicians and pharmacists. It's called trial by fire. You'll get used to the accent very quickly."

The other line started to ring. Lydia interrupted the woman on the phone. "OK. I'm going to put you on hold for a minute." She pushed the hold button and got up and moved over to the desk in back of them. It was vacant most of the day, unless Mrs. Ajit wanted to use it; which she started to do more often in the late afternoon. Kathy's desk was also in back of the front desk, but diagonally across from it. Beth had heard Kathy, Lydia and Dr. Arvind Ajit make references to "the back office." Beth thought there was a literal back office somewhere, but she quickly learned that "the back office" was just a reference to the two desks in back of the front reception desk. Behind the desks that comprised "the back office" was a counter that was always cluttered with miscellaneous paperwork, binders, and a couple cartons of even more lab supplies. Under the counter were cabinets that contained paper for the copier; rolls of paper for the prescription printer; and rolls of labels for labwork. Other than that, the cabinets were stuffed with more miscellaneous paperwork, binders, envelopes and old phone books. There were half a dozen drawers, only one of which Beth used; and that contained menus from various local restaurants that the doctors and staff ordered lunch from. It was usually Lydia who would get the calls from pharmaceutical sales reps, who would call the day before they were scheduled to bring lunch. They would ask Lydia what everyone wanted to eat the next day. Either Lydia or the rep would call the restaurant and place the order. Occasionally, this duty fell to Beth if the rep called in the afternoon. Beth had been instructed to tell the reps to order food for 10 people, even though there was only a total of 5 people who ate lunch at the office—just 2 of the 3 doctors (Dr. Vishnu went home for lunch), Lydia and Mrs. Ajit. But they ordered for 10 people so there were plenty of leftovers. The third person on staff worked in the mornings from 8:00 until 11:30. Her name was Ann Lange and it was her job to do the paperwork for patient referrals to specialists. She had a few other miscellaneous duties such as filing. Beth hadn't even met her yet and would only see her when she had to cover Lydia's shift. Ann and Lydia were both obese; but whereas Lydia was soft spoken and dressed nicely with feminine touches; Ann was unattractive with a very gruff manner. She kind of grumbled hello in response to a greeting and, other than that, she never initiated a friendly greeting or any other conversation. She seemed to prefer to stay below the radar in order to avoid the possibility of being assigned any additional work, other than what she was expected to do. Ann never left for the day before she loaded up her Tupperware container with food. And she had first dibs on the food because she attacked it as soon as it was delivered.

Within the relatively small "back office" area, were the 3 rolling filing cabinets that were filled with charts from floor to ceiling. One of the 3 filing cabinets was entirely filled with charts for patients with the last name "Patel" because it is such a common Indian name. A tiny shredder was crammed into the corner so the only open space was room enough to walk between desks. When Beth pulled charts from the bottom shelves, she had to turn sideways to fit into the tight space between the filing cabinet and one of the "back office" desks. Beth tried to look away whenever Lydia tried to squeeze herself into that space because she inevitably revealed the upper portion of her backside as she bent down.

After a few hours answering the phones, Beth was certain she would incur damage to her hearing because most of their patients talked so loudly into the phone. It seemed they thought their broken English would be better understood if they spoke loudly. Often Beth held the receiver slightly away from her ear, but she didn't do it all the time, despite the discomfort, because she didn't want to appear rude or disrespectful toward their patients.

She liked the triage message system. It was all on the computer, so it was much faster to type in a message to the doctors rather than writing it out on a message pad. Lydia instructed her: "Give Dr. Arvind all messages regarding screenings; i.e., MRIs, CT scans, Xrays and prescription (script) refills. Give Dr. Vishnu all messages regarding prior authorizations from insurance companies, and all lab results. We don't even see most of the faxes because they are sent directly to the doctors via computer. Dr. Vishnu has to respond to these. Faxes received the old fashioned way—via the copier/fax—are also tended to by Dr. Vishnu, unless they're for Lansdale Labs, in which case we put them in this manila folder with Mita's name on it."

When Beth received a call from a patient or a pharmacy stating they needed a refill on a prescription, she would open the electronic medical record and attach the message to the patient's electronic chart.

When the doctors sent a response to a triage message, Beth would see a little orange box light up at the bottom of her screen, next to the word triage. She quickly discovered that, although Dr. Arvind was sent script (prescription) refill requests, he would often confer with Dr. Vishnu before filling it. When they were finished seeing patients at the end of the day, Beth would frequently hear Dr. Arvind asking Dr. Vishnu for his opinion about a diagnosis and/or drug therapy.

Each doctor completed a Patient Visit Summary that was embedded in the patient's electronic medical record. These were completed after each patient visit, but Beth noticed that the summaries for patients seen by Dr. Vishnu had the electronic signature of Dr. Deepak Ajit (so it appeared they had been seen by Dr. D. when they had actually been seen by Dr. Vishnu).

Beth began to notice the same with prescriptions, whether it was for blood pressure medicine or antidepressants or pain medication. The electronic record always showed the electronic signature of Dr. D. instead of Dr. Vishnu. Beth thought there was something odd about that so she planned to ask Lydia about it whenever it was just the two of them at the front desk.

It didn't take long for Beth to notice other things that just gave her a bad feeling in her gut—like the prescription printer on the right side counter of the front desk. Beth would hear a prescription printing out and a moment later, Dr. Vishnu would come out of the exam room and escort the patient to the front desk. He would pick up the script that had just printed and reach over the counter to take a pre-printed stamp that sat on Lydia and Beth's desk. He stamped the script and handed it to the patient; the patient left. Beth discovered the stamp was Dr. Deepak Ajit's signature. So even though Dr. Vishnu saw the patient and prescribed the medicine, the Visit Summary and the prescription each had the electronic or (in the case of the printed "hard copy" scripts) the signature stamp of Dr. D.

Beth never got a direct answer from Lydia, when she asked her about something the doctors did, or something she and Lydia were required to do, that didn't seem quite right. Lydia would typically just raise her eyebrows and make a frown, as if to say, my lips are sealed. If she did answer, it was nothing more than a whisper of, "Don't ask me. That's just the way they do things."

Beth felt awkward about asking him, but by Friday afternoon, she decided she would try to chip away at some of the mystery. A script had just printed out and she stood up from her seat and leaned over to her right, in order to see what the prescription was for. She could see it was for Oxycodone (a potent narcotic pain medicine that is sold illegally and known by various street names; one of the more obvious ones was Oxy). Then she heard Dr. Vishnu's voice as he opened the door to his exam room at the end of the hall. She quickly sat down again and busied herself with the work in front of her. After the patient left, she asked Dr. Vishnu, "Why do some scripts get sent by computer to the pharmacy and others are printed here at the front desk?"

Dr. Vishnu said, "Most of the scripts for pain meds have to be printed out and taken to the pharmacy by the patient."

Beth didn't understand the logic of this. Dr. Vishnu apparently sensed that she was confused. He said sternly, "Patients can abuse pain medications. They can become addicted or they may try to sell the meds. So it's important to prevent that." Then he walked away at his usual brisk pace.

Beth thought, "He must think I'm stupid or naive or both. That's illogical, because the opposite is true. If a script is sent via computer to a specific pharmacy, it would be the best way to prevent illegal behavior." She had an idea. She looked at her computer screen and did a double click on the name of the patient, who was just seen by Dr. Vishnu.

But she couldn't open the file because it was locked—that meant that Dr. Vishnu was most likely in the patient's electronic medical record (or chart) at the same moment. He was probably typing in the Visit Summary. Beth would have to wait a little while before she could access the file.

Later that afternoon, when Dr. Vishnu was seeing another patient, Beth returned to the electronic chart and clicked on it. This time it opened. As usual, it indicated the patient was treated by Dr. Deepak Ajit. Then she scrolled down to the section for medication. It was blank. There was no record of a prescription being written for Oxycodone. Beth tried to make sense of it. But the phones began to ring incessantly and she was so busy that she pushed it out of her mind for the moment.

Later that day, Beth overheard a patient say to Kathy, "I hear you're going to retire soon." Beth was surprised to hear this. She turned to look in Kathy's direction.

Kathy said, "Yeah. I'll be leaving at the end of June."

Beth said, "Kathy, I'm so disappointed. Even though we've only worked together for a week, you're such a nice person."

Kathy smiled. "Thanks Beth. But it's time. I've been with Dr. Deepak for 25 years now."

"You're kidding?"

"No. I'm serious."

The patient talked to Kathy for a few minutes and when she left, Kathy rolled her chair closer to Beth and whispered, "It hasn't always been easy with Dr. D, but it's gotten a little tougher with Dr. Arvind." Beth just grinned. She wasn't sure what to say. She didn't want to offend anyone, since she was the new kid on the block.

"By the way," Kathy started, "We hired someone to do the billing. I'm going to start training her on Monday. Her name is Ruth McBride."

Beth asked, "Is Ruth going to be the new Office Manager or is she just doing the billing?"

Kathy whispered, "No. They're so cheap; they're not going to have an Office Manager for the time being. So Ruth won't have all the same job responsibilities that I had. She'll only do the billing."

Beth asked, "Who's going to do the other stuff?"

Kathy said, "It seems that Dr. Arvind wants to have control of everything that goes on here. In most offices, the front desk handles incoming faxes and some other things that he wants to do. I don't think he trusts anyone and he wants to have his hands in everything that goes on here. He probably wouldn't even have you and Lydia working at the front desk if he could help it, but he just doesn't have time to do to do it all."

Since Kathy was opening up a bit, Beth asked, "Do you get along with Dr. Arvind?"

Kathy said, "Oh sure. He just doesn't have much of a personality so he takes some getting used to."

"Yeah. I know what you mean. He's very aloof. I thought maybe it was just me—you know, since I just started I thought he might just be a little standoff-ish because I'm new."

Kathy said, "Oh no. You're right. He's not friendly at all. Well, what can you expect, he's a spoiled kid."

Beth just grinned. Now she wanted to ask Kathy about Dr. Vishnu but she hesitated because she had noticed that Kathy was apparently very tight with Dr. Vishnu. They would often chat quietly at Kathy's desk and Kathy could often be found talking with Dr. Vishnu in his office at the opposite end of the hall. Since he had already complained about the Ajit's a few times, Beth surmised that Dr. Vishnu felt like an outsider to what was essentially a family business—father/son and mother with her lab downstairs. Dr. Vishnu liked gossip and if Lydia, or a sales rep, or even some of his patients, complained about one or more of the Ajit's, Dr. Vishnu was right there to join in. But Beth had also heard Dr. Vishnu gossiping with Dr. D. or even with Mrs. Ajit. It seemed Dr. Vishnu liked to play both sides; so everyone thought he was their confidante; but not Beth. She could already see there was something shady about him. Beth started to say, "I was wondering about . . ." but just then a patient walked up to the front desk and that was the end of their conversation.

Chapter 15

CHARLES MUST HAVE fallen asleep because his room was dark when he woke up. He looked over at his digital clock/radio and saw that it was 11:16 p.m. As he sat up, he could hear voices coming from downstairs. He slowly opened his door and crept to the top of the staircase. His mother was talking to someone. Then he heard his father's voice. He made his way downstairs and rubbed his eyes, and then tried to appear casual as he entered the kitchen.

"Hey Charlie!"

"Hey Dad." They hugged each other briefly and Charles said, "You ready for the Phils on Saturday?"

"You bet I am. Wouldn't miss it for the world my man."

His mother was sitting at the kitchen table, looking like she was pretty wasted as she sipped from her wine glass. She fumbled with her pack of cigarettes until she pulled one out. She said, "You two and your Phillies. They haven't won a game yet this season, have they?"

Charles said in a defensive tone, "They're 2 and 4 mom. They have a whole season left to play. Besides, they always win their home games."

"Well good for them." She sounded drunk.

Charles's father asked, "Hey, what are you doing up at this hour Charlie?"

He said, "I fell asleep on my bed while I was reading something for school."

"I can't tell you how many times I've done that," his father said with a laugh.

Then his mother garbled, "Yeah. There ya go Charles. A great example—that man."

His father apparently felt obligated to be responsible at that moment so he said, "Maybe you better get back to bed Charlie."

"Alright. Are you staying?"

There was an awkward silence for a moment as his father glanced over at his mother and then turned to Charles and said quietly, "I don't think so man. Not tonight. But I'll give you a call Thursday night and we'll figure out what time I should pick you up on Saturday. Hell, it's probably a better idea if I just stay here Friday night."

Charles smiled. He liked that idea. "OK. Well, goodnight Dad." Charles was swinging an imaginary bat in his room, until he finally got into bed again.

When he sat with Lydia on the activity bus the next day he asked, "Do you want to meet at the mall again on Friday?"

"Sure."

"Good. Let's just plan on meeting at 7:00 again at the same place— the fountain at the front entrance."

"OK."

It was time for Charles to get off at his stop. When he stood up, he suddenly remembered and turned to Leah, "Oh wait! My Dad said he might stay over on Friday night so . . ."

Leah suggested, "Do you want to meet on Saturday night instead?"

"That's a great idea. That way I can tell you all about the Phillies game."

Leah smiled and said, "Alright. Hey I think you better get going." Apparently Charles hadn't noticed the bus had stopped and the driver was looking back at them through the giant rearview mirror.

"Oh crap! I'll call you tomorrow."

He saw his new neighbor as he neared Mrs. K's house.

Beth waved and then called out to him, "Hey Charles. Wait a minute."

"Hi. Is Mrs. K. still here?"

"No. She's already moved out."

Charles said, "Oh gees, I never said goodbye. She was a nice lady."

"Yeah. You know she still lives nearby at Haverford Arms."

"Yeah that's right." He didn't really know what that was but, from the sound of it, it was probably a place where old people went to live. Beth noticed him looking at the yard and she asked, "Would you still be able to cut the grass for me each week?"

"Sure." Charles was happy to hear "each week;" because he'd have some money to pay for movies or food when he meets Leah at the mall.

Beth asked, "Would you be able to cut it this Saturday?

"No. I can't this Saturday because I'm going to the Phillies game with my Dad."

"What about Sunday?"

"Yeah. Sure. Sunday's good."

"Alright. I'll see you on Sunday afternoon."

"OK. Bye."

On Friday, Charles sat at the kitchen table eating his burger and fries. He couldn't stop checking the time on the clock above the sink. He was wishing the time away—like somehow 20 minutes would go by—like magic—in between bites of his burger. He was sure that any minute his dad would walk into the house and call out "Charlie!" The question had been on his mind since he got home from school, but he dreaded asking his mother because he could just hear her mean and nasty response. He decided he wouldn't ask her. He would just wait it out. He thought, "He'll probably just show up around 6:00 or 7:00, so why bother asking her."

"Why do you keep checking the time? . . . *Charles!* . . . *Hello in there!*" his mother said loudly.

"What? What's wrong?" he asked.

"You've been checking the clock over there ever since you sat down to eat."

It seemed there was no point in pretending anymore, so he asked, "Did Dad call you today?"

"Now why in hell would he call me today? Unless he needed money or a place to crash cause his latest girlfriend threw him out."

Charles's stomach knotted. He hated to hear his mother talk about his father that way. But what hurt the most, and he wasn't even conscious of it, was the suggestion that his father was only interested in what he could get from *her*. She didn't even mention that his father was coming over to see *him*. He said, "Why do you have to say that?"

"Because it's true."

Charles curled up the paper that had been wrapped around his hamburger. He balled up the paper; stood up and shouted at his mother, "No it's *not* true. He comes here to see *me* and to hang out with *me*!" Then he threw the ball of paper across the table and shouted, "You're just jealous 'cause he doesn't come here to see you!" Charles choked back tears as he yelled, "And it's your fault 'cause you have to ruin everything!"

Now his mother shot up out of her chair and waved her finger at him saying, "Don't you dare talk to me like that! "I'm the one who keeps a roof over your head. I'm the one who takes care of you when you're sick and feeds you and washes your clothes and I'm the only one who really loves you!" She covered her mouth, as if it would make the last few words go back.

Charles shouted through his tears, "Yeah, well Dad loves me too. What do you know about it anyway! You always ruin everything. I hate you! I'm gonna ask Dad if I can go live with him!"

She was going to apologize but now she was hurt by *his* words. Charles had already left the kitchen and she could hear him stomping up the stairs when she muttered, "Yeah, well, good luck with that."

When the phone rang around 7:30, Charles bolted out of his room and into his mother's bedroom to grab the phone. He thought, "I knew he would call. What's she going to say about it now." He mumbled, "Bitch" just before he answered.

"Charlie?"

"Oh Leah, hi."

"You sound like you almost wish it was somebody else," Leah said.

Charles was surprised he hadn't even been thinking about her. "No. No. I just . . . well I thought it was my Dad calling. He said he might come over tonight but I guess he'll just wait until tomorrow and pick me up before the game. I can't blame him for not wanting to be around my mom."

Leah asked, "Did you have a fight with your mom or something?"

"Yeah, well, kinda. But, um, I don't want to talk about her. Did you ask your mom if she can take you over to the mall tomorrow night?"

"Yeah. She said it's no problem."

They talked for about a half hour and finally Leah said, "Have fun at the game tomorrow and I'll see you at the mall, by the fountain, at 6:30."

"OK. Great. Bye Leah." Charles ended the call and then a thought occurred to him. "Wait a minute! I can't live with my Dad because I'd have to go to a different school. Guess I'm stuck living here." He went back to his room and laid back on his bed and soon fell into a fantasy about the next day. He could hear the crack of the bat. He could see Chase Utley hit a home run; he would jump out of his seat; his Dad would jump up too; the whole crowd on its feet—cheering; and finally Chase slides into home plate. He high-fives his Dad and, after several minutes, they sit down again. Charles takes a long sip from the straw popping out of his 30 ounce Coke; hot dog wrappers and peanut shells crushed beneath his sneakers . . . hours later, the Phils win it with a score of 9 to 3. They spend the whole ride home talking about the game. He doesn't even have time to talk to his mom when he gets home. He has to hurry because his Dad agreed to give him a ride over to the mall. He runs up the stairs and takes a shower; puts on his jeans and a good dose of Axe deodorant before he pulls his new Phillies t-shirt over his head. He runs his hand over his close-cut hair as he looks at himself in the mirror. Then he sees a wide grin on his face. He didn't even know it was there. As he runs down the stairs, he thinks, "This is probably the best day of my life." Soon, he was fast asleep.

Beth did a cat stretch on the floor of her bedroom—bending her lower back one way and then the other. With hands and feet on the floor, she lifted her knees and moved her hands toward her ankles, and then slowly lifted her upper body until she stood straight, and then put her hands on her hips and bent herself backwards until she couldn't go any further. "Ahh . . . that feels good." She stood up straight again and then stretched her arms into the air. Jake stretched on the rug and made a happy yawning sound. "Ready for a walk?" Beth felt refreshed after a good night's sleep; even though it was in a sleeping bag with lots of blankets. Her bed would be delivered that afternoon. She was surprised to see that it was almost 9:00. She never slept that late. But then she realized she had been up until about 1:30 in the morning, unpacking boxes after she had cleaned the house to her satisfaction. She had lived alone before and for now it felt good to be by herself, with her dog. She was at peace. She didn't have the typical Saturday morning anxiety about what Henry's mood would be that day.

Beth started to walk down her relatively short driveway with Jake. It was the first time she had a driveway. It was the first time she had a garage for that matter. The driveway wasn't a long, curvy blacktop that lead to the double or triple garages of a suburban McMansion. It was just a simple, straight path to an old garage that didn't even have an automatic door.

Beth turned to the right and saw her neighbor Charles sitting on the bench on his front porch. He was wearing a baseball cap, and he was tossing a ball back and forth, into his baseball glove. Beth waved to him and he waved back with a smile. Beth thought, "He's a cute kid." It felt good to have someone to wave to already. She wondered if Charles was on a local baseball team. She noticed there weren't any other kids around and she hoped he had someone to play with.

Later that morning, Beth was on her way to Walmart. She had to buy a few household items, and she hoped she might find the perfect shower curtain at a reasonable price. She was surprised to see Charles, still sitting on the bench on his front porch. It felt like déjà vu because he was still tossing a baseball into his glove. Beth looked at the clock on her dashboard. It was 11:45 a.m. She looked in his direction to wave, but this time he wasn't looking up.

When she got back from Walmart, it was almost 1:00. Charles was sitting on his front curb, looking dejected. Beth slowed down as she neared him and said, "Hi Charles." She could see that something was wrong, when he looked at her. "Are you OK?" she asked with genuine concern. He just mumbled, "Yeah" and continued to toss stones across the street. Beth tried to think of something to say; hoping she might get an idea of what was wrong. "Are you still going to be able to cut my grass tomorrow?" But as soon as the words came out of her mouth, she thought she might know what was wrong. She remembered Charles had told her he wouldn't be able to cut the grass on Saturday because he was going to a baseball game. She asked, "Hey, what time do the Phillies play today?" He didn't answer. He got up from the curb but looked at the ground. Then he mumbled, "They play at 1:00." Then he turned and started to walk toward his house. "Poor kid; looks like somebody really disappointed him," Beth thought.

Charles looked down the street one more time before he entered the house. Maybe his Dad would pull up any minute.

"Come on. I'll make you a sandwich." His mother spoke in an unusually nice tone of voice, so Charles found himself following her into the kitchen. "How about a toasted P&J sandwich?" She didn't wait for a response. She just pressed down on the lever of the toaster and the bread disappeared into the hot coils.

Charles slumped into a chair at the kitchen table. He took off his baseball cap and put it on the seat of the chair next to him. He stared off into the distance beyond the kitchen window until the unfamiliar aroma of toasted bread caught his attention and he watched his mother smear peanut butter and jelly onto each slice. She cut it in half and put it onto a plate. Then she poured him a glass of milk. She brought the glass and the plate over to the table and placed them in front of him. He waited until his mother turned toward the kitchen sink before he took a bite of the sandwich. He had called his father half a dozen times that morning, but all he got was his voicemail. The first couple of times he didn't leave a message. But the third and fourth time, he had said, "Hey Dad. I'm waiting right outside the house for ya. Can't wait to see our Phils." While he watched his mother rinse out the coffee pot, he thought, "Maybe she's right about him. Maybe . . ." He pushed the thought out of his mind. Then his mother started to speak; but now her tone of voice had the same anger in it that he was used to, "I told you he's no good." Charles had just started to swallow a bite of his sandwich, when he suddenly gagged. He jumped out of his seat. He thought he might throw up, but after a few seconds, the nauseous feeling subsided. He shouted, "Don't say that Mom! Don't say it. I don't care about a stupid baseball game anyway!" Charles ran upstairs and slammed his door. His mother shook her head and then lit a cigarette. She had lost her marriage and now she could see she was losing her son. She walked into the living room and turned on the television. She needed something to distract her. She wished it wasn't Saturday. It was going to be another long, slow weekend. She went back to the kitchen and poured herself a glass of wine. She felt sleepy as she drank the last mouthful. She slumped into a comfortable position and thought, "I could use a nap anyway."

She had fallen asleep on the couch when Charles woke her up. "Mom. I need a ride to the mall." Her immediate reaction was resentment. She was about to say something, but she stopped herself.

"C'mon Mom. I have to go. I have to meet Leah at 6:30."

She sat up slowly. "What time is it anyway?"

Charles said, "It's time for you to take me to the mall. Come on Mom, please."

"Alright," she said. She was actually glad Charles had something to look forward to. She thought, "Why should he be miserable too. Maybe he'll be smart enough to let go of the bastard."

Matt Howard, David Reilly and a few of their friends had been drinking beer in the parking lot of the mall. "This is getting fucking boring," David said.

"Yeah. Let's go check out the ponies inside."

They entered the mall by the food court. David Reilly grabbed Matt's arm and said, "Hey there's my buddy Chuck with that little bitch Leah!"

"Where?"

"Over there."

"You've gotta be fucking kiddin me!" Matt said.

As they neared their table, Matt felt a jealous knot in his chest. Leah and Charles were holding hands and laughing.

David Reilly called out, "Hey Chuckie, wanna fuckie?"

Charles turned around with a start. He couldn't believe it. David Reilly had no reservation about tormenting him in public. When they reached the table, David ran his hand over Charles's head and then tugged on his ear.

"Hey! Quit it!" Charles said.

Leah looked up at Matt in nervous anticipation. She could see he was becoming increasingly enraged as he stared at her. Finally he said, "So did you tell him the big news?"

Leah swallowed hard. Her heart was beating wildly.

"Well . . . did you?"

"Don't Matt. Please don't." Leah was saying as she stood up.

Now Charles stood up. He was afraid of what Matt might do to Leah. "Leave her alone," he pleaded.

David Reilly giggled. "Ooo . . . look at the mad 'n bad boyfriend. I didn't know you liked girls too Chuckie."

Charles took a swing at David, but he missed when David backed away.

"Whoah. Take it easy big boy."

"Did you tell him about your little package?" Matt said.

Leah shrieked, "Shut up Matt!"

Charles asked, "What? What are you talking about?" He looked at Leah. "What?"

Matt blurted out. "She's pregnant Charlie. And I'm the one who fucked her!"

Charles leaped toward Matt but two of his friends grabbed Charles's arms. Matt was saying, "On second thought, maybe I'm *not* the daddy. Maybe you've been fucking her too."

Leah was screaming and crying, "Stop it Matt! Stop it, please!"

By now a small crowd had gathered to see what all the commotion was about. Then two men in blue shirts, with a mall security badge, grabbed Matt. "Let go of me man. Let go of me!" Matt shouted.

Charles looked at Leah and pleaded, "Is it true? Are you . . ." but he couldn't say the words.

Leah just shook her head and cried, as a couple of strangers led her to a chair.

The mall security men were escorting Matt, David and their friends to the exit. "Come on. Move along guys. Either you leave now, on your own, or we call the police."

Charles was breathing heavily. Someone must have guided him to the chair he was sitting in, across from Leah. He watched the two women stroking Leah's hair and Leah was blowing her nose. Charles naively assumed Matt made all that up. Now he was worried about Leah. He asked her, "Can I borrow your cell phone?"

Leah took it out and handed it to him with a hopeful look on her face. It seemed that Charles thought Matt was lying.

Charles called Leah's mother. "Mrs. Godwin?"

"Yes. This is Mrs. Godwin. Is there something wrong?" Mrs. Godwin recognized Charles's voice and she didn't like the sound of it.

Charles said, "Don't worry. Leah's OK. But I think you need to come to the mall and take her home—I mean take us home—if you don't mind."

"Sure. Sure. I'll be right there but, what happened? You sound upset."

Charles said, "It's just that Matt Howard and his friends saw us and I guess Matt wasn't too happy to see Leah with someone else and he got . . . well, he said some things that were . . . inappropriate I guess."

"Alright honey. I'm on my way."

"Thanks Mrs. Godwin."

Charles walked over to Leah. The women who had been sitting with her asked Charles, "Are you OK?"

"Yeah. I'm fine. I called your mom Leah."

She looked up at him and grinned. "Thanks Charles."

"She's on her way to pick us up."

Leah was happy to hear him say *us*. Now she was certain he didn't believe Matt.

Once they were outside, Charles put his arm around Leah's shoulder and gently asked, "Is it true?"

Leah turned and gave him a surprised look. Thoughts were racing through her mind. She could stick with her plan and wait and just get Charles to have sex with her. If she told him the truth, he would probably still be in love with her. He just seemed to be that kind of a guy. Then she thought about her mother. Her mother would freak out about the pregnancy but she was adamantly against abortion. Maybe she would be relieved to know that Leah was too good a person to have an abortion. If she told her Mom in the car on the way home, with Charles in the car, her mom wouldn't freak out as much. She looked at Charles.

"Leah, please tell me the truth. Please."

She thought, "He looks so sad . . . so . . . pathetic." She hesitated. She felt like she would burst from the pressure of the moment. She couldn't stand it. Then she heard herself blurt out, "It's true. I'm sorry." She started to cry on his shoulder.

"It's OK. It's OK." Charles said, "Did he . . . did he rape you?"

Suddenly Leah stopped crying and looked up at Charles. She hadn't thought of that! She felt a surge of guilt as she started to answer. She thought, "No. I can't accuse him of rape. God! They'll arrest him. But I . . ." Then she heard herself saying, "He didn't attack me, if that's what you mean . . . but I guess he forced me because he said it was the only way he would believe that I loved him. And, at the time, I thought I did love him . . . oh Charlie." Leah began sobbing.

"It's OK. It's OK Leah. I'm here." Charles had no idea how dire the situation was—Leah was in junior high school and pregnant.

Leah's mother pulled up and Charles got into the backseat with Leah. He listened to her tell her mother everything, through halting speech. Finally, her mother said, "Oh Leah. How could you let this happen?" But Charles sensed that she was more understanding than angry. She reached her arms out toward Leah, who moved forward and held on to her mother as they cried.

After a few minutes, Mrs. Godwin said, "Don't worry. We'll get through this. Somehow we'll get through this."

"Thanks Mom." Leah sniffled, as she leaned back into the seat.

Mrs. Godwin started to drive. Leah reached over for Charles's hand. They held hands, but Charles found himself looking out the window. He felt a strange emptiness, even with Leah holding his hand. He noticed Mrs. Godwin had said nothing to him. She didn't even look at him. He began to feel like an outsider in all of this. And sure enough, when they reached his house, Mrs. Godwin turned and said, "Thanks for calling me Charles. I'll take care of Leah from now on."

"OK." He could feel her pushing him away with her words. He got out of the car and watched Leah turn and wave to him as they drove away. He walked up to the front door and saw the television light flickering in the living room. He knew his mother would be sleeping on the couch. He quietly shut the door and peaked into the living room. Sure enough, an empty wine glass was on the coffee table and his mother was fast asleep. Charles turned off the television. His mother stirred for a second but didn't awaken. Charles slowly made his way into the kitchen and looked at the darkness through the kitchen window. He felt numb. His father, and now his girlfriend, had each managed to break his heart in one day. He replayed the scene from the mall and wondered how he could even go to school on Monday. But then he remembered he had to do the stats for the tennis team and stay for his Algebra tutoring. Then he replayed the scene at the locker room the other day. He thought, "He was probably just trying to help. Why did I make such a big deal out of it? He may be the only real friend I have." He fought his better instincts because he was desperate for a father figure; desperate for someone to talk to about Leah. Mr. DeLeon was the only person he could tell. He turned the kitchen light on and looked at the wine bottle sitting on the table. There was still a little bit left in the liter bottle. He lifted it to his lips and swallowed a mouthful and stood waiting for something to happen. He swallowed a bigger mouthful and still nothing. He put the empty bottle back where it was on the table. He thought, "She'll never notice. Even if she does, she'll think she drank it." Then he remembered the time he caught his mother putting a bottle of vodka under the kitchen sink, in back of the dishpan. She didn't know he had seen her. He opened the cabinet and sure enough, there it was. He took it out and was happy to see that it was more than half full. He unscrewed the cap and took a swig and then another and another. He felt dizzy as he screwed the cap on and put it back. He lost his balance for a second as he started up the stairs but soon he was passed out on his bed. He woke up a little while later feeling sick to his stomach. He barely recognized the feeling that he was going to throw up, when it started to surge up uncontrollably. He ran into the bathroom and knelt by the toilet. He made it there just in time. When he finished, he felt relieved, until he stood up and felt his head pounding. His stomach contracted and he gagged. He quickly leaned over the toilet, but nothing came out. He made his way back to his bed and got under the covers. He thought, "Never again. That stuff is nasty. How can she drink it?"

Charles was silent in the car on Monday morning, as his mother drove him to school. He had barely spoken a word to her on Sunday. She assumed he was still upset about the baseball game so she didn't press him for conversation. As he got out of the car he said, "I'm staying for tennis team and then Algebra so I'll be home around 5:30."

"Alright. See you then."

Charles went through the motions all day—going from class to class and wondering when he would see Leah in the hallway. His feelings about her seemed to change from moment to moment. He felt anger, sadness, confusion and, by late afternoon, he had idea. He thought, "I'll marry her. Her mom likes me. She'd probably let me move in with them." But then he remembered the tone of her voice when she said, "*I'll take care of Leah from now on.*" He shook his head and thought, "It's a stupid idea anyway." He must have been looking at the floor instead of where he was walking because he was startled when he heard David Reilly sneak up beside him and say, "Leah's back with Matt so now I have you all to myself again. Let's fuck Chuck." Charles backed away from David in disbelief. "What are you talking about?" "I'm talking about you and me Chuckie boy."

Charles was unfazed by the abuse. He needed to know if he heard him right, when suddenly Matt rounded the corner with Leah walking next to him. Leah quick looked away, but Matt gave him a dark stare as he passed. It took a minute before Charles realized his mouth hung open. He swallowed hard.

"Told ya. It's me and you now Chuck." David Reilly tapped his butt and Charles yelled, "Get off me you homo!"

With that, David Reilly shoved him to the floor. Charles started to get up, as David Reilly and his friends stood there laughing at him. David taunted, "Ahhh, did I upset my little boyfriend?"

Charles felt sick to his stomach, as he watched other kids passing in the hallway, just staring at him.

David said to his friends, "Come on. Let's get out of here." Fortunately, there was a restroom across the hall and Charles forced himself to walk to it, even though he wanted to run. He went into a stall and shut the door. He wiped the tears and sweat from his face. He mumbled, "Oh God. Oh God." He looked at his watch. He felt relief. It was almost 3:00. All he had to do was get to the gym. The thought of Mr. DeLeon made him feel safe. He opened the stall door slowly. He was afraid David might have snuck into the restroom and was waiting to jump him. He finally exhaled when he saw the empty room. He slipped into the hallway that was busy now with students slamming their lockers and gathering their belongings before heading for the buses. He made it to the gym without anyone bothering him and he was relieved when he saw Mr. DeLeon in the distance by the office.

"Hey Charlie." Mr. DeLeon's expression changed to concern as Charles neared him. "Are you OK man?"

"Yeah. Yeah. Well, no. Can I talk to you?"

"Sure. But let me get the guys started on their drills. Just wait for me in the office."

After a few minutes, Mr. DeLeon returned to the office and sat down. "Hey what's up man?"

Charles spoke in a halting manner initially, but once he got going, everything just gushed out of him. By the time he finished, Mr. DeLeon had maintained an expression of fatherly concern. He said, "Charlie, you've had a bad couple of days. I don't think it gets much worse than that. And this guy, David Reilly, sounds like a real prick. But don't give it another thought. I'll make sure he doesn't bother you anymore."

Charles relaxed a bit and finally sat back in his chair.

Mr. DeLeon continued, "As far as Leah . . . man that really sucks. I know how much you cared about her. I know you don't want to hear this now, but you've got to move on. I know you can't imagine that now because your feelings are raw, but you're a good looking guy. You're smart. Hell, we've even got you doing well in Algebra now." Charles made a half smile.

Mr. DeLeon continued, "As far as your Dad . . . well . . . that's a tough one." Charles hoped he wouldn't say anything bad about his father. Mr. DeLeon said, "Look man, I had a lot of issues with my father—some of it is pretty ugly. But I got through it. Look, your Dad probably has a good reason for missing the game. I'm sure he'll come around soon." It seemed Mr. DeLeon was saying everything Charles needed to hear. He felt comforted. He felt calm.

Mr. DeLeon stood up. "Come on. Let's get your mind off things and go do our job with the team."

Charles liked the way that sounded. *Our* job. Not like Mrs. Godwin . . . or his mother . . . or even his father . . . Charles felt like he belonged.

When practice ended, Mr. DeLeon said, "Let's take a break from Algebra today. Why don't we play a little tennis?"

"But I . . ."

"Don't worry Charlie. I'm sure you can play better than you think you can."

They stood on opposite sides of the net and Charles hit the first couple balls into the net.

Just before he set up another serve, Mr. DeLeon said, "Just tilt your racket up a bit and hit it a little harder this time. When you slam the ball around, it's good for the soul." Mr. DeLeon laughed and Charles smiled. It was the first time he felt somewhat happy in a few days.

Thirty minutes later, Mr. DeLeon said, "Alright. I don't want you to push it too hard. Let's hit the showers."

Charles realized he was covered in sweat. He followed Mr. DeLeon into the locker room and Mr. DeLeon took a couple of towels from a closet. He tossed one at Charles. "Here. I'll just grab another team shirt so when you're finished, you can wear that home."

The shower heads lined the tiled walls of a large open room. Mr. DeLeon had already started running the water by the time Charles was standing a few feet away from him. Mr. DeLeon had already begun soaping himself up when Charles glanced over at him. Mr. DeLeon gave him a big smile. Charles grinned and turned toward the tiled wall. He liked the way the hot water felt as it pulsated against the back of his neck and then his back and his arms. He lathered himself up and breathed in the hot steam as he rinsed his hair. When he opened his eyes again, the room was fogged up with steam. He looked up at the shower head to see how he could turn it off. Mr. DeLeon must have noticed because he heard him say, "Don't worry. There's a master switch. I'll take care of it."

Charles left the shower room and began to towel off. He put his underwear and his jeans back on. Mr. DeLeon walked out of the shower room with a towel wrapped around his waist.

"Oh right. Let me get you that shirt."

Charles waited by the bench. A moment later, Mr. DeLeon handed him a shirt. "I think this is the right size."

Charles lifted the shirt over his head. He pulled it down over his jeans and said, "It fits." He looked at Mr. DeLeon. He was surprised how serious Mr. DeLeon looked. "What's wrong?" Charles asked.

"You've gotta tuck that in man."

Charles had a flash of déjà vu. He remembered the last time Mr. DeLeon had said that. But he pushed the thought out of his mind. Mr. DeLeon was a good guy after all. He felt embarrassed that he had even imagined that he was a little weird. He unbuckled his belt and unzipped his pants. But in a moment's flash, Mr. DeLeon was standing behind him and he put his hands on Charles's hips. "Come on Charlie." He tried to sound playful. "I guess I have to help you with this." Charles was confused. Mr. DeLeon gave the shirt a yank downward and Charles felt relieved. He realized Mr. DeLeon was just straightening the shirt for him. But then he saw his towel fall to the floor, and in what seemed like one swift motion, he had pushed Charles underpants downward and pulled Charles against him. Charles screamed when he felt the pain of Mr. DeLeon's hard penis.

"Ahhh Charlie. Charlie." Mr. DeLeon was panting.

Charles screamed, "Stop! Stop it! Stop!" He struggled to free himself.

He heard a loud groan come from Mr. DeLeon, as he released him from his grip. Charles fell to the bench. He was sobbing.

Mr. DeLeon was saying, "Charlie, it's OK. It's OK." He reached out to touch his back and Charles jumped to his feet.

"Stay away from me!" He screamed. He tried to back away when he realized his pants were twisted around his legs. He hoisted them up. He was trembling as he nervously tried to zip his pants. Mr. DeLeon moved toward him. "Stay away from me or I'll kill you!" He ran out of the locker room without a shirt. He looked across the gym and ran toward the exit sign. Once he was in the hallway, he turned to see if Mr. DeLeon was chasing him. He wasn't. He ran as fast as he could toward the front doors of the school. But there were no activity buses waiting for him outside. He looked to the left and then to the right and just started running.

He had already run a half mile, before he realized he was cold. His teeth had been chattering, but he only noticed when he rubbed his arms for warmth. It was a gray, cloudy day and rain started to drizzle. But Charles kept running, and soon he neared his neighborhood. He hoped his mother wouldn't see him enter the house. But by the time he reached for his front door, he didn't care. The television was blaring and the aroma of cigarette smoke wafted in the air. Suddenly Charles felt the urge to pee as he ran up the stairs to the bathroom and sat down on the toilet. He was panting and trembling. He rested his elbows on his knees and held his head in his hands. When he got up, he turned to flush the toilet and saw blood in the toilet bowl. "Jesus Christ!" He felt pain and touched his anal area. When he took his hand away, there was blood on it. He turned the water on at the sink and washed his hands. He let the water run as he leaned on the sink and cried. After a few minutes, he stood upright and looked at his hysterical expression in the mirror. "Why?" He cried out as he raised his fist and punched the mirror hard. Glass shattered. He fell to the floor.

By then his mother ran up the stairs and was pounding on the locked bathroom door. "Charles! Open the door this minute! What's going on in there? . . . Charles! . . ."

Through the blur of tears, his eyes became transfixed by a particularly large shard of glass. He took a deep breath . . . grabbed at it and pulled it across his throat.

* * * *

Beth was shocked to see police cars at Carrie's house. She got out of the car and heard Jake howling. She hurried inside and quickly wrapped his harness around his chest; attached the leash and shut the door.

A couple of police officers were standing by their car in the street. "What happened?" Beth asked.

They looked at her with trepidation. Beth said, "I live a couple houses down . . . right there." She pointed toward her house.

"Apparently there's been a suicide," one of the officers said.

"Oh my God! Who was it?"

"A young boy who lived here with his mother."

Beth's heart sunk in her chest. "Oh God . . . Charles? He . . ." Her eyes filled with tears. "I just moved in last week . . ." she started to cry. She felt embarrassed. She hardly knew him.

One of the policemen said awkwardly, "It's OK miss."

She took a breath. "Thanks. I was just going to say that I met him when I was first looking at the house. He was such a nice, friendly kid. In fact, he cut my grass yesterday."

The officer asked, "Did he seem upset?"

"No. Not at all. Oh . . . wait a minute. On Saturday I saw him in the morning sitting on his porch and he waved to me. But later that day, he was sitting on the curb looking like he lost his best friend or something. I think he was supposed to go to a Phillies game. But it couldn't have been that. I guess there were other things going on."

The officer said, "Well, off the record, we talked to his mother and she said she suspected that he might have been bullied because he didn't want to take the school bus. She had to drive him to school in the morning. But, there's only so much you can do. I'm sure he still saw the kid at school."

Beth said, "It's so horrible the way kids bully each other these days. I mean, it's not like it hasn't always happened but now it just seems so much worse."

"Unfortunately, it can destroy a kid. Look what happened here." The officer asked, "Do you want to go up to the house to see his mother?"

Beth said, "To tell you the truth I haven't met her yet. I met Charles because he was friendly with the lady who used to live in my house. Maybe I should go say something though."

The officer said, "It might be helpful to her if she feels like she has a neighbor who cares. She's apparently divorced from the kid's father and, when he showed up at the house about an hour ago, all hell broke loose."

Beth asked, "Is she OK?"

"Yeah. There was just a lot of screaming and yelling going on, so the guys who were already here gave us a call as backup. A traumatic situation like this can drive people to do crazy things."

Beth looked toward the house. "Is it OK if I take my dog with me?"

"Sure. As long as he's friendly."

"Oh yeah. He's fine."

"Go ahead then."

A few police officers were milling around inside the house and their radios intermittently transmitted loud voices across the threshold. Jake's tail was wagging as he jumped up playfully toward a policeman. "Hey, how you doing Buddy?" The officer spoke in a respectfully quiet voice. Beth said, "I'm a neighbor . . . I was just going to say something . . ."

The officer said, "Here, I'll hold him for a minute. She's right in there."

"Thanks." Beth felt a familiar sensation of being a protector as she approached the woman, who was apparently Charles's mother.

She sat down on the couch next to her. "I'm Beth. I just moved in last week."

The woman's eyes were red and swollen. She gave Beth a limp handshake as she said, "Hi. I'm Carrie. I'm . . ." She started weeping.

Beth moved a little closer to her and gently touched her shoulder. "I'm . . . I'm so sorry about what happened."

Carrie cried out, "Oh God I can't believe this. Why? Why would he do it?" After a couple minutes, she settled down, but then she started to say, "By the time I got into the bathroom, there was so much blood !" She was crying hysterically again.

Beth knew there was nothing she could say. She waited. Carrie calmed down a little and swiped at the box of tissues next to her. After a moment, she was about to light a cigarette, when she caught herself and looked at Beth. "Do you mind?"

"Oh no. Not at all."

They sat there silently for a few moments. The officer who had been holding Jake's leash, slowly entered the room. "Hey. Come here you." Carrie started petting Jake. "He's a sweet dog." She looked toward Beth, "Is he your dog?"

"Yeah." Beth was happy that Jake seemed to give Carrie a momentary pleasure.

The officer looked at Beth and said, "We need to talk to Carrie for a few minutes."

Beth could see this was her cue to leave. She asked the officer, "Do you have a piece of paper and a pen?"

"Sure."

Beth wrote down her phone number and handed it to Carrie. "Just call me any time."

Carrie choked up. She couldn't speak, as she took the piece of paper from Beth. She just nodded.

Beth whispered, "Thank you" to the officer and left.

When she got home, she nestled into the corner of the couch and cried until she could no longer breathe through her nose; it had become so congested from her sobbing. As she pulled tissues from the box in the bathroom, she looked in the mirror at her puffy eyes and inflamed nose and mouth. She thought she looked ugly from crying so much, as she listlessly wandered from the bathroom, and back to the couch. She was crying for Charles but also for herself and all the loneliness and sadness she had been trying to push out of her mind lately. She could see Charles that day as he stood on the driveway—the shy grin on his sweet, young face. More tears fell, as she clenched her hands around the sopping wet tissues.

Chapter 16

A month later

RUTH MCBRIDE HAD finished her training as the Billing Manager, and Kathy would be gone by the end of the month. But there was another change to the office staff; Mrs. Ajit had begun to work at "the back desk" from about 11:00 in the morning until around 4:00 in the afternoon.

"Doesn't she run Lansdale Lab anymore?" Beth asked Lydia.

"Yeah, but she said she's trying to sell the Lab business. She hired that mousey guy, George, as her assistant."

"Oh; that's who that guy is." George would often come up from the Lab in the afternoon and sheepishly stand in the tiny space between Beth's work space and what was now Mrs. Ajit's desk in back of her. He didn't dare approach Mrs. Ajit until she acknowledged him. He spoke in an almost inaudible tone, so Beth could never quite hear their brief conversations. He was in his mid-50s, about six feet tall, slim build, and not a bad looking man; but he was very shy and awkward; and he was White, which apparently made Mrs. Ajit confident that she could trust him.

Mrs. Ajit's hours just about coincided with Ruth's hours, although Ruth worked from 12:00 noon until 5:00 p.m.

When Beth arrived each day at 1:30, it was the last half hour of the doctors' two hour lunch break. Lydia sprang out of her chair immediately, unless she was in the middle of a conversation with a patient or perhaps a sales rep who was lingering a bit too long after their lunch with the doctors. If the food was still in the kitchen, that's where Lydia headed; unless the leftovers had already been moved to the catch-all exam room at the far end of the office; in which case Beth could chat with Lydia there to get caught up on anything Lydia considered to be of importance that happened during morning office hours.

Beth followed Lydia so they could talk in relative privacy, since Mrs. Ajit was always around now. Beth said, "I don't get it. Mrs. Ajit sits in a chair next to Ruth for about an hour every afternoon and they are apparently discussing patient billing. So is Ruth leaving already or is Mrs. Ajit going to be the Office Manager, now that Kathy's retiring?"

At the mere mention of Mrs. Ajit's name, Lydia rolled her eyes. But unlike Beth, Lydia always called her by her first name—Mita. Lydia said, "Let me put it this way; I think Mita now considers herself the Office Manager, even though nobody actually gave her the job. She didn't get along with Kathy and now that Kathy's leaving, she's basically given herself the job."

"How does that go over with Dr. Arvind? I mean, he wants to have control of everything doesn't he?"

"Yeah, well, he's gradually taking the reins, if D ever lets go and actually retires. But Mita thinks she's entitled to the job simply because she's his mother . . . you know, she's often said she's responsible for D's success so I guess that makes it *her* practice."

"Really?"

"Oh yeah. You'll see. Now that she's working in back of you, you'll find out what she's really like. Excuse the expression but, she thinks her shit don't stink."

They both laughed a little. Lydia continued. "She's always had her nose in the billing part of it. That's why she didn't get along with Kathy. But Ruth isn't going anywhere; not yet anyway." Lydia giggled and said, "Poor Kathy. She was the Office Manager, but she had 4 peoples' hands in the billing and once Arvind started, it grew to 5 people."

Beth asked, "Why are all of them involved with the billing?"

"It has something to do with the Medicaid patients and the billing codes . . . I don't know."

Beth had the feeling Lydia *did* know. Ironically, like Dr. Vishnu, Lydia played all sides and when she wasn't having a tete de tete with D in the kitchen, she was whispering with Dr. Vishnu.

If he chose to stay at the office rather than go golfing, Dr. D's habit, during the last 15 minutes of his lunch break, was to heat up two cups of tea in the microwave oven. He strolled over to Mrs. Ajit and handed her a cup; at which point Dr. Vishnu would join them as he slipped into his labcoat again, after returning from his lunch break at home. The three of them laughed and chatted in an Indian language, as if they were the best of friends.

Apparently some dynamics of human behavior stay the same from elementary school to the workplace; regardless of the profession or education level of the people involved. Whenever three or more people are involved, there's a competition for top dog. Beth had experienced being a new employee a few times during her life. Long term employees sized up the new person and likewise, the new person cautiously decided which coworker they wanted to befriend. If Kathy had stayed, she would have been the coworker Beth chose to befriend because she had a pleasant and professional demeanor and there was something about her that reminded Beth of her mother. Kathy even had a similarly beautiful Irish face; and oddly, that same demure affect that insinuated she was keeping a secret.

In fact, there *were* secrets to this medical practice that would slowly unravel; gradually chipping away at Beth's naivete.

During the course of the afternoon, Dr. D did more socializing than actually treating patients; just as Lydia had told her. He was the go-to doc for the pharmaceutical sales reps; and there were usually 8 to 10 of those stopping by each day. It was obvious they were sales reps because they were dressed in stylish suits or tight-fitting dresses; they were all good looking; and they were always smiling as they gave that inquisitive facial gesture, as if to ask, "Is it OK if I go back there?" which referred to the kitchen—the designated place for their visits. They would fill the sample bins for their products with tiny, white bottles filled with a 7 day supply of their drugs. Whenever Dr. D escorted a patient back to the front desk after he had seen them, he would peak into the kitchen to see if a rep was waiting; at which point he would chat with the sales reps for 20 minutes at a shot. Of course, Dr. Arvind appreciated this, since he had no interest in spending his valuable time with the pharma sales reps, whom he often referred to as idiots.

Dr. Vishnu wasn't so happy about how little work Dr. D did each day. Dr. Vishnu would often complain to Beth, "When I'm bringing my patients back to my exam room, I can hear him chatting with the same patient for 45 minutes. He picks and chooses who he wants to see."

"Really?" Beth would say; in a voice that she hoped would empathize with Dr. Vishnu's exasperation. His eyes would widen and he'd say, "Watch. The next time he comes up," he moved his arm in a back and forth motion between Dr. D's exam room and the front desk. "He'll walk up and subtly look into the waiting room and see who's there. Then he'll decide if it is somebody he wants to see." Then his frustration would morph into an angry tone and he'd say, "I see 8 or 9 patients to his one!" Often Beth would listen to Dr. Vishnu complain. She thought it was inappropriate that he divulged so much information about the Ajit's—like the time he whispered to Ruth and Beth that Mrs. Ajit had once had a nervous breakdown because, as he put it, "she's inclined to severely depressive episodes." He said the cause was her marriage and her attitude—her marriage because Dr. D spent as little time with her as possible (Dr. Vishnu recounted the time that Mrs. Ajit was beside herself because Dr. D had left his family in the Bahamas; only two days into their vacation, because he was bored and wanted to return to work); and her attitude because she came from a wealthier family in India than Dr. Ajit's family. India is a very class conscious society as Dr. Vishnu pointed out. He went on to explain that Mrs. Ajit came to the United States before Dr. D to further her education and to work, which elevated her status in the eyes of Indian people; and it gave her a feeling of superiority. She felt entitled to be paid attention to and even revered. She had a Masters Degree in Biochemistry and was working at the Cleveland Clinic when she met Dr. D, while attending a medical conference. She left her career behind to raise their two children, while

Dr. Ajit started his practice. According to Dr. Vishnu, Dr. D had a difficult time establishing a patient base as an Indian doctor in a mostly
White area, some 30 years before; so he would do all he could to attract
patients to his practice by making house calls and seeing patients at any
time day or night. For many years, he worked 12 to 13 hours a day to
supplement his income due to his initially tiny family practice. He had
been a prison physician at Graterford Prison nearby, which required
him to see patients there every other week for a half day. He did that
for about 15 years. Additionally, he became an attending physician at
half a dozen nursing homes, which meant he had to visit patients at
each nursing home once a week. (Until recently, Dr. D, like all family
practice physicians, visited all of his patients in the area hospitals. Now
hospitals have full time staff physicians—called Hospitalists—and it is
only specialty physicians who make hospital rounds). Dr. D became a
school district physician conducting sports physicals; and he even contracted with a local bus transportation service to do their employees'
annual physicals.

Beth once naively admired Dr. D when he said of Medicaid patients, "If we don't take care of them, who will?" That was before she
realized Medicaid patients were good for business. An individual patient with Medicaid did not result in a livable reimbursement to the
doctors, but when a large volume of patients were Medicaid and/or
Medicare, the profits grew exponentially; and volume was what Dr.
Vishnu was capable of producing. Unfortunately, he did so by twisting
the well intentioned programs into an illegal money-making scheme.
Dr. Vishnu would stand just to the right of the front desk, in the patient
waiting area, and speak in a rapid-fire pace in Hindi to a huddle of
3, 4 or 5 Indian people who listened with rapt attention. Beth would
hear the English words Medicaid or Medicare as he handed them their
Medicaid or Medicare application forms. Many patients applied for,
and received benefits from, both Medicare and Medicaid. (Medicaid
is intended for U.S. citizens who are the working poor or who have
no job at all. Medicare is intended for U.S. citizens who have worked
for many years and thereby earn the benefit for themselves and their

spouse when they become senior citizens). For Medicaid, Dr. Vishnu apparently told them what to write for the reasons they allegedly could not work because Beth would see application form after application form with similar wording. Dr. Vishnu was coaching them on how to falsify the paperwork. Dr. D would then sign a dozen forms at a time, because they required an original signature of a physician. As usual, Dr. D had never even seen the patients because they were seen by Dr. Vishnu. The patients showered him with platitudes in the Hindi language and Beth could tell by their gestures of head bobbing up and down and from side to side, that they were infinitely grateful. Right or wrong, Indian patients trusted Indian doctors.

All of this was strictly for the benefit of ultimately increasing business by sending more patients their way because of the wildfire pace at which word of mouth spread in the Indian community.

Most patients were not U.S. citizens, and Beth wondered how they were getting the social security numbers needed to complete the application forms for Medicare and Medicaid.

A small number of patients did not participate in the Medicaid/ Medicare scam because they thought it was wrong, while others did not participate for less honorable reasons. They believed that paying cash was the best way to stay below the radar. They carried large wads of cash in their pockets and stashed money at home because they didn't want to establish a bank account. They didn't have credit cards, or anything else that created a paper trail.

The relatively few, well-to-do Indian patients in the practice, were seen by Dr. D or Dr. Arvind; and not by Dr.Vishnu. These were the patients Mrs. Ajit made time for, with few exceptions. She became a different person in these moments because her voice took on the pleasant, relaxed tone of a woman at ease with "her own kind." Even her own sister (who lived in the area but had not married well and was not well educated) would nervously try to catch Mrs. Ajit's eye, when she signed in at the front desk; but Beth would watch her expression wither as her sister realized that Mrs.Ajit did not have time for her. It seemed Mrs. Ajit wanted the few upper class Indians in their practice, to have the impression that the Ajit's only worked as physicians to provide an admirable service to the Indian community. That was far from the truth.

The illicit practices were initially so nuanced, that Beth just occasionally had the feeling that something wasn't right. But the frequency caused them to seep into her consciousness and, once she was aware; they grew exponentially and so blatantly, that Beth could not even fathom such a level of narcissism on the part of the doctors that allowed them to perceive themselves as beyond reproach and above the law.

One of Beth's job duties was to verify whether or not a patient who said they had health insurance; really had active health insurance. She did this for patients scheduled to be seen the next morning. Lydia was required to do the same for each patient seen in the afternoon. The website used to verify health insurance is entitled Navinet. To access this service, they entered their practice identification numbers and then entered the insurance identification number for a particular patient, along with the date of birth, thus allowing the name of the patient to pop up on the screen, as well as an indication as to whether or not the insurance was active or inactive.

Insurance co-payments were collected by Beth or Lydia, before the patient was seen. If the patient was paying cash for the visit, they would pay after the visit. Dr. Vishnu escorted the patient back to the front desk where he would write a code number on a sticky note and put it in front of Beth. The code number corresponded with a dollar amount. If Dr. Vishnu forgot to place a sticky note in front of Beth, she had to walk back to Dr. Vishnu's exam room to ask for the code number. The use of the code number allowed him to avoid the awkwardness of saying an amount due, in front of the patient.

An older, Indian woman was periodically ushered into the waiting area by an Indian man whom Beth frequently saw at the office, when he escorted this woman's husband or other patients to the office. The man, like others who served as patient escorts by driving them to the office, was notably more friendly and outgoing than typical Indian patients, who tended to quietly say hello when they signed in for an appointment (sometimes not even uttering a word but rather slightly bobbing their head in a culturally typical yes-but-no fashion). Those few patients of a higher class and income level would not say hello at all or would do so in a patronizing fashion; because Beth, as a White front desk receptionist, was below their class level and not worth the expenditure of energy to befriend.

The older Indian woman, with the escort, was noted as "self-pay" (paying cash for the visit) so Beth was surprised when, after she was seen by Dr. Vishnu, the escort handed Beth an insurance card with *his* name on it and said, "Give this to Dr. Vishnu."

Beth went back to Dr. Vishnu and asked what she should do with the man's insurance card. Dr. Vishnu said, in his usual quiet, instructive tone, "Yes. That is for her medicine. I'll take it."

Apparently, Dr. Vishnu wrote a prescription (script) for medicine and sent it to the pharmacy with the name of the escort on the script; so even though the medicine was for the woman, the escort's insurance company was paying for it.

That same afternoon, Beth took a call from a man who identified himself as Jaikishin Patel. He said, "My foot doctor said I need a letter from Dr. Ajit to prove I have diabetes so I can get special shoes."

Beth said, "I need your date of birth so I can look up your chart."

He said, "My date of birth is 8-4-45."

Beth brought up his chart on the screen and said, "It looks like you have Cigna health insurance; is that right?"

"Yes."

"And what is the name of your podiatrist—your foot doctor?"

He gave Beth the information and she said, "OK. I'll give a message to Dr. Arvind Ajit because he handles these issues and then we'll get back to you."

"Thank you."

Dr. Arvind responded by telling Beth to "write a short note for the patient verifying that he has diabetes."

She did this on the computer template that automatically added Dr. D's signature at the bottom. When she called Jaikishin back to tell him he could pick up the letter, he said, "Thank you because I don't even have insurance. I have to use my son's insurance."

Beth was alarmed at this and asked, "What did you say?"

Jaikishin repeated something about how he "needs these shoes" (he had a heavy accent).

She said, "No, I mean; what did you say about using your son's insurance?"

He said, "No, no, nothing. Can you just send the letter to me in the mail?"

"We usually ask patients to pick up letters." (Beth had been instructed not to mail letters because of the cost of postage. However, they made some exceptions).

Jaikishin said, "But I have trouble walking and I can't drive."

This seemed like a reasonable exception, so Beth said, "OK. I'll put the letter in the mail. Can you verify your address?"

He gave his address. When Beth finished the call, she went into the Navinet website and entered the Cigna insurance identification number and it brought up the name of Jack Patel with a date of birth of 5-11-85, and the same address as Jaikishin. She then opened the electronic medical record for the date of birth 5-11-85 and the chart for Jack Patel popped up. Jack's last office visit was 11-11-08 (two years before). Later she told Dr. Arvind that Jaikishin was apparently using his son's health insurance. He didn't react. He seemed to behave as if he hadn't heard her and just changed the subject.

The lack of continuity of coverage at the front desk was beginning to make sense to Beth. It worked to the advantage of the doctors that Beth and Lydia couldn't possibly discuss every issue with a patient in the few minutes they had together before Lydia left for the day.

The practice had no nurses; no medical assistants; no medical technicians. All of the duties that are typically performed by such medical professionals fell to Lydia and Beth or the doctors themselves. This allowed the doctors to reduce costs by eliminating the need for employing other healthcare professionals. It also gave them control of every aspect of patient care (and no other care professionals around to ask questions).

Every medical practice has its share of blood drawn on any given day—usually by a nurse or a medical technician. But Ajit Medical Center did an extraordinary amount of bloodwork. The doctors drew the blood themselves and then inserted the blood-filled tubes into racks on the front desk. Lydia did not wear gloves, as she showed Beth how to process the blood tubes—spin them in the centrifuge, label them and insert accompanying paperwork into a small plastic bag. Most of these bags were then sent to Labwork Diagnostics for processing. (When the sales rep for Labwork Diagnostics brought new information about reduced prices for uninsured or under-insured patients who could go directly to Labwork Diagnostics to have blood drawn, the patients were never informed about it because FBT (Fasting Blood Test) appointments were a major source of income for the practice.

Beth confessed to Laura, "I always put on a pair of gloves before I empty the trash and I really don't want to handle the blood tubes and urine cups without gloves."

Lydia said, in a maternal tone, "That's perfectly alright. You do whatever you're comfortable with." She took a box of latex gloves from a side shelf under the left side of the desk. "Ooops. This is almost empty. I'll get another one." Beth put on a pair of gloves and Lydia got up to get another box out of the supply closet. When she returned, she said, "I just remembered something *very important*" (she shivered with drama.) "When you make appointments for fasting blood tests (FBTs), make sure the patient isn't going to hold up the docs with other issues. In other words, it has to be an FBT appointment only—not a sick visit. The docs just want to draw the blood and move on to the next patient. They don't want the patients holding them up with a lot of questions. Just get them in and out. OK?"

Beth asked, "How do I prevent someone from combining an appointment for a sick visit with an FBT?"

Lydia said, "We just train our patients. If they call for an appointment because they're sick, just tell them we're booked in the morning and we don't have any available appointments, so they have to come in the afternoon. Now, if it's someone who really needs to be seen right away, you can make an exception; but you'll learn that in most cases, you can put them off until the afternoon. The docs want the mornings reserved for FBTs. See, we have many, many diabetic patients and the docs have to test for sugar levels in the blood. So these patients have to fast and can't eat before the blood test. They can only be seen in the morning because most people have to eat by lunchtime. The docs want to schedule as many FBT appointments as they can."

"So does that mean Saturday morning appointments should only be for FBTs?"

"Yes. Definitely. Just like mornings during the week—they just want to get them in and get them out so they can keep moving. Again, there are exceptions. If someone calls that morning and sounds really, genuinely sick, you can make an appointment for that morning."

Beth sat silently. The doctors were charging patients' insurance companies and Medicare/Medicaid for appointments that were really nothing more than the doctor drawing blood and getting the patient out the door again. She asked, "What happens if they start asking the doctor questions?"

Lydia laughed. "Trust me. They know how to nip it in the bud and cut them off. Usually they'll say something like, 'We're really backed up today. Why don't you make an appointment to review all your meds or whatever the issue is. Or sometimes they'll pretend they got paged. Believe me; docs know how to give patients the brush-off."

Lydia turned toward the centrifuge to the left of the desk. "Now the centrifuge holds six blood tubes. The docs fill two tubes for each patient. The larger tube gets put into the centrifuge and the small tube with the purple cap doesn't have to be spun. But make sure you label the tubes properly so you have the right name on the tubes. The docs will process a requisition for the lab to inform them about what to look for; like sugar levels; electrolyte balance; and cholesterol levels." Lydia opened a plastic bag that was a bit larger than a sandwich bag. "Put the blood tubes in here with the folded lab requisition." She then opened a much larger plastic bag—about the size of a kitchen trash bag and it was bulging with the smaller bags inside. She said, "Put all of the bags into this bag."

Beth said, "Wow, that's a lot of bloodwork."

Lydia giggled and said, "Yeah. Oh, and the courier from Labwork Diagnostics comes by each day and picks this up. He'll come right up to the desk counter to get it. But, for the labwork you process during the afternoons, evenings and Saturday mornings, you have to put it into a metal milk box container just outside the office door. You know—the ones you've seen when you go out to empty the trash. A courier comes by again at night to pick up the labwork in the metal box."

Lydia stopped to take a gulp from her coffee cup and then continued, "Labwork Diagnostics processes the bloodwork at their central labs and then sends the results electronically to Dr. Vishnu, who then calls the patients with results." Beth often overheard him on the phone in the kitchen, where he sat at the table with his laptop, leaving message after message for patients that "the results were good and we'll see you next month." Now and then she heard him tell a patient their cholesterol level was high or the sugar level was high; in which case the patient was instructed about a change in dosing or frequency of their medication.

The patients were instructed by the doctors to leave the cups with their urine samples at the front desk, where Lydia trained Beth to label them according to what the doctors were looking for; i.e., infection (in which case the lab would look for bacteria in the urine) versus assessment of kidney function (in which case the lab tested for micro-albuminaria—protein content in the urine). It was important to look for the presence of protein in the urine of diabetic patients because their kidneys were at risk of progressive deterioration. *So many* of their patients had diabetes; that it seemed like *all* their patients had diabetes. Beth thought it must have had something to do with the diet of Indian people. What she didn't know was that the doctors were falsely classifying most of their patients as "diabetic" so Medicare or Medicaid, or insurance companies, would pay for blood tests every month. The patients didn't question the frequency of blood tests because they trusted the doctors.

Beth learned how to use a plastic pipette to extract a urine sample from the urine cup; deposit it into a tube, and then label it appropriately. Lydia had instructed Beth to toss the leftover urine into the toilet and then throw the container into the trash can under the front desk. If a doctor was looking for testosterone levels in the blood, Beth used the same method to extract a blood sample from the blood tube after it was spun in the centrifuge. The excess blood, in a small tube with a rubber stopper, was just tossed into the trash under the desk. Everything, including bodily fluids, went out with the regular trash. The only exception was a sharps container on the counter in each of the doctor's exam rooms. They disposed of used syringes in these tiny red containers. More than once, Beth saw these containers stacked on top of each other by the back office door. Once, after they had been there for several days, Beth asked Lydia, "Who takes care of disposing of the sharps containers?" Mrs. Ajit happened to be at her desk at the time. Lydia shrugged her shoulders and seemed to be at a loss for an answer, so she looked toward Mrs. Ajit. Mrs. Ajit looked uncomfortable and started fidgeting with something on her desk. Finally, she said, "I don't know. Dr. Vishnu is supposed to take care of that." Later that day, when Mrs. Ajit had gone for the day, Beth played dumb and asked Dr. Vishnu, "Am I supposed to be throwing the sharps containers out?" He said, "No. No. Mrs. Ajit takes care of them."

On Monday and Friday, Beth's hours were shorter so it was still light out before daylight saving time when she emptied the trash. One night she saw a partially ripped open trash bag in the large trash can and she could see red sharps containers. The practice did not even care to go to the expense of properly disposing of syringes.

Not all blood tests required fasting; so there was a fair amount of labwork to be processed during the afternoon and evening shift. Quite often, when a patient came in for an appointment because they weren't feeling well, the doctor would take blood samples. Beth knew this was odd because she had *never* had to get a blood test because she wasn't feeling well. When she had turned 40, her doctor had given her a prescription to go to a local lab to get bloodwork done to check her thyroid function and cholesterol levels. The doctor did not have his nurse take a blood sample in the office; much less draw blood from her himself.

Beth commented to Lydia, "I'm surprised all this labwork doesn't raise any red flags with the insurance companies or Medicare and Medicaid."

Lydia said, "Oh that reminds me. Dr. Arvind uses the electronic medical records to query patient information and he's started to compile a list of Medicare/Medicaid patients who failed to come in for their regular FBT appointments. He's going to send a copy of the list to you and I, and he wants us to call the patients to schedule appointments for them."

Beth said, "OK. Sure. No problem."

One afternoon, Beth had spoken to yet another Indian woman who reacted nervously and spoke haltingly, in response to Beth asking to speak to her mother—one of the patients on the list compiled by Dr. Arvind. She began to realize there was always one of two standard replies. If they were honest, the answer was always: "She's in India now. She'll be back in April." The answer was April if the call was made during the late fall or winter months. The Indian patients on Medicare/Medicaid typically wintered in India from October until March or April because they hated the cold winter in the States. Others went to India for 4, 5 or 6 months at various other times of the year.

The other reply Beth heard more often, because so many patients knew how to *beat the system* was, "She's not here right now. She's living at my brother's house for a couple months." The *brother's house* was usually New Jersey or New York. Now, this was probably true in some cases, however, more often, the person had returned to India and they didn't want to divulge the lack of residency in the United States; while they maintained *active* status with Medicaid and/or Medicare. Often the answer was, "She's outside now but I'll tell her to call you." Beth learned the expression, "she's outside" did not mean the person was just outside in the back yard or on the front porch; it meant the person was not at home; or not even in the country. The patient never called back; until months later, when she or he came back to the United States for healthcare; stayed with relatives or friends for 4 or 5 months and then went back to India again. Beth was angry after making a few of these calls. Mrs. Ajit had gone for the day; Dr. D had left around 10:00 a.m. to play golf; and Dr. Arvind and Dr. Vishnu were busy seeing patients. Beth turned to Ruth and said, "Shouldn't a person have to live in the United States, in order to receive Medicaid and have worked in the United States to get Medicare?"

But before Ruth could answer, they heard, "Gooooood afternoon Beth." It was the easily recognizable, loud tenor voice of Vipul Amin. He was a know-it-all; a braggart and he could B.S. with the best of them. He would immediately launch into a monologue and expect the office staff to listen attentively.

"Hi Vipul. How are you today?" Beth did her best to make him think she liked him; even though she dreaded the feeling of being sucked into the quick sand of one of his soapbox lectures about Indian culture.

Vipul had told them he worked for the U.S. government as a civil engineer ; so Beth assumed he must be independently wealthy because he couldn't be making a salary that was large enough to cover all of the traveling, dining and entertainment that he bragged about. In addition, he said his daughter attended the University of Pittsburgh and would be going on to medical school; and his son was studying international business at the University of Virginia.

Vipul said, "Oh Beth, my allergies are killing me. You know, where my family comes from in India I never had any problems with allergies. In fact, it is the same region the Ajits come from and the people from this area . . ."

Beth feigned interest and was certain she'd be rescued from listening to him at any moment by a phone call.

". . . and Dr. Vishnu's father was a well known surgeon. He had his own hospital . . ."

Now Beth *was* interested but the phone starting ringing and she barely answered that call, when another line began to ring. She had been on the phone for several minutes and, by that time, Vipul had seated himself in the chair beside Ruth's desk, which was supposed to be for the use of patients who had a question about a bill. Vipul was complaining about the cost of 3 drugs that his mother was taking for her high blood pressure and diabetes. Beth heard bits and pieces of what he said "and can you believe Medicare only covers . . . ."

Dr. Arvind had finished with a patient, whom he escorted to the front desk. When he saw Vipul, Dr. Arvind struck his usual stance of leaning on one hip, with hands in his pockets and a tolerant grin.

After Dr. Arvind took Vipul back to the exam room, Ruth said, "You know, he's complaining about how much Medicare doesn't cover for his mother's meds, but she's shouldn't even be getting Medicare because she's never worked in this country! And by the way, yes, you're right, a person is supposed to be a U.S. citizen and a resident, in order to be entitled to Medicaid and Medicare."

Beth turned toward the entrance when she heard the familiar beeps of a package tracking device. It was either UPS or Fed Ex. The UPS guy usually came in the morning to deliver cartons of lab supplies for Lansdale Lab and the Ajit medical practice. A couple times a month, UPS delivered a large Styrofoam container used for shipping Hepatitis B vaccines—for White patients. Beth had learned that Indian patients were not accustomed to being vaccinated. Dr. Vishnu had shared that children in India are not vaccinated, as children are in the U.S.

The Fed Ex guy arrived around 5:00 p.m., and he was always there to pick up a package, rather than deliver one. The Fed Ex package would always mysteriously appear on the left side counter of the front desk some time during the afternoon. Since it was always already sealed and labeled for pickup, Beth began to wonder who was leaving it there. She tried to be discreet because it was obvious that whoever was doing this, didn't want or need her assistance. The Fed Ex guy punched numbers into the beeping electronic gizmo. The location of the package on the counter was within Ruth's peripheral vision and Beth didn't want Ruth to see her snooping. When Ruth turned to gather up her things to leave for the day; Beth lifted the package to hand it to the Fed Ex man, while simultaneously asking him how his day was going; she read the return address label. It said, "Harry Vishnu, Lab Examiner, Superior Mobile Labs . . . San Diego, CA" and it was going to a lab in Kansas. Beth was stunned, "*Harry* Vishnu, *Lab Examiner* . . . and a lab business in *San Diego, California?*"

That night, after everyone had gone for the day, Beth took out the trash and put the labwork into the metal box. When she got back inside, she went into the mysterious exam room that was set up like all the other exam rooms, but it was only used by Dr. Vishnu for patients who weren't on the day's schedule. He saw them either late in the day or sometimes on Saturday mornings. (Beth never had a reason to go in there unless it was to empty trash from the can that was positioned at the entrance to the room). She peered into an open cardboard box on the counter of the exam room. It contained the plastic wrappings of syringes; used syringes; and lots of small bits of gauze with blood on them. Next to the box was a stack of lab kits. She hadn't seen a lab kit like this in any of the other exam rooms. She realized this room was apparently for "*Harry* Vishnu, *Lab Examiner*" for his *Superior Mobile Labs* business.

Not long after that, she began to find, on occasion, a carelessly discarded tube of blood in the trash can in Dr. Vishnu's office.

Like so many things in the office, Beth wondered how long it had been going on and why it took her so long to notice; although she had only worked there for a couple months. Now that she had discovered *Harry* Vishnu's lab business, she began to take notice of regular visits by a professionally dressed, Chinese man, who would often arrive around 6:00 p.m. on a Tuesday or Thursday—the days they had evening hours. He would bring young, Chinese couples with him. They never had an appointment on the day's schedule; nor were they patients of the practice. The Chinese man would just come up to the front desk and say, "Can you tell Dr. Vishnu that Jim is here."

The same routine would happen with a particular Indian man who would show up with young Indian couples. He would saunter into the office waiting area—always smiling and charming when he showed up in the evening, or late afternoon. He didn't even bother to say, "Tell Dr. Vishnu I'm here." He would just take a seat in the waiting area with the couple he had brought to the office. When Dr. Vishnu came up to escort a patient out or to take a patient back, he would interrupt what he was doing; excuse himself; and escort the Indian man and the couple back to his office or that exam room, where they would emerge from about ten minutes later. When Beth went into Dr. Vishnu's office to empty the trash at the end of the day, she took notice of neatly staggered packets of paperwork sitting, always on the right hand side of Dr. Vishnu's otherwise cleared desk at the end of the day. The Chinese man and the Indian man were life insurance agents and the paperwork was for potential life insurance policy owners. Apparently, "*Harry Vishnu, Lab Examiner,*" would either see the customers in his office; in that mysterious exam room; or *Harry* would travel to their homes to draw a sample of their blood. Three or four lab kits were also on the desk most nights. Each kit had 3 tubes in it, which were sometimes empty and sometimes filled with blood. The paperwork indicated that *Harry* was apparently taking a blood sample from people who were applying for life insurance policies in the amount of $500,000 and quite often for as much as $1,000,000. Beth figured that the insurance companies wanted to be sure the potential customers were not about to die from a disease before they issued them a life insurance policy. The form indicated a date and time that *Harry* had taken the blood samples or a date/time when he was scheduled to take blood samples either at the office or at the person's home. As she looked through the paperwork, she learned that it was usually the names of a married couple, who were taking out life insurance policies on each other. The dates of birth were always for people in the age range of 35 to 40 years old and the names were always

Indian or Chinese. But one time Beth recognized the name on the paperwork as being that of an elderly White man, who was frequently in the office for morning FBT appointments. She thought, "Why would someone that old be getting a life insurance policy—it's a wonder it would be approved."

One night Beth saw a different type of paperwork on the desk of *Harry* or *Dr.* Vishnu or whoever he really was. It was the name of another elderly White patient who had been with Dr. D since his practice started. Attached to the paperwork was a list of names clipped to a manila folder. Beth brazenly opened the folder. It contained plans for an anniversary party for the elderly gentleman and his wife, and a handwritten note inside was thanking Dr. Vishnu for his help in planning an anniversary party for the elderly couple. "That's really odd," Beth thought. "Why would Dr. Vishnu plan an anniversary party? Maybe they like Indian food and he just referred them to an Indian caterer or something."

She looked at a few other papers in the folder and then she froze. There was a list of the old man's friends who were veterans of WWII and a notation to indicate those who should be invited to the party. A line was drawn through several names with a handwritten notation "deceased." She wondered, "What if he used their social security numbers for illegal immigrants? He must have some way of obtaining social security numbers for all these Indian people who falsify Medicaid and Medicare paperwork."

Chapter 17

THE FOLLOWING MONDAY Beth had to work both the morning and afternoon shifts because Lydia had the day off. She had just finished in the restroom, when she saw Mrs. Ajit looking through the bags of bloodwork that were accumulating at the front desk. She took two of the bags and she seemed startled when she turned and saw Beth standing there. Mrs. Ajit said, "I can take care of these in my lab because they're cash paying patients. If they don't have insurance or Medicare, I can do the labwork."

Beth just said, "OK."

Mrs. Ajit continued, "I can process bloodwork for Medicare patients in my lab, only if it is sent to me by another physician. I can't process Medicare labwork for this practice because it is considered a conflict of interest."

Later that morning, the granddaughter of an elderly patient, Eleanor Hahn, called and said, "My grandmother said she was just there the other day, but when I stopped by to check on her this morning, she said she's not feeling well. Is there any way you could fit her in?"

Beth recognized her as a long time patient and, although she had been instructed to schedule only FBT appointments in the morning, she felt certain that Eleanor Hahn met the criteria for an exception to the rule.

Eleanor was seen by Dr. Arvind and then he walked her to the front desk and dropped off a tube of blood and said to Eleanor, "We'll let you know how the INR looks." (This referred to a check for healthy blood clotting time—an indication of cardiac function). Beth heard Eleanor's granddaughter ask her, "Didn't you just have that done?" She didn't hear what Eleanor said in response as they were leaving the office. Dr. Arvind then said to Beth, "You can send that to Lansdale Lab downstairs for my mom." But Eleanor had Medicare and Highmark (an Independent Blue Cross insurance).

He must have noticed Beth's expression, so he asked, "Is something wrong?"

Beth remembered Mrs. Ajit saying, just that morning, that she cannot process Medicare labwork for the Ajit Medical Center because it is a conflict of interest. She started to answer but decided against it, "Ah no, I . . . ah nevermind."

"Hey George. How are you?" Dr. D put his hand on George's shoulder and grasped his hand warmly. After their greetings in the waiting area, George always turned to Beth and said, in his Russian accent, "I've been his patient for 30 years. He's a good man!"

"Oh, I know he is." Beth would answer; doing her best to sound genuine.

George had Medicare and American Continental Insurance. His bloodwork was always sent to Lansdale Lab.

Dr. Arvind brought up bloodwork for Anand Uhbay and said, "This goes to Lansdale Lab." Anand had Aetna Medicare, but Beth did as instructed.

And so it went. Eventually, Mrs. Ajit would just boldly rifle through the labwork that was going to Labwork Diagnostics and pull some of them; saying, "Oh, this one's Medicare, I can take that." Beth was getting used to all of the contradictions.

"Oh my God! We're all going to jail!"

The first time Ruth blurted this out, and the next twenty times she did so; she said it with a half giggle and her skin blushed a bright red on her face. Mrs. Ajit was never present when Ruth said this; nor were the doctors. If Beth wasn't on the phone or talking to a patient, she would turn toward Ruth and ask, "What do you mean?" But nine times out of ten, Ruth would just look toward Beth and shake her head; bite her lower lip insinuating worry; shake her head again; and yet say nothing more. Ruth seemed to enjoy getting Beth's attention and then gaining even more interest by offering no explanation for her outburst. Or she would often say, "Unfortunately I need this job because I've had a heart attack; I have a rod in my spine; I have diabetes; and my husband's company is laying people off."

Over time, Beth had heard Ruth run through her list of maladies innumerable times, but she was progressively more disturbed every time she made the comment about going to jail. She said, "Ruth, we're all part-time employees, so is it worth going to jail for a job that doesn't provide health insurance and doesn't even pay much?"

Ruth said, "Well at least I'm making a little bit of money so we could buy groceries if my husband gets laid off. He's a 59 year old, White male, so what are the chances of him finding another job?"

Beth said, "He's not the only one with few prospects. I'm happy to have a job because I'm 52 now and, not only are there few jobs around; but employers want to hire young people to pay them less or they're afraid someone 50-plus is going to have health problems and that will increase their insurance premiums. They can't ask you if you have kids in an interview, but they assume you do at a certain age and that worries them because they figure they're going to have to pay for your kids' healthcare. Everybody's hiring people part-time so they don't have to pay insurance. But in the end, it's also age discrimination and you're never going to be able to prove that."

Most of their conversations were cut short by phones ringing or patients arriving for an appointment.

"Ajit Medical Center. Can I help you?" Beth said.

"Hi. I need Dr. Arvind to re-write a prescription for Adderall 10 mg. Instead, I need 15 mg twice a day. I mean. No. I need 10 mg instead of the first one he wrote for 15 and it has to be for 90 pills."

He sounded agitated and confused and this was typical of young 20-somethings (or younger) who called for more of the drug Adderall.

Beth said patiently, "First, I need your name and date of birth so I can look up your chart."

"Sure. My name is Daniel Kelly and my date of birth is 4-27-90."

"OK. I have your chart in front of me. It looks like you were just here this morning, right?"

"Yeah. So Dr. Arvind gave me a prescription for Adderall 15 mg twice a day and a prescription for Adderall 25 mg time release capsules. But I think I must have dropped them out of my pocket somewhere, so I need him to write the prescriptions again."

Adderall is a drug used to treat ADHD (Attention Deficit Hyperactivity Disorder) because it increases the ability to focus, but it is also abused by young people as a stimulant. There were about a dozen young, White patients in their early 20s who called frequently for refills of Adderall prescriptions and, just like the patients getting their scripts for Oxy (Oxycodone) and other narcotics, the doctors never questioned the frequency of refills. In the case of pain meds and depressant meds, Beth could hear the intoxication in the voices of these patients. Some were so far gone, they slurred their words. She told the doctors about it but they never reacted with any interest in her observations.

Instead, Dr. Arvind and Dr. Vishnu gave them exactly what they wanted—paper scripts in lieu of sending an electronic script directly to a particular pharmacy. These patients would then go to more than one doctor's office, in order to acquire multiple paper scripts that can be filled at various pharmacies, with no electronic trail. Then the patients turn around and sell the drugs on the street or on college campuses.

Beth typed a message with Daniel's request. Dr. Arvind's response was simply, "Done. Tell him he can stop by to pick up the new scripts." Now Daniel had multiple scripts for a stimulant drug.

Beth had seen patterns of behavior within the general patient population, as well as with individual patients. One of those patterns was the Friday afternoon phone calls from pain med seekers; calling in to ask for a script for Oxycodone (usually pretending they didn't remember the name of "that pain medicine" or they couldn't quite pronounce it, "I think it's pronounced Codomen or Odomen . . ." Of course that part may have been true because they only knew the street name for the drug. They would have a calm façade on the initial phone call but inevitably call 3 or 4 times to ask "has Dr. had a chance yet to write that prescription?" all while doing their best not to appear anxious and impatient; yet calling back or just stopping in and saying "OK. I'll just wait here if you don't mind," as they were obviously chomping at the bit to get their narcotic meds. Beth wondered if they really thought everyone else was so stupid or perhaps their brains were getting so wasted, they couldn't remember the various excuses they used and re-used—like the patients who said they were carrying their medicine bottle in their backpack and "someone mugged me on the bus" (more than one patient used that excuse for needing more meds); or the woman who said she was having a barbecue and accidentally spilled her Oxycodone pills into the grill. Two patients said their apartment was robbed and "they took my pain medicine."

One day when Beth arrived for work, a young couple was sitting in the waiting area. Lydia quietly explained to Beth, "The guy's name is Aazim Khan and him and his wife were already seen as new patients by Dr. Vishnu."

Beth said, "I thought Dr. Arvind saw all the new patients."

Lydia said, "Well, sometimes, but actually when Aazim arrived, he told me his wife needed to see a doctor too. Then he asked if we have any female docs and I said no, but I told him Dr. Vishnu is an older man. Then he said it would be OK for his wife to be seen by him."

Beth asked, "Why?"

Lydia explained, "Muslim men don't want their wives to be seen by a male doctor—let alone a young, good looking man like Dr. Arvind. So when these Muslim women make appointments, you should schedule them with Dr. Vishnu. In fact I always schedule all the Muslim patients to be seen by Dr. Vishnu."

Beth asked, "How do I know they're Muslim when they call to make an appointment?"

"Well, that's the thing. You don't know, but sometimes you can tell by the names—like this guy Kahn. And lots of them have the first name Mohammad or they just say their name is M.D." Lydia giggled a little and said, "When I first started here, I saw 'M.D.' next to a lot of names on the patient charts and I thought the docs had a lot of doctors for patients—because of the M.D."

They both laughed a little. "So M.D. is short for Mohammad?"

"Yeah. Oh and the wives always have a different last name. I think it's like they keep their family clan name or something. So his wife's name is Aara Muzaffar."

"OK. So why are they still here if Dr. Vishnu saw them?"

Lydia said, "They're waiting for the results of a pregnancy test that they're doing downstairs" (*downstairs* refers to Lansdale Lab). Lydia continued, "I was too busy to collect the payment for her visit. So here's a lab requisition that Dr. Vishnu created for Lansdale Lab, indicating that Aazim was having his CBC and CMP panel done; even though he really didn't have his blood drawn. It was simply a way for Mrs. Ajit to bill for the labwork done for his wife's pregnancy test. Aazim said he has Aetna insurance and he gave me his insurance identification card; but his wife isn't covered by his insurance for some reason. Aazim owes $35 as his copay for the office visit and his insurance will pay for his blood test, which is really *her* pregnancy test. And you have to collect $90 from Aazim for his wife's office visit because she is a cash paying patient."

Beth rolled her eyes and smiled. Lydia did the same. Beth said quietly, "I just got here and already my head is spinning."

Lydia giggled and said, "Yeah this place will do that."

As they stood face to face for a moment, Beth asked, "Are the Muslim patients Indian or is it just the Hindi patients who are Indian and the Muslim patients consider themselves Muslim the same way Jewish people consider themselves Jewish and don't say they're Russian—even though they're ethnically Russian Jews, but culturally they consider themselves to be Jewish and not Russian?"

Lydia laughed out loud and said, "Jesus Beth, now you've got *my* head spinning."

Beth smiled and shook her head in frustration as she sat down in the chair warmed by Lydia. She was about to take the phones off the lunch time answering service, when Lydia announced, "Oh, Dr. Arvind passed his medical board exam." She looked around to be sure the doctors and Mrs. Ajit were out of earshot and she added in a low voice, "He took it a few times, so it's good he finally passed."

Beth had been instructed to check that each patient's address and phone number were up to date; so when Nand Patel arrived for his appointment (even though he had just been in recently) Beth had to ask, "Is there any change to your home address or phone number?" She noticed Nand's wife walk toward Ruth's desk.

Nand said, "Do you want my *actual* address or my insurance address?"

She said wearily, "Your *actual* address is supposed to be the same as your insurance address."

Nand's nonchalant demeanor suddenly changed. He said, "Oh, well that's what I meant. My address is 2100 N. Line Street in Lansdale." He also gave his apartment number. Beth recognized the street address as one frequently given by Indian patients. Apparently there were apartment complexes in Lansdale and Hatfield where most, if not all, of the residents were Indian. Athough Beth knew that many of them actually lived in those very overcrowded apartments (as Dr. Vishnu had described); she suspected that others just lied about where they lived and used those street addresses and zip codes that indicated to state/federal agencies the low income level of that demographic. There had to be a reason why they lied about where they lived.

After Dr. Vishnu took Nand back, Beth told Ruth about what Nand had just said.

Ruth said, "Well his wife, Kinari was talking to me while he was talking to you. I had called her because her insurance rejected our claim for her last visit. So she said we had the wrong birth date for her."

"Oh my God! Not another one."

Ruth laughed and said, "Oh yes. Another one. So now I'll resubmit the claim with her new date of birth."

Beth just shook her head and turned to answer her phone.

"Hi Beth. This is Mrs. Martin."

"Hi Mrs. Martin." It was a young Muslim woman who always made appointments for her husband's parents. She had obviously Americanized her last name. And, as is typical with young Muslim women, her last name was different than her husband's last name. But her in-laws were Safia and Habib Khan—the same last name for an older Muslim couple. Beth wondered if, at some point, Muslim women were allowed to take the same last name as their husbands—maybe after a certain number of years of marriage.

Mrs. Martin said, "My mother, Safia Khan, is returning from India next week and I want to make an appointment for her because she is not feeling well."

Beth opened the chart and saw a note from the previous October. It read, "Mrs. Martin asked that Dr. Vishnu call her Monday or Tuesday with the results of Safia's FBT because she is leaving for India for 6 months." Safia had Coventry Cares/Health America (a Medicaid insurance).

Beth made the appointment for Safia. When she finished the call she turned to Ruth and said, "These patients live in India for the winter and then return to the United States in the spring for their doctors' appointments—paid for by our federal and state governments with the tax dollars of working Americans! There are people—American citizens—who cannot get Medicaid insurance because the government can only pay for so many bodies and yet these Indian patients leave our country; don't contribute to our economy; but they get Medicaid!"

Ruth shook her head, saying, "I know. I know."

Beth glanced down the hallway to be sure none of the doctors were heading toward the front desk and then she asked Ruth, "Why does Dr. Vishnu do all of his paperwork and scripts under the name of Dr. D?"

Ruth almost licked her chops and said, "He doesn't have a license to practice medicine."

"You're kidding!"

"No. He told me he was a general surgeon in India and then moved to Australia for a few years, before he came here."

"How did he wind up working with Dr. D?"

"Apparently they go to the same temple and they got to know each other. So Dr. D hired him and the deal is something like, he doesn't get paid as much as he thinks he deserves, but then he knows that he's lucky Dr. D covers for him and he never had to get his license to practice medicine because he does everything under D's name."

"Do the patients know?"

Ruth said emphatically, "No."

"So *that's* why he stamps the scripts with Dr. D's signature." She sat for a moment and then said, "This place is starting to make me sick."

Ruth laughed and said, "Well, you can see one of the doctors!"

Some of the pieces were starting to fit. Beth had observed how Dr. Vishnu enjoyed flaunting his knowledge of the finer things in life to the office staff. Travel, dining, wine, cars, higher institutions of learning—he knew and, in most cases, experienced the best in all categories. Beth had wondered, "So why would a renaissance man like Dr. Vishnu choose a sleepy town like Lansdale to settle in?" The White people, who chose Ajit Medical Center as their doctors, were not well-to-do. The practice seemed to draw White patients from nearby communities who had lived in the area for generations of low to middle income families, who thought a drive into Philadelphia was an excursion. Now she could see that the insidious growth of the Indian population made it easier for Dr. Vishnu to stay below the radar in a population of people who *also* wanted to float beneath the radar.

The next day Beth asked Lydia, "Do you know Dr. Vishnu doesn't have a license to practice medicine?"

Lydia flushed but didn't address it directly. Instead, she said, "Yeah that reminds me. The pharmaceutical sales reps usually come by in the mornings, but if you get a rep in the afternoon who asks for information about Dr. Vishnu, just tell them he's a P.A."

"A Physician's Assistant?" Beth asked.

"Yeah. Because otherwise they'll ask for his state license number to enter into their computer and you don't want to have to get into an explanation about any of that."

Beth was annoyed. She looked at Lydia and said, "And the patients don't know, do they?"

Lydia shook her head, as if to say "No."

Beth said, "That explains why all the pharma reps are always inviting Dr. D to dinners; because he's got *2-doctors' worth* of prescriptions being written under his name."

Lydia said, "Yeah. But ironically, Dr. Vishnu is the one who goes to all the pharma dinners."

Beth said, "As long as pharma companies are getting scripts written for their products, they don't care whose writing them. As long as the pharmacy is filling them, it's not a matter they have to get involved with."

On her drive home that night, Beth wondered, "Why are they so sure that no one on their staff is going to be alarmed by all the unethical and illegal stuff they do?"

She remembered learning about the caste system in India. The way she understood it, the caste system classifies people according to birthright. The family you are born into determines your place in society based on wealth, education and profession.

Beth thought, "They see Lydia, Ruth and I as below them. They assume we're too slow witted to pay attention to the fraudulent things they do. Even if they gave any one of us enough credit to notice what's going on, they know at least Ruth and I desperately need our jobs so why would we risk losing our jobs by blowing the whistle on them? After all, Kathy knew as early as my interview with her that I have an abusive husband, and I needed a job quickly. She said she told Dr. Arvind about my *situation*. Ruth has all kinds of health problems and she's worried that her husband might get laid off. The one I can't figure out is Lydia. She said her husband is an accountant with his own business and she doesn't *have* to work; she just *wants* to work. But it seems she has a new blouse or a new piece of jewelry on everyday; so I guess this job gives her play money . . . but if she doesn't need the job, shouldn't that be more of an incentive to report what's going on here? . . . and what about Kathy? She must have known what was going on after so many years . . . I think most people don't care about anything that doesn't directly affect their lives . . . and it starts when you're a kid . . . families hide the dirty laundry . . . looking the other way is part of our culture . . . Oh, who am I kidding with the holier-than-thou attitude . . . I didn't report Henry to the police in exchange for him sending me money every month."

As she rounded the bend into her neighborhood, Beth saw her neighbor Carrie getting out of her car. She followed her impulse to stop. She got out of her car and walked up to her; "Hi Carrie. How are you doing?"

Carrie frowned. "I'm doing as good as can be expected."

After a few minutes of small talk, Beth fought an impulse to ask Carrie if she found out anything more about *why* Charles did it. Then suddenly she heard herself asking, "Did they find out who was bullying Charles?" She regretted saying it when Carrie immediately welled up with tears and said, "The bus driver came forward and identified one kid who had gotten into a fight with Charles on the bus, but what can they do? The kid gets in a little bit of trouble and then it blows over and life . . . or I should say *his* life goes on." Her eyes were filled with tears when she looked at Beth. "Would you like to come in for a minute and talk?"

"Sure." Beth looked toward her house and Carrie noticed and said, "Oh, it's OK; you probably have to walk your dog."

"No. No really. He can wait a little bit."

Beth was surprised to see how sparsely furnished the house was, as she stood in the living room. She hesitated when Carrie turned to walk toward the kitchen.

"Come on," Carrie said, as she motioned for Beth to follow her. "Would you like a glass of wine?"

"Ah, sure, if you're having one."

Carrie reached for two glasses and put them on the kitchen table. "Sit. Sit down. Make yourself comfortable." Carrie popped a stopper off of a half empty liter bottle of white wine. She poured enough to fill each glass.

"Thanks," Beth said.

"Do you mind if I smoke?" Carrie asked.

"No. No go ahead."

Carrie lit a cigarette and took a long drag and held in the smoke until it streamed from her nostrils. "I found out something else that may have driven Charles to do what he did."

Beth remained silent.

Carrie said, "One night there's a knock at my door. It was still early; maybe 7:30 or something. Anyway I was dosing on the couch in there and I thought to myself, who could that be at this hour?" She made a wry smile and said, "I figured it wasn't my asshole ex-husband because he never knocked before he came in. I should have taken his key away a long time ago." She took another long drag and then drank down some wine like it was water. Then she continued. "So I peak out of the curtain at the front door and I see this woman standing there with a young girl. So I open the door. Under the porch light I can see that the young girl looks upset. You know that look when the mascara is a little runny under the eyes?"

"Yeah. I know what you mean."

"So I say, "Hello. Can I help you 'cause by then I'm thinking maybe their car broke down or something; I don't know." She drank down what was left in her glass and asked Beth, "Do you want another?"

Beth held up her glass that was still half full and said, "No. No thanks."

Carrie got up from the table and emptied the wine bottle into her glass. She put her cigarette out in the ashtray and immediately lit another one. "Well anyway I open the door and this young girl says, "Hi Mrs. Rowan. Can I talk to you for a minute?" And meanwhile her mother—I mean I assumed at this point that it was her mother—she's just standing there looking like she just lost her best friend. Well, since the girl called me by my name, I knew this must be the girl Charles was always meeting at the mall. So I said, 'Sure. Come in;' so the two of them come in the kitchen with me and I told them to have a seat. Then the girl sits down and starts to say something and then bursts out crying! So finally her mother says, 'I'm sorry Mrs. Rowan but my daughter is really upset about . . . about what happened to Charles.' I could tell she didn't know how to word it. So then I felt kinda bad for her and I just sat down next to the girl and put my hand on her arm and said, 'It's OK. Are you Leah?' And she looks at me all teary-eyed and says, 'Yes.' Now all this time I was thinking that she just wanted to meet me and she probably felt bad because for all I know, she never came to the service we had for him at the church. You know, it was just a small thing with his old man and me and some of our relatives who are still around; and probably a couple of his father's girlfriends for all I know . . ." She finished her cigarette and then pushed it hard against the ashtray. She picked up the empty wine bottle and said, "Jesus! These things go fast!" She got up from the kitchen table and opened the cabinet under the sink and knelt down to reach into the back of the cabinet. She pulled out a bottle of vodka and looked toward Beth with a devilish smile. As she stood up with some effort, she exhaled and said, "Hallaleuiah! Thank you Jesus." She looked toward Beth and said, "You want some?"

Beth finished her wine and felt a little buzzed. She didn't want to look like a prude but she really didn't want to drink anymore, so she finally said, "No. But you go ahead."

Carrie poured the vodka until it filled half of her wine glass. She must have felt a little self-conscious because she looked at Beth and said, "Hey, I know I'll cut down after a while but right now, it seems to be the only way I can sleep at night." Carrie sat down again and said, "Well, as it turns out, this girl Leah said she thinks she might have caused . . . how did she put it? . . . she said something like, 'I think I might have been the reason Charles did that' and then she starts sobbing. And I mean, she can't stop and I felt sorry for her for about a second, but then I took my hand away from her arm. Well I must have had some weird look on my face because her mother is now touching *my arm* and trying to comfort me I guess. I felt like I had the wind knocked out of me for a minute but then I finally said, 'What do you mean?' But this girl Leah can't stop crying, so then I yelled it . . . 'what do you mean?' And then she looks at me with her face all twisted up from crying and says that she thinks Charles was in love with her but then he found out she was pregnant from another boy. Well at that point, I just slumped back in my chair. I looked at her for a minute and I felt this anger inside me and I was tempted to slap her. I think I may have even raised my hand . . . I don't know . . . but then a minute later I just started crying. And then like three nutcases, we were all sitting there crying. Finally, Leah's mother pulled herself together and kind of calmed the two of us down and we just sat there . . . just not knowing what to say . . . but at the same time, not even caring that we were just silent. And the next thing I know I was saying, 'Thanks for coming to talk to me' because . . . I guess I was just glad to know another piece of the puzzle. I mean I still think that bullying stuff had something to do with it. And another thing I thought of right away; in fact that's why I was ready to rip his father's head off the day . . . *that* day . . . was that his goddam father didn't show up for the big Phillies game he was so excited about and I told Charles, 'Don't get too excited about it' . . . but of course he didn't listen . . . well . . . kids, you know . . . they can only take so much . . . they don't even know what they're doing sometimes when . . ." She started to cry and Beth moved to the chair next to Carrie and put her arm around her. After a few minutes, Carrie sat back and pushed her hair out of her face. Beth got up and tore off a couple of paper towels from the rack above the sink. She handed one to Carrie to wipe her face. "Thanks Beth. Thanks for listening to me."

"Of course. It's the least I can do Carrie."

"Well I just start rambling and . . . God what time is it?" She turned to look at the clock and said, "Jesus! You better take care of that dog of yours. I hope he didn't already make a mess in your house."

Beth said, "Oh he'll be alright. Don't worry about it."

"Let me walk you to the door Beth." They walked to the front door and Beth had just opened it, when Carrie said, "Hey, how do you like living here anyway?"

"Oh, it's good. Yeah. I like it."

Carrie asked, "Are you a nurse? I see you leaving for work on Saturday mornings in scrubs?"

Beth said, "No. I just work at the front desk in a doctor's office. I just had the idea to ask if I could wear scrubs to work because it would save money on buying clothes. The other receptionist doesn't wear scrubs but I like it."

"It's a good idea. And you don't have to waste time in the morning figuring out what to wear."

"Yeah, right."

"What's the name of the doctor?" Carrie asked.

"Ajit Medical Center. It's a father and son and another doctor—Dr. Vishnu. Have you heard of them?"

Carrie said, "Oh yeah. I have an older lady friend who goes to them. She's lived in Lansdale all her life and at this point, all she has to talk about is her health."

Beth asked, "What's her name? I might know her."

Carrie said, "Eleanor Hahn."

"I know who she is!" Beth said. She's a regular.

"That doesn't surprise me." Carrie said.

"What . . . what does she think of them—I mean Dr. Ajit."

"As far as I know she likes her doctor. It must be the father because he's been her doctor for years. She said he's hard to understand because he has a heavy accent. I guess they're Indian or something like that?"

"Yeah. They're Indian."

Carrie asked, "Do you like working for them?"

Beth was tempted to say no but instead she said, "They're OK. Anyway, it's a job, right?"

"I hear ya. Well, listen, I'll let you go. Your dog is probably itching for a walk."

Beth laughed a little and after an awkward pause, she said, "Well, take it easy and I'm right next door if you need me."

"Thanks Beth. Goodnight."

As Beth walked to her car, she could smell the aroma of cigarette smoke in the cool evening air coming from Carrie's direction as she stood smoking on her front porch.

Beth became more depressed as the evening wore on. She finished washing her dinner dishes and stood looking at one plate, one fork, one knife and a frying pan in the dish rack. The last time she talked to Henry on the phone he told her he was driving to Rhode Island to pick up oxygen tanks that he had bought on eBay. His new hobby was deep sea diving. He asked Beth if she wanted to join him on a trip to Florida where she could learn how to dive. It was an easy "no" for Beth because there were recent stories in the news about husbands killing their wives while diving in the depths of the ocean. This, of course, did nothing to endear her to Henry. The conversation had escalated into an argument, with Henry yelling into the phone and not allowing Beth to get a word in edgewise once he was off in a rage. He hung up on her after he said, "Maybe I'll call you when I get back from Florida."

Beth picked up the phone and then hung it up. She picked it up again and dialed.

"Hello?"

"Hi Mom. It's Beth."

"Oh Hi honey. How are you?" Beth was happy to hear the warmth in her mother's voice.

"Good. I was wondering if it would be OK if I drove down the shore on Saturday after work and stayed overnight."

"Sure. Let me just check with your father."

Beth listened to her mother move the phone away from her face and ask faintly, "Is it OK with you if Beth comes down on Saturday?" Beth hated the way her mother was so old fashioned that she could never give a definitive answer or make a decision, without first consulting her husband.

"Yeah. Why not?' Beth heard her father say.

"Beth?"

"Yeah?"

"Your father said it's OK."

"Oh good. Can I bring Jake?"

Again her mother moved the phone away from her mouth and asked her father the question. Then she said, "Yeah. He said it's OK to bring Jake." Then she quickly added, "But you have to put him in a crate when you're at the beach."

"OK." Actually, Beth hated to put Jake in a crate. The only reason she had one was for her stays at the shore house. She told her mother she would probably get there in the late afternoon on Saturday.

On Friday night, Beth packed a suitcase for the shore. On Saturday morning, it was raining lightly but she didn't let that change her mind about going to the beach. She needed a changed of scenery more than anything. She rushed to get out of the house by 7:10 a.m. She would have to swing by the house after work to get Jake, his crate and her suitcase.

Chapter 18

O N SATURDAY MORNINGS, Beth arrived at the office just before 7:30 a.m. The parking lot was always empty at that hour, except for one of Dr. Vishnu's vehicles—whichever one he decided to drive to work. He had a van; a yellow motorcycle that he drove in spring and summer when weather allowed; at least two Mercedes cars (one was "previously owned," and he bought that for his 16 year old son); and an older, non-descript Toyota sedan.

Lydia had told Beth that Dr. Vishnu was always the first doctor to arrive everyday and the last doctor to leave at night.

It was usually the same routine. Beth would unlock the door to the office building (because Dr. Vishnu always locked it again after he entered) and then she walked up a small flight of stairs and unlocked the door to their office (again, because Dr. Vishnu would lock the door behind him).

Often, an Indian couple was just leaving Dr. Vishnu's exam room and their discomfort at Beth's arrival was palpable. After all, office hours didn't start until 8:00 and the couples never had scheduled appointments. It was always the same routine—the couple would slowly approach the front desk, but never stop to check out as most patients do. Instead, the woman forced a pleasant grin, while the man did not even look at Beth; as they continued toward the exit. Dr. Vishnu would catch up with them and they chatted in Hindi for a few minutes. They always left before Dr. Arvind arrived. By now, Beth figured it was related to his life insurance lab business; but sometimes she wondered if Dr. Vishnu might have performed abortions.

If Dr. Vishnu wasn't conducting one of these mysterious early morning patient visits; Beth smelled the aroma of Indian food coming from his office when she arrived. She would call out, "Hello Dr. Vishnu," but he never answered so she assumed he was quietly eating his breakfast. She stopped calling out "hello" when she realized he might be praying; after she noticed a small statue of what she assumed to be a Hindu god on his bookcase; ironically sitting behind his stack of Fed Ex envelopes and paperwork for his lab business. The statue was only 3 inches high and it was a skinny, gilted gold man with multiple serpent-like arms. There were small pieces of paper near the statue, with handwritten prayers. Some of the writing was English and some was written in an Indian language.

When he emerged from his office, Dr. Vishnu would say in a very friendly voice, "Good morning Beth. How are you today morning?"

"Good. How are you Dr. Vishnu?" They would chat for just a couple of minutes and then he continued down the hallway to his exam room. She couldn't figure out why someone, who obviously spoke English very well, would use the phrase "today morning." She heard him use the phrase with patients and she began to think he did it to sound quaint. Dr. Vishnu and Dr. Deepak Ajit played the role of old-fashioned country doctor-types for their few White patients. They certainly fit the part physically—Dr. Vishnu appeared pleasingly plump beneath his white lab coat and his bald head and glasses gave him a wise, professorial air. Dr. Deepak Ajit had an easy, warm smile, and he could chat up anyone with the ease of a smooth salesman. Conversely, their demeanor with Indian patients was clearly more authoritative. The Indian patients seemed to revere them in much the same way that most Americans used to revere doctors. For the many patients who had some sort of scam going, (whether it was Medicaid/Medicare or insurance fraud; or abusing or selling prescription meds), they were quite cognizant of the doctors' power to enable their schemes.

Dr. D's life was naturally immersed in the Indian culture but, with the White patients and pharmaceutical sales reps, he spoke of his passion for golf to show that he deferred a good portion of his leisure time to a White man's hobby. Beth thought they made quite a perfect business trio because the addition of Dr. Arvind Ajit brought them into the new world of healthcare with updated technology—electronic medical records and a new computer system—and new contracts with the care management divisions of insurance companies that were mutually lucrative by driving patients to the office to maintain wellness.

Beth discovered that Dr. Arvind's forte included "ghost appointments." She would notice, at the end of most days, the names of half a dozen patients pop up onto the computer screen as if they had appointments at 3:30; 4:00; 4:30; etc.; yet Beth knew those patients had never been to the office that day. By creating appointments and visit summaries, Dr. Arvind could then bill the insurance carriers for the appointments. He knew his patients would never pay attention to the benefit summaries they received in the mail from their insurance company. As long as the "balance due" indicated $0; they just discarded it.

As the only son, Dr. Arvind would inherit his father's medical practice and all of his patients; so he didn't have to try to win people over with his personality. However, he wanted to drive new patients to the office to increase his income. He did so by prescribing the medication they wanted, whether it was for legitimate use or illegal abuse. He wrote scripts for narcotic pain medication; amphetamines; drugs for ADHD (and other stimulants), anti-anxiety meds (and other depressants). Once the word got out that a doctor didn't hesitate to prescribe these meds to patients (even on their first visit to the office as a new patient, which is always a red flag for abuse) the number of new patient visits grew.

One of the two patients scheduled for the 8:00 time slot walked up to the front desk.

Beth said, "Good morning Carol."

She grunted at Beth, "It's not a good morning until I have my coffee." Since morning appointments were for fasting blood tests, some of the patients were a bit grumpy because they hadn't eaten or had their morning coffee.

"Is your address and phone number the same as last time?" Beth asked.

"Oh yeah. I've been living in the same house in Lansdale for 35 years and I'm not leaving until they have to carry me out."

Beth laughed a little.

Dr. Vishnu stood at the entrance to the waiting area and motioned for Carol to come back. "How are you today morning?"

Carol repeated, "You know me. I'll be better when I'm done here and I can have my coffee."

Beth heard the slight beep that went off whenever the back door was opened. She turned to the left and was surprised to see Dr. D and Mrs. Ajit walking in. Neither of them typically worked on Saturday. Beth asked, "Isn't Dr. Arvind coming in today?"

Dr. D said, "No. He and Bijal (his wife) are going to New Jersey for the weekend to visit her parents."

"Well, it's nice to see you here," Beth lied. She knew she wouldn't get out of there until close to 1:00 because Dr. D was always slow to write up his clinical visit summaries, which included the lab requisitions that accompanied the blood tubes that Beth processed and labeled. That was one good thing about him seeing fewer patients than the other doctors—less visit summaries that he had to write and that Beth had to wait for.

"Hi Mrs. Ajit. This is a surprise."

Mrs. Ajit made her way over to her desk with her usual limping gait. "I have to finish up some billing work." It was odd for Mrs. Ajit to make a statement that was so indiscreet. Although she had become more visibly involved in the billing since Kathy retired, Mrs. Ajit apparently had the unlikely hope that Lydia and Beth wouldn't know just how involved she was. They wanted Beth and Lydia to think that Ruth was solely responsible for that job even though Beth often heard Mrs. Ajit asking Dr.

Vishnu about a patient visit and they would sometimes disagree about a code used to indicate the purpose of the visit. Insurance companies and Medicare/Medicaid paid more or less for a patient visit, depending upon the code used. Most often, there was more than one reason (thus more than one code) for a patient visit. Mrs. Ajit could view the codes (used by the doctors) on her laptop and she would adjust the codes and then bill the insurance company or Medicare/Medicaid accordingly; always adding bogus codes to increase their reimbursements.

A young woman walked up to the front desk. "Hi. My name is Nita Patel and I have to see Dr. Vishnu."

Nita did not have a scheduled appointment. She was apparently in good health and quite pleasant.

Beth said, "Well, we're very busy this morning. Are you sick?"

Nita said, "My husband talked to Dr. Vishnu last night and he said I could come to the office this morning at 8:00."

Beth said, "OK. I guess Dr. Vishnu forgot to tell me. When he finishes up with the patient he's seeing, I'll tell him you're here."

"OK. Thanks." They chatted for a few minutes and Nita mentioned that she "went swimming this morning." Beth opened her chart, in the meantime, and said, "I can see that you haven't been here in a while so I'll have to update your records. Do you have health insurance?"

Nita said, "No. I'll pay cash."

Dr. Vishnu was not at all surprised when he saw Nita. In fact, he took her to his exam room, ahead of the next scheduled patient. When he finished seeing her, Beth heard the prescription printer going. It meant Nita was getting a script for pain medication or some psychotherapeutic drug. She got up and glanced at the script before Dr. Vishnu had a chance to snatch it up and stamp it with Dr. D's signature. It was a prescription for Oxycodone (a narcotic pain med) with a quantity of 90 tablets and 3 refills.

Dr. Vishnu said to Beth, "Nita needs a work absence note."

"Oh sure." Beth opened the template for a work absence letter and Dr. Vishnu dictated, "Nita was involved in a motor vehicle accident and injured her left ankle; possible fracture. Advised 5 weeks off with bed-rest. Patient will get Xray of left ankle and return to office in 5 weeks." After the letter printed, Dr. Vishnu stamped it with Dr. D's signature. Beth was certain there was never any motor vehicle accident. In fact, if a patient *was* in an auto accident; she and Lydia were required to get their auto insurance information so the auto insurance carrier could be billed for the visit.

Beth asked, "Do you have auto insurance?"

Dr. Vishnu said, "No. No. That is not necessary. It's OK. Just give her the work absence letter."

Beth handed her the letter and Nita said, "Thanks sweetie." She turned and walked toward the front door in a perfectly normal gait, with absolutely no indication of an ankle injury. Beth suspected that Nita and her husband were going to India for 5 weeks.

About 2 hours later, Catherine Duggan called. "Call me Lee," she reminded Beth in her husky smoker's voice.

"Oh that's right. Sorry Lee." Catherine or "Lee" was the wife of a successful local businessman, Howard (Buzz) Duggan. His business was horticulture and landscaping. Their employees were mostly Hispanic, with the exception of a couple of their children who had gotten involved in the business. Lee said, "I'm having one of my guys bring over Ishmael. I already talked to Dr. Vishnu on his cell, and he said he'll squeeze him in. Just charge his visit and any prescriptions to my insurance." When her two Hispanic employees showed up, one of them pointed to the guy next to him and said, "This is Luis." Luis was holding a wet towel against one of his eyes. Beth figured that he served as Luis's interpreter. She said, "Lee said his name was Ishmael." The interpreter looked confused. Then Beth realized that "Ishmael" was probably just code talk between Lee and Dr. Vishnu. The interpreter handed Beth a piece of paper with the name of an insurance company and a patient identification number. Beth brought up the chart for Lee Duggan and sure enough, it was *her* insurance identification number. Like many patients, Lee used her personal health insurance identification card like a credit card. They didn't think twice about handing it to one of the doctors (or to Beth or Lydia to give to the doctors) to charge someone else's prescription or office visit to the health insurance of another. Just before he took Luis back, Dr. Vishnu whispered to Beth, "Just put this on the schedule as an office visit for Lee." So now, even the clinical visit summary would reflect an office visit for Lee Duggan, for whatever malady Luis suffered from. Luis left the office with his interpreter, along with one of those printed prescriptions for narcotic pain medicine, which would be paid for by Lee's insurance company.

Throughout the morning, 8 patients came in to pick up their monthly prescriptions for Oxycodone. Narcotic pain meds, if prescribed responsibly, are intended for short term use; but in this practice, long term use was the norm; and refills of narcotics were routine. Many patients were getting refills after just 3 weeks or less in some cases.

"Good morning. How can I help you?" Beth asked; even though she knew why the woman was there. The pharmacist from Top Shelf Pharmacy in Hatfield, named Prejah, was standing in front of her. She came in at the beginning of each month for the same reason.

"I'm here to pick up the prescriptions." She was an Indian woman (late 30s or 40-ish years old) who always bore the typical coy expression of young Indian women. Several months ago, when Beth had just started working there, Prejah had introduced herself as a pharmacist, who owned Top Shelf Pharmacy with her husband—also a pharmacist. She came in every month to pick up 3 prescriptions: one for Oxycodone and two for different strengths of Fentanyl patches. The prescriptions were allegedly for the same patient, Madhu Patel.

Dr. Vishnu had just brought a patient up to the front desk when he saw Prejah and they stood by the tiger painting in the waiting area and chatted heartily for several minutes in Hindi. When they finished,

Prejah approached Beth with a facial expression of contrived pleas-
antness and said, "Dr. Arvind said he would have my scripts ready to
pick up this morning." Beth looked in the little black box for scripts
but didn't find anything for her. She said, "I'll have to ask Dr. D. about
this." Just then, Dr. D came out of the kitchen and saw Prejah and said,
"Oh, here, Dr. Arvind told me you were going to pick these up today."
He took out his prescription pad and wrote out 3 scripts, which Beth
intercepted before she handed them to Prejah. As Dr. D spoke to her
in Hindi for a few moments, Beth looked at the scripts, 180 tablets
of Oxycodone and the other two scripts for each of the most potent
strengths of Fentanyl patches at a quantity of 60 each.

One day Beth had decided to ask her local pharmacist about the
dosage and quantity of Oxycodone and Fentanyl that Prejah was getting each month. She didn't want to tell the pharmacist the real reason
she was asking so she made up a story that her grandmother was getting hospice care for terminal cancer and she wanted to understand the
appropriate dosage of those drugs because she was worried the hospice
nurses might be giving her grandmother too much.

The pharmacist explained that the combination of a narcotic pain
med, along with Fentanyl patches, was an extremely potent combination of therapy for pain relief. He cautiously remarked, "In fact, it's a
drug cocktail used only at the end-of-life stage."

Yet Prejah had been coming in each month for the same prescriptions, allegedly for the same patient. Beth thought, "If Madhu Patel
existed, her liver and other organs should be donated for scientific
research due to their ability to metabolize a toxic drug cocktail for so
long, while supporting the other bodily functions of an allegedly near-
death patient."

It didn't make sense that a pharmacist, who owns a pharmacy,
would drive over to the doctor's office in a nearby town to pick up hard
copy prescriptions because it would be much more efficient to receive
the scripts electronically. The only possible reason is that they did not
want an electronic trail. Beth felt certain the medicine, allegedly for

Madhu Patel, was being sold to other patients and maybe Dr. Arvind was getting a kickback.

It was close to 1:00 by the time Beth finished her paperwork and then took out the trash. One good thing about Dr. D working on a Saturday was that he dragged the trash cans to the corner of the property, where it sat ready for Monday pickup. Dr. Arvind apparently considered that duty to be below him and Beth was the one who had to drag the large trash cans to the corner on Saturdays. She went back inside to wash her hands and lock up. In fifteen minutes, she was home, where she quickly ate a peanut butter and jelly sandwich and then packed up her car. The rain had continued all morning and a sudden downpour drenched her and Jake in the brief time it took to get into the car.

Until she reached the Ben Franklin Bridge, her mind had been cluttered with a growing discomfort about working for Ajit Medical Center. So far, she hadn't gotten any nibbles on the resumes she was sending out for jobs she had applied for on the internet.

It wasn't until she was on Route 55 going south, that she started to relax. She was looking forward to seeing everyone. It wouldn't be a *beach/bars/boys* kind of weekend. Those ended long ago. Nowadays it was an opportunity to visit with her brother and his wife and play on the beach with her nieces and nephews. They brought the kids to the shore almost every weekend; so if Beth wanted to see them, she had to endure her parents and her sister as part of the package. After all, it was their house. Her sister and her parents had bought the house in North Wildwood, New Jersey almost 20 years before. The opportunity arose when their daughter-in-law's grandparents had the need to sell it quickly. It seemed her grandfather had suddenly taken a turn for the worse mentally. He was always an opinionated guy, but he had begun to turn violent when others disagreed. And the monsters he saw in the yard at dusk were probably just ghosts of his dead war buddies, but he hit his wife again and again on the day she said he was imagining things. She had to move out to a small apartment, and he spent the rest of his life in a Veterans Administration nursing home. Beth was surprised to hear her sister-in-law's family talk so openly about the domestic abuse; and even take action against it. It was very different from the way Beth's family hid their own dark secrets of domestic violence.

The house was in the quiet, family section of North Wildwood and it was one of several holdouts from the 1950s. So far, there were just three tear-downs in the 4 block radius that surrounded it. Three-story, cookie-cutter houses, with large wooden decks in the front, replaced the old, two story, flat-roofed Cape Cods with the original wide siding and concrete porches.

A house at the shore was a lifelong dream for Beth's father and a good real estate investment for her sister Laura, who had become a successful career woman. It wasn't enough that Laura had always been their obvious favorite; but now she made it possible for them to realize their dream of a shore house. Laura was now a financial consultant who traveled globally to research investments for her firm. She made a huge salary and worked 14 hour days; but for all of her travels and money, she was oddly content to spend a great deal of her free time with her parents. She socialized with a few coworkers and had the occasional, short-lived romance. From what she told Beth, Laura apparently rarely had problems with the men in her life. In fact, it was quite the opposite of Beth's experience. Men seemed to chase Laura, while Beth chased men; and it was Laura who did the breaking up, while Beth had her heart broken again and again. Beth even secretly thought that she was better looking than Laura so she couldn't understand why men treated her so badly. She finally decided it must have had everything to do with the fact that Laura was a "daddy's girl" and women who are treated well by their fathers will expect the same treatment from the men in their lives; whereas, Beth always felt her father's cold resentment, even though she tried to convince herself that he loved her. As a teenager, there was something in his hugs and kisses that disturbed her—the affection felt fake and his physical closeness felt scary. She wanted him to love her but she didn't want him near her for more than a moment.

She could never understand why she didn't like to be in the house alone with him but fortunately those occasions were rare.

There was still something that bothered Beth about Laura's relationship with her father. Her mother would have bouts of atrial fibrillation; usually at the shore house. Her father would take her to the hospital where she would be observed until her heart beat returned to normal. Once, they kept her overnight and Laura was pouring her father's coffee the next morning, as they chatted and laughed together. When Beth walked in on the scene, which would appear perfectly normal to most people, it gave Beth a disturbing feeling. The two of them looked like husband and wife. It turned her stomach. Maybe it was because Laura had told Beth about a weekend at the shore during the winter months when she had joined her parents to check on the house to see how it was faring in the snowy weather. "We didn't want to turn the heat on upstairs, so the three of us slept in Mom and Dad's room." There was just one double bed in their room.

Beth had been horrified. "What? Why didn't you sleep in one of the other bedrooms?"

Laura gave her a familiar blank look. Beth repeated, "You slept in the same bed with Mom and Dad?

"Yeah."

Beth just shook her head.

The shore house was the domain of these three close allies. Her mother still fawned all over Laura and the shore house was a chance for Laura and her father to take turns holding court. While Beth played with the kids in the ocean and built sand castles on the beach, Laura sat with the adults and chatted all afternoon. Happy hours started at the beach in the late afternoon and continued back at the house. That's when Laura would brag about her latest travels and what she had managed to accomplish at work since they last saw each other. After a couple martinis, her father took over as the center of attention and that's how it went for the rest of the night.

For all the pain he caused her, Beth knew there was no one more important to her mother than her father; and Beth grew to understand this was a burden for her father. Although she was beautiful and intelligent, her mother was so insecure and anxious that it crippled her. Her life's purpose seemed to be keeping tabs on where her husband was at any time of the day or night. One of the things Beth's mother had cried to her about years before was, "Your father doesn't even let me have any friends." Beth now believed that it was her mother's choice not to make time for friends because her mother worried if she went out to socialize with friends, it would mean that her husband could go out and socialize with friends—like the old saying: "What's good for the goose is good for the gander;" so her mother chose to stay at home and they only socialized with family or with the occasional neighbors. Beth was sadly aware that she was the same way with Henry. She was clingy and anxious and ironically, the more abusive he was, the more anxious and clingy she became.

Ever since he retired, her father couldn't leave the house without her mother feeling anxious about where he might really be going. At least when he worked, she believed he was at work. He called every night when he was leaving the office to let her know he was on his way home. On the few occasions when he had to travel for work for a couple of days, they had horrific fights because her mother would accuse him of lying about where he was really going. Her mother constantly repeated the telling of the infamous fight when; as her mother tells it, "He said he had a dinner meeting for work and he came home at 2:00 in the morning with lipstick on his collar." Beth wondered which violent fight was a result of that incident.

Beth always had an uneasy feeling that her mother was befriending her competition with Laura and that feeling was somehow validated when Beth saw her mother behave the same way toward Eileen, the daughter-in-law who could do no wrong in the eyes of her father. Lots of families have them—the daughter-in-law who becomes the crush of the father-in-law. Eileen was his new favorite. The one thing Beth liked about this was that Eileen trumped Laura in his eyes. Of course, that was only until Eileen wasn't around and Laura was. He seemed to have his favorite-of-the-moment.

Eileen managed a restaurant in center city Philadelphia and she apparently knew all there was to know about gourmet food and wine. She was sociable and charming, and quite attractive to boot. But the icing on the cake was the filet mignon and lobsters that she brought to the shore for everyone to feast on, each time she visited with her brother and their kids. Her father would often say, "I'm at the age where eating and drinking are the only pleasures I have left." Everyone would laugh (even her mother, who failed to see the irony in it, or maybe she did, but the statement made her feel safe—like women and sex were in the distant past).

When her brother and Eileen, and their kids, descended on the place every weekend, it was Beth who became the scapegoat for tension. Her mother was not the sort of woman who should have been hosting a gang of adults and children at a shore house. She was rigid, routine, obsessive compulsive and cheap. Children running through the house; leaving half empty soda cans behind (that she had paid for); chasing each other through the shrubs outside and occasionally breaking a screen or knocking over a hidden bucket of stinky sea water that contained their treasures of sand crabs, guppies or dead frogs, raised her mother's ire. Sometimes she yelled at the children, but usually, she took it out on Beth. "Did you leave this glass of juice on the table?" "Did your dog break this screen by jumping on it?"

"*No!*" Beth would cry out emphatically. "Are you kidding? . . . Isn't it obvious that one of the kids did it Mom?"

Then her mother would say, "Don't you talk to me like that!" and she would turn to Beth's father, angry or teary-eyed and say, "Do you hear how she talks to me?"

Her father was only too quick to end the hassle. He didn't want to hear her mother goading him on; the kids got on his nerves too; and he wanted to enjoy the drinking and eating parts of the weekend without the interruption of her mother's complaints.

Beth was an easy target and it was certainly no loss if she packed up and left. She had insidiously become the dark sheep of the family. And she felt it. They made her feel like she was a big loser; or maybe she already felt that way, but the shore weekends managed to confirm it. She had a troubled marriage; a job well below her education level; and she was a subliminal reminder of her parents' dark past. She didn't stand a chance. Her father would make the "ugly face" at Beth. His eyes squinted and he grit his teeth as he came at her, "We're not going to put up with your shit Beth. You either cut it out or you can leave."

"Alright. I'll just leave!" she would cry out as she grabbed at her belongings and shoved them back into a suitcase.

"Good. The sooner the better," her father would reply.

It would have served her better to move away from her parents and her sister and just enjoy superficial holiday visits; but Beth wanted to be around her brother and his kids because it seemed they brought the only joy into her life. Now she only ventured to the shore house a few times during the summer season; always hoping for a better outcome. She was so worn out emotionally, that she was certain this would be a good weekend. She had no fight left in her. She would let her mother yell at her and blame her for whatever she was angry about this weekend. Beth promised herself she would let it all roll off.

She could smell the sea air coming off the bay. After a slow drive down Atlantic Avenue for 30 blocks, she turned left onto Magnolia Avenue, where she searched for a parking space. The street was quiet because everyone was at the beach at 4:30 on a Saturday afternoon— almost everyone.

"Hi Mom," Beth said tentatively, while trying to assess her mother's mood. She had been dozing in a chair on the porch with a paperback book in her lap.

"Hi honey," her mom said sleepily.

"Can you do me a favor and hold Jake's leash for a minute while I use the bathroom?"

"Sure." Her mother stayed in the chair and slid the leather strap of Jake's leash over her hand. Jake wagged his tail and put his paw on her leg. Her mother pet him and he thought this might mean he could jump onto her lap.

"No. No. Get down."

Beth said, "Jake, stop it. He's just happy to be out of the car."

"Did you run into traffic?"

"Yeah. I guess it's all the families heading down for a week of vacation and you know they always get a late start on Saturday by the time they pack up kids and bikes and everything else." Beth looked at her watch. "I guess it added another half hour to the drive so it wasn't too bad."

"Are you heading down to the beach?"

"Not at this point. By the time I walk Jake and feed him and get my stuff out of the car, they'll all be heading back."

Her mom said, "I don't know about that. The girls (referring to Laura and Eileen) just came back for snacks and wine and beer for a happy hour on the beach."

"Oh," Beth sounded interested, until she thought about stuffing Jake into a crate while she pranced down to the beach. That would mean trouble; because he would start yelping and that would surely set her mother off. She changed the subject, "Hey mom, I *have* to go to the bathroom so . . ."

"Well go. Go. I'm not stopping you."

It was a little after 5:00 by the time Beth had settled in and by now, her mother was sitting in the living room watching the news.

"Can you believe a guy walked into the gas station at 50th Street and Atlantic Avenue and robbed the guy at the counter and then hit him over the head with a hammer?" Her mother was always quick to report the latest horror story in the news.

"Oh my God, did he kill him?"

"No. In fact, the guy tried to chase the robber but he was bleeding so heavily that he passed out near the gas pumps and one of the customers called 911. And now they're saying he was released from the hospital already."

Beth shook her head. "It's a crazy world isn't it? You know the other day I . . ."

"Shhh!" Her mother waved her hand at Beth. "Let me hear this." Her mother was transfixed by what sounded like the beginning of a story about another horrific crime.

At the commercial break, Beth tried to change to a more pleasant subject. "Is everybody down this weekend?"

"Yeah. We've got a full house as usual, so you'll have to sleep on the couch."

"OK. No problem." Beth was never allotted a room at the shore house to call her own. Her brother and Eileen had a bedroom and their kids had their own room too. Her parents slept down the hall from them. Long ago, the house had been converted into a duplex so the staircase to the second floor was on the outside of the house. Her sister had her own separate apartment on the second floor, with two bedrooms. Beth rarely opted to stay in that second bedroom because, on the few occasions she did, an argument inevitably broke out between her and Laura over some petty issue. One time Laura was angry because Beth was getting ready to leave on Sunday night without first cleaning Laura's toilet and shower. Beth argued that she had only used the toilet twice—once during the night and early Sunday morning. The rest of the time she had used the toilet downstairs. She hadn't even showered in Laura's bathroom because she liked to use the outside shower.

"Anything new with you?" her mother asked.

For a moment, Beth was tempted to tell her mother about all the craziness at work. With everyone else out of the house, it seemed like a good, rare opportunity to have a heart-to-heart talk. She felt a little awkward about broaching the subject. Her mother was likely to tell her to just do her job and don't worry about what's going on around her. "It'll only get you into trouble, so stay out of it" she could hear her mother saying. But she wanted to get it off her chest. Still, there was the possibility it could turn out to be disappointing.

Beth leaned forward on the couch where she was sitting next to her mother. She turned toward her mother and said, "Mom, can you believe one of the doctors at work doesn't even have a medical license?"

"How do you know that?" Her mother asked calmly.

"This woman, Ruth, who does the billing told me."

"Well how does she know?"

"She said Mrs. Ajit, the older doctor's wife, told her."

"Well, who knows, that's probably true with a lot of these foreign doctors."

Beth thought, "There she goes, making light of the problem so she can just change the subject; like that'll make it go away."

Her mother thought, "Oh no. Here she goes again, sticking her nose where it doesn't belong and, in the end, she'll be the one who gets into trouble."

Beth said defensively, "No Mom. I mean, yeah, it happens, but it's got to be illegal to treat patients and lead them to believe that you're a licensed physician when you aren't."

"Just let it go Beth."

"Well there's other stuff going on too."

"Like what?" her mother said with irritation and doubt in her voice.

"Like insurance fraud—people sharing health insurance cards like credit cards; and people lying about their identity."

"What do you mean, lying about their identity?" Her mother sounded like the defense attorney for the doctors.

Beth stood up. She didn't want to sit next to her mother anymore. She started to get loud. "They change their dates of birth in order to qualify for Medicare and they get Medicaid for headaches and hemorrhoids and they don't even live in this country!"

Her mother looked at her quizzically. Beth wasn't sure if she was really listening to what she was saying. She continued in the hope of getting a reaction. "They use false dates of birth, and they use the names and social security numbers of people who died or . . ."

Her mother interrupted, "Don't get involved in this Beth."

Beth was incredulous, "Why?"

"Shh . . . Shh" her mother reached for the remote and squinted to find the volume control. "Wait, I wanna hear this." She turned the volume up so loud that it infuriated Beth.

"It's just like you Mom to pretend bad stuff isn't happening—just brush it under the rug or hide it in the closet and don't let anybody think that anything is wrong. You're like all the women of your generation who . . ." She stopped herself.

"Who what?"

Beth's heart was pounding. She knew she had crossed a line. She was silent for a moment.

Her mother remained seated, but finally lowered the volume on the remote and snarled, "You know, you've had a bug up your ass for the past 40 years and no wonder you can't find a decent job and you can't get along with your husband."

Beth welled up with tears and flopped into a chair and started to cry. After a moment, her mother said, "I'm sorry."

Beth looked at her and said, "Do you know that the little boy next door to me committed suicide because he was being bullied at school?"

Her mother swallowed hard and her voice got shaky with emotion. "I know. You told me. But what does that have to do with this?"

Beth was crying. "Wait a minute. I have to blow my nose." She walked into the bathroom to get a tissue. She blew her nose and wiped her face and quickly returned to the living room because she feared her momentary absence would be an easy out for her mother—a chance to turn up the volume on the television again.

She stood in front of her mother and pleaded, "I'm trying to say that it just seems that everyone looks the other way and that's why there's so much bad stuff happening in this world."

Beth was hopeful that she had touched a nerve, as her mother's silence seemed to indicate. But then she blurted out, "Oh grow up Beth."

Beth's heart sunk. "Are you *serious*?"

"You're at the shore, so just shut up and have a good time."

"God! I can't believe how cold you are to me after all those times when I defended you."

"Defended me from what?"

"From Dad; that's what!" Beth glared at her.

Her mother glared at her for a moment, and then snarled, "You're my daughter, so I have to love you; but I don't like you."

Beth stood still in stunned silence.

"Now go somewhere and let me watch the news in peace."

Beth left the room and went into the kitchen and poured herself a glass of wine from a bottle that was already open. Then she quietly opened the back door and took Jake with her to sit in a chair on the back porch.

It was almost 7:00 when she heard the kids' voices and soon the whole group of sandy, happy people, with tousled hair and wet bathing suits was milling around the small, grassy yard surrounding a large patio. As usual, everyone seemed to talk at once.

"Hi Beth. I didn't know you were coming down."

"Whose showering first?"

"I will."

"Wow. That's a first. He must be growing up."

"Hi Aunt Beth."

"Hi sweetie."

"Do you wanna beer?"

"How are you Beth?"

"Good. Good. How are you Eileen?"

"Hi Beth."

"Hi Dad."

"Hey, I don't want to ruin the party, but what are we having for dinner?"

"Ice cream!"

"Hey, you'd like that wouldn't you?"

"Yep."

Eileen said, "I marinated some chicken in the fridge."

"Well fire up the grill."

"Dad, it's a gas grill. It won't take long."

"I know. But let's get it started."

"You just ate about 3 pounds of cheese and crackers at the beach!"

"Yeah, but now I want real food."

"How come you didn't come to the beach Aunt Beth?"

"I just got down a little while ago and by the time I walked Jake and everything I just decided to sit outside."

"With your glass of wine?"

"Yeah, why not?"

"You guys were doing the same thing at the beach."

"So why didn't you join us?"

"I guess I was lazy. Plus I didn't think you'd be down there this late or I would have gone down."

"Aunt Beth, can we take Jake for a walk?"

"Yeah, but . . ."

"Not now. You have to take your shower first."

"Ahh mom."

Sometimes the happy chaos provided the diversion needed to change a subject or break up tension. That night, it made it easy for Beth and her mother to subtly avoid each other and even wish each other goodnight in passing, as Beth settled under a blanket on the couch, and her mother reminded her father and brother to lock the back door whenever they came in to go to bed. The two of them would sit out there talking way past midnight.

In the early morning, her parents discreetly opened and closed the bathroom door, as they took turns showering and dressing for the 8:00 mass. They appeared in the living room—her father in pressed khaki pants and a crisp, striped shirt—her mother in an ankle length beige skirt and a pink polo shirt under a white crocheted sweater. They whispered good morning and quietly shut the front door. It was only 7:40, but her mother was obsessed by the idea of getting a good parking space that would provide a clean getaway for their early departure from mass. Beth credited her mother with giving her the great gift of faith. It was the one true thing, outside of her family, that her mother confidently held dear. She often repeated the story of how she dragged her father to church, after years of ambiguity on his part, after his father's sudden death of a heart attack at the age of 42. Yet it now seemed that her mother was more preoccupied with avoiding the crowds in the church parking lot because she insisted they exit the mass immediately after receiving Holy Communion. To Beth, this was the only deeply personal part of the mass because each person could just kneel or sit and quietly say the prayers and thoughts they held in the depths of their own hearts. It was an escape from the communal prayers spoken throughout the mass that often lethargically sputtered from their mouths, as rote words; apparently devoid of any thought or feeling.

Beth felt a sense of relief when her parents left the house. For the next hour, freedom reigned. Even though it led to nothing more than adding as many scoops of coffee as she wanted to, to the pot that was for caffeinated coffee, it felt good. Her mother had a separate coffee maker for her parents' decaffeinated coffee and, if she happened to be in the kitchen when Beth was making coffee, she hovered over the scene like a hawk and would predictably cry out, "My God! How many scoops of coffee are you putting in there?"

Beth read a book with Jake snoozing by her feet. And slowly, one by one, the children emerged with messy hair, sunburned faces and twisted pajamas. Within minutes, cartoons blared; wrestling matches ensued; and balls were tossed across the living room.

Eventually, the grownups schlepped into the living room; saying good morning with a yawn as they continued on to the kitchen for a cup of coffee.

"Are you going to church?"

"Yeah."

"Which mass are you going to?"

"What do you think hun—should be try to make the 10:00?"

"10:00?" one of the kids would whine.

"What's wrong with the 10:00 mass?"

"I wanna go to the beach?"

"Do we have to go to church?"

"Yes, we have to go to church."

It happened so often that Beth had begun to expect it; although she never took it for granted. Just when she felt overwhelmed by difficult challenges in life that made her miserable or heartbroken, the sermon at mass on Sunday struck the perfect chord to bring her back to a feeling of hope.

This Sunday was no exception. The muddled singing of the parishioners was drowned out by the choral leader, whom everyone had agreed sounded exactly like Barry Manilow—that is, if Barry had become a lounge singer. Her brother whispered, "Don't forget to tip your ushers," and Beth giggled. The priest read the gospel and everyone got cozy as they sat back in anticipation of his sermon. Beth was surely not the only one who secretly yearned for a sense of direction and a feeling of reassurance. The priest used the news of the day to make his point—the pedophile assistant football coach at Penn State University, who had sexually assaulted young boys for many years; and the disturbing finding that others knew about it, but looked the other way. "All it takes for evil to exist is for good men to do nothing." Beth could feel her heart move in her chest. Then, the priest repeated that powerful sentence with a slow cadence. "All it takes . . . for evil to exist . . . is for good men . . . to do nothing."

Now Beth had chills. At that moment, she knew what she had to do. She thought, "I'm going to contact the FBI. I'll go on line and find out how to contact them. I think they'll be interested in hearing about Ajit Medical Center."

On her drive home Beth thought about the sermon again. "How sad to think of so many young people being abused . . . who knows how many children have been sexually abused and never tell anyone about it . . . and how many children live with violence in their homes; either as witnesses or as victims. . . why is it that some, like Laura, can just turn over and go to sleep when it's happening . . . how could she go back to sleep when Dad was hitting Mom? Then they rewarded her for it . . . maybe Henry and people like him know that people like me want to escape but we're too afraid to leave. We're children afraid in our own homes or children unloved in our own homes; so how can we be brave enough to face an even scarier world . . . so we meet someone who seems nice and easy at first . . . easy to know and easy to love . . . we admire their confidence and strength and we crave it because it's missing in us. To the evil ones, it must be blatantly obvious that we're hungry for a friend . . . for love . . . for leadership—a father figure who is the good, strong protector that we've longed for . . . . . . then when abuse happens we're so desperate for love that we forgive them again and again and even find a way to blame ourselves for their behavior . . . after all, this is how we were taught to live as children."

Traffic was building up and it seemed to be heavier going toward the Walt Whitman Bridge. Beth changed lanes until she was far enough on the left to take the exit for the Ben Franklin Bridge instead. She thought, "I better start keeping a journal of what's going on at the office." She had crossed the bridge and was stopped to pay the toll. She took a few dollars from her wallet and looked out of her open car window at the setting sun. She shook her head and quietly said out loud, "There's just one problem. Dr. Arvind will kill me if he finds out I'm the one who told the FBI about what's going on at Ajit Medical Center." The car in back of her beeped the horn and she moved forward.

Chapter 19

ON MONDAY MORNING, Beth searched the internet and found a phone number for the FBI. She felt confident as she listened to the phone ring.

"Federal Bureau of Investigation, how can I help you?"

Beth said, "I work as a Front Desk Receptionist at a medical practice and the doctors and their patients are committing insurance fraud. They are also prescribing lots of narcotic pain meds and I think they're gaining a lot of new patients because the word is out. And . . ."

The woman interrupted her. "Where is this practice located?"

"In Lansdale, Pennsylvania."

"OK. Let me give you the phone number for the FBI office in that area."

"Thank you."

Beth called that number and repeated her introduction. This time the woman said, "Can I have your phone number?"

After Beth gave her the number, the woman said, "I'll pass this information on to someone and you can expect a call back."

Fifteen minutes later, Beth's phone rang. "Hello?"

"Hi. This is the Montgomery County office of the FBI."

"Yes?"

"An agent will be getting in touch with you in the next day or two. Is there any particular time that is best to contact you at this number?"

"Mornings are better because I go to work in the afternoon."

"OK. Good enough."

"Thank you."

"You're welcome. Goodbye."

On Tuesday morning Beth's home phone rang at 8:30 a.m. The caller ID indicated a private number. Beth hoped it would be him and it was. "Hello?"

"Hello, Beth?"

"Yes."

"This is agent Tim Booker with the FBI."

Beth highlighted some of what had been going on at Ajit Medical Center and then Tim said, "I'd like to meet with you Friday morning, if that's good for you, and we can discuss this further."

"Sure. Friday morning is good any time. I don't leave for work until 1:00."

They set up a time and Tim said, "It's good that you called us about this. Sometimes we don't know these things are going on unless somebody gives us a heads up."

Beth had a self-satisfied grin on her face. She felt validated.

On Friday morning she exercised early, then showered and dressed for work, even though she had a few hours before she had to leave. She was expecting Tim Booker at 9:00 a.m. She didn't hear the car pull up but she heard car doors shutting and she peaked through the window blinds and saw two men in business suits casually make their way from their car toward her door. She felt a flutter of butterfly wings in her stomach as she stood silent and waited for the knock on her door. She opened the door and Tim said, "Hello Beth?"

"Yes."

"I'm Tim Booker and this is Jim."

Beth immediately felt comfortable with the two clean shaven, professional looking men, but still she asked, "Can I see your ID?"

"Sure." Tim immediately produced something that looked like a wallet which opened up with a big, golden FBI badge on the right side and Tim's thumbprint-sized photo on the left side. Jim did the same.

They each held it up to Beth's eye level—the same way they do it on television. Beth said, "Thanks" and then moved aside so they could enter.

Tim sat on the couch and Beth sat in the chair across from him. Jim did not sit down but rather stood next to the couch and listened intently. Tim said he had brought the other agent with him as a matter of standard procedure because he had to witness Tim stating the standard legal blurb that she was not to collect patient information other than that which Tim deemed as pertinent to the investigation; this was in keeping with HIPPA, Health Information Patient Privacy Act. Information collected by Beth about the Ajit Medical practice would pertain to the areas they were looking into; i.e., Medicaid/Medicare/insurance fraud; abuse of narcotic prescriptive authority; and other matters that came to Tim's attention that he deemed as warranting further investigation. Tim then used his smart phone to pull something up on the screen. As he did so, he told Beth he had to read something to her regarding the standard parameters of her work with the FBI as an Informant. The term Informant made Beth a little nervous because it brought to mind the Hollywood depiction of Informants being found out and killed by the mafia or corporate kill-for-hire types. She only heard the last part of what Tim was reading, ". . . and your work with the FBI does not allow you to live outside the laws of the land." Tim looked at her and said, "But if you get a traffic ticket or something like that, I might be able to help you out."

Beth grinned. Then Tim said, "Do you agree with these parameters as set forth by law?" Beth said, "Yes." Tim said, "OK. You just have to sign this," and he handed her his smart phone and a stylus and Beth signed on the green signature line on the screen. Tim looked at the paperwork that Beth held in her lap and said, "OK. Now we can talk about what you have for me today."

Beth handed him the notes she had typed up and reiterated most of the information contained in her notes until she finished with ". . . but I just can't figure out how they're getting so many social security numbers for these people, and then this whole lab business that Dr. Vishnu; or should I say Harry Vishnu, is running."

Tim grinned and said, "Well, you're not supposed to figure all of it out; that's what we do. But I can tell you that there is a vast underground market for obtaining and selling social security numbers to people entering this country illegally."

Beth said, "Why do politicians and the media focus on people entering the U.S. illegally from Mexico? What about all the people entering illegally from India?"

Tim didn't answer her question. Beth would get used to his manner of only addressing information that he felt she needed to know. Instead he said, "There's a number of ways that social security numbers are obtained, and they don't have to be the numbers of deceased individuals. The numbers can be obtained from various business databases by individuals on the inside of a particular company or organization. It's not just low level employees, but professional software developers, engineers and doctors who buy and sell hundreds of social security numbers at a time. As far as the lab business, there's a black market for selling the blood of healthy individuals for a variety of purposes. But we'll look into that too."

When Tim seemed to be rapping up their brief meeting, Beth felt compelled to say something more and, rather nervously she said, "I feel like I'm serving my country in a way because these people are doing so many illegal things and I'm sure I still don't know the half of it. What bothers me the most is that good people aren't getting healthcare because they can't afford the monthly insurance payments or they don't qualify for Medicaid, and yet these people who aren't even U.S. citizens are ripping us off and the doctors are helping them to do it; because, in the end, they make money. And, as far as all these narcotic pain meds and other drugs, there's got to be crime going on in the community that's a result of all that."

Tim had been nodding to show he was listening intently and Beth found it reassuring, but she suddenly realized she was nervously rambling, so she stopped and the three of them stood. Tim handed her his business card and said, "You can start sending stuff to my email address. But of course, send it through your personal email on your home computer. Don't send it from their computer. When you make copies of pertinent information, mail it to me once a week, so you're not running to the post office every day." He smiled and they walked toward the door, and then he turned to Beth and said, "Just start keeping track of anything that seems *off*—like some of the things we've talked about today—and shoot me a quick email about it when you get home."

Beth grinned. "OK. I will."

As Beth drove to work that day, she felt a new sense of purpose. She felt the calm of self-satisfaction as she got out of her car in the parking lot. She didn't feel any guilt as she neared Dr. Vishnu, who pushed the kickstand of his motorcycle into place, as he removed his helmet. "Hi Dr. Vishnu." He nodded hello and smiled.

Beth went up the small set of stairs to their office. The back door beeped as she opened it, causing Lydia to glance in Beth's direction, as she continued talking to the pharmaceutical sales rep, who had brought lunch to the office that day.

Beth sat down and slipped her shoulder bag into its usual space to the left of her chair. (There would be many times over the next several months when Beth would discreetly slip her notes and copies of pertinent information into this bag).

Later that afternoon, Ruth, once again blurted out, "Oh my God! We're all going to jail!"

Beth turned so that Ruth could see she was on the phone. She had come to the conclusion that she didn't particularly like Ruth; yet she felt a connection with her because Ruth, unlike Lydia, did not seem to be the type of person who would just look the other way. Although Ruth had only worked there for a few weeks and Beth had worked there several months, Ruth had worked in medical billing for other physician practices, so it didn't take long for her to see that Ajit Medical Center was breaking the law.

The patient said to Beth, "I have to change my date of birth in my files." It wouldn't be the first time and it definitely was not the last time that an Indian patient wanted to change their birth date.

Beth asked, "Why do you want to change your date of birth?"

"Because there was a mistake made and I have to change it."

As usual, there was no valid explanation.

Beth asked, "What is the date of birth you gave us originally?"

"It was 2-10-58."

Beth typed in the date of birth and opened the chart on the screen. "OK, I have your file open."

"I have to change my date of birth to 2-10-48."

"OK. I just changed it for you."

"Thank you."

Dr. Arvind Ajit walked by her desk. Beth said, "Dr. Arvind, why do we allow patients to change their date of birth? Isn't that unusual or . . . I mean . . . doesn't it raise any red flags? I mean, it's not like it's a difference of a month or day being transposed. The patient I just spoke with made a change that added 10 years to his age!"

Dr. Arvind shrugged and said, "It's no big deal. Sometimes patients make mistakes. Just change it if they ask."

The change of birth date just happened to make him 65 instead of 55; thus making him eligible for Medicare.

Beth looked at a Medicaid form for patient Bala Patel. There was a sticky note on the form and Lydia had written, "Bala will pick this up this afternoon." Under the reason why Bala cannot work, it said, "Bala Patel cannot work due to hemorrhoids." Beth sat there holding the form in disbelief and sighed heavily.

Ruth said, "What's wrong?"

Beth said, "Guess why this patient is getting Medicaid insurance?"

"Why?'

"Because she has hemorrhoids! Can you believe it? She's 32 years old, and the doctors are approving her Medicaid application that says she is *ineligible* to work and therefore *eligible* for Medicaid because she has hemorrhoids! The worst part is that it's not the first time I've seen this as a reason for not working on these Medicaid applications."

Ruth just shook her head.

By 3:30, Beth needed a cup of coffee. She had a chance to leave the front desk for a minute and go pop a Keurig pod into the machine in the back room. She was walking back to her desk, when she saw that Dr. Vishnu was whispering with Ruth, as he stood by her desk. Dr. Vishnu turned toward Beth and said, "Ah, that coffee smells good."

Beth smiled. "It tastes good too."

Ruth said to Dr. Vishnu, "Hey, we were wondering about these dates of birth."

Beth was happy Ruth put him on the spot.

"What do you mean?" Dr. Vishnu asked.

Ruth said, "The patients are always changing their dates of birth."

Dr. Vishnu seemed to relish the moments when he could instruct them about the Indian culture. His body lurched forward a little with enthusiasm and his tone became professorial. He said, "Yes. In India, it's not like here. We can easily change our date of birth. In fact, I have two birth dates."

Ruth said, "You're kidding?"

Beth was fascinated.

Dr. Vishnu giggled and said, "My father wanted me to be eligible for college a little early, so he just changed my date of birth. So I have my actual birth date in November and a separate birth date."

Ruth asked, "So which one do you use here?"

He said, "My actual birth date in November."

Mrs. Ajit had quietly walked up behind Dr. Vishnu. Apparently she had been in Dr. D's office down the hall. She abruptly interrupted the conversation and started talking to Dr. Vishnu in Indian. Beth and Ruth stole a glance at each other and got back to work.

A very refined, older Indian woman, Bhakti, came in for an appointment, as she did every few months. She wanted to be seen by Dr. D. Mrs. Ajit told Beth that Bhakti had not only grown up in the same town in India, as Dr. D, but they had dated for a period of time and remained friends over the years. Bhakti brought her sister, who was visiting from India. While Bhakti was seen by Dr. D, her sister (with symptoms of a urinary tract infection) was seen by Dr. Arvind. Later, Bhakti chatted with Mrs. Ajit at her desk. Dr. Arvind came out of his exam room, where her sister was being treated, and he told Bhakti he wanted to prescribe an antibiotic for her sister.

Bhakti said, "OK. Just put it on my insurance."

Later, when Beth looked at the clinical visit summary for Bhakti, she saw that Dr. Arvind had gone into her electronic chart and added the antibiotic to her list of prescribed medicines. The script was then sent electronically to the pharmacy as being prescribed for Bhakti and paid for by Bhakti's health insurance company; even though the antibiotic was actually going to be taken by Bhakti's sister, who was visiting from India.

That same day, patient Jayesh Patel was seen by Dr. Vishnu for a work physical. Apparently, he was a healthcare worker because he was required to get a booster shot of the MMR vaccine. Dr. Arvind had gone into the kitchen/sample room where there was a half-size refrigerator used for storing vaccines and allergy shots. He discovered they had no MMR vaccines in stock. By now, Dr. Vishnu was standing in the hallway and Beth heard Dr. Arvind tell him to send a script for an MMR vaccine to the pharmacy. Later in the day, after Dr. Vishnu had left to attend a dinner hosted by a pharmaceutical rep; Jayesh Patel called to say, "I went to my local CVS and the pharmacist told me they don't carry the MMR vaccine."

Beth tried to be helpful and suggested, "The doctors use our local Lansdale Quality Pharmacy all the time. Let me call them to see if they carry it. Can you hold?"

"Sure."

The pharmacist said, "I told Dr. Arvind before that I don't stock the MMR vaccine. We don't order it because it's too expensive to stock in small quantities. But tell Dr. Arvind I can do him a favor and order it but he'll have to reimburse me. The smallest quantity I can buy is a 10 dose pack because that's the way they're sold. And it's about $500 for the 10 dose pack."

"Alright. I'll check with Dr. Arvind and see what he wants to do."

Dr. Arvind was visibly irritated, which happened frequently each day; so it was just a matter of how angry or how irritated he was. He said, "No. No way. I'm definitely not buying it. Tell Jayesh he'll just have to shop around and go to a few other pharmacies to find out who stocks it."

Beth called the pharmacist to tell him Dr. Arvind didn't want to buy it. Then she called Jayesh Patel to tell him to shop around. Jayesh wasn't happy about that.

"Let me talk to him," Jayesh said impatiently.

Beth walked back to Dr. Arvind's exam room, where he always sat working on his laptop, when he wasn't seeing patients. "Dr. Arvind, Jayesh wants to talk to you."

"Tell him I'm with a patient."

Beth started to walk back to her desk.

"Nevermind. I'll talk to him." Dr. Arvind walked into the hallway and snatched the receiver from the phone on the wall.

Beth didn't hear the conversation because she had phone calls from other patients in the meantime. On his way out the door, Dr. Arvind handed Beth a letter he had just printed out. He told her, "Jayesh Patel is going to stop by for this letter tonight."

"OK. Goodnight Dr. Arvind." Beth was shocked when she read it, "To Whom it May Concern: Jayesh Patel had an MMR vaccine administered at this office on . . ." Since the whole issue had become a hassle that Dr. Arvind didn't want to deal with, he just lied and stated that he had given Jayesh an MMR vaccine that day.

Beth made notes of all this for Tim Booker and sent him emails each night with the information.

Most faxes were sent electronically to the doctors' laptop computers, but faxes for Lansdale Lab were received via the office fax number and they printed out on the copier. Beth picked up a small stack of papers from Briarleaf Nursing Homes. It was a regional group of nursing homes and Lydia had told Beth that Mrs. Ajit had contracts with four of the local ones to do their labwork. The multi-page list contained names and social security numbers of residents in the nursing homes who needed labwork processed. There was also an asterisk next to many of the names. Beth turned to the last page to find the key which would explain what the asterisk meant. The asterisk was an indication that the nursing home resident was deceased and no longer needed labwork. Beth put the list into the mail bin for Mrs. Ajit and she took note of it when Dr. Vishnu nonchalantly took that same list out of Mrs. Ajit's bin; made a copy of it; and then put the original back into her mail bin. Beth thought, "That's probably one of his sources to get social security numbers for patients getting Medicaid and Medicare, who aren't citizens."

One afternoon a young, White patient (named Vincent) arrived a little late for his appointment with Dr. Vishnu. The appointment type was "Procedure." Vincent was always very chatty with Beth but since he had arrived a few minutes late, they didn't chat until after his appointment. By then, Vincent was wincing in pain. He said, "Man, he really got me."

Beth asked, "What do you mean?"

"He took a chunk out of my foot!"

"What?"

"He was removing a wart from my heel and Dr. Arvind came in the room at one point and said, 'It smells like a barbecue in here' and I looked at my foot and it looked like he took a chunk out of it!"

Beth could see that Vincent almost thought it was comical so she assumed he was exaggerating a bit. When he left, she tried to open his chart in the computer but it was locked because Dr. Vishnu was apparently in the chart typing in a visit summary. Beth waited a while and later she was able to open it. The visit summary comments were: "electrocauterized a large wart from left foot heel." Beth recalled Ruth telling her that Dr. Vishnu had been a licensed surgeon in India. She began to notice that many minor surgeries were performed by Dr. Vishnu. All appointments were scheduled at 15 minute intervals but the "Procedure" appointments were allotted 30 minute time slots.

"Procedure" appointments were always seen by Dr. Vishnu but, ever since Dr. Arvind became board certified, the visit summaries now indicated that Dr. Arvind had seen the patient and performed the procedure.

A patient was seen by Dr. Vishnu for "right hand middle finger pain, swelling and pus secretion . . . removed possible foreign body from finger."

Many more surgical procedures were performed by Dr. Vishnu with patient visit notes that included, "removal of a cyst on upper back; patient was recently treated for MRSA." Beth knew that MRSA (Methicillin resistant staphylcoccus aureus) was a very dangerously contagious microorganism. However, on the nights of Dr. Vishnu's surgeries, when Beth emptied the trash in his exam room, it contained bloodied gauze, bloodied exam table sheets , gloves, bandages, gooey tissues, paper towels and gloves—all of which, as usual, went out with the regular trash instead of in a hazardous waste container.

"Ohhh no!" Ruth said in a semi-hysterical tone. My favorite patient will be here any minute." Beth had seen his name on the afternoon schedule so she knew who Ruth was talking about—Ashraf Dahtar. Beth dreaded his office visits too because he was rude, loud, obviously misogynistic (judging from the way he spoke to Beth and Ruth), and he wreaked of body odor. He wore a large, white turban on his head and a white cotton tunic that was the length of a gown, ending just above his ankles. He wore a vest over the tunic and sandals (even in the winter time).

Beth was learning about Indian and Muslim culture by observing the patients. She wondered if there were different levels of intensity in the Muslim faith, that found it vain to shower, or to dress in regular street clothes; because there were other Muslim patients—men and women—who wore the same type of white cotton tunic/gown and sandals every time they came to the office and may very well have not showered in between office visits. They were typically 50-somethings and older. The younger Muslim men always had the same beard that looked like a chin strap and was never trimmed—perhaps also a statement against vanity. There was the group of 4 young women who wore ornate saris and veils. They used the prefix "Miss" before their names. Beth assumed this was to show the world they were young virgins. They were always accompanied by a middle-aged man, who wore the typical white tunic, sandals and a large turban. He approached the front desk and did all the talking for the young ladies, who didn't speak unless Beth spoke to them—which she always did on purpose because she resented their subordination by this man, who had a forboding air about him. These young women claimed to be sisters. They gave dates of birth that conveniently reflected sisterhood—18, 19, 20 and 21 years old but Beth was certain they were younger and it would actually be more unusual if they were *honest* about their age. They came to the office frequently and gradually became bold enough to walk up to the front desk unescorted. They stood together as a cluster, as if joined at the hips, and they giggled as Beth spoke to them. She tried to discern if the giggles were youthful exuberance or exhilaration about these few moments of inhibition; as they were briefly tethered only by the man's watchful stare.

There is a sacred Muslim holiday (which is actually several days) known as Ramadan, when Muslims have to fast from sunrise to sunset—no food and no water until after sunset. Some Muslims still visited the doctor during this extended holiday. There was a young woman who came in with a toddler. Her tunic hid the fact that she was pregnant, although she mentioned it to Beth when she signed in for her appointment. Her facial skin tone was sallow and she looked tired and listless. Her lips were partially cracked with dryness. When she bent down to pick up magazines that her child had scattered on the floor, she seemed to catch herself as she stood upright. Beth asked, "Can't you eat anything during Ramadan, even if you're pregnant and caring for a toddler?" The woman grinned at Beth's naivete and said, "No."

Ashraf Dahtar constantly argued with Beth and Ruth about paying his bills. Whenever Beth asked him for his copay or to pay a balance due, he flashed into a rage and said, "I have insurance. I do not have to pay anything." He wasn't the only patient who believed this or pretended to believe it. Ashraf and others would argue that having insurance meant a person had no copays and no deductibles. And so Ashraf's bills were mounting because he refused to pay his copay every time he came in; and Ruth had to call him to try to collect payment. He usually yelled at her, until he eventually hung up on her.

Ruth said, "I'll have to ask him about his back due bills—that ought to be fun." She lowered her voice and said, "I think Dr. Arvind is afraid of him because he doesn't put up with nonpayment of bills with any other patients."

Beth had a (possibly hysterical) suspicion that Ashraf might be grooming terrorists. Often, Ashraf came into the office with four or five young Muslim men and he paid cash for their office visits—this from a man who became infuriated at the mention of paying $20 for a copay. He always pulled out a wad of cash that apparently consisted of nothing less than $100 bills, because Beth watched as Ashraf opened up the wad of money and he licked his way through the $100 bills while counting. The young Muslim men would be seen as new patients, just so they could get the required physical they said was necessary to get a driver's license. Beth thought this was odd since she had never heard of anyone needing a physical for a driver's license. Over time, Beth estimated there were at least 2 dozen young men who came in for the same reason. When one of the men said, "I need a physical for my pilot's license," Beth did her best to appear unfazed, but her imagination gave way to frightful memories of 9-1-11.

At almost 2:10, Ashraf Dahtar entered the office with 5 young men. Ashraf was always late for his appointments. As usual, all five of the men were scheduled as new patient visits; being seen for physicals to get their driver's licenses. Each of the five men would have to pay $90 (the cost for a "New Patient" office visit for anyone paying with cash). After they had all been seen, Ashraf approached the front desk and pulled out his wad of money. He was apparently going to pay for these men, as he did with other young men he brought to the office. Beth said, "That will be a total of $450 for today."

Ashraf exhaled heavily with annoyance but, he started to pull out $100 bills. Ruth, who had not yet approached Ashraf about his lingering debt to the office, finally got up and stood behind Beth's chair. Ruth was intimidated by Ashraf's rages, but she must have felt reasonably safe with Beth, and the front desk, in between them. She started to speak to him about the money he owed. He suddenly stopped handing the money to Beth and stood up very straight and angrily declared, "This is not true! I do not owe you any money. I have insurance." By now, after so many arguments with Ruth, he *had* to understand the concept of copays and deductibles, etc. Dr. Arvind happened to come up front at this moment. While Ashraf argued with Ruth, Dr. Arvind surreptitiously whispered to Beth, "Did he pay for today yet?" Beth shook her head "No." Dr. Arvind mumbled, "Just charge him $70 for each patient today, instead of $90." Beth said, "OK" and Dr. Arvind took a waiting patient back to his exam room and shut the door. Meanwhile, Ashraf and Ruth had reached a momentary stalemate; so Beth said, "Dr. Arvind said it will be just $70 for each patient today instead of $90; so your total is $350." He did not speak or look at Beth as he angrily pulled out a total of four $100 bills. Beth took out $50 from the petty cash box and handed it to him.

Ruth started to speak to him again and Ashraf suddenly stood back a little from the front desk; lifted his arms into the air and, looking up toward the ceiling, cried out, "May God curse this office!" The five young men had already shuffled out the front door and then Ashraf turned and made his exit.

Beth's nerves were a little rattled by the scene but, for some strange reason, she suddenly found it comical. She turned to Ruth who had become beet red, and was apparently beside herself. Ruth said, "I . . . I . . . I can't take this . . . I've gotta sit down . . . I" and she sort of staggered into the kitchen. Beth followed her and tried to calm her down. "Don't let him get to you."

Ruth said, "Oh my God, he's crazy. I don't need this."

Beth said, "You know for some reason he reminds me of the mafia-wannabe-types."

Ruth looked at her quizzically. Beth said, "You know, only now it's Muslims who play the 'I know a terrorist' card, instead of Italians who play the 'I know somebody who will hurt you' card? You know what I mean?"

Ruth just stared at her. Beth couldn't understand why Ruth didn't see the humor in it. So she continued, "You know, like the Italians who say 'I've got a friend who's got a friend. . .' insinuating mafia connections, only now it's Muslims who are like 'I gotta friend who's gotta friend who. . .'" Ruth gave her an obligatory grin, at which point Beth gave up and returned to the front desk.

Chapter 20

THE NEXT DAY it was peculiarly quiet in the office area, when Beth arrived. Ruth sat at her desk trying to look busy, and Lydia nibbled on food at the front desk. Beth had noticed that Ruth didn't respond to her when she said hello. Lydia shoved a big forkful of food into her mouth and then stood up and motioned to Beth to follow her, as she headed toward the back room.

Lydia did an about-face as soon as she entered the room and said with drama, "Ruth gave her 2 weeks notice this morning!"

"What! Seriously?"

Lydia said, "And lucky us, Mrs. Ajit is going to officially take over the billing job."

"What about Lansdale Lab?"

"She said she's hoping to sell it to Norris Lab—that's why she's so nice to the rep from Norris Lab. She wants him to think she's going to send bloodwork to them for processing, but she really just wants them to buy her lab. She's convinced the rep to bring some higher level people to his next lunch here."

Beth made a disgusted look and said, "Why would anyone want to buy her lab? I couldn't believe it the first time I saw it. I had to go down to tell Mrs. Ajit there was an urgent phone call for her from one of the nursing homes she goes to, to draw blood."

Lydia made a disgusted look and said, "Oh, I know. It's disgusting. It's dirty and smelly."

Beth said, "And there's stacks of papers everywhere and that dirty sink . . . and then when I was leaving her lab through the physical therapy office, I started to walk up the stairs and I was surprised to see the mess under the stairs—piles of papers and boxes stuffed with manila folders—talk about a fire hazard."

Lydia giggled. "Oh yeah. Kathy told me that mess under the stairs is Mrs. Ajit's filing system for Lansdale Lab."

The both laughed a little; then Beth said, "Hey, why did Ruth say she's leaving?"

"She said her health hasn't been good and her husband just got promoted so . . ."

"Oh that's good because I know she was worried he might get laid off when his company was bought out by another company."

The back door beeped and Dr. Vishnu walked into the office. Beth asked, "Does he know?'

"Know what?" Dr. Vishnu hoped it was good gossip.

Lydia said, "I was just telling Beth that Ruth is resigning."

"Oh yes. I know. We'll miss her." Then he giggled and left the room. It was obvious he was being sarcastic when he said Ruth would be missed.

Beth had just finished scheduling a patient for his next appointment. "OK. So here's a reminder card and we'll see you in two weeks."

The older Indian man smiled and bobbed his head in the typically ambiguous yes/no gesture. The man had barely gotten out the front door when Ruth blurted out, "Oh God. That head bobbing says it all, doesn't it?"

Beth turned around and gave her an inquisitive look—just to be politically correct; she pretended she had no idea what Ruth was talking about. "What do you mean?"

Ruth said, "They all speak with a forked tongue so it figures they can't even shake their head yes or no; it's just that vague *maybe yes; but then again, maybe no.*"

"Hello Beth."

She turned around and saw the head of a middle-aged Indian woman—so petite that her stature just about surpassed the height of the front desk. Beth said, "Hello Tabaik."

Tabaik looked tired and even lethargic; the way she placed her forearm on the counter, and leaned against it as she signed in. Tabaik was scheduled as a "Sick" visit. Her insurance was KHPE (Keystone Health Plan East). She worked as a Research Assistant at Merck & Co., Inc., a local pharmaceutical company.

Tabaik said, "I think I need a B12 injection because I've been very tired lately and I don't know why. You know, vegetarians are lacking the B12 vitamin, which is found in red meat."

Beth thought that was interesting. She said, "Oh, thanks for telling me. That explains why so many of our patients get B12 shots."

Tabaik smiled and said, "Yes, most of us are vegetarians."

Beth would later send an email to Agent Tim Booker: "I have evidence that the doctors are double billing . . . and after Tabaik was seen by Dr. Vishnu, he came up to the desk and said to me, 'OK, that will be 2 appointments for today—one for a B12 shot and one for an MVA' (Motor Vehicle Accident). So I had to create an additional appointment on the schedule with the visit "types" as Dr. Vishnu instructed. Two clinical summaries were done. One states reason for visit, 'Complained of neck, upper back and shoulder pain going down both arms, slowly getting worse; started after MVA. (Note: Tabaik never mentioned anything about being in pain or about having a car accident). The second visit summary states: 'Patient presents for B12 injection.' Both visit summaries had the electronic signature of Dr. Arvind Ajit, who hadn't even been in that day because of settlement on his new house; and it was Dr. Vishnu who saw the patient."

When Tabaik stopped at the front desk to make her next appointment for a B12 shot (the doctors give 1 injection per week for 4 weeks and then once a month for as long as needed), Tabaik said, "I'll have to call you later with my auto insurance information."

Beth wrote to Tim: "I think Dr. Vishnu and Dr. Arvind tell patients they can be seen several times for an MVA because this allows them to bring the patient back in and double bill. Tabaik has Keystone Health Plan East; so her B12 injection visit was charged to KHPE, and her MVA visit was charged to Erie Insurance (her auto insurance carrier). Tabaik gave the date of the MVA, which was 6 months prior to today's visit."

Each subsequent visit, Dr. Vishnu reminded Beth, "Don't forget to show this on the day's schedule as 2 appointments for Tabaik—one for B12 and one for MVA." On one of her visits, Dr. Arvind saw Tabaik and Beth wondered what he would do. Sure enough, Dr. Arvind did not ask Beth to create two appointments for the same patient, he just did it himself. Beth saw that he had gone into the schedule for the day and added a second appointment for Tabaik and created two clinical visit summaries: one stated, 'Patient presents today for B12 injection.' The other summary stated, 'Patient presents for follow-up treatment of injuries sustained in MVA' and the B12 injection visit was charged to her medical insurance and the MVA visit was charged to her auto insurance. Beth wrote to Tim, "Dr. Arvind apparently thinks I don't notice these things."

Whenever Takesh Patel came to the office, he was accompanied by 2 or 3 Indian men who seemed to be his assistants. The entourage always came on a Friday. Interestingly, they all wore beige khaki pants and blue oxford shirts. Beth liked their crisp, oddly Americanized, preppy look. They were clean shaven and pleasant, but with an air of superiority she had come to expect from Indian and Muslim men.

Takesh and his men, did not even approach the front desk. One of the men would nod hello to Beth, and whereas the other two men were sometimes absent from the scene, this man—Manendra Patel was always with Takesh. They never had a scheduled appointment. They just sat in a row of chairs facing front; and waited until Dr. Vishnu happened by; at which point he would immediately rush to greet them warmly.

The first time, and every time Dr. Vishnu brought the men toward Beth—either to go to his exam room or, more often, to his private office at the back—Dr. Vishnu would say to Beth, "Takesh is a priest at our temple." The first time he did this, Beth was impressed and respectfully said hello. But her respect soon dissipated as she puzzled over the voluminous quantities of pain meds Takesh and his friends were getting—all tied to a particular pharmacy in Northampton, PA with the name of the same Indian pharmacist on the bottles.

Their residence was ironically in Bethlehem, PA, (presumably where the temple was located) and about an hour's drive from Ajit Medical Center. And what irritated Beth more than anything, was the games they played with their Medicare and Medicaid insurance. Their visits with Dr. Vishnu had the air of social visits rather than doctor visits; but of course Medicaid and Medicare were billed for doctor visits.

Beth started referring to them as the "temple guys" in her notes to Tim Booker. Their loss of innocence (in Beth's eyes) started one Friday night. And she wrote to Tim about it:

"I went into Dr. Vishnu's office to empty the trash, as part of my normal daily job duties. I saw a wrinkled plastic bag on his desk and I opened it. There were large plastic bottles inside. I took them out and placed them on Dr. Vishnu's desk. The labels said LIQUINOPRIL, quantity 180 tabs. I recognized it as a high blood pressure medicine. But something told me to open it and look at the tablets inside. I unscrewed the cap on the first bottle and gently poured about a half dozen tablets into my palm. The large tablets had a tiny imprint that said Oxycodone. I opened the other bottles and found the same thing. The patient's name on all of the bottles was the same—Manendra Patel and the date of birth was 3-12-48. I went back to my desk to find out who the patient was (because the name was a common Indian name that a lot of the patients had). I saw the address and I was shocked because it is one of the "temple guys" that come in to see Dr. Vishnu; usually without an appointment. As I was doing this just before 6 pm on Friday,

I was alone in the office, when suddenly, the back door alarm beeped because someone was entering. My heart leapt to my throat and then pounded in my chest, until I turned and saw it was a woman looking for New Day Physical Therapy. I did my best to sound nonchalant, even though I thought a squeal of fear might come out when I opened my mouth. "Oh, their office is downstairs."

A few minutes later, the back door alarm beeped again. This time I was annoyed because I figured it was the same woman. My mouth must have dropped open when I saw it was Dr. Vishnu. He said, 'I forgot something.' Keep in mind, at this point, there were 3 large medicine bottles lined up on his desk. My heart was pounding and I immediately felt sweaty. My mind raced for an excuse. He came out seconds later and did not look back at me, as he opened the back door and said, 'Goodnight' as he left. After a couple minutes of stunned silence, I went into his office and saw the bottles as I left them—lined up on his desk. I put them back into the wrinkled plastic bag and went back to my desk and finished scribbling the information on a piece of paper so I could send it to you. I think Dr. Vishnu had forgotten to take those bottles of meds with him to deliver to someone over the weekend. But when he saw the bottles lined up on his desk, he knew something was up. I think I might have blown my cover!"

Tim didn't respond to Beth's email until Saturday morning. He simply wrote, "Don't worry about it. Just keep sending me stuff."

Chapter 21

ETH'S PHONE RANG mid-morning on Monday. Lydia said, "I just
got a call from my daughter's school that she's not feeling well, so
I have to leave a little early to go pick her up. Can you come in around
12:00 instead of 1:30?"

Beth said, "Sure. I can be there by noon."

"Thanks Beth. I really appreciate it."

When Beth arrived at the office, Lydia said, "I'm so sorry Beth."

"It's OK. I don't mind at all."

Lydia left and Dr. D, Dr. Arvind and Mrs. Ajit were apparently in
the kitchen for a pharma rep lunch with the door closed. Ruth was at
her desk so Beth took advantage of the moment of privacy and walked
up to her and said quietly, "What's the real reason that you're leaving
this madness?"

Ruth grinned and said, "There's just so much that goes on here that
I really can't take it anymore. I mean, I've worked at other doctors' offices and they all play games with billing codes here and there to make
more money, but this . . . this is just . . ." She looked over her shoulder.

Beth said, "They can't hear us. They're in the kitchen having lunch."

Ruth seemed hesitant to continue—as if she was thinking about
how much she should tell Beth. After a moment, she relaxed and decided she wanted to talk. "One day, I'm on the phone and Dr. Vishnu
is standing by my desk—like he has to tell me something. I covered the
mouthpiece and whispered, 'This is going to take a while. Do you need
something?' He said, 'Add these to the charts' and he put two Medicaid

insurance cards on my desk. I assumed he wanted me to add them to the charts of a couple of patients. But I looked at the names and saw that the Medicaid cards were for Dr. Vishnu and his wife Kijal.

"What!" Beth covered her mouth self-consciously after she realized how loud her response was.

Ruth laughed a little and said, "I know, it's crazy. But, OK, so I scanned the cards into the charts of Dr. Vishnu and his wife; and I notice the effective date on both, is the first of this month."

Beth asked, "So what does the effective date have to do with it?"

Ruth said, "Think about it! We just saw Kijal when she stopped in the other day and she looked fine. I mean, she's never friendly to us, but she looked fine right?"

Beth said, "Yeah. She looked fine and she said she had just gotten back from . . ." Beth gasped and then continued, "She said she just got back from being in India for . . . I don't know—how long was it?"

Ruth said, "I don't know, but it seems like every time Dr. Vishnu mentions her, he says she's in India. I know he said she hates the cold here. So, anyway, I look at her chart and see an office visit with Dr. D, two months ago—now you know she was in India 2 months ago—but it's one of their 'made-up appointments.' In fact, I'm sure Dr. Vishnu wrote up the clinical visit summary even though it has the electronic signature of Dr. D. They created a paper trail to make it look like she had returned to the States much earlier than she actually did. See, they all lie about going to India because Medicaid becomes inactive if they're out of the country for a long period of time. If they don't tell anyone they're out of the country, then Medicaid coverage remains active. So, in Kijal's case, they created an appointment to make it look like she's been back in the U.S. for 2 months. Her Medicaid is conveniently effective the first of this month, which is when she actually returned from India. But, I mean, here she is—the wife of a doctor—getting Medicaid health insurance? And I can't figure out how Dr. Vishnu qualified for Medicaid, unless each of them used fake social security numbers."

"Oh my God. This is just . . ." Beth was at a loss for words.

Ruth continued, ". . . and did you know that Dr. Vishnu is going to India to settle his father's estate, which is worth millions?"

"What!" Beth was incredulous. "How did you find that out?"

Ruth obviously enjoyed the attention she was getting over the shocking details. "Mrs. Ajit told me. She said his father died a year ago and something about they had to wait a year for tax purposes before they could settle the estate. Anyway, she said Dr. Vishnu is now extremely wealthy because he is inheriting everything his father owned, which includes a hospital in India."

Beth shook her head. "Oh my God. You have to laugh or you'll cry. I mean, a doctor, inheriting millions; probably keeping it in India for tax purposes, and he and his wife are getting Medicaid in the good old USA—perfect!"

Ruth's phone rang, so Beth returned to her desk and began looking over some paperwork and messages that Lydia had left for her. Ruth had finished with her call and she walked over to Beth's desk.

Beth said, "Here's another example of a patient starting the paperwork for Medicaid while she's in India. Her name is Sipal Dhokshi and Lydia sent a message to Dr. Arvind, 'Sipal said she filled out forms for Department of Welfare while she was in India and dropped them off at our office today. She needs Dr. Arvind to write on the form that her thyroid medication is medically necessary." Beth turned to look at Ruth, who was shaking her head.

Beth said, "But you know what really scares me?"

"What?"

"I think some of them are carrying TB back and forth from India."

"TB?"

"Tuberculosis. Yeah; apparently TB is still very common in India. They don't get any kind of vaccines there, as far as I know; and I've seen notations on patient's charts that they have a history of TB."

Ruth said, "You're kidding!"

"No. I'm not. I think TB is like cancer and goes into remission but can resurface later. The scary part is that we've had a lot of young Indian women, and even some young men, who are going to the local community college for nursing and medical assistant jobs. One of the requirements for admission to college; or to get a job in nursing for that matter, is to get a PPD test—you know, a skin prick on the forearm with needles that tests for Tuberculosis. The patient gets the skin prick and then returns to the office 2 days later to have their arm *read*. If the area with the needle pricks is red and inflamed, it requires a chest Xray to verify the presence or absence of TB. But there have been times when a patient doesn't even come back to the office 2 days later to have their arm looked at; and the doctors will just tell me to write a note that the result was negative for TB. This one guy was in the other day, what was his name . . ." Beth looked at the schedule of patients. "Here he is—S.K. Fahitma. Let me bring up his chart. He was seen by Dr. Arvind. The clinical visit summary states, 'S.K. finished nursing school and will start working at a nursing home soon; patient has history of TB, but a letter from his Pulmonologist, Dr. Rajesh Patel, states, 'no active disease and no latent disease can be identified.'" Dr. Arvind instructed me to give a letter to S.K. indicating the results of his PPD test were negative, even though S.K. didn't come in 2 days later to have his arm read. The nursing home where he's going to work will never know that S.K. has a history of TB. I mean; maybe he doesn't have TB anymore; but what if he does? The guy is going to be working at a nursing home with vulnerable, elderly patients!"

Ruth said, "Well, I'm outta here soon. I just can't take it anymore." Ruth walked over to the restroom and shut the door.

Beth sat for a minute looking around the quiet office. She thought to herself, "I just hope the FBI does something to stop all this madness."

That night, when Beth put the trash out, she was surprised to find the parking lot completely dark. Apparently both lights were out. Fortunately, there was a window on the side of the building facing the parking lot, so there was enough light to feel comfortable on the path to the trash cans and back again to the office building. She went back inside and left the restroom door partially open while she washed her hands. She was drying her hands, as she rounded the corner of the restroom door and saw a man standing there. "Hhhuuhh!" she gasped for breath. The man squinted behind his thick glasses. He looked as embarrassed as Beth felt, because of her squeamish reaction. "Sorry," the man said. "I just wanted to get a signature." He was wearing his Fed Ex uniform and held out an electronic board for Beth to sign. She put her hand on her chest and said, "I'm sorry. You just startled me. I guess I forgot to lock the front door. As she scribbled a signature she commented, "I don't remember you ever coming this late." He handed her a large Fed Ex envelope and said, "Yeah. Only on Thursdays though. There's usually no one else here when I come by around 9:00 p.m." Beth's eyes widened in surprise. She asked, "Why do you come by at that hour? And who lets you in?" But as the question came out of her mouth, she anticipated his answer. He said, "Dr. Vishnu lets me in; although most of the time he's waiting for me in his car. He sure works late." Beth knew Dr. Vishnu wasn't working at the office until 9:00 because he was always gone before 7:30 on their late nights. But he lived around the corner and was obviously driving back to the office to get the Fed Ex delivery. "What was in the envelope?" she wondered, as she handed him his electronic signature board. "Thanks. Have a good night mam." Beth glanced at the clock as she followed him to the door. It was 8:10 p.m. She asked, "Why did you come early tonight?" The Fed Ex guy turned and said, "Excuse me?" Beth said, "You told me you usually come around 9:00 and I wondered why you came early tonight." He replied, "Hey, I just deliver the packages mam. The dispatcher told me to be here around 8:00 tonight. I don't why." Beth just grinned and then locked the front door behind him." She thought, "That's strange. Dr. Vishnu told Fed Ex to deliver an hour earlier than usual, which just happens to be the time I usually leave the office, and the lights are out in the parking lot." She quickly gathered up her things and left through the back office door, just seconds after punching in the code for the security alarm. She locked the door to the office building because New Day Physical Therapy did not have hours that night. She walked to her car at the far end of the parking lot and just as she was getting into her car, she saw something rush past the passenger side window. Her heart was pounding. Then she heard, "It's OK. I got him." She recognized the voice of the man who lived in a house on the other side of the parking lot. He often tossed a ball to his dog once the parking lot was empty of cars, other than Beth's. "Hi Bill," Beth could hear a nervous tremor in her voice so she tried to correct it and sound casual, "How are you?" She eased herself into the driver's seat and started the car before he had a chance to answer. Bill could talk for a half hour about the weather and Beth had gotten ensnared in conversation with him more than once. He was pleasant enough, but by the time she saw him at the end of a day, she was tired and just wanted to go home. She opened her window and leaned her head out to be sure the dog wasn't standing near her car as she slowly reversed out of the parking spot. Bill had grabbed his dog by the collar and said, "I'm good. Hey what happened to the lights?" Beth said, "I don't know. Maybe they forgot to pay the electric bill." They both laughed and Beth drove out of the parking lot and stopped to look left and right before she turned onto Main Street.

She spotted a shiny, silver Mercedes parked on an angle across the street in the lot of the buildings owned by Dr. D. It seemed odd since the people who rented the apartments in those buildings had little, economy cars. A Mercedes in their parking lot looked out of place. She knew it wasn't one of the doctors' or Mrs. Ajit's because all of their Mercedes cars were navy blue and each had a couple of years on them. Beth made a left hand turn and, as she passed the sleek car, the headlights flashed on and the car pulled out onto the road behind her. She worried, "Is he *following* me?" Her eyes went back and forth from the road in front of her to the rearview mirror, where she hoped she would see the Mercedes turn at the traffic light ahead. The street lights at the intersection, along with her rear brake lights, provided enough light for Beth to see the man driving the Mercedes in back of her. It was the face of a handsome, middle-aged Indian man. When the light turned green, Beth proceeded straight and the Mercedes did too. She drove about two more miles and the car stayed in back of her. She thought, "Oh God. I think he's following me!"

She saw the lights of a parking lot up ahead on the left. It was a row of little shops that would surely be closed at this hour, but the restaurant was open and she could see a few cars in the lot. "I'll pull into the restaurant parking lot and that way I'll lose him." As she neared the parking lot, she made a quick left turn without using her turn signal. Her heart jumped to her throat when she saw the Mercedes do a similar fast turn and his headlights were now brightly shining in her rearview mirror. She had to slow down to a crawl because two people were crossing in front of her and headed toward the restaurant. She murmured, "Thank God," because she was certain the man in back of her wouldn't suddenly ram into her if there were witnesses around. As the couple cleared out of her way, she swallowed and thought, "What do I do now?" She rounded the bend and the road inclined to a small hill. The Mercedes was still behind her. She gripped the steering wheel tightly and took shallow breaths . . . as the road sloped downward she saw an exit on the other side. She could make a right hand turn, but she would have to stop at the red light just a few yards ahead. "What if he jumps out of his car when I stop at the light?" She made a right turn but didn't see headlights behind her. The Mercedes must have stayed in the parking lot. The light turned green before she had to come to a complete stop, so she was driving a little too fast into the turn, and her car screeched. She cringed because she didn't want to draw attention to herself.

For a moment, there was darkness in her rearview mirror, except for the glow of the traffic light that was now fading in the distance. She breathed easy until she saw headlights flash again in her mirror. "Maybe it's not him." There was a red light up ahead. "Shit!" She had hoped it would turn green so she wouldn't have to stop. She gently hit the brake and slowed down well before the intersection. Just as she came to a stop, the light turned green and by then she could see there was a pickup truck behind her. "What if he's behind the pickup truck?" She proceeded straight and the pickup truck followed but, a moment later, she saw his turn signal flashing just before he turned onto a side road. There were headlights behind her again. She knew there was a Wawa up ahead at the next intersection. "I'll pull into the Wawa parking lot and stop for a few minutes to see if the car follows me in there." The light was green as she approached the next intersection so she drove straight and then quickly turned right into the brightly lit Wawa lot. She turned her head to the left and saw that the car behind her at that point had been an old Buick. She exhaled, "Thank God." She decided to sit for a minute because it felt like a safe oasis as she watched people putting gas in their cars or walking out of the store with soda and candy. She hadn't spotted the silver Mercedes among all of the traffic coming and going, so she finally pulled out and made her way home.

She took Jake for a very brief walk—just enough time for him to do his business. Then she shut the door and locked it and pulled all of the blinds shut. She poured herself a glass of wine and sat down at her computer to write an email to Tim Booker. She described every detail of what had happened, including the mysterious return of Dr. Vishnu to the office on Thursday nights to meet up with the Fed Ex guy to receive an envelope. For a moment she thought of offering to double back to the office on Thursdays and hiding out to try and figure out what Dr. Vishnu was doing, but after being followed tonight, she decided against it. She thought to herself, "Tim should be the one figuring out what's going on during the night." She sent the email and turned off her computer and then poured herself a second glass of wine. She snuggled under a blanket with Jake on the couch and fell asleep with the television on. It was 4:00 a.m. when she woke up hearing the phone ringing. Jake barked at the sudden noise and Beth felt her heart pounding. She was almost afraid to look at the caller ID as she thought, "It can't be good news at this hour." Then she saw the number. It was Henry. She felt relieved but for some reason, she pretended not to know who it was. "Hello?" she said in her best, "I just woke up from a restful sleep" voice. Henry said, "Hi sweetie. I'm sorry to call at this hour but I couldn't sleep." Beth asked, "What's wrong?" Henry said, "I've just been thinking about you and about us and I miss you. I'm scared. I don't know what's happening to us. I mean we haven't seen each other in a while and I wanted to know if you want me to drive down this weekend." It seemed like Henry had a sixth sense. He always knew when Beth was the most vulnerable. She had been so frightened before she fell asleep and now she felt safe hearing the love and warmth in Henry's voice. She said, "I'm glad you called. I miss you too and I would love it if you drove down this weekend." Henry said, "Alright. I'll leave tomorrow morning around 11:00, after I get some stuff done around here. It's better to leave late morning and avoid rush hour anyway."

The next morning Beth was getting ready to ride her stationary bike when the phone rang. She figured it was Henry saying he just woke up and still had a lot to do before he left so he would have to leave later than planned. Henry had a knack for overestimating how much he was capable of accomplishing in a given amount of time. If he left at 11:00 from New Hampshire, he would arrive Friday between 6:30 and 7:00 in the evening.

The phone rang a second time as she picked it up and saw the caller ID was "private." She knew it would be Tim Booker responding to her email. He always called around 8:30 in the morning."

"Hello?"

"Hi Beth. It's Tim."

"Hi Tim. Did you get my email?"

"Yeah. It's normal for people to get a little paranoid when they're working with us as an Informant."

Beth was surprised by his nonchalant reaction. She wanted him to be as alarmed by it as she was. She said, "It was just so weird to see a luxury Mercedes pull out of the parking lot of that crummy building; and the guy was definitely Indian; and he even followed me into the restaurant parking lot." As she heard herself speaking, she realized she was trying to convince Tim that her fears were justified and she might still be in danger.

Tim said, "I wouldn't worry about it. But I will have one of my guys follow up on that strange 9 p.m. Fed Ex delivery to Vishnu." What Tim didn't tell Beth was that there was no courier pickup of the patient bloodwork that Beth put out into the metal box each night and on Saturdays. Dr. Vishnu was driving back to the office and taking the bloodwork out of the metal box. It was the blood of relatively healthy people that he could sell for various purposes on the black market. Tim's investigation had discovered that *Harry* Vishnu's lab business with a return address label of San Diego, CA, was nothing more than an exam room in Lansdale, PA. The life insurance business was also a scam. The Chinese guy and the Indian guy were recruiting people who trusted them simply because they were the same ethnicity. The life insurance company didn't really exist; other than the address where clients sent their checks each month; and that address belonged to Dr. Jakar Guptalinian, who became involved with their life insurance business after finishing a four year prison sentence for selling narcotic pain meds and practicing without a medical license. Tim suspected the Fed Ex envelope delivered each night was likely a cut of the profits for Dr. Vishnu and his Chinese and Indian *life insurance agents.*

As for the mysterious 5:00 p.m. Fed Ex pickup each day, from *Harry* Vishnu, *Lab Examiner;* those were in fact the blood tubes *Harry*/Dr. Vishnu took out of the metal box the night before; and also the blood obtained from life insurance clients. The lab in Kansas really did exist. It was one of several, on the black market, for the sales and distribution of blood from healthy people. The buyers varied from people who needed clean blood samples; i.e., athletes who were using performance enhancing drugs; or, to companies conducting clinical studies where a clean blood sample could skew the study results to their advantage; or ironically, to seriously ill people who wanted to buy life insurance policies for their loved ones.

Beth felt frustrated. She wanted to know more. Tim was certainly a man of few words, whether it was in person; on the phone; or an email response. He had that stereotypical "just the facts mam" way about him. She respected Tim for what he did. He was a hero of sorts. He probably risked his own life on a regular basis. But she wished he would give her a more definitive opinion about where all of her reporting would lead. Will they be able to prosecute them? How long will this reporting have to go on before they have enough incriminating evidence? And how long will they get away with everything? Or will they just *get away with everything?*

Finally, Tim said the usual, "Just keep sending me stuff."

Beth asked, "Is the information I'm sending helpful?" She wanted feedback and maybe even a pat on the back.

Tim said, "Yeah. It's good stuff." After a momentary silence, she sensed he wanted to get off the phone; and she knew she might have to live with unanswered questions for a long time.

Finally, Beth said, "Thanks for calling Tim. I'll keep sending you emails."

"Sounds good. Thanks."

"Bye Tim." She wondered, "What if he's wrong? What if I really *am* in danger because they have a hidden camera that I don't know about and they've seen me writing notes and putting copies of paperwork into my bag? And what about that night when Dr. Vishnu came back to the office and saw the bottles of Oxycodone that I had discovered and left sitting out on his desk. He's not stupid. He must suspect something."

She walked back to her stationary bike and bent down to tighten the tension on the wheel, when she suddenly stood up straight and covered her mouth. The thought had teased itself into her mind before, but, she had hoped she would forget it. But there it was again and this time she said it out loud; as if that might provide an answer , "What if Tim isn't an FBI agent? What if . . . oh God . . . stop it Beth. You really are getting paranoid!" She turned on the radio and blasted music while she exercised.

On Friday evening, there was a chill in the air as it grew dark, and she was just too hungry to wait for Henry, so she put some leftovers on a plate and popped it into the microwave. Three beeps let her know it was finished, but at the same moment, Jake started barking. She ran to the front window and saw headlights in the driveway. She turned on the outside light and watched Henry get out of the car.

As he came through the doorway, Jake's tail was wagging as he jumped on Henry. "I think he missed me."

Beth laughed. "Yeah it looks that way."

"I missed him too." Then Henry leaned toward Beth and kissed her. He said, "It's a nice place you have here."

"Thanks."

"I smell food."

"Oh. I just heated something up in the microwave cause I'm starved. Did you . . ."

"No. No. Don't worry about me. I ate something on the road. Go ahead."

Beth poured each of them a glass of wine and they sat and talked at the kitchen table while she ate. They lingered there for a while when Henry sat back and took a deep breath and said, "Beth, I was talking to a guy that I go diving with and can you believe he got into a similar situation with his wife."

Beth was apprehensive because she had a sense where this was going. "What situation?"

"Let me finish. Let me finish." Henry paused dramatically and continued, "Well I guess, like you, his wife watches Oprah and the housewives of Ocean County and . . ."

He knew her hot buttons and why he pushed them was a mystery. Beth was immediately angry. She said, "You know I don't watch any of those housewives shows and Oprah isn't even on anymore; well she is, but on another network that I don't even watch . . ."

Henry raised his voice, "It doesn't matter what show little miss watches, they're all the same . . . how to twist a guy by the balls and . . ."

"What are you talking about? Why are you getting into all this? I thought you wanted to see me."

Henry jumped up from his chair and shouted, "I do. I love you but it's clear we cannot live together and I found out that I better get my record expunged if I ever need to look for another job."

Beth stood up, "So that's why you came here! You want me to lie and say you never hit me!"

Henry made a pained expression and then shouted, "You pushed me to it! It was your fault. You wouldn't leave me alone. And now I have a criminal record for domestic abuse in the state of Delaware that happened half a dozen years ago, but it will follow me for the rest of my life!"

Beth said, "Wait a minute. Why are you talking about it as if there was only one incident? What about all the times since then that you hit me or punched me?"

Henry yelled, "I'm talking about Delaware because that's the time you called the police and they hauled me away and now I have a record of an arrest for domestic violence."

"You told me to call the police that night because you said you'd rather live in jail than live with me!"

Henry shouted, "Well, what did I do? I pushed you. It's not like I slapped you across the face. Now that's the ultimate means of control."

Beth said, "First of all, you did a lot more than push me. You punched me in the arms and chest and head for God's sake. And you did the same in Massachusetts. Now all of a sudden a *slap across the face* is the worst thing to do? Well, you've done that half a dozen times too."

"When?"

"Well let's see. You slapped me across the face when we went to Rhode Island to pick up the rigid inflatable boat that you bought on eBay. You slapped me so hard that I had a cut above my nose where your ring cut me. I had to tell my family that I bumped into the doorway on your friend's boat when I was going down below. And when we went to Martha's Vineyard to stay with George and Diane and you didn't want to go shopping with them so you drove us around through the woods. I tried to keep quiet because I knew you were in one of your moods and I didn't want to set you off, but all I could think was, why isn't he driving on the main road; why is he driving through these backwoods? I actually thought you might be trying to drive me somewhere to kill me. So when I finally said, 'why aren't we on the main road?' you slammed on the brakes and slapped me hard across the face. Oh and the time I was taking a turn driving on a trip to Maryland and you kept ranting about how I never want to try anything because you were mad that I didn't want to take diving lessons. So I finally take an exit to get off the highway because I'm so shaken up from you yelling at me for 45 minutes and as I pull off the exit you slapped me across the face again! Do you want me to go on?"

Henry screamed with rage and got close enough to Beth that spittle flew into her face. "You bitch! You are trying to fuck up my life. I want a divorce and I never want to see you again."

Beth was afraid Henry might lose it at any minute. She backed away from him and walked into the living room so she could get near the door. She cried out, "Why? Why am I so stupid? I actually believed you! I thought you wanted to come see me because you missed me."

Henry said, "I did miss you but I forgot what a bitch you are!" He started to open the front door when, strangely, Beth suddenly felt less afraid of *him* than the man who followed her the night before. She heard herself asking, "Where are you going?"

"I'll stay in Maryland tonight. I don't want to be near you."

As he opened the door Beth said limply, "Well I may have been stupid enough to make excuses and just keep living with it, but I am not going to lie and say it never happened."

Henry turned around and started toward Beth. She backed away as he raised his fist into the air. She saw her cell phone on the table and grabbed it. Henry stopped and they stared at each other for a moment until Beth said in a low voice, "You come any closer and I'll call the police."

Henry shook his head and uttered, "You bitch." Then he turned and headed for the door and slammed it shut. Beth slumped to the floor and sat there until she cried herself out. She finally got up and went into the bathroom to get some tissues. She looked at herself in the medicine cabinet mirror and saw a familiar pathetic woman looking back at her. Suddenly, Jake started barking and the front door opened.

"Henry?" There was no answer. She banged the bathroom door against the wall when her shirt caught the doorknob as she turned to leave the room. That momentary distraction made her think he might have answered and she didn't hear him. "Henry?" She called out again as she started down the hallway; but now she heard the silence. She thought, "It must be Henry because Jake isn't barking anymore." She took another step. Her heart was pounding. She stopped to listen and her hand was trembling as she brought it to her face and cupped her mouth; as if she didn't want her breathing to be heard and then, in that moment of complete silence, she heard a sound like a shoe moving across the carpet. She turned to go into the kitchen and head toward the back door, when she realized someone was behind her! She was about to turn around when she felt something slam against her back.

She dropped to the floor. Now Jake barked and ran toward her. The bullet had pierced her spine. He pointed the gun toward Jake; hesitated; but then pulled the trigger. Blood silently pooled across the floor. As Beth lost consciousness her hands, which were so often clenched in worry and fear, opened.

The car slowly eased out of the driveway.

Epilogue

H ENRY WAS QUESTIONED by police and then released. Beth's murder remained an unsolved mystery.

Tim Booker turned the FBI report over to the District Attorney's office. They were certain they had enough evidence to make arrests at Ajit Medical Center.

Laura moved in with her father when Beth's mother died just a year later.

David Reilly was bullying a new kid at school.

Mr. DeLeon lived on to share terrible secrets with many other young boys.

All it takes for evil to exist is for good men ... *and women* to do nothing.

www.ingramcontent.com/pod-product-compliance
Lightning Source LLC
Chambersburg PA
CBHW030913120626
46554CB00001B/128